PRAIS

GAME OF STRENGTH AND STORM

BOOK 1 OF THE LABORS OF GEN

A 2021 Junior Library Guild Selection

"[A] fast-paced, magical, action-oriented story with a conclusion that points to more adventures to come."
—*Kirkus Reviews*

"Fast-paced and full of imagination, this glittering twist on Greek mythology surprised me at every turn. The heroines are brilliant, the tasks are brutal, and I cannot wait to be immersed in the world of Olympia again!"
—*Marissa Meyer, #1 New York Times* **best-selling author of**
The Lunar Chronicles and *Heartless*

"[A]n intriguing fantasy series starter. . . . Menard's rapid pace and sympathetic characters make for a sweeping adventure."
—*Publishers Weekly*

"[A] fast-paced, suspenseful, magical adventure with a satisfying twist on Greek mythology."
—*The Bulletin of the Center for Children's Books*

"*Game of Strength and Storm* is a spellbinding twist on a classical myth set in a universe teeming with diverse creatures, people, and cultures, while drawing from both the best and worst of our own world. The pages flew by, and I can't wait for more!"
—**Erin Beaty, author of** *The Traitor's Kiss*

CLASH OF FATE AND FURY

RACHEL MENARD

THE LABORS OF GEN #2

CLASH OF FATE AND FURY

RACHEL MENARD

flux®

Mendota Heights, Minnesota

First Edition
First Printing, 2023

Book design by Karli Kruse
Cover design by Karli Kruse
Cover illustration by Sanjay Charlton (Beehive Illustration)

Flux, an imprint of North Star Editions, Inc.

This is a work of fiction. Names, characters, places, and incidents are either the product of the author's imagination or are used fictitiously, and any resemblance to actual persons living or dead, business establishments, events, or locales is entirely coincidental. Cover models used for illustrative purposes only and may not endorse or represent the book's subject.

Library of Congress Cataloging-in-Publication Data
Names: Menard, Rachel, 1979- author.
Title: Clash of fate and fury / Rachel Menard.
Description: First edition. | Mendota Heights, Minnesota : Flux, 2023. |
  Series: The labors of Gen ; #2 | Audience: Grades 10–12.
Identifiers: LCCN 2022043720 (print) | LCCN 2022043721 (ebook) | ISBN
  9781635830828 (paperback) | ISBN 9781635830835 (ebook)
Subjects: CYAC: Adventure and adventurers--Fiction. | Mythology,
  Classical--Fiction. | Cerberus (Greek mythology)--Fiction.
Classification: LCC PZ7.1.M4699 Cl 2023 (print) | LCC PZ7.1.M4699 (ebook)
  | DDC [Fic]--dc23
LC record available at https://lccn.loc.gov/2022043720
LC ebook record available at https://lccn.loc.gov/2022043721

Flux
North Star Editions, Inc.
2297 Waters Drive
Mendota Heights, MN 55120
www.fluxnow.com

Printed in Canada

To my partner: Barry, my Pollux, my hero, thank you for letting me lead the way while you light my path. I never would have found my way in the dark.

CHAPTER 1
GEN

The air at the prison smelled like fire, sweat, and despair. Gen stood outside the gate, shifting from foot to foot while her sharp-toothed chaeri leaned against her leg. Her elderly pet could normally sleep anywhere. *Here* he stood with his hackles raised and his fangs exposed. He knew this place wasn't safe. Gen knew it, too, and for four years, her father had been rotting behind these black stone walls.

Gen knelt and ran her fingers through Chomp's purple fur.

"It will be all right," she said, to reassure herself more than her sharp-toothed companion. Whatever bravado she'd brought with her as the infamous Hydra-Slayer had disappeared as soon as she'd set foot on this black isle. She felt like a child again. Helpless. Weak. Alone.

On the two black towers at either end of the wall sat two Gargarean guards—hulking gold beasts. They kept their eyes and lightning cannons trained on the space between Gen's eyes. Unwavering.

The Empresses had promised Gen her father, not for keeps, but for a respite in their palace while she completed two more deadly labors for them. They wanted her to find the fabled golden apples of Hesperides and capture the Cerberus, favored pet and vicious guardian of the Elysium Emperor. In exchange for her agreement to complete the two tasks, the Empresses had told Gen her father could stay in the palace instead of the prison until she returned. But the longer she stood outside these gates, breathing in the stench of the prison, waiting under the glare of the Gargarean guards, the more she worried she had made another mistake.

While the Empresses were true to their word, their words were rarely true.

Beyond the gate, the front doors of the prison ground open with a shuddering creak. Two more guards appeared, dragging a thin, limp figure between them. Gen's muscles tightened. She hadn't seen her father in four years, not since he'd left her and supposedly murdered a roomful of Gargareans like these. He'd been sent to this prison, never setting a foot outside these grimy black walls until today.

One of the guards holding Alcmen released him to crank open the gate. Alcmen hung from the other guard's arm, a burlap sack sagging over his face onto his shoulders. Gen craned her neck to see through the bars. Her father was too thin, bones jutting out from his elbows and knees. Scars marked his forearms and shins.

He had been in here for four years, tortured.

The gate squealed open, and the guard holding Alcmen shoved him through. Alcmen stumbled over his own feet and skidded across the dirt, landing at Gen's boots.

"Get out of here!" The guard spat at him before pulling the gate shut.

The muscles in Gen's arms surged, and the bands of silver that twined her skin shone like starlight. After a visit to her mother's home island of Mazon and a battle with the great Hippolyta, Gen had absorbed more strength and speed from the island itself. She could easily wrench those bars apart and slap the crooked teeth out of that Gargarean's foul mouth.

She could do it, but she chose not to. The Gargareans didn't matter. Not anymore. The only thing that mattered was getting Alcmen far away from here.

She grabbed her father by the bony elbow and lifted him from the ground. He stood shakily. Chomp sniffed his boot, then bared his teeth and snarled.

"Shh." Gen tapped the chaeri with her boot. Yes, Alcmen smelled terrible. But he was still her father.

Carefully, she grabbed the edges of the burlap sack and lifted it over Alcmen's head. A gaunt figure looked back at her, squinting in the sun. Black-and-gray stubble marked Alcmen's sharp jawline. A new scar ran across the top of his forehead in a jagged line, and his greasy hair hung heavy in his face. Knots twisted in her stomach. He did not look like the Amazing Alcmen, ringmaster of the most famed circus in all of Olympia. He looked like he had been dredged out of a refuse bin.

She had come too late. She had lost too much of him.

"Hello," she whispered.

His clouded eyes locked onto hers and, slowly, his mouth stretched into a grin. "It's you."

Unease slipped off Gen's shoulders like a discarded jacket. "I wasn't sure you'd recognize me."

He ran his gnarled fingers through her silver hair. "Of course I would. Oh, Zusma, how I've missed you."

The knots in Gen's stomach returned tighter than ever. He thought she was her mother. Did he not remember? Zusma was dead.

"No, it's me. Gen. Your daughter." She hated that she had to explain it.

Alcmen's smile dropped. "Gen." He tried on her name as if it were the first time he was uttering it. "Of course, Gen. My darling Gen." The smile he gave her this time was much smaller than the one before.

She gave him a strained smile of her own. She had known he would have changed in these past four years, in the same way she had changed. However, she hadn't expected the great Alcmen, most renowned MindWorker in the Empire, to be this . . . small.

She took a breath and caught another waft of the rot emanating from the other side of the prison's walls. She coughed and took Alcmen's hand. Being on this foul island certainly wasn't doing him any good. He needed fresh air. A change of clothes. Some more colorful scenery.

"We have to go," she said.

"I'm free?"

"Yes," she said, a half-truth. She couldn't bear to tell him the entire truth. If she didn't satisfy the Empresses' last two requests, or if she died trying, they would send him right back here.

She tried not to think about what would happen if she *did* complete them. The Elysium Emperor would certainly come to reclaim his lost treasures, inciting a war between the two empires, a war Olympia would most likely win with the Cerberus in hand. But no one really won a war. Many would die. Entire islands could fall.

The Empresses had already played Gen once. They'd told her she could have Alcmen if she defeated the better half of ten tasks, and she'd done it. She'd defeated the Lion, rescued the young woman Livia Kine, cleaned the horrid stables of Elis, retrieved the belt of

Hippolyta from the Mazon Queen's own demented fingers, caught the Thracian Mares, and defeated the Nine-Headed Hydra, which had been at least the Forty-Headed Hydra by the time she had crushed it.

She had won, but in the end, the Empresses changed the rules. They'd declared her competitor the winner instead and given Castor control of the StormMakers' island of Arcadia. Soon, all of Olympia would be flooded with lightning cannons like the ones perched on the rocks of this isle. And Olympia would need them, with war coming.

Gen didn't want to start a war, but if the Empresses wanted one, they would have it. She had made the only deal she could, her servitude for Alcmen's freedom.

She dragged Alcmen toward the small black-sand beach, and the Gargarean guards above aimed their cannons at her shoulders.

The Empresses had sent their orders. She was allowed to take Alcmen and bring him to the capital island of Athenia. However, she could never trust a Gargarean. They had killed most of the Mazon race—including her mother.

Alcmen seemed to remember Zusma's loss now.

"You golden brutes!" he shouted at the Gargareans. He jerked on her arm, trying to wrench out of her grasp. "I will kill you all for what you've done!"

Gen tightened her arms across his chest and dragged him forward, while he kicked and clawed to break free, his nails raking across her arms.

"Please, stop," she begged. She understood now why the guards had brought him out with his face covered. He was almost feral, scrambling to get away from her.

"They're monsters," Alcmen spat. "All of them."

Gen had spent years trying to convince people that Alcmen had been wrongly accused of murdering a roomful of Gargareans. His innocence would be harder to prove if he tried to scratch out the eyes of every Gargarean he passed. Even if Gen wanted to do the same.

"I know." Gen squeezed his hand. "But now is not the time." She turned to the sea. *Come get us. Now*, she called to her whale, and Andromeda answered promptly. *On my way.*

Before Gen had set foot on this isle, she'd dropped three of her silver hairs on the whale's tongue to strengthen their mental connection. Gen used this connection to express her urgency. They needed to get off this island before Alcmen had another outburst or the Gargareans above decided to blast them with lightning regardless of the Empresses' orders.

Andromeda broke through the ocean's surface and swam into the shallows. She opened her mouth, and water ran from her pale pink-and-blue iridescent skin. Gen dragged Alcmen onto the whale's soft tongue while Chomp scrambled along behind them.

"Let's go," Gen told the whale as soon as they were inside. Andromeda promptly closed her mouth and wriggled back into the sea.

Gen sat on the whale's fleshy tongue and pulled Alcmen down with her, holding him tight. He had stopped screaming and struggling, but he still felt poised to strike. Chomp settled on Gen's other side, snarling at Alcmen as if he were a stranger.

In the pale pink-and-blue light of the whale's insides, Gen felt the same way. She barely recognized the man beside her. He marveled at the whale as if he hadn't spent the better part of his life riding inside one. This wasn't how things were supposed to be. She'd gone to the prison to retrieve the Amazing Alcmen. Not this . . . shadow.

He can heal. He just needs time.

"Is this *my* whale?" he asked.

"No." A familiar ache struck Gen in the chest, a wound that would never fully heal. "He died." She didn't want to upset Alcmen further by telling him the truth—that the old whale had been murdered by Castor's minions in the first part of the Empresses' game, an act Gen would never forgive.

"Oh," he said softly. "I'm sorry to hear that."

His body relaxed, and she loosened her arm around him. She curled her fingers into Chomp's purple fur to smooth down his raised hackles.

"How much do you remember?" she asked. "From before."

"Before what?"

"Before you went to the prison."

Her father stared thoughtfully at his hands, turning them back and forth. "I remember your mother. I remember the day I met her, when I brought my circus to Mazon for our one and only performance there. I was the one in the spotlight, but it felt like all the light in the tent shone upon her." A small smile graced his lips.

Gen's spirits lifted. Despite what he'd lost in that awful prison, he had not lost his great love for Zusma, which was proof he was still in there. Gen just had to peel away the darkness to find him again.

She didn't ask him about the supposed murders. She didn't have to. She already knew her father couldn't have killed the Gargareans. The whole accusation said he'd used his mind magic, his blood, to take control of the Gargareans and force them to murder one another.

But MindWorkers like him, like her, didn't have that kind of power. Especially when under duress. If Alcmen had been anything like he was now ... well, it would have been absolutely impossible.

To work that kind of mind magic, the MindWorker would need complete control.

Not that anyone else would believe her. They would see Alcmen like this and make their own assumptions, and Oracles be damned if he threw another fit in front of a Gargarean. Unfortunately, Gen wouldn't be able to watch him; she was expected to set off for the last two labors soon and leave him behind.

We're here, Andromeda whistled. Gen gripped Alcmen's arm as the whale rose out of the water.

Andromeda had more spirit than the old whale. With one flip of her tail, everything flew backward, including Gen, Chomp, Alcmen, and the leftover fish bones in her mouth from lunch. Then she launched herself into the shallows, and they all flipped forward. Gen planted her hand in something slimy, and Alcmen laughed.

"It's been a while since I've had a ride like that," he said.

His laughter warmed her soul. It had been so long.

Gen sat up and plucked a piece of seaweed from her jacket. She helped Alcmen to his feet, and Chomp shook the excess seawater from his back. They emerged from the whale's mouth to the white shores of Athenia, the grand capital of the Olympian Empire.

In front of them, the golden spire of the Empresses' palace rose into the clouds. Despite its shimmering beauty, Gen saw it for what it was—a pretty prison. She had been staying there for the past weeks, entertaining the Empresses until Alcmen's release could be arranged. The Empresses had had to do some negotiating to smooth things over with the Gargareans. They were not happy Alcmen was being freed, but Gen frankly didn't care.

She turned to the whale. "Go get something to eat, Andromeda. I'll call you if I need you."

The little whale flipped her tail, splashing water on Gen's boots. Gen shook it off and took Alcmen's hand.

"We're on Athenia," he said. "Are we playing a show?"

"No." He was drifting again, into a place where she couldn't follow.

Gen had spent the last four years daydreaming about the future, about this moment. She'd imagined Alcmen strolling from the prison in a black suit, as confident and tanned as he'd been the last time he'd performed in their circus. That Alcmen had been nothing more than a dream, built out of fond memories. He would never be the same. Not exactly. She could only hope to bring him closer to something she recognized.

They walked through the luscious gardens, gaining stares from the workers as they passed. Gen kept an iron grip on her father's elbow and tightened it as they approached the bridge leading to the palace. Two Gargarean guards stood there, watching them with snarls on their lips. The Gargareans might have agreed to release Alcmen, but they were a people known for their tempers. Not their diplomacy.

"Please don't," Gen whispered to Alcmen, who'd tightened like a cord about to snap. She pulled him across the bridge, not making eye contact with either Gargarean. Chomp followed at her heels, growling. Alcmen remained stiff, but he didn't break. They made it across the bridge without incident.

Gen exhaled and pressed on the golden doors to the palace, marked with the four diamonds of the Empire. Each diamond stood for one of the Oracles who had created Olympia and the isles: Hecate, Oracle of the Spirit. Tartarus, Oracle of the Sky. Ponos, Oracle of the Earth. Keres, Oracle of the Mind.

The diamond on the left represented Keres, the Oracle who had given Gen and Alcmen their MindWorker abilities. It had been scratched raw with a blade. Gen narrowed her eyes. It had not been like that when she'd left earlier this morning.

She stepped onto the polished floors of the palace and walked quickly for the stairs, keeping her hold on Alcmen. Servants swarmed the hall, dusting priceless statues and watering hanging plants. They turned as she and Alcmen passed, eyeing the trail of dirt and fleas they left in their wake. Before anyone else spotted Alcmen, she needed to help him wash up and change.

She brought him up three flights of twisting stairs and pushed open the door to her suite. It included two bedrooms, a sitting room, and, thankfully, a bath.

"Pollux!" Gen called.

She poked her head into the second bedroom, the one Pollux slept in some nights. Most nights, they stayed up late talking until she fell asleep with her head resting on his chest while he stroked his fingers through her hair. The room felt empty without him, dismal without the sound of his violin echoing off the walls.

Half a year ago, she would have laughed if someone had told her she would be dating a StormMaker. Now she couldn't imagine life without him.

When Gen had lost the Empresses' competition, Pollux had been set free. His sister, Castor, had won the right to inherit Arcadia in his stead. Without the burden of being the future Storm Duke, Pollux could stay here with Gen.

So where was he? And where was Bale?

Gen opened the liquor cabinet and found a few full bottles inside, which meant Pollux's assistant hadn't been there yet to empty them. She wandered back to her bedroom and spotted a note on the bedside table.

Dearest Gen,

My father sent a messenger. He needs me on Arcadia immediately. I don't know why. I only know it is urgent. I'm sorry to not be there when Alcmen arrives. This hurts me as much as it must hurt you, but as you know, if I ignore my family, things only get worse. I'll be back as soon as I can. I am already missing you terribly.

Love Always,

Pollux

Gen crushed the note in her silver fingers. Even freed from his inheritance, Pollux would always be at the beck and call of his family. But that was the nature of the StormMakers. They took what they wanted when they wanted it without care for anyone else.

Alcmen stood in the sitting room, staring into nothingness. The StormMakers were partly responsible for him being like this. They'd given the Gargareans the bottled lightning that had killed Gen's mother, and Gen would never forget it. Just as she'd never forget that Castor was exactly like them. During the Empresses' competition, Pollux's twin murdered Gen's previous whale simply to keep Gen out of the game.

Pollux had suggested Gen ask Castor for help on these final two tasks. Gen would rather get help from a fire-breathing crocodile. She'd be less likely to get burned.

"What are you looking at?" Alcmen peered over her shoulder at the crumpled letter in her hand.

Gen shoved it into her pocket. "A letter from a friend. It's nothing. Let me get the bath ready."

Her father absolutely couldn't find out she was dating a StormMaker. Not yet.

She went into the bathroom to fill the tub with one of Pollux's bottled rainstorms, keeping even that hidden from her father. He might have a fit if he saw her using StormMaker rain.

After Gen filled the tub, she hid the vial under a pile of towels, lit the heater, and called her father inside.

"The bath is ready. I'll let you get washed and changed." She pointed to a set of clothes folded neatly on the chair beside the tub. She had picked them out herself, a fine linen suit like one Alcmen used to own.

Now, though, she wondered if it was too big. Alcmen had lost so much weight. He peeled off his shirt to reveal sharp bones prodding through his scarred skin, and she looked away.

"I'm right outside if you need me." She left the bathroom and closed the door.

In the sitting room, she slumped into a plush armchair and held Chomp in her lap, stroking his fur. Alcmen's flesh held so many scars. Thinking about what could have happened to him in that prison made her muscles burn with Mazon strength. She wanted to crush everyone who had hurt him. But that wouldn't make him better.

She wondered if he would ever get better. Had the Empresses known what she would find behind those prison walls? They must have. The Olympian rulers knew all that happened in their empire.

When the door to the bathroom opened, Gen sat upright. Alcmen looked slightly more like himself. Though the new suit did hang off his bones, the grime was gone from his skin, his scraggly beard had been removed, and his hair no longer hung in greasy tangles around his chin. His formerly ink-black hair now held long streaks of white, not unlike her own streaks of silver. Except hers came with power. His came with age.

"You look better," she said.

"I feel better." He sat in the armchair across from her, and this time, Chomp didn't snarl. A good sign. Alcmen took her by the chin and stared hard into her eyes. "When did you get so big?"

"I don't know." Tears filled her eyes. She didn't feel big. She felt like a child again, waiting for her father to pick her up and throw her in the air.

Alcmen released her and folded his hands in his lap. He rubbed his thumb over one of the raised scars on his knuckles. "I want to apologize to you. I said I'd come back, and I didn't."

"That wasn't your fault." She took his hand and covered the scars with her palm. "We're together now. That's all that matters."

He raised his head and smiled at her. She forced a smile in return. She would be the one leaving him this time when she set off on her labors for the Empresses, and it occurred to her that she might never come back.

"Why do you look so worried?" Alcmen asked.

"No reason." She slid her hand from his. "You should get some rest. We can talk later."

She didn't want to burden him with her problems. She could handle this. She would collect the Empresses' prizes and return for Alcmen, and they would start rebuilding their lives. She was the Hydra-Slayer after all. Could capturing the Cerberus be that much harder? As she gave Alcmen one last false smile, she thought, *This was all for nothing if you don't find some way to finish it.*

CHAPTER 2

CASTOR

astor leaned through the open window and inhaled the sweet air of Arcadia. It always smelled like fresh rain and wet leaves. The last few raindrops from the recent storm rolled off the roof and splattered onto her windowsill. She touched them with her fingertips and held them to her nose. She loved that smell—the smell after a storm. It meant everything was clean. A fresh slate for something new.

She would be that something new. She would be the rain that washed away the patriarchy that had controlled Arcadia for far too long—as soon as her father decided to retire. If he stayed as angry as he was now, though, he would never retire. He would live forever simply to keep her from taking what was hers.

In the past four weeks since he had been notified by the Empresses that Castor would be his heir, he had spent every moment sending pleas for a retraction. When the Empresses had refused, he'd messaged all his friends and allies, begging them to stand with him against the Olympian rulers.

No one would stand with him. The Empresses' word was law, and everyone else understood that. Soon her father would too.

Through the fading rain, a white orb came soaring toward her— her ghostly assistant returning to her in a hurry. Castor had told Delia to keep watch for anything unusual. The Duke wasn't the only one displeased with the change in heir. Most of the male guards didn't like that she would be taking over, either. Until she could make her own staffing changes around here, she had to watch her back.

"What is it, Delia?"

The ghost bobbed in front of her. "There's someone here to see you. A visitor."

"Who?" Castor reached to her belt for a vial of lightning.

To win the Empresses' game, Cas had made some promises. To get the Boar to leave the people of Psophis, she'd promised him all of Arcadia's less respectable shipping contracts. She'd also sent him on collections for overdue accounts. Technically, she didn't have the authority to do that yet. She'd forged the Duke's signature on the contract. When her father was in a more reasonable mood, she would tell him.

Today was not that day, and Cas couldn't have the Boar showing up here unannounced.

"It's the pirate," Delia said. "The one who stole the ship."

"Adikia." Castor released her lightning and touched her lips where the thief had kissed her once.

Then she removed her entire storm belt and hid it in a drawer. She couldn't trust the thief not to lift a few storms. Adikia had incredibly sticky fingers.

"Thank you, Delia." Castor took the wooden box from her pocket and held it open.

Delia made something like a sigh before she flew into the box, and Castor sealed the lid. Delia had been doing more of that as of late—sighing, dawdling, and answering with sharp retorts. Contrary to popular belief, Castor didn't have complete command over the spirit. But she did have complete command over Delia's box, which gave her complete command over Delia's fate. If Cas broke the box, Delia would forever be a lost soul, wandering silent among people who couldn't see or hear her. She would lose the magic that kept her somewhat corporeal.

Maybe Castor had to remind the ghost of her likely fate if she kept testing Castor's patience. Later, though. She had company coming.

Castor set the box on the vanity, picked up her silver hairbrush, and ran it through her long, pale hair. She pinched her cheeks, pursed her lips, and turned for the door, waiting for her guest to be announced.

Adikia likely came to ask her for gold. She had freed Castor from her father's guards when he'd tried to pull her out of the game. She would want to be compensated for that. Castor looked forward to haggling. Heated negotiations always made her feel alive.

Something slammed against the window.

Castor spun around to find a hand grasping the windowsill, followed by Adikia's body tumbling over. As the pirate spilled to the floor, her pockets jangled with coins, and she left a smear of grime on the white rug.

Adikia stood and straightened her belt. It hung loose on her hips with a crossbow dangling from the side. Her wet linen blouse clung to her skin and hung open over her chest, revealing her sharp collarbones. Castor's gaze settled there, on the divot above the bones.

"That was quite the climb," Adikia said. She lifted her lavender eyes, split in the middle by long pupils. Then she pulled off her hat and shook rainwater onto the rug beside the stain she'd left behind. If anyone else had barged into Castor's room like this, she would have flung them back out the window with a gust of wind.

Adikia, however . . . something about her brazenness delighted her.

"Do you have something against doors?" Castor tapped her foot on the floor.

"No." Adikia ran her hands through her tangled lavender curls. "I have something against the forty guards standing outside yours."

"I do too." Castor grabbed the carafe of wine sitting on her bedside table and poured some into a glass. "Something to drink?"

Adikia took the glass and drank its entire contents in one swallow. A drop of red wine ran from her lips. Castor brushed it away with her thumb, then licked it from her own finger.

"What brings you to Arcadia?" she asked.

"You did." Adikia roamed the room, poking through random papers and jewelry scattered on Castor's dresser. She picked up a silver bracelet, and Castor pulled it from her fingers.

"You came for payment, for saving me?"

"No." Adikia smiled. "Not particularly. But if you want to give me some coin, I won't refuse it." She grabbed a sapphire necklace from the jewelry box and held it to her neck, admiring herself in the mirror. "I think jewels agree with me, don't you?"

Castor admired her too. She ran her fingers over the line of shimmering purple scales that ran down Adikia's neck, between her shoulders. Adikia turned around, her full lips pouting, and Castor kissed her.

Adikia kissed her back. Hard.

Castor's fingers curled around Adikia's shoulders as her lips parted. The pirate grabbed her by the hips and pushed her down on the bed. Lightning rushed through Castor's veins. She reached for Adikia's belt, breathless. This whole thing with the Empresses and the labors had left her strangled. Now it was like she could finally breathe.

Adikia ran her tongue down Castor's jaw to her neck. "If I had known I would get a greeting like this, I would have come sooner." Her breath curled in Castor's ear. Chills ran down Castor's spine.

She almost had Adikia's belt removed when someone knocked on the door.

"Damn the Empresses," she whispered. Then she called out, "I'm busy! Come back later." Much later. Cas planned to take her time.

"Lady Castor, the Duke requests your presence immediately." Leto's voice cooled her fire to pure ice. Her father's most loyal and annoying guard had the worst timing. He'd captured her on Ceryneia and would have ruined her chances in the Empresses' game if Adikia hadn't stepped in.

Castor kissed Adikia one last time before she slid out from under her and ran her fingers through her tangled hair.

Adikia stretched out on the bed like a cat and picked at a loose thread in the coverlet. "Should I be jealous?"

Castor laughed. "No, but if you shoot him with your crossbow, I will pay you dearly."

Leto knocked again. "Lady Castor, your father is waiting!"

"I will be right there!" she shouted back.

Adikia reached for her crossbow. "Didn't I already shoot him once?"

"You did. Unfortunately, you didn't kill him." The shot through Leto's arm had saved Castor and left the annoying guard with a perpetual ache in his shoulder that he constantly complained about. If Leto had succeeded in turning Cas over to her father, she would be in bed with disgusting Memnon right now, playing dutiful wife to the heir of the Tegean mines.

"I can always try again." Adikia slid out of the bed and aimed her crossbow at the closed door.

"Some other time," Castor said. Until her father came around, Cas didn't want to upset him any further. Assassinating the head of his guard wouldn't go over well. Leto would get his due though. Soon enough.

Castor looked in the mirror and smoothed down the wrinkles in her blouse before picking up a vest and buttoning it tight to her waist. Pale blue velvet to match her eyes. Then she replaced her belt of storms. Adikia came up behind her and planted her lips on the back of Castor's neck. It sent heat through her stomach.

"Will you be here when I get back?" Castor asked, already knowing the answer.

"Doubtful," Adikia said.

"Then I'll see you when I see you."

Adikia picked up her rain-soaked hat and placed it on her head. "You'll see me soon enough."

Castor leaned in close to her, inhaling the smell of charred wood and salt air in Adikia's hair. Then she reached into Adikia's pocket and removed her sapphire necklace.

"Not this one," she whispered. "I like this one." She brushed her lips against Adikia's cheek before pulling back and clasping the necklace around her own neck. It had been a gift. From her father.

"I'll remember to steal something less valuable next time." Adikia tilted her head and climbed back through the window. Castor leaned over the sill, watching as the pirate shimmied down the thick vines that clung to the side of the manor.

Leto knocked again. "Lady Castor!"

She spun around, furious that he had interrupted her small moment of joy. She stomped across the room and flung open the door. Leto stood there, hunched and yellowing, like a rotting tree dressed up in the black rubber armor of the Arcadian guard. That armor was likely the only thing holding together the sack of bones and sagging skin.

"How dare you!" she spat. "May I remind you, Leto, that you work for this family, not the other way around. If I make you stand outside my door until you collapse, then I will do so, and you will patiently wait. Do you understand?"

He smiled at her as if she were a petulant child. "I work for the Duke of Storms, not for you, my lady. He asked me to collect you immediately."

Heat rushed to Castor's cheeks. "Perhaps you missed the announcement that I am his successor."

"As long as he is the Duke, I serve him. If you ever take that place, then I will swiftly resign."

"Only if you are alive to do so," she said. "How is that wound in your shoulder? You seem to be moving more stiffly these days."

His smile dropped, and the familiar vein at the top of his yellowed forehead pulsed in an erratic rhythm. Castor smiled and sauntered by him. He hated that she had escaped him on Ceryneia, with the help of Adikia and the arrow she'd slammed through his shoulder. Two young women had taken down the head of her father's guard. Proof the old ways were weak.

Even so, Leto and people like him wouldn't let go of tradition. As long as her father refused to accept that she was the heir and not Pollux, they would continue to fight her.

Leto stayed behind her as they walked across the polished wood floors of the manor. The long hall to her father's office led right under the painting of the Othonos family tree, long-held rulers of the Arcadian isle. At the top of it, her ancestor Tyrus glared down with faded blue eyes.

This was all his fault. He was the one who had made it so control of the island could only pass from father to son. Well, this wall was running out of room for men. Time to make a new family tree. When this manor was hers, Cas was going to have that wall stripped.

Leto lingered when they reached her father's office. Castor turned to him. "You can go now. You've done your duty. I'm here."

"I want to see you safely inside, my lady."

"Oh, I think I'm in better shape to step over this threshold than you are. You look tired, Leto. You should rest." If her father started shouting at her as soon as she opened the door, she didn't want Leto to hear it.

His expression twisted. "As you wish, my lady." He made his way toward the stairs, bones cracking the entire time.

Cas took one more breath before her father's office. This used to be her safe space, where she would go to be heard and admired, lovingly patted on the head and praised for her ingenuity. It was always Pollux who came here to be shouted at and berated.

Her brother had warned her this would happen if she won her game. She hadn't believed him.

She pulled open the doors.

Duke Tyndareus, his long white hair loose around his face and deep frown lines marring his forehead, spun around and snapped, "What kept you?"

Castor strode into the room and closed the door behind her.

"Leto. He moves so slowly these days. We had to stop twice so he could rest. Maybe it's time he retired."

"Hmm." The Duke rubbed his chin. "I will talk to him about it later. We have bigger things to worry about."

"What's wrong?"

He grabbed a stack of papers from his desk and thrust them at her. "What do you plan to do about this?"

Castor shuffled through the papers. She didn't know what this was. She saw a promise of a fifty-thousand-coin tithe. Was her father trying to buy her out again? He had already tried this several times, offering her piles of gold, the manor, control of the mining contracts . . . a million promises if only she would relinquish her claim on Arcadia. But why would she accept a portion of it when, one day, she would have it all?

She pulled out one of the papers and swallowed when she read the top.

This is the certified engagement contract between Lord Memnon Cirillo of Tegea and Lady Castor Othonos of Arcadia on this, the eighteenth day of . . .

Castor didn't need to read any more. That contract had been a mistake, a hasty decision she'd made immediately after the Hydra, when she thought she'd lost the Empresses' game. She had agreed to marry Memnon to control the ore and keep a thumb on her father. Thank the Oracles things had turned out as they had. The thought of Memnon pawing at her with his sweaty palms and foul breath made her want to rip the skin from her bones.

"I've resolved this issue. The engagement is off."

Her father snatched the papers from her. "Not according to this contract. Is this not your signature right here?" He pointed to her script on the bottom line. "Did both parties agree to terminate?"

As soon as the Empresses had declared her the winner, Castor's first stop had been to Tegea, to throw Memnon's engagement ring in his face. On her way out, she'd shouted, "I would rather cut out my eyes than marry you!"

He hadn't officially agreed to terminate, no, but she'd assumed Memnon would let it go once he'd heard the Empresses' decree. It was not in his best interest to challenge the future Duchess of Arcadia. Arcadia was Tegea's best and *only* customer. Memnon had as much to lose from a dispute as she did. Also, her failure to marry him before the end of the year entitled him to half her dowry and three percent of Arcadia's profits. Not a bad consolation prize.

But the papers her father thrust at her suggested Memnon was going to be a thorn in her side. He wanted everything the contract had promised: marriage to her within a calendar year, her entire dowry, and her legacy—10 percent of Arcadia's annual profits. Not to mention he would have equal reign of Arcadia as her spouse, once it became hers.

Impossible. She would never allow it. If she had to relinquish more of her dowry to make him go away, she would. But the StormMakers had leverage too. They were the only buyers of the Illumium mined on Tegea. Without the StormMakers, Tegea was an isle of worthless rock.

"It doesn't matter," she said. "He can't force me to marry him, and his choice is either to sell us the Illumium or not sell it at all."

"There is plenty more he can do, Castor." Her father rubbed his temples. "He could double the price of Illumium. Triple it. There is a clause in our trade contract that nullifies our agreement if we ever breach a contract with them." He shook the papers at her. "This is a breach of contract!"

Lord Atreus of Tegea had put the note in their trade contract himself: *If the StormMakers are found to be in breach of any agreement, all terms of this contract are null and void and will be renegotiated.*

"We always have contract negotiations," Castor said. "We will get through it. They need us as much as we need them. Their Illumium is worthless without us."

"Without them, our storms are useless!" The Duke threw the papers in the air. They scattered across the floor like snow. "Do you realize what you've done, Castor? You've ruined this island. You've destroyed everything we have built over centuries with one selfish choice!"

"You always look at change as ruin. You're the one holding Arcadia back!" They could do and be so much more. If only her father would let them.

He pinched his nose. "Do you know why I never named you heir?"

"Of course I do. It's because of the stupid doctrine." She jabbed a finger at the offending parchment hanging behind glass on the wall. It was as frail and yellowed as Leto. One breath, and it would crumble to ash.

"No. It's because you're selfish. You're a selfish child. You think only of yourself and nothing of our island."

Castor closed her fist. "This island is all I think about."

"You think about having it, not running it. It's always been a game to you."

"And you think Pollux would be better?"

"It's not even a question. Of course he would."

Castor's breath caught. Their father despised Pollux. He had said as much on multiple occasions. He was lying. "You're just angry I defied you."

He shook his head. "Always about you. You continue to prove how inadequate you would be as leader of this isle. Your brother has exactly what you do not: patience, the ability to think outside of himself, and the willingness to adapt and listen to other people. Yes, he needs some guidance—"

"Some guidance?"

Her father raised an eyebrow. "At least I know he can accept criticism. You can change the direction of a storm, Castor. What you can't do is move a mountain. You will sink this island if you take control. Pollux will . . . keep it afloat. At least until his own heir assumes command."

Pollux's heir? As her father spoke, Castor watched her island slip through her fingers, going straight from Pollux to his presumably bratty child. No, wait, it couldn't. The Empresses had already spoken. Her father couldn't do anything about the succession, not without defying the Empresses and incurring their wrath.

Castor smiled. "It doesn't matter what you think. I won the Empresses' game, and they declared me irrefutable heir to Arcadia."

The Duke laughed. "You didn't win that game. Everyone knows the Mazon killed the Hydra. She should have won. They are playing you. They are playing all of us, and you are so foolish, you've let them do it."

Castor's smile dropped, replaced by a heavy knot in her throat. Truth clung to her father's words, truth she didn't want to hear. She had been there, in the swamps of Lerna. She had watched Genevieve tear the monster apart to save Pollux. Technically, the Mazon *should* have won.

But none of that mattered. The Empresses had spoken, and they had spoken for Castor.

"Whatever their game," she said, "they've decided to name me future Duchess, and there is nothing you can do about it."

Her father slowly clapped his hands. "Then congratulations, dear daughter. Once you've bankrupted the island, you will have inherited a pile of ash." He smoothed back his stray white hairs. "Lord Atreus and Memnon will be here this afternoon. I assume, as future Duchess of Arcadia, you will want to do everything in your power to protect our relationship with Tegea. So, you will beg Memnon and his father for forgiveness and begin making your wedding plans. Do you understand?"

Castor's face burned hot. "We shall see about that." She spun on her heel and pushed through the heavy doors. After all she had done for this island, all the business deals she'd made, the new ventures she'd started . . . it was never enough for her father.

She would kill Memnon before she would marry him, then dig up the Illumium with her bare hands. She would not let anyone tell her what to do anymore, she would not let this island fail, and she would never, ever give up her claim to it.

CHAPTER 3
POLLUX

A s his winged horses cut through the pale blue sky on a direct path to Arcadia, Pollux sat back in his gilded chariot and pressed his fingers against the strings of his new violin. He slid his hand up and down the neck, and the vibrations hummed through his bones. The new violin was nice. Likely of higher quality than his old one. The Empresses' own MetalBenders had made it under his instruction, and he had watched every second of the crafting.

But something was off. It was too new, the strings too tight. The neck didn't have the same subtle wobble that Pollux had come to appreciate in his old violin. He had played that violin for almost a decade. This one wouldn't feel like his for a few more years at least. But it was better than nothing.

He formed the positions for "The Tyrant." The song was about his father, of course. Pollux never performed it. It was private, his soul laid bare. It was a song he often thought of when he received an unwelcome summons from the Duke.

Pollux should have been there for Gen today. Instead, he soared across the sky, beckoned by a note from his father. The Duke hadn't released any details as to why he needed Pollux so urgently. But then his father rarely spoke his intentions. He didn't have to. He was the infallible Duke of Storms, leader of all Arcadia. He snapped his fingers, and everyone came running.

Except for Cas. Despite his sister charring off half of his face and smashing his old violin, among other things, in order to win her game, a part of Pollux was pleased she had managed to subvert their father's rules. He could never be too angry when someone found a way to put the Duke in his place.

"Thank you for coming with me," Pollux said to his companion, Bale. Not really a servant, even though Pollux did pay him. Pollux didn't know what to call Bale, or even much about Bale at all. All he knew was that Bale's presence put his mother at ease, because it meant Pollux didn't travel alone, and Bale's presence put *him* at ease, because he kept other people away with his sharp tongue.

Bale shrugged. "That's what you pay me for, isn't it?"

"I actually pay you for your honest conversation."

Bale raised a blue eyebrow. "You want an honest conversation? You should have thrown your father's summons in the trash."

"That might be a bit too honest," Pollux said.

"You asked for my opinion." Bale pulled back on the reins to slow the winged horses as they neared Arcadia. In the distance, the frosted peak of Ice Mountain rose into the clouds. It was always the first thing Pollux saw when coming home.

"He's still my family," he said. "He always will be." He couldn't change that no matter how much his father tormented him.

"Then he should invite you to visit, not demand it." Bale ran a hand through his hair. "Why do you do it, Pollux? You don't need him. You are out of the line of succession as of recently, and you make enough money with your violin. Why do you still let him push you around?"

Because it's the only way I know how to deal with him, he didn't say. "I want to see Cas anyway. I need to talk to her."

"Sure."

It was impossible to deceive Bale. He was too perceptive, and Pollux didn't hide his emotions well.

But Pollux wasn't lying about wanting to see Cas. If Gen was getting her father today, the Empresses would want her to leave for Elysium soon. Despite Gen not wanting to ask Cas for help, Pollux didn't want to set out for the enemy empire with no plan and no resources.

Gen had a habit of being impetuous. Pollux loved that about her . . . except when it put her in the way of deadly monsters. Cas, on the other hand, plotted and planned everything. She might have some ideas or advice to help them complete the Empresses' tasks or find a way out of them. It bothered Pollux that the Empresses were so eager to start a war with Elysium. The two empires had been at peace for centuries. Why did they want to disturb it? Why did they want *Gen* to be the one to do it?

Cas would know. She had a mind like the Empresses', always after coin and power.

The chariot jerked downward. Pollux gripped the side to keep from falling to his death.

"Sorry about that," Bale said as he pulled the reins to the left.

They circled the gardens outside the manor. The house itself rose from the top of a green hill in a mix of oiled wood and ornate stone. Pollux felt hopeful and sick when he saw it, his usual feelings when returning home. He wanted to see his mother and talk to Cas, but he couldn't forget that his father had summoned him here. And probably not for a good reason. Pollux couldn't recall a time he had been summoned by his father that didn't have him sobbing afterward.

"You're useless."

"Why can't you be more like your sister?"

"Do you have no concern for your legacy?"

"Why couldn't I have been given another son?"

Pollux shook his head to drive the noise out. He wasn't a child anymore. He also wasn't set to be his father's protégé. Cas had won her game. She would inherit the legacy. And Bale made a good point. Pollux didn't need the Duke. He had Gen. He had his music. And he had the sickening guilt that taking what he wanted meant abandoning his family and all of Arcadia for his selfishness.

Bale brought the chariot down in the open field outside of the manor walls. The wheels hit the ground hard. Pollux held tight to his violin to keep it from dropping over the side. Even though he didn't love this violin, he didn't want to start from scratch again.

Bale pulled back on the reins, and the horses came to a stop about fifty yards from a small farmhouse on the edge of town.

"That wasn't your best landing." Pollux brushed the dust from his sleeve. His hand grazed the edge of his neck where skin rose in round scars, a reminder of his sister's temper.

"You could always control the horses yourself." Bale stepped out of the chariot and led the horses over to the farmer's trough to drink.

"If I did that, we probably wouldn't land at all," Pollux admitted. He was not the best with horses. Not that he didn't like them or appreciate them. He just lost focus when he was in charge of things. The horses would likely fly clear across the Empire before Pollux noticed they were going in the wrong direction.

"Then don't complain about my landings." Bale picked up his rucksack and flung it over his shoulder. "I'm heading into town."

"You're not coming with me to the manor?"

Bale's answer came in a laugh over his shoulder as he made his way to the short stone buildings that circled the manor. Pollux could smell roasting honey cakes and salted nuts and wished he could go with Bale. Instead, he turned to the manor house, and dark music played in his head.

As usual, the sky over Arcadia held the perfect number of clouds, enough to cover the sun every now and then and not so many that he grew cold. A gentle breeze blew across the fields, rustling the stalks of wheat in the farmyard. The weather on Arcadia was always in perfect order. Rain when needed. Sun when preferred. A feat easy to achieve when over half of the residents had been gifted with the power of storms by the Oracle Tartarus.

Pollux asked the farmer who owned this plot if he could keep an eye on the horses.

"Of course, Lord Pollux," the man said, and bowed. Pollux tried to give him a few coins, but the man refused.

They had their own stables at the manor, but if Pollux needed to leave in a hurry, it would be easier to leave from here. It wouldn't be the first time he had snuck away from his father. He had a routine, various places he kept his chariot so he could escape quickly and discreetly.

Coward. The word crept into his thoughts, unbidden. He preferred to think of himself as a conflict avoider.

He made his way up the cobblestone walk to the Illumium gates of the manor. Beyond them, his childhood home loomed. He raised his eyes to the pitched roof and the angled glass windows. From the outside, it looked like an oversized farmhouse, something quaint and cozy.

It was all a ruse.

Pollux pushed through the gates into the garden. He wove

around the grand fountain in the center of the walkway and headed toward the carved doors. They were already open. One of the maids swept dirt from the stoop.

She stopped sweeping as he passed and ducked her head. "Lord Pollux, so good to see you home."

"It's good to be home," he lied. Coming home always felt like his punishment for leaving.

He stepped inside and smiled when a familiar click of heels moved toward him.

"Lux, darling, is that you?"

Some of his anxiety subsided at his mother's voice. This was why he always came back. For her.

"It *is* you. Come here." She hurried across the floor, carrying with her the scent of rose petals. As usual, her long white hair was tied into two braids, one twisted at the top of her head as a holder for her Illumium crown, the other hanging long down her back. Pollux used to sit and watch her braid her hair, and Castor would call him "a pathetic mother's boy," which wasn't entirely untrue.

He held out his arms, and his mother wrapped hers around his waist. He leaned into her shoulder and took a deep breath. He wanted Gen to meet his mother. One day it would happen. But not today.

His mother pulled back and frowned as she touched his scarred neck. "I wish I knew where I went wrong with her," she whispered.

"You let her spend too much time with Father." Pollux squeezed her hand and pulled it away from her face. "Where is he?"

"Where do you think he is?" she said.

"His office," Pollux muttered. If Cas planned to take over Arcadia one day, the hardest part would be prying their father out of his leather chair.

Heavy, loud footsteps approached from the kitchen. Pollux turned and sighed as Soter plodded toward them. The guard looked as if he had added pounds of muscle in the last few weeks. What did he eat to keep doubling in size?

"Excuse me, my lady"—Soter bowed to Pollux's mother—"but I must steal Lord Pollux from you. The Duke requests his presence immediately."

"Of course," she said, and kissed Pollux's knuckles. "Be good, my son."

"I'll try."

She picked up her skirts and walked softly toward the drawing rooms. Behind him, Pollux felt Soter's breath on his neck. The Duke had sent Soter after him during the first part of the Empresses' game, and Pollux had scrounged up what little authority he had to send Soter away. Soter must have gotten an earful from the Duke when he'd returned to the manor without him.

"I want to apologize," Pollux said, "for lying to you when you came to fetch me."

"It is your right to do so. You are the Duke's son," Soter said in a voice that was colder than ice. "Your father is waiting." He gestured to the grand stairwell.

As Soter began to walk upstairs, Pollux grabbed his sleeve.

"Soter, wait." While he didn't want to rekindle their childhood friendship, he also didn't need more animosity in this house. "Do you remember when we spent the day rolling fruit down these steps to see which ones made the biggest mess when they hit the floor?"

Soter cracked a bare smile. "I do. I also remember the scolding Lydia gave us when she saw the fruit smeared all over the rugs."

Pollux rubbed his neck. The only person who could yell louder than the Duke was the head of house, Lydia.

"I also remember," Soter continued, "scrubbing fruit off the floors for hours while you got a slap on the wrist and a piece of cake, *my lord*. Can we continue on now?" He thrust his hand toward the stairs.

"Yes, of course."

He was a fool. Despite what he did, he would always be *Lord of Storms*. He couldn't erase all the wealth and privilege he'd grown up with, even if he discarded it all now. People like Soter wouldn't forget, or forgive, and Pollux wasn't sure he deserved any forgiveness.

At the top of the stairs, he turned left and shied away from the looming painting of the Othonos family tree. He felt his ancestor Tyrus glaring down at him with his cold blue eyes.

Tyrus had been the first Arcadian ruler to discover that the Illumium from Tegea could be used to hold and transport storms. He'd also declared that Arcadian succession would go from father to son, a law Castor recently broke by "winning" her game with the Empresses.

Tyrus must be turning in his grave. Good.

Pollux's own portrait was at the bottom of the family tree. He avoided it as he passed. He knew he looked like a stuffed doll in that high-collared shirt his father had insisted he wear for the painting.

When they reached the doors to his father's office, sweat broke out on Pollux's skin.

"Here you are, my lord. I take my leave." Soter bowed his head and backed away.

Even through the thick Illumium doors, muffled voices escaped. Loud voices. Angry voices. Pollux gripped his violin with white knuckles. He tried to remember what Bale had said to him. Pollux didn't need his father anymore. His father needed him. Pollux was only here as a favor.

He rapped his knuckles on one door before he pushed it open. Over its creaking, the shouting temporarily stopped. But tension hung in the room thicker than fog.

The Duke sat behind his desk, lording over the scene, per usual. His white hair was pulled back into a tight knot, and unfortunately for everyone in the room, he wore his black coat. Never a good sign. His black coat was his Furious Cloak, as Pollux used to call it. It had more pockets. Held more lightning.

Castor sat in the chair opposite him. Her face was blank, but her hands curled around the arms of her chair, knuckles white—a storm cloud about to burst. In the chair to her left sat Lord Atreus, the head of the Tegean isle. He wore a gray jacket over a red vest that had been buttoned crookedly. He must have left Tegea in a hurry.

To his left sat Lord Memnon, Atreus's eldest son and Castor's former fiancé. Pollux remembered him from when they'd been children. He was a bully. He used to sneak extra tea cakes from the kitchen and blame the serving boys, who then took the beatings in his place.

"Finally, you've arrived," the Duke said. "Sit down, Pollux, and help us talk sense into your sister."

"It's too late." Lord Atreus stood up. "I have been insulted enough, and your daughter is far beyond sense. Because of our longstanding relationship, Tyndareus, I was willing to give you a second chance. I see now, that is impossible."

"Atreus . . ." The Duke stood, almost pleading in a voice Pollux had never heard his father use. "Let Pollux and me speak with her privately. I'm sure we can change her mind."

Pollux had clearly arrived late. He had no idea what was happening, but he did know that once Castor had made up her mind about something, no one could change it.

"I'm sorry, old friend, but you are out of time." Lord Atreus took a deep breath and blew it out slowly. "We have another buyer for the Illumium who has offered more coin. This visit was merely a courtesy."

Castor stood, nostrils flaring. "That's not possible. You're bluffing! You don't have another buyer."

Atreus looked at her like she was a barking dog. "I do, young lady. And seeing as how you've released us from our contract, I feel no guilt about selling to this other party. If you were family, things would be different."

Pollux began to piece things together. This was about the engagement, a marriage that would be much more appealing to Atreus now that Castor was set to be Duchess. Cas could be right—this could be a bluff. If she was wrong, Arcadia was about to lose its entire business.

A small part of Pollux wanted to laugh. This was exactly what his sister and father deserved. But Cas looked broken by the news, as broken as she had looked stumbling away from the Hydra's lair.

"Lord Atreus—" Pollux began, not sure what he would say next.

"Enough." Atreus held up his hand. "Come, Memnon. We have other business to attend to."

Memnon curled his lip at Castor. "Your loss," he said under his breath as he stood.

"I can guarantee it will be yours," Castor retorted with enough venom to widen Memnon's beady eyes.

"Atreus," the Duke said, coming out from behind his desk. "I'll go to the Empresses. I'll ask them to force the marriage."

"If, by the grace of the Oracles, you succeed, then perhaps we can talk." Atreus gave Castor one last look. "But I highly doubt it."

Pollux did too.

As soon as the doors shut, the tension in the room rose even further.

"You little fool!" the Duke shouted at Cas. "You have ruined us. You will go after Atreus immediately and tell him you've reconsidered. You will marry Memnon."

"I will not," Castor snapped. "Atreus is bluffing. You could see it in his face. He doesn't have another buyer. He is trying to force my hand."

"What if he's not bluffing? What will you do then? Without the Illumium, we have nothing, and if there is another buyer, we have no room to renegotiate the contract." Their father slammed his hand on the desk, and Pollux involuntarily twitched. "Our storms only have power if we can keep them. If we can sell them. We cannot lose the Illumium."

Pollux's hands trembled as they always did when their father lost his temper. Except this time, oddly, it wasn't aimed at him.

"Father," he said. "You can't make her marry him."

"What would you have me do instead?" the Duke snapped. "None of this would be happening if you'd only laid claim to the role that was already yours. You invited your sister to take it with your weakness."

Ah, there it was. The insult Pollux had been waiting for.

The Duke paced the floor in his well-worn grooves. "You leave me no choice, Castor. You made this mess yourself, and I can't let our people sink with your bad decisions. I will appeal to the Empresses. They may not have changed their minds about you being my heir, but they *can* force the marriage. The Empresses are one of our most important customers. If the Illumium is at stake, they will act. They will not want to lose their supply of lightning."

"Then they can act as easily against Tegea," Castor said, "and force Tegea to sell it to us."

"If, by the Oracles, you can convince them to do that, then be my guest. But I guarantee, it will be far easier for them to strong-arm one stubborn girl than an entire isle. I warn you, if we lose our supplies, you will never see the inside of this office until I am long gone, and until then, I will make life very difficult for you. Restrict you to the grounds. Cut off your funds. Take away your access to the storm vaults."

"You're playing right into Atreus's hands," Castor said coolly, except her voice cracked ever so slightly. "I guarantee it's a bluff, and once things have settled, we can begin the real negotiations. No one is taking our Illumium."

"That is your greatest flaw, daughter," the Duke said in an even colder voice, without any cracks. "You made this personal. Just remember, the Empresses can take Arcadia away as easily as they granted it, and I'm certain, once they discover you won't be able to restock their supply of lightning vials, they will make some swift changes. You will have lost everything."

Castor's face flushed. "We shall see about that, Father."

She spun on her heel and made for the door. She slammed it hard enough behind her to rattle the family portrait hanging on the wall. It swung three times before it settled at an odd angle over the fireplace. Pollux's painted face stared back at him crookedly.

"She is impossible," the Duke snapped. "For the life of me, I can't figure out why the Empresses would give her the duchy."

"They must recognize her strength," Pollux said.

"She has no strength. It's all stubbornness and spit."

The muscles in Pollux's arms tensed. He hadn't come here to listen to his father insult Cas. "Did you need me for anything else?"

"I need you to make your sister marry Memnon."

Pollux bit back a laugh. As if anyone could force Castor to do something against her will; as if Pollux would have the smallest chance at being the first. Even if he could make Cas marry Memnon, he wouldn't. Memnon was a horrible person, and Castor would make relations between their two isles worse as his wife.

Pollux grabbed his violin and made for the door. "I'll be gone for a while, so I won't be able to respond to any future summons."

"Where are you going?" the Duke said. "I need you here."

"As I am no longer the heir apparent, I am taking advantage of my secondary status to travel. I will see you when I get back." Pollux ducked his chin and left the room before his father could explode into his usual series of curses. As Bale had said, Pollux no longer owed his father anything.

In the hall, Pollux glanced quickly down the stairs to the front doors, to freedom and to Gen. That was where he should be going, but instead he kept walking straight, toward his sister's room. As much as he wanted to abandon this place, he knew he could never abandon Cas. Barely a month as the heiress and she'd already gotten herself into trouble. The least he could do was tell her what was coming: war.

CHAPTER 4

CASTOR

Vile, disgusting Memnon, Castor thought as she charged down the hall. She itched to burn, break, or smash something.

Her father would always control her. Even when she had won everything.

She would never marry Memnon. Even if her father locked her in her room, took away all of her coin, and had his foul guard Leto follow her everywhere she went. Even if he appealed to the Empresses and they vowed to sink Arcadia into the sea. She would find a way out of it. She wanted to lead Arcadia for her freedom. If she didn't have that, she had nothing.

But she was worried for no reason. It was a bluff. There was no buyer. This was a battle of wills, and Atreus and Memnon would break long before she did. Arcadia had enough of the ore in storage that they could last the winter at least. And *if* there was a second buyer—maybe she could convince them to use another metal for their purposes.

Because Illumium wasn't special to anyone except the StormMakers, and all of Olympia's StormMakers were here. Who else would want it?

"Cas."

Her shoulders curled to her ears, and she spun around and reached for her nearest vial of lightning. Lux, hurrying down the hall toward her, caught the movement and skidded across the polished floors. His hand immediately flew to his neck and covered the scars there. The ones she had given him at the stables.

She released her vial and took a breath. She appreciated him trying to stand up for her in their father's office, but she hadn't forgotten how he had betrayed her in the Empresses' game by siding with Gen. She was also just *not* in the mood. "What do you want?"

"I need to talk to you."

"There is nothing to talk about." She turned and kept walking.

Lux caught up and fell in step beside her. She lifted her chin. He'd outgrown her sometime during the year they'd turned thirteen, stretching taller and leaner, like a reed in the wind. She hated that he was larger than she was.

"There is something to talk about," he pressed. "Something important."

Castor quickened her pace. "What? Are you here to apologize for forcing me into this position? I wouldn't have been so desperate to sign that stupid marriage contract if you hadn't teamed up with Genevieve to defeat me."

"I think after burning my face and destroying my violin, we can call it even. I want to help you."

"I don't need your help."

"I have information you might want."

She slowed. "Talk."

"I can't talk about it here."

Castor rolled her eyes and kept walking to her room. He followed. In listing off all of Pollux's wonderful leadership characteristics, the Duke had forgotten "persistent."

Castor knew she held on to her claim on Arcadia by a spider's web. Like her father had said, the Empresses could take it away as easily as they'd granted it, and everyone knew Castor had won the contest on a technicality.

You didn't win that game. Everyone knows the Mazon killed the Hydra. She should have won.

If Cas had killed the Hydra, her father wouldn't be harassing her about marriage contracts. Or bragging about Pollux. He would be in awe of her skill and power. He would *want* her to be in command.

Castor entered her room and slammed the door behind her. Or tried to. Pollux caught it with the edge of his boot before it closed. If he didn't have those scars, she would have burned him twice by now.

She picked up her wooden box. "Delia!" she shouted.

"Yes, Lady Castor," the ghost replied from inside the box.

"Lord Atreus and Memnon are on their way back to Tegea right now. Follow them and listen to their conversation. I want to know who is buying the Illumium, if anyone, or if this is all a trick to force me into marrying. I need to know everything that is said."

"Someone else is buying the Illumium?" Delia asked.

"Yes," Cas hissed. "Now go. I need answers, and fast." She cracked the window, and Delia soared through it. Castor would get to the truth soon enough, and then she would plan her next steps.

Best case, there was no buyer, and negotiations could reopen with marriage off the table. There would possibly be some price increases, but Castor could handle them, especially with the Boar and his men making claims on late payments.

Worst case, there was another buyer, and her father's appeal to the Empresses to force the marriage contract would be successful. She would kill Memnon before she married him, which would only make things with Tegea worse. And her father was right. The

Empresses were unlikely to force Tegea to sell. In their same position, she would force the easier mark: her.

She shook her head. She couldn't get ahead of herself. First, she needed Delia to come back with her news. Castor couldn't solve the problem until she knew how deep it went.

She turned to find Pollux toying with a bracelet from her dresser. She snatched it from him and shoved it in a drawer. Why was everyone handling her jewelry?

"Why are you still here?" she asked. "I thought I made it clear we have nothing to talk about."

"We have a lot to talk about." Pollux paced her room the same way their father did, chin high, shoulders back. "The Empresses have given Gen another chance to save her father."

Castor raised an eyebrow. "Good for her."

"But she has to do two more labors for them: get the golden apples of Hesperides and capture the Cerberus."

"You're joking." Castor sank onto her bed. This was worse than the first round of tasks.

"I wish I were."

"Then it's obvious. The Empresses don't want Gen to succeed. They don't want Alcmen out of prison. That's why they keep asking her to do the impossible."

"No. They let her have him. Today. He's staying at the palace while Gen goes after the apples and the Cerberus."

"They let him out?"

"Yes." Pollux sat cautiously beside her and set his violin by his feet.

This was interesting news. If the Empresses weren't making

excuses to keep Gen from Alcmen, then what did they want? Did they want her dead?

No. They had much easier ways of killing someone. They kept a garden of poisonous plants. If they wanted her dead, all they had to do was serve her tea. Well, if they didn't want Gen dead, and they didn't want to keep Alcmen in prison, then they wanted something else.

"A war," Castor said. "They want to start a war with Elysium." Sending Gen after the Elysium Emperor's prized treasures would easily accomplish that.

With impending war, no doubt the Empresses would be looking for lightning, which Cas couldn't provide without Illumium. But if the second buyer was a hoax, then this would be a golden opportunity for renegotiations. Both she and Atreus would make a fortune from a war. It would be a bad time to be battling against each other.

"Why would they want a war?" Pollux said. "What do they have to gain from it? We've been at peace with Elysium for years."

Castor shook her head. Pollux never thought big enough. "If they win it, they get another fifty islands, all the Elysium resources, and taxes from all the conquered people."

"But if they lose, we'll have Elysium forces here in our waters, and Cas . . . I don't want to be the reason why Olympia falls."

"Don't be obtuse, Lux. The Empresses don't start things they will lose." They were like Castor in that sense, playing to win. "That's why they want the Cerberus."

The Cerberus was how the Elysium Empire had won the old wars. Their Oracle Arai had gifted the Emperor with the Cerberus, and once it burned a thousand Olympian ships, the two empires declared a ceasefire, negotiated a treaty, and vowed to remain in their own borders from then on.

If Gen took the Cerberus, that would tip the scales. If Gen *died* while trying to take the Cerberus, the Empresses could always claim Gen had gone rogue, and they'd known nothing of her plans. They could keep the peace.

It was genius.

"Why the apples, then?" Pollux asked. "What are they for?"

That was tricky. The golden apples were part of Elysium lore, rumored to be magical, indestructible. One apple planted could grow another golden apple tree that would produce golden fruit for an eternity.

The Elysiums had four Oracles: Arai, Oracle of Malice; Nyx, Oracle of Night; Phoebe, Oracle of Prophecy; and Gaia, Oracle of Growth. Gaia supposedly gave the late Emperor Hadrian the apples as a wedding gift, and because he didn't want anyone else touching them, he had them hidden on an island. The Oracle Nyx offered up her own daughters to protect them, witches named the Hesperides. The apples were supposedly impossible to find and even more impossible to reach. Only the current Emperor would know where they were.

"Maybe they plan to mold it into armor," Castor said. "Is Gen going to do it?"

Pollux sighed. "You know Gen. She'll go to the end of the world for Alcmen, and I worry this time she won't make it back." He looked Cas hard in the eye. "What would you do if the Empresses asked you to go into Elysium? Would you go?"

Would she? If it could end her problem with Tegea and finally earn her father's blessing?

Months ago, she would have said yes. She'd never failed at anything. However, recently, she'd made too many mistakes. She couldn't afford any more setbacks.

"You'll never be able to sneak into Elysium," she said, not answering his question. "Even if you ride in that whale underwater, Emperor Nessos has eyes. Instead of avoiding them, you should go directly into his line of sight. Visit him under the guise of friendship. Come up with some fake message from the Empresses that you were sent to pass along. Work your way inside and see what you can find. Then plan your next steps."

"Cas, he's going to kill us if we do that."

"He's not going to kill you." *Not immediately.* "Nessos isn't cruel like the Empresses. He has nothing to prove. Elysium was the winner in the last wars, not the loser. He'll know killing you could incite fury from the Empresses, and he doesn't want a new war. He could lose, and he wouldn't be willing to give up his status."

Pollux looked down at his hands, chewing on her advice. While the Emperor likely wouldn't kill him immediately, the Elysium Empire held many other dangers. Other monsters like the Cerberus gifted from the Oracles, poisonous fruits, dangerous waters, unmentionable sea creatures . . . if Pollux tailed after Gen this time, he might not return.

"You're a fool if you go," she said.

"What? You just said—"

"I know what I said, but you're not Gen. If you find the Cerberus, it will tear you to pieces. It's selfish of her to ask you to go."

Pollux narrowed his eyes. "She didn't ask me. I want to go."

"Because you're a fool."

"Of course you would think caring about another person is foolish."

Their father's words echoed in Castor's thoughts. *"You think only of yourself and nothing of our island."*

"I am thinking of you! Trying to keep you from killing yourself!"

"If I'm a fool, it's because I thought you might help." Pollux picked up his violin and made for the door.

"I am trying to help. What did you think I would do? Tell you how to vanquish an immortal beast? Or find magic apples?"

"No, Cas. You did exactly what I knew you would—focus on what *you* need. Best of luck with your Illumium. Maybe I will see you when I get back." He slammed the door behind him. Castor picked up an errant boot and threw it at the closed door. It left a black mark on the wood.

Castor lay back on her bed and pulled her pillow to her face. She closed her eyes and breathed in the lingering seawater and wood-smoke smell that Adikia had left behind. Then she screamed into the fibers. Her life would be so much easier without other people in it.

As she pulled the pillow away from her face, Delia sailed through the open window, blinking feverishly. Castor sat upright.

"I have seen Lord Atreus and his son," Delia said.

"What did they say? What do they want? Is there another buyer?" Castor dug her fingernails hard into her palms.

"Yes," Delia said with a lift in her voice, as if she was delighted to deliver her news.

Castor gritted her teeth. "Who?"

"The Empresses."

Heat rose from Castor's collar. "The Empresses? Are you sure?"

"Yes, Lord Atreus said it himself: 'We need to get in contact with the Empresses and let them know the marriage is null. They can have their Illumium.'"

Castor twisted the vials on her belt. Why would the Empresses steal her metal? Why did they need it? It was only good for—lightning.

It all clicked into place. Gen's quests. The Illumium. Oh, those foul Empresses. They had set Castor up. They'd given her the win, knowing she would break her engagement with Tegea. Knowing Lord Atreus would then sell *them* the metal. They would need it to hold all the lightning required to win the war that Gen and Pollux were about to start. And without control of the Illumium, Arcadia would be forced to supply the Empresses with *all* their lightning. No price gouging. No competition.

Arcadia would lose their other customers, and once the war was over and the Empresses no longer needed their lightning, Arcadia would be destitute.

Castor pulled a vial of lightning from her belt and released it. The blast struck the ceiling, leaving a black scorch mark and the scent of smoke in the air. She pulled the lightning back into the vial and tucked it on her belt.

"Into your box!" she shouted at Delia. Once the spirit had soared inside, she sealed it shut and grabbed another handful of storm vials. She needed to speak directly to the Empresses. She could not lose control of the Illumium, even to them.

Cas ran from her room and stormed down the manor steps. She burst through the front doors and caught up to her brother, walking through the gardens.

"Pollux!" she shouted.

He turned around. "What? Are you here to insult me again?"

"No. I need a ride," she said, near breathless.

"You have to be kidding."

"The Empresses are the ones buying the Illumium, Lux. I need to stop them." She would have to figure out how on the way there. "Please," she added.

Lux predictably softened. He was so easily manipulated. It took only a few kind words or, in Gen's case, a pair of dewy brown eyes to control him.

"Fine. You can come," he said. "But I think it's best if we don't speak on the ride."

"Agreed." She had nothing more to say to him, but she had plenty of words for the Empresses.

CHAPTER 5

GEN

Gen sat by her father's bed while he slept with Chomp curled into his side. Asleep, he looked almost like the man she remembered. Awake, he was a near stranger with confusion on his face and fear in his eyes. And he wouldn't be asleep forever. She would have to figure out a way to make him better . . . after she completed her last tasks for the Empresses, of course.

Outside, a dark shadow passed over the gardens—Pollux's chariot. Gen rushed from the room and down the stairs. A small part of her had worried he wouldn't come back, not because he wouldn't want to, but because his horrid StormMaker family would have forced him to stay behind.

She raced through the gardens and reached the stables. A cloud of dust plumed in the air. She squinted, searching for Pollux and his two winged horses, Nimbus and Eclipse. They were new; Castor had lost his last horses when she'd burned down his old chariot.

A tall, willowy shadow broke the haze. Gen smiled and ran to meet Pollux, then stopped. "Castor?"

Pollux's twin stomped from the stables with a scowl on her face and a belt filled with storm vials. In her blue vest, silk blouse, and sapphire necklace, she made Gen feel like a child playing dress-up in her tailored jacket and velvet pants. She looked as vicious as when

Gen had last seen her in the Empresses' solarium, gloating that they had named her winner of the contest.

"What are you doing here?" Gen demanded.

"That is none of your business." Castor lifted her chin toward the top of the palace behind them.

"It is all of my business," Gen said. "Where is Pollux? What have you done with him?"

"Why would you accuse me of doing something with him? Aren't *you* the one planning to take him into the Cerberus's lair?"

Gen flinched. How did Castor know about that?

"Pollux can make his own choices, at least with me." Gen had told him he didn't need to come with her, but possibly not with as much sternness as she could have used. The truth was, she wanted him with her. They both worked better together.

"That's hilarious," Castor said. "He is so deluded by you, he can't even think straight. Are you poisoning him with your mind magic?"

"No, of course not." Gen clenched her fists tighter. "I will ask you this one more time. Where is Pollux?" If Castor, or anyone in their family, or anyone in the entire Empire for that matter, had touched one strand of his white hair, she would crush them to dust.

"Causing trouble already, I see." Bale emerged from the stables with an empty ale glass in hand.

Gen's shoulders relaxed slightly. More when Pollux followed, appearing mostly unharmed except for the anguish written on his face.

"I thought I told you not to speak," Pollux said to his sister.

"Enough of this. I have my own business to attend to." Castor flipped her hair over her shoulder and stalked past them into the gardens. Gen didn't unclench her fists until she could no longer see the back of Castor's adorable boots.

"I thought she had done something to you." Gen pressed her palm to the scarred skin on Pollux's neck.

"No." He put his hand gently on hers and pulled it away. "Nothing more than the usual insults and demands."

"Despite what you might think," Bale said, "we are capable of handling ourselves when you're not there."

Gen raised an eyebrow. She would believe that more if Bale didn't smell like the inside of a tavern. She turned back to Pollux. "Why did your father call you home?"

"Why do you think?" he said. "Problems with Castor. Memnon is trying to hold her to her marriage contract. She refused, so they are breaking their contract with Arcadia for Illumium and selling it to the Empresses instead."

"The Empresses want the Illumium? Why?"

"From my vast experience in dealing with power-hungry and controlling rulers, my guess is they want to force Castor to supply them with lightning for the war they're planning with Elysium."

Gen chewed on her lower lip. This was no less than Castor deserved. She had stolen the win in the game, killed Gen's whale, and burned Pollux. It had seemed unfair that after doing all that, she would get exactly what she wanted. But Castor's misfortune didn't fix any of it. Gen had been happy to let Castor take Arcadia and leave her Pollux instead.

"Where's Alcmen?" Pollux asked, peering into the gardens for a sign of him. "Is he here?"

Pollux was one of the few people who had remained loyal to her family's circus even after Alcmen's downfall. Right now, he looked like an eager fan, waiting for the show to begin. Gen didn't want to take that away from him. Not yet.

"He's upstairs. Resting. Chomp is with him."

"I'm sure he must be exhausted. I can't wait to meet him. Do you think he would sign one of my old ticket stubs?"

"We can ask him later." Much later.

Behind them, someone cleared their throat. Between the shrubs stood the Empresses' head servant, Gregor. He had crept up on them without making a sound, and with his gray skin and matching gray suit, he blended in seamlessly with the shadows. Gen assumed that was why the Empresses kept him; he could be everywhere and anywhere and move like smoke.

"Lord Pollux and Mistress Genevieve," Gregor said. "The Empresses request your presence in the solarium—immediately."

"If I'm not needed," Bale said, "I am going to stay as far from the solarium as possible." He made a quick bow and ran through the gardens to escape.

Gen wished she could follow. Being summoned to the solarium never ended well. The last time she had been pulled into a formal meeting with the Empresses, they told her she'd lost the game she had actually won, Castor would be taking over as heir of Arcadia, and Gen would have to capture a massive three-headed fire-breathing dog and find legendary apples to secure her father's freedom.

"They are waiting." Gregor urged them to the palace.

Gen took Pollux's hand. He held his violin with his other. *Always better together*, she told herself.

They crossed the stone bridge into the palace and followed Gregor into the solarium. He pushed open the doors to reveal Castor there, waiting. Gen didn't know if Castor had been summoned, too, or if she had barged her way in there unannounced. Neither answer would surprise Gen.

"What are you doing here?" Castor snapped.

"We were summoned," Pollux said.

Castor sighed and rolled her eyes. "Whatever it is can wait. I need to talk to them about my Illumium first."

Gen crossed her arms. Perfect. Castor would put the Empresses in a bad mood before Gen could ask for what she wanted: time. She couldn't leave her father here alone with them, not how he was. The Alcmen she had known as a child could have handled himself anywhere. This one couldn't handle himself at all.

Gregor left the room and, moments later, reappeared through the dais doors. He bent at the waist and waved his hand in a flourish. "Presenting Their Exalted Highnesses, the esteemed rulers of Olympia, the Red and Crystal Empresses."

He shifted a curtain aside and pulled the gilded doors wide. Red and Crystal stepped out together, wearing a custom gown of glittering red and white. It twisted together in a swirl on the skirt and came up high behind their necks, forming spikes behind Crystal's blond hair and curling into flames behind Red's. Their gowns all had to be custom made to perfection to fit to their single body.

Rumor in the palace was the last dressmaker hadn't given one of their gowns enough room to twist, and it ripped during an important meeting. The next day, that dressmaker's bloated body was carried out of the palace wrapped in bloody sheets.

Gen couldn't leave Alcmen in a place like this, not alone.

The Red Empress wore a silver bracelet with a chain. On the other end of that chain crouched a young man. Gen forced herself to look at him. That man was only here because she'd freed Mr. Percy from his gambling debts with the Lion. In exchange for that service, Mr. Percy had to give the Empresses his eldest son for the year.

He stared back at her with haunted gray eyes, and Gen flinched. The Empresses held everyone by a chain, even if it wasn't always so obvious. If the Empresses requested a favor, the reply was "yes" if you wanted to see another day. "No," and you would end up like the dressmaker. Or worse. The Empresses had killed entire families, settlements, and towns in their rage, and they had enough powerful supporters to keep their place.

Little people like Gen and Mr. Percy's son could only hope to avoid them. But it was too late for that. They had both been seen.

"Welcome," Red said as she sat down.

"So good to see you all together," Crystal added. "We missed you at supper last night, Mistress Genevieve, Lord Pollux."

"I apologize, Your Majesties. We took supper in our rooms," Gen answered.

The Red Empress laughed. "You two do spend quite a lot of time in *your rooms*." She tugged on the chain, and the end of it cut into the neck of Mr. Percy's son. Gen closed her fists.

"And Lady Castor, we have been expecting you. Not this quickly, though. News does travel fast, doesn't it," Red said.

Castor pressed her lips together and glared daggers. Gen had seen that look before. Then it had chilled her to the bones. Now she appreciated not being the subject of Castor's hatred—not that she planned on becoming a Castor fan anytime soon.

"I count three," Crystal said. "We seem to be missing a guest. Gregor!"

"Apologies." Gregor rushed from the room, and Gen chewed her lip, waiting to see who their next guest would be. Surprise visitors from the Empresses were rarely good.

The doors opened, and Gregor entered the room with a half-dazed Alcmen, dredged out of sleep.

Gen sucked in a breath and held it as her father blinked, looking around the room. *Please stay calm. Please stay calm.* His gaze came into focus when he spotted Castor. His face changed from a confused mask into murderous rage.

"StormMakers!" He lunged, biting into his wrist as he did.

Castor reached for her nearest storm vial. Gen slid across the solarium floor toward her father. Pollux went for Castor.

Gen snatched Alcmen's arm. He spat on her and struggled to break free. On the dais, the Empresses watched with cruel smiles. They had already known what would happen. They had planned this for their own entertainment.

"Stay away from me, MindWorker!" Castor shouted.

"I'll kill you, StormMaker!" Alcmen spat back.

Gen used as much strength as she dared to hold him without snapping his arm. Screaming and spitting, with blood running down his fingers, he looked exactly like the unhinged murderer everyone thought he was.

"Father!" She gently shook him. He looked from Castor to her. She pressed his face between her palms, a knot forming in her throat. "Please," she begged. "We're in front of the Empresses. You can't act like this."

Confusion dropped over his face. She could see him struggling to make sense of anything, of everything, like a child lost in the woods.

"I'm sorry," he whispered, but they were just words. He wasn't sorry. She held tight to his wrist.

Pollux kept his distance, horror written on his face. Gen had been afraid of this. Pollux had been the last person to think Alcmen was still amazing. Now the word "murderer" hung on his lips.

No one believed in Alcmen anymore.

No, that wasn't true. Gen still believed in him. The prison had done this to him. All he needed was time and space to heal, and she could give that to him when she truly set him free.

"My word." The Crystal Empress fanned herself. "That was uncalled for."

"The years in prison have been hard on my father," Gen said. "He will get better."

"While you are away on your errands, Genevieve, we will make sure Alcmen gets the best of care," the Red Empress said, tugging on the chain that held Mr. Percy's son.

The Empresses called capturing the Cerberus an errand, as if he were a mouse or a lizard she could shove into her pocket. Gen could be gone for weeks, months . . . forever. "This is what I would like to ask you, Your Highnesses. My father needs me. Here. I was wondering if I could postpone—"

"Absolutely not," the Red Empress said. "It's been enough time as it is. We can't wait any longer."

"We have fulfilled our end of the bargain," the Crystal Empress said. "Do you not think us capable of handling one man?"

No, she didn't. "Can't you—"

"No," the Red Empress snapped. "We have been generous enough, have we not? While we have been working to secure the safe release of your father, have you not stayed under our roof? Eaten our food?"

"Ingrate," the Crystal Empress added. "You give her everything, and she keeps trying to take, take, take."

"Agreed," the Red Empress said. "You will set out tomorrow, Mistress Genevieve, and we won't hear another word about it. Your father will be perfectly safe with us."

"Perfectly safe," the Crystal Empress echoed, running her fingers through the pale blue hair of Mr. Percy's son.

This was Gen's final, unspoken warning. "Of course, Your Majesties. I'll leave tomorrow." She squeezed Alcmen's hand.

The Red Empress turned. "Now, Lady Castor, what is it we can do for you?"

Castor stepped forward, her glare sharper than before. "I'm here to talk about the Illumium."

The Red Empress smiled. "What is there to talk about? Lord Atreus has recently been freed from the confines of his contract and has received a better offer on the metal."

"From you," Castor snapped.

"It's nothing personal. Just business," the Crystal Empress said.

"You have time to settle the matter of your contract," the Red Empress said. "As we hear it, you only have to go through with your marriage to Lord Memnon."

"It would be quite the pairing," the Crystal Empress said. "The future Duchess of Arcadia with the Lord of Tegea. You would be unstoppable."

"I do not need Memnon to be unstoppable," Castor said through her teeth. "What I need is my metal."

"I think you mean *our* metal," the Red Empress said.

"I can offer you a discount—"

The Red Empress held up her hand. "You *will* give us a discount, especially since we will be providing the metal containers for your lightning. A third of your normal price should be more than generous."

All the color left Castor's cheeks, turning them a pure, alabaster white. "You will bankrupt our island."

Did Castor deserve this? Yes. Still, Gen didn't like to see it. Castor was one of the fiercest women she knew, and if the Empresses could break her, they could break anyone.

"Of course, we cannot force you to sell us the lightning," the Crystal Empress said. "But it will be quite useless to you, if you have nowhere to store it."

Castor clenched her fists. "Half price."

"Thirty-five percent," the Red Empress said. "And that is our final offer. I suggest you take it."

"Done," Castor said in the barest whisper. Then she turned on her heel and left the room.

"Is there anything else?" Crystal asked. "Or are we done here?" She said the words as a challenge.

Gen shook her head. The Empresses exited through the dais doors, and Gen exhaled. She supposed it could have been worse. At least they were all alive. For now.

Pollux turned to her. "I need to go—Castor—"

"Go," Gen said. She wouldn't begrudge him chasing after Castor now. Besides, she had her own family issues to manage.

She led Alcmen back to their rooms. Chomp woke up when she opened the door. She sat down on the bed and called him into her lap. She stroked her fingers through his fur. Alcmen ran a hand through his hair. Blood crusted his arm where he had bitten into his own skin. What had he planned to do? Feed Castor his blood? Gen had spent much of her life trying to be exactly like the Amazing Alcmen, the dashing and beloved ringmaster. Now she felt ashamed of him.

"What is happening?" he asked. "Why are the StormMakers here?"

"A lot has changed since you've been gone."

"The StormMakers haven't changed. They are still coin-hungry killers."

Gen couldn't entirely argue that. "Pollux isn't."

"The Duke's son?"

"He helped me save you from prison. He risked his life to keep me alive. Neither of us would be here without him."

"Then I suppose I owe him my gratitude," Alcmen said, unconvinced.

"Pollux is a performer," Gen added. "A gifted violin player. You will have to hear him play. He headlined a sold-out show at the Lion's Den."

"Really?" Alcmen smiled, and his eyes flashed with the barest twinkle, the one he used to get before their own performances.

"We've talked about performing together," Gen continued, wanting to hold on to this Alcmen, shining through the haze. "I always thought our show could use some music."

He scratched his chin. "Not a bad idea. The show could use a refresher. Some new acts too. You know the last time we performed, I heard a stagehand say he'd seen a gryphon just north of Deimos."

"We should look for it," Gen said. "I've never seen a gryphon before." If Alcmen had gotten this news almost five years ago, it was likely the gryphon had moved on. It didn't matter, though; what mattered was sitting here with her father, talking about a possible future. It meant he believed there could be one.

"They're wily creatures," he said. "One's not about to soar by your windows. They nest high in the mountains and are as likely to tear the skin from your bones as they are to bite off your head."

"We can go after it together," she said, "when I get back. I have to leave for a while." She set Chomp on the rug and brushed purple fur from her pants.

"Where?" Alcmen cocked his head.

Gen stared at him, but he seemed completely oblivious. In his rage against Castor, he hadn't even heard the Empresses' decree.

"The Empresses want me to get some things for them, and you have to stay here." She gestured to the fine room: the satin bedsheets, the plush armchairs, and the wide windows. With three full meals a day and some fresh air, it would be far better than the prison, even if he did have to stay here with the wicked Empresses.

"That's ridiculous. I'll come with you."

"You can't." *Because you're collateral*, she didn't say.

"Gen, what do you have to do for them?" Her father was lucid enough to know she wasn't telling him the truth, at least not all of it.

"They want me to go to Elysium to get the golden apples of Hesperides and the Cerberus, which means—"

"That's preposterous. You can't chase after the Cerberus." He spoke to her as if she were still that knobby-kneed little girl he'd left behind.

"I have to, or the Empresses will send you right back to prison." She turned to face one of the paintings hanging on the bedroom wall. It showed the Empresses in a stylized form, their faces pieced together in large, colorful shapes.

"Then let them send me back."

"I can't do that."

He shook his head. "Gen, why would you agree to something so foolish?"

"Foolish?" Heat burst on her cheeks. "What choice do I have? After you left, I spent the last four years hiding in the shadows, trying to stay alive. People hate us. Our names mean nothing now. I finally gained some of their respect when I killed the Hydra, but it won't last. I need the Empresses to clear your name if we ever want a chance again."

"You're doing this for the fame?"

She reeled back. Maybe she had been doing it for the fame once. Not anymore. Not for a long time.

She stood up to face him. "I'm doing it so I don't add 'traitor to the Empresses' as one of my crimes. So I have a chance at a life again without getting pelted with rotten fruit or being called 'monster' behind my back." If he wasn't going to be the Amazing Alcmen anymore, *she* needed to be more. She needed to be the one to keep their small family from falling to pieces.

Alcmen leaned against an armchair. "This is all my fault. I shouldn't have left you."

"You're right, you shouldn't have. But you did. You made this mess, and now I have to clean it up."

"You won't survive it, Gen. The Cerberus? It will destroy you."

"They said the same thing about the Hydra."

"You're not—"

"What? Strong enough? A good enough MindWorker?"

He took a breath. "You're just a little girl, and there are things you don't know, things you don't understand."

"No, there are things *you* don't understand." She shook her head. "I'm not a little girl anymore. I stopped being a little girl the second I became an orphan. You weren't the only one who suffered, Father. I won't go into exile again. I can't. I'm going to Elysium, and I'm going to finish this whether you like it or not."

"Gen, I won't let you go. I already lost your mother. I won't lose you!"

"You didn't lose me! You gave me up when you left home and didn't come back. You don't get to be the parent now." She scooped up Chomp and left the room, slamming the door behind her.

Leaning against it, she closed her eyes, tears running down her cheeks. She buried her nose in Chomp's fur. Even if she did survive to return with the Cerberus and the apples, it would take more than that to fix what was broken between her and Alcmen.

CHAPTER 6

CASTOR

Castor stormed from the palace. She raged through the gardens and snatched the Empresses' pretty little flowers from their pretty little beds. Her hand raked through a rose bush, and the thorns cut her palm. She cursed at her bleeding hand and slumped onto a stone bench.

Tears burned in her chest. But she wouldn't cry. She would not cry. Crying meant she had been defeated, that she had failed to lead Arcadia, and she couldn't have failed so soon. She'd only been named heir weeks ago. She was supposed to take Arcadia to glory, not lose more than half of their income.

"Those horrid women," she spat. "I wish they were both dead."

"Careful where you say that."

Her brother made his way toward her through the gardens. Cas quickly swept her hand through her hair and cursed her stinging palm. When had he become the calm, confident sibling and she the pathetic mess?

Pollux sat beside her and set down his violin.

"What are you doing here?" she snapped.

"Making sure you don't burn down the gardens."

"They're not worth the lightning," she said, and realized that was true. Without a steady supply of Illumium, the StormMakers would have to conserve what they had. Vials would have to be saved and reused, reserved for their strongest storms.

"Arcadia can survive on less coin, Cas. This isn't the end of the island."

"Survival isn't good enough. It's not good enough for me, and it's not good enough for Father, either. He will find a way to have me unseated or married to Memnon." The only thing worse than being broke would be marrying that fool.

"The Empresses won't let that happen. If you marry Memnon, they don't get their discounted lightning."

She glared. "That is not helping, brother."

"I don't know what I can do. But I'm sure you'll figure it out." Pollux picked up his violin.

"That's all you have to offer? You're not still going with Gen to Elysium, are you?"

"Of course I am."

Fool. "But Arcadia is in trouble. You need to be here."

"Gen is in trouble."

Castor plucked a rose thorn from her thumb. "She's going to lead you to your death."

"She's not the one who burned me. Twice." Pollux's fingers touched the scars along his collarbone.

Castor flinched. There were only so many times she could call it an accident. "You saw Alcmen in there," she said instead. "He's insane. He's not worth the trip."

"I was never doing it for Alcmen." Pollux turned his chin to the palace. "And I'd rather fight for someone I love than for some worthless title. You want my advice? My name and fortune have never done me any good. If anything, they have only brought me down, and they will bring you down, too, Cas."

"Arcadia isn't worthless. It's everything to me." It was her land, her name, her identity, her strength. She couldn't let it fall. "If only I had another supplier for the Illumium, this could all be solved."

"The only Illumium in the Empire is on Tegea," Pollux said.

"Then I need another metal." But they'd tried all the base metals, consulted the best MetalBenders. Nothing else worked. Only the Illumium could hold the storms.

"Best of luck to you, Cas. I'll see you when I get back." Pollux nodded to her once before he stood up and started down the garden path. As usual, her brother had been no help.

Castor pulled a loose thread from her blouse and wrapped it around her finger over and over again until her skin turned purple. Was there a metal they hadn't found yet? Maybe something deep underneath one of the isles or under the water or in—

Elysium.

That was it. There wasn't a metal in this empire she could use, but Olympia wasn't the only empire. The golden apples. Oracle-made. Indestructible. The seeds from one apple could grow an entire orchard. Arcadia could have its own source of metal. She would never have to work with Tegea again.

Of course, she'd still have to sell the Empresses their blasted lightning at 35 percent, at least until her golden apples flourished. Then she'd have more room for negotiations. But in the long term, she would save a fortune from not having to pay out for Illumium. This could save her. This could save Arcadia.

She chased after Pollux and caught him before he reached the palace bridge. "I want to come with you to Elysium."

He spun around. "What?"

"The apples. That's the metal I need. If I have one apple, I can save Arcadia."

"Then I'll bring you one back," Pollux said. "You don't need to come with us."

"Yes, I do." She wouldn't leave the fate of Arcadia to Gen and Pollux. Yes, they'd done fairly well in the Empresses' game. But Castor also charred half of the Hydra heads for Genevieve. If she failed in her quest or was eaten by the Cerberus, Castor would never see her golden apple. She needed to get it for herself.

"You can't come," Pollux said.

"You need my help."

"Gen doesn't trust you, Bale doesn't like you, and I have some serious concerns about it too. Also, how do you expect to hide a golden orchard from the Empresses?"

"I won't need to hide it. They won't care what I do as long as I supply the lightning they need." They never told her she couldn't find a new metal source. "This is my answer, Lux. It's the answer for everything. With a free source of metal, our profits will double, triple. Arcadia will be more powerful than ever, and—" Their father would realize that *she* was the right choice, the only choice. "I need this."

He shook his head. "It's not my decision to make, Cas. It's not my venture."

Genevieve. This was her venture. Castor would have to appeal to her.

Castor marched across the bridge into the palace, smoothing her hair and straightening her blouse. She knew how to negotiate. In exchange for one small apple, Genevieve would get Castor's leadership and, more importantly, her lightning. Gen would be getting the better end of the deal.

Castor caught Gen coming down the stairs with her purple dog. The girl's red cheeks and swollen eyes suggested she had been crying.

"I need to talk to you," Castor said.

"About what?" Gen wiped a smear of tears from her cheek.

"Let's find another room." She led Genevieve to a nearby sitting room, filled with overgrown plants and various pieces of artwork. Paintings hung side by side on the walls, several featuring the Empresses drawn separately in supine poses and airy gowns. The word *tacky* came to the forefront of Castor's mind.

"What do you want?" Gen asked. Her dog growled with the same intensity. Castor wondered if it would be so brave with her boot in its mouth.

"It's more of an offer to you. My help in your venture to Elysium."

She laughed. "I didn't think you helped anyone besides yourself."

Castor gritted her teeth. Maybe Genevieve would respond better to the truth. "I need an apple. I need another source of metal. The golden apples are the only possibility."

"Why should I help *you* get an apple?"

"I would be the one helping *you* get the apples."

"Then why are you the one in here asking for favors?"

Castor's hand dropped to her belt of storms by reflex, then she pulled it away. She could chase the apples on her own and avoid Genevieve and the Cerberus altogether. But as her father had said, *Everyone knows the Mazon won the game.* Castor knew it too. If she wanted to reach the apples, she would need Gen to beat the monsters out of her way.

"This is my last chance for Arcadia," Castor said, "and it's your last chance for Alcmen. You help me get an apple, I'll help you get the Cerberus, and we can both keep my brother alive."

"I can't trust you. You killed my whale. You burned your brother."

"You tried to drown me in manure!"

"Only after you tried to cook me!"

"Your father just tried to blood poison me in the solarium." Castor hadn't missed that attempt.

"*Your* father sold the weapons to the Gargareans that killed my mother." Genevieve shook her head. "What will stop you from burning me or throwing me into the sea once you have your apples?"

Nothing. Nothing her brother's girlfriend could trust. "What would stop you from snapping my arms or breaking my neck?"

"I don't want to hurt Pollux."

"Neither do I," Castor said. "Not anymore. We have one thing in common. Two if you consider we both need to get into Elysium and out alive. Yes, I had your whale killed, and I'm sorry. We can take a ship into Elysium. You can keep your new whale here, safe and sound. I play to win, Gen, you know that. Now imagine I'm playing on your team."

Genevieve considered. Despite her appearance, the Mazon wasn't a fool. She knew her chances of success increased greatly if they worked together.

"We'll need a MetalBender, for the apples," Gen said.

"I can get a MetalBender," Castor offered.

"No, I don't trust anyone you'll find. *I'll* get the MetalBender."

"Then I'll get us a ship." Castor knew exactly where she could find a ship, and it came already equipped with an attractive purple-haired thief. "Meet me on Stymphal in three days with your MetalBender. We'll sail from there." She headed toward the door.

"Castor," Gen said.

Castor turned and raised an eyebrow. "Yes?"

Genevieve made a show of cracking her knuckles. "If you hurt Pollux in any way on this trip, I will crush you."

"We don't have to worry about that." Castor had no intentions of hurting Pollux, and she had less intention of letting Genevieve get close enough to touch her. "Three days," Castor repeated as she left the sitting room. Now to find Adikia and the *Hind*.

CHAPTER 7

POLLUX

Pollux made his way slowly to the palace, on alert for the crash of a vase, or a bolt of lightning. It never came. Instead, his sister met him on the palace bridge looking determined and, dare he say it, happy?

"It's done," Castor said, still walking as she spoke. "I'll be coming with you to Elysium."

"You got Gen to agree?"

"What can I say? I'm an excellent negotiator. I'm off to secure us a ship. I'll see you on Stymphal in three days." Cas made for the stables.

Pollux continued toward the palace. He knew how his sister negotiated, and it usually involved lightning and threats.

He'd thought for sure Gen would have told Castor to stay behind.

He went upstairs and found Gen in his room, on his bed, with Chomp. She chewed on the end of a pen and had a leaf of paper resting on her knees. She looked unharmed. Thoughtful.

"You agreed to let Castor come with us?" he asked.

Gen looked up and blinked. "It was a mistake, wasn't it?"

"More of a surprise." He sat on the end of the bed, and Chomp raised his head to growl. Pollux gave the dog a wary glance. He didn't think the creature would ever warm to him.

"I am well aware she could decide to try and kill me halfway through the trip," Gen said. "I also know she's desperate. I saw her in front of the Empresses. She will do everything she can to get those apples. She'll do things that I can't or won't do."

"I know that." He had seen the things Cas was willing to do for his entire life. He had scars from some of them. "You can't turn your back on her for a second."

"I know. I've made that mistake before."

Pollux stretched out on the bed and leaned against the cushion beside her. The page in front of her had one name written at the top. *Flek*. He made a face. "What are you writing?"

"We need a MetalBender to get the apples. I'm making a list of possibilities."

"And all you have is Flek?" The handsome Croecian had taken them in when Castor had shot down Pollux's chariot. The handsome Croecian also had a crush on Gen.

"The only other MetalBenders I know are here, and in service to the Empresses. Or they were old acquaintances of Alcmen's that are no longer speaking to us." She set the pen and the parchment aside and pressed her fingers to her temples.

"How is Alcmen?" he asked, warily. The man he'd seen in the Empresses' solarium had not been the ringmaster he remembered from childhood, commanding a tent filled with magical creatures in a black suit. He'd looked more like the murderer people painted him to be.

"He's not himself. I'm sorry I didn't warn you. I guess I wanted to hide the truth a little while longer." Gen dropped her hands. "He doesn't want me to go to Elysium, which is exactly why I have to go. He's in there. Enough to care what happens to me."

Her white blouse fell off her shoulder, exposing the tanned skin on her collarbone, marked with a long silver stripe. She leaned her head on Pollux's shoulder. Her hair cascaded down his arm, and he ran his fingers through it. She sighed as she traced small circles with her finger on his leg.

Pollux curled his arm around her shoulder. Music played in his thoughts. One of his older songs, when Gen had just been a girl in a sequined jacket performing with her family. Back then, he had never thought he would be here with her like this. He hadn't even dared to imagine it. He wished he could stay here forever . . . well, not exactly here. He would prefer to be out of the palace and out from under the Empresses' thumbs. He didn't want to admit it, but with Castor's help, he had more faith that his dreams of the future were possible.

Or Castor could crack them both in the back with lightning and leave them for dead. He never knew what to expect with his sister.

Gen twisted to face him, her nose almost brushing his, and Pollux breathed in her sweet smell of sugar and fresh-cut grass. He ran a finger down the silver stripe that curled around her cheek and pressed his forehead to hers. She tilted her chin upright, and he kissed her, carefully.

This was the piece they hadn't yet worked out, how to be together without her mind magic affecting him. He wanted to be with her. He wanted her to know him, but through practice—a lot of very enjoyable practice—he had learned how easy it was to lose himself with her. Not that he planned to stop any time soon.

He ran his fingers through her hair and tasted her lips. She melted into his chest and curled her leg around his, pulling him in even closer.

His throat released a moan. He wrapped his arms around her, running his hands down her back to her thighs. When her lips parted, and the end of her tongue found his, Pollux felt the connection snap into place. This was when her magic took hold of him, and if he wasn't careful, he could dump every pathetic thought he'd ever had right into her mind.

She slid her hand underneath his shirt. Pollux played one of his songs in his head. It kept him focused on something other than her warm fingers trailing across his stomach.

When they'd first kissed, he'd sensed Gen's feelings too. With more practice, she had improved at holding them back. Occasionally, he caught a glimpse of her thoughts, but they were usually focused on what they were doing, which only made it harder for him to exercise any control.

Gen broke their kiss, but it didn't matter. Her mind magic would hold for the next few hours anyway. Since the damage was already done, he had no reason to go back. He kissed the underside of her jaw, down her neck, following the line of silver that ran there. She exhaled a small gasp, and Pollux lost his place in the song.

He had to recollect himself. He sang it louder in his head. *Duh-duh-dum, dee-dum-dee-dum.* Sweat beaded on his skin. He wasn't sure how long he could do this. He also didn't want to stop. He had waited years to be with Gen like this, and here she was. The only thing keeping him from her was his own fear.

Gen kissed him again, more aggressively this time, and Pollux lost all control. The frail wall he'd been using to hold everything in place shattered. Across their mind connection, he sent her everything. Every daydream he'd had about her, every insecurity about his looks, every fight with his father, including the one when he was eight years old, when his father had struck him so hard, he'd wet his pants.

He found himself right back in that room with soiled pants, sobbing into his hands until his mother came to him.

She had put her arm around his shoulders. *"Your father loves you. You know that, don't you?"*

"No, he doesn't!" he'd shouted back at her. *"He doesn't love you, either."*

He could still see the hurt on his mother's face, but it had been the truth. His father didn't love her. His mother had been a prize, the most beautiful woman on Arcadia with a wealthy family and hefty dowry. His father had simply wanted to own her. And he did.

"I can't." Pollux pulled away from Gen and buried his face in his hands. He couldn't bear to look at her after that.

"I'm sorry."

"It's not your fault." His pulse still throbbed with heat and anger.

"I'm trying. I was hoping I could talk to my father . . ."

Pollux was not excited about Gen getting advice about their love life from her father, but anything would be better than this. Unfortunately, he didn't think Alcmen was ready to have that talk with Gen.

If only Pollux could keep his thoughts more guarded. He wasn't even sure why his mind had gone to that moment. Further proof he couldn't escape his family, even when they were leagues away. They had left their mark deep on his psyche.

Gen rubbed his shoulder. "Do you want to talk about it?"

He raised his head. "That is the absolute last thing I want to do."

Shame burned on his cheeks. He was here with the girl of his dreams, except she had the power to see all his most embarrassing moments, his worst nightmare, with a kiss.

"Why don't we take a look at your list of MetalBenders?" He reached over her and retrieved the pen and paper from the floor.

Having Flek's name at the top of the list was worse than the page being empty. Pollux was sure if Flek were here with Gen instead of him, the MetalBender wouldn't have to avoid kissing her. He probably didn't have any embarrassing memories to share.

Pollux wrote the name *Nicholas* below Flek's, then quickly scratched it out. Nicholas was one of the Arcadian MetalBenders. He often made repairs to Pollux's violins. He also had been burned by Castor once in a fit of rage when he'd failed to seal one of her lightning canisters properly.

Pollux wrote another name, then put a line through it. And another.

All the MetalBenders he knew either hated his sister or were employed by his father. They couldn't be trusted. Flek remained the only unmarked name on the page.

"You can't think of any, either?" Gen asked. "I suppose Flek is our only choice, then."

"I suppose he is." Pollux did his best to hide his emotions. He was still connected to Gen through their last kiss—not as strongly, though, and he had much better control at the moment. He didn't want her to know how much he dreaded being stuck on a ship with the good-looking MetalBender for the duration of the trip. He already felt as if his relationship with Gen hung on a sour note. If he kept shoving his old memories and thoughts at her, soon enough she'd see something she couldn't overlook.

It will only be for a few weeks, he told himself. *I will get better control of my thoughts, Gen and I will be free of the Empresses, and everything will be perfect.*

CHAPTER 8

CASTOR

Winging away in Pollux's chariot, Castor smiled as the wind whipped through her hair. She needed a ship. A crew. She also couldn't be stuck on a boat with her brother and his girlfriend for months without some sort of a distraction. Adikia could solve all three problems.

Adikia. She could already smell the Borean girl's scent of wood-smoke, sea salt, and danger.

Castor opened the wooden box on her belt. "Delia!"

The spirit floated from the confines of her box and hovered. "Yes, Lady Castor."

"I need you to search for Adikia and the *Hind*."

"Again?"

"Yes," Castor hissed.

"Why?"

"It's none of your business."

"It is my business if I will be doing the searching."

Delia's behavior hadn't improved. In fact, it had gotten worse. This current attitude bordered on full-blown rebellion, something Castor couldn't stand.

Castor held up Delia's box, wrapping her fingers tightly around it. "Remember, if I crush this box, you will be trapped in limbo for all eternity."

"And if you crush my box, you will have no one to search for lost ships."

Delia had her there.

Castor tightened her grip, hard enough that a crack ran down the box's center. "Don't try me, ghost. You know I have no patience, and you have more to lose than I do."

The spirit blinked rapidly. "Yes, Lady Castor. Of course, Lady Castor. I'll find the ship right away."

That was better. "Start with Plutos and work your way back to me. I'll be on Ceryneia."

"Yes, Lady Castor."

The small white orb flitted into the darkness with renewed fervor. Fear was an excellent way to exert control, but it didn't last. Eventually, Delia would call Castor's bluff, and Castor would either have to follow through with her threat, crush the box, and lose her ghost, or think of another way to reestablish her dominance.

This was another symptom of Castor's downfall. She had lost so much respect, she couldn't even command the allegiance of her indentured ghost servant.

Castor pulled the horses through a swath of low cloud cover, and the isle of Ceryneia came into view. A misty rain pattered the side of the chariot. She didn't have a spare vial to trap it, but she held out her hands and used her storm magic to keep the rain away from herself. She didn't want to wander the market soaked through.

She brought the chariot down near the stables and paid a stable hand three gold pieces to keep the horses watered and ready to leave. As soon as she found Adikia, or Delia returned with news of the thief's whereabouts, she needed to leave. Three days didn't give her a lot of time to find the thief and head to Stymphal.

Castor squeezed through the crowded market aisles. Rain drummed on the tops of the tents. People sloshed through muddy puddles, and glowing lanterns lit the dim alleyways. A bubble of dry air followed Castor wherever she went.

She pushed by a MetalBender's booth of small metal sculptures, pausing when she saw one of the Hydra. It was not at all how the thing had actually looked. The teeth weren't sharp enough or long enough, and all the heads were the same size.

Cas clearly remembered the center head, the strongest, being twice the size of the others. Sometimes she saw it in her dreams, lunging for her, and sometimes in her dreams, she was able to char it to ash with lightning before it reached her. Other times, she couldn't, and she woke up in a sweat right before it swallowed her. Still other times, she dreamed things how they actually happened—Genevieve crushing the thing with a crab claw before it could strike her.

Those were her least favorite dreams. She hated remembering the after, when she thought she had lost.

You didn't really win, though. Father doesn't think so. No one thinks so.

Castor walked on. She might have been granted her title by the Empresses' game, but she would soon prove it belonged to her regardless. Once she had her apples, and Arcadia became more profitable than before, no one would question her.

From the market, Castor made her way to the docks. Ships lined up on the piers with their sails unfurled and their lanterns lit. Down the road, she spotted an inn. It was getting late. If she didn't find Adikia here, she'd have to buy a room for the night and rest until Delia came to find her. Walking among the gray wooden ships, it looked like that would be her plan.

Until she saw it.

The sleek white hull of the *Hind* gleamed among the other dingy ships. Castor ran her hand along the polished wood, as happy to find the ship as she was to locate its captain. For the short time she had used the *Hind*, prior to giving it to the Empresses to claim her win, Castor had marveled at the ship's speed and comfort. There was no finer ship in the Aegean Sea.

A ship this fine didn't deserve to be in the hands of the dry-humored man who actually owned it. This ship belonged to Adikia, which was why she'd stolen it again only days after it had been returned. Castor remembered hearing that the ship had been retaken and knew Adikia had been behind it.

Castor smoothed down her vest and tucked the sapphire necklace underneath to hide it from the thief. However, if things went the way Castor hoped they did, she soon wouldn't be wearing this vest. Or the necklace.

She smiled as she made her way up the gangplank. Adikia wasn't on deck, so she went below and heard noise beyond the door of the captain's quarters. She opened the door and froze, ice and fire flooding her veins at the same time.

Adikia turned to her from the rumpled covers of her bed, where she had been deep in the skirts of a woman with long red hair and flushed cheeks.

"That's a surprise," she said calmly, as the other woman re-adjusted her dress and smoothed down her hair.

Castor didn't know what to do. She couldn't move or look away, even though she didn't want to see this. She had no right to claim Adikia for herself—she knew that. But she didn't want to know what the purple-haired thief did after climbing out of Castor's window.

She had to speak. Or light the ship on fire. Or *something*.

Castor cleared her throat. "Adikia, I need to speak with you when you're done with . . . whatever this is." She waved her hand dismissively and stepped back from the cabin. She hurried up the steps and clutched her stomach. She didn't know if she was going to be sick, or if she was going to pitch that red-headed woman in the water as soon as she emerged. No, not the redhead—Adikia was the one to blame. She was the one who made Castor feel like this: embarrassed, ashamed, worthless. Did Adikia not realize what an honor it was for the Heiress of Storms to show her favor? Why would she waste that favor on someone else?

The door to the cabin opened. Castor dropped her arms and contorted her face into an expressionless mask, an easy task for her. Pollux claimed that was her natural state. *"You're like ice,"* he'd said to her on more than one occasion.

Adikia and that other woman emerged, giggling. Castor raised her hand to her belt and tapped her fingers on a vial of lightning. Adikia pulled the woman in for a kiss and swatted her on the backside. More giggling. Castor ground down her teeth.

"Thank you for a lovely evening," Adikia said, pressing her hand to her stomach to give the woman a gentle bow.

"You are quite welcome." The woman returned her bow and swung around to face Castor. Her smile immediately fell. She clutched her hands to her chest and hurried from the ship, scrambling down the gangplank.

The corner of Castor's mouth lifted ever so slightly.

"I wasn't expecting company." Adikia ran her brown fingers through her tight purple curls.

"I wasn't aware I had to announce myself, considering you'd let yourself in through my window."

Adikia leaned on the railing beside Castor. She reeked of sweat and cheap perfume. The odor made Castor sick.

"Do we need to talk about this?" Adikia said. "I like you. A lot. But I didn't think this was anything serious. Just messing around. Girls like you and me don't have happy endings, you know?"

That depended on what she considered *happy*. Castor would have been quite happy to see that other woman with her dress in flames. "I'm not here for that. I mean, I would have come for that, except I don't take second place. Ever. You should consider that *your* loss. You wasted your time with a cheap thrill when you could have had so much more. You're a petty thief, Adikia, chasing after rocks when you could have gold."

"Oh." The look on the pirate's face told Castor her insult had made its mark.

She released a breath. "I do have a business proposition for you, though."

"What do you have in mind?" Adikia raised an eyebrow.

"I need your ship. And a captain. I'm going into Elysium with my brother."

"Elysium? Why?"

"Chasing treasure. Something much more valuable than rocks."

"What is it?" Adikia asked, practically salivating.

"The golden apples."

Adikia remained still for a breath, then broke into a laugh and leaned over the edge of the ship. "The golden apples? They're a children's story."

"Are they?" Castor challenged. "It's fine if you're too afraid to go. I'll take the ship and find another captain."

Adikia let her fingers fall to the crossbow hanging from her belt. "No one captains this ship but me."

"I think the man who owns the ship would beg to differ. Should I send him a message and tell him where he can find his stolen ship? He might be more open to selling it to me."

Adikia tapped her fingers on her crossbow. "I've heard a few whispers that Tegea is undercutting you on Illumium. You think the apples will replace it, don't you?"

Castor frowned. "Where did you hear that?"

Adikia shrugged. "Your window wasn't the only one unlocked at your fancy Arcadian manor."

Damn the Oracles. "So what if I do."

"Then I know exactly what getting those apples means to you."

Castor chewed on the inside of her cheek, trying to keep her face as unresponsive as possible. "One hundred thousand in gold. Half before we leave, the other half when we return."

Adikia laughed. "Nice try. What was it you said? I shouldn't chase after rocks when I can have gold." The thief tapped her chin. "If we find the apples, I want five percent of Arcadia's annual profits."

This time, Castor laughed. "That's ridiculous."

"I'm not done. If we don't find the apples, then I'll take your one hundred thousand in gold, and before you threaten to turn in my ship, ask yourself if the man who keeps getting it stolen will really let you take it into Elysium. I don't think so. I don't think you'll find many who will. So, what is it, Castor?"

Castor stepped toward the gangplank. "I could buy a fleet of ships for less."

"Ships that could outrun the Elysium forces? Come on, Castor, you know this is the best ship, and I'm the best captain for it.

Otherwise, you would have bought a shiny new ship long before you came looking for me."

Castor swallowed. "Two percent of the profits, and only if we find the apples and return them here safely. Fifty thousand in gold if we don't."

"You just offered me one hundred thousand a minute ago," Adikia said.

"It was fifty thousand in advance. Fifty on return. If we return with the apples, you get much, much more." Castor ran her finger across the top of her lightning vials. "I suggest you take it. I'm losing my patience, and your value is beginning to lessen."

Adikia looked stung by the remark, enough to agree. "Deal."

Castor hesitated, then took Adikia's hand, lifting it brusquely up and down. "Prepare to sail. I need to retrieve my things from my chariot and sell the horses. I won't be too long. We should leave tonight. We have to meet my brother and Genevieve on Stymphal in three days."

"The MindWorker is coming along?" Adikia asked.

"Is that a problem?" Gen was more essential to this venture than Adikia and her ship. If the Empresses didn't get what they wanted, then Castor wouldn't be able to take her piece of it. Which meant they would have to get the Cerberus too.

"No, no problem," Adikia said, "as long as she keeps her blood to herself."

"I'll make sure she does."

Castor walked down the gangplank, stiff and straight, holding herself together until she reached the shore and stepped out of Adikia's sight. Then her shoulders dropped, along with the corners of her lips. This night wasn't going at all how she'd intended. *She* should have been with Adikia in the captain's cabin this evening. Not that other woman.

Gen didn't have to pay Pollux to follow her everywhere. He did it by choice. He did it even when Genevieve tried to convince him not to.

But is that the kind of person you want? Someone like Pollux?

Castor gagged. No, absolutely not. She wanted someone like Adikia. But she wanted that someone to be chasing *her*, to catch *her* in bed with someone else and feel like . . . this.

Castor made her way back through the market and to the stables. She cleaned out the contents of her chariot and offered to sell the horses to the stable owner for two thousand in silver. Not even a quarter of what they were worth, but they hadn't been her horses anyway.

She pocketed the coins and asked the stable owner for a pen and parchment.

Dearest Father,

I am leaving for a while to settle the problem with Tegea. Pollux is coming with me. When we return, we will have no worries about the Illumium or Lord Atreus and his foul son Memnon. Arcadia always has been and always will be my first priority. Maybe when you set aside your own ego, you will be able to see that.

Future Duchess,

Castor Othonos

She folded the letter and handed it to the stable boy. "Make sure this reaches the Arcadian manor."

"Of course, Lady Castor."

She tilted her head to him and made her way back to the docks. She'd long since abandoned the fight against the weather. The mist fell onto her wet blouse and even wetter hair. She debated whether she should force Adikia to remove herself from the captain's cabin. But then Castor would have to sleep in sheets that smelled like discount perfume. She would rather sleep in the brig.

A white light cut through the hazy rain and market crowds. Delia coasted toward her and bobbed in front of her face. "I've found the *Hind*. It's here."

Castor rolled her eyes. "Yes, I'm well aware of that. More proof that your usefulness is wavering." She opened the box. "Get inside and think about that the next time you want to challenge me."

The spirit drifted into the box, and she snapped the lid shut. Hopefully that would be enough to remind Delia of her place.

CHAPTER 9

GEN

Gen paced the beach while Chomp gnawed on a piece of driftwood. She glanced up at the palace window, where she'd left her father behind with a terse "Goodbye," afraid a longer conversation would lead to another argument and more heartbreak.

She couldn't do anything for him now except make sure the Empresses never sent him back to prison.

Bale emerged from the gardens and made his way to the beach. His blue skin shone brightly in the early morning sun. It wasn't like him to be the first one up and out. Usually, he was the last one to crawl out of bed.

"You seem eager to leave this morning," she said.

"Not as eager as you." He dropped his duffel bag into the sand.

"I wasn't sure if you would be coming with us."

Bale shrugged. "I have nowhere else to be."

Gen rubbed her toe in the sand, wary of starting an uncomfortable conversation, and even warier of postponing it. "Bale, can I talk to you about Pollux?"

Bale raised an eyebrow.

She laced her fingers. "It's about when we're together."

"I don't want to know."

"Please," she begged. "You're the only other MindWorker I know besides my father." She glanced back at the window. She couldn't talk to Alcmen about this. She couldn't talk to him about anything.

"Don't say that so loudly," Bale growled.

He kept his identity as a MindWorker a secret and with good reason. After Alcmen's arrest, MindWorkers weren't the most trusted people in the Empire.

"I'm sorry," Gen said in a lower voice. "It's just—when I kiss Pollux, I know what he's thinking, and I try not to listen, but it's impossible when he's practically shouting at me, and I thought you might have some advice."

Her father had taught her everything she knew about her abilities. But he'd left her before they'd gotten to the kissing lesson. She wondered what else he could have taught her. What else was she missing?

"Easy," Bale said. "Don't kiss him."

Gen sighed. That was what worried her, that Pollux would reach a point where he was afraid to kiss her because of what she saw. Not that she judged him for his thoughts, but with those thoughts came his shame for having them. If anyone should be ashamed, it was his family, for treating him the way they did. If she ever met the infamous Duke of Storms, she would have a thousand words for him and none of them would be kind.

"I was hoping you would have some other advice," she said.

"I don't. If you recall, I made my girlfriend drown herself through a kiss."

She remembered. Bale had urged his late girlfriend into the sea to swim after her lost boat, and she hadn't come back. Gen knew he hadn't meant to harm his girlfriend. Just like she didn't want to harm Pollux.

"You're not influencing him, are you?" Bale asked.

"No, I can't. If *you* recall, I'm not as powerful of a MindWorker as you are." She could probably nudge Pollux on some issues, but she wouldn't. She wanted him to be with her by choice, whole and absolute.

"There are other ways to influence someone without using magic. Be careful with him, Gen. He's vulnerable."

"I'm trying to be careful," she said. "Is there a way to control it? Can I kiss him and not use my magic?"

"No," Bale muttered. "You can't turn your magic on and off, Gen. It's a part of you. The only way to stop using it would be to rip it free of your body. Sorry to be the bearer of bad news."

"I—" Gen quickly closed her mouth as Pollux emerged from the gardens looking annoyed. Pollux didn't know Bale was a MindWorker, and Gen didn't want him to know she'd been asking Bale how to kiss. He would be mortified.

"She stole my chariot," Pollux muttered as he approached.

"What?"

"Castor. She took my chariot and stranded us here."

Gen worried this would be the first sign of many that letting Castor come was a mistake.

"Well, we're not stranded." She turned to the sea. She had planned to release Andromeda here, but they would need the whale a little while longer.

Can you come get us, please? Gen called to the whale.

Andromeda rose from the sea. The water rolled down her pink, iridescent side as she opened her mouth wide.

Gen picked up Chomp and carried him across the shallows into Andromeda's mouth. She set him down, and he found a place to nap in a pile of half-digested fish bones. Overhead, yellow and blue lights crackled across Andromeda's insides, the sign of a freshly fed infinity whale. Gen sat on her tongue, and Pollux settled in beside her. Even after several trips inside an infinity whale, Pollux still tried to avoid the seaweed and fish bones, knowing full well he would be covered with them in moments.

Bale stepped in with his rucksack and gave Gen a side glance. *"Be careful with him,"* it said. She tipped her chin to say she would. She cared about Pollux as much as Bale, if not more. Though in a very different way. Bale plopped onto Andromeda's tongue, and Gen turned her attention to the whale.

"Take us to Quisces, please," Gen said. "Where we found you."

Oh, I remember that, Andromeda said.

Gen dropped two hairs onto Andromeda's tongue to strengthen their tie, and the little whale shot through the water. As suspected, the seaweed and fish bones in her mouth flew back and landed on all of them. Pollux sighed as he plucked seaweed from his pants. Bale laughed.

Gen opened her bag and removed a small tin. She opened the lid and pulled out a mound of white fluff, whisper moth cocoon husks. They would need the husks to visit Quisces.

"Thank you," Pollux said as he took two pieces and shoved them deep into his ears.

She didn't need to kiss him to know what he was thinking. He hated Quisces. The isle was home to a species of caterpillar that could cause deafness and death. Also, Flek lived there. She and Pollux had spent hours trying to think of another MetalBender who could join them on their trip. They had filled a page with crossed-out names. Only Flek's name remained.

Flek liked Gen, she knew that. She realized he was attractive, too, but not in the way Pollux was. Not to her, at least. Pollux had her heart and always would. It wasn't something Flek could steal away.

As Andromeda rose out of the water, Gen passed cocoon pieces to Bale, then stuffed some in Chomp's ears and her own. Soon, the whale's skin vibrated with the sound of the caterpillars, but Gen couldn't hear it. The cocoon husks snuffed out all sound.

She grabbed her bag and Chomp and carried them across the whale's tongue. Bale and Pollux followed, and they stepped onto a familiar white beach.

Go eat, Gen told the whale through their connection. *I'll call you when we're ready.*

Andromeda wriggled back into the water. Gen tried to keep her thoughts away from their eventual goodbye. They would need one last ride to Stymphal, then Gen would set the whale free. She couldn't have Andromeda anywhere near Castor or the Elysium waters. She had no idea what creatures or hunters they would find in the foreign seas.

Gen slung her bag over her shoulder and waved Pollux and Bale toward the village. They circled around the blue lake and up a rocky gravel path to another hill. On the other side, the town of Croecia spread across the fields in rows of simplicity. Thatched wood-and-stone houses sat on either side of the marked road, while goats and chickens wandered freely in the middle of it. Nothing living on this island could hear. It was how they all survived the shrieking caterpillars.

Gen took Pollux's hand. His palms were clammy, his fingers tense. She offered him a smile. What was the benefit of being able to connect to his mind if she couldn't convince him she was his?

At the end of the main road, they found Flek's workshop with him inside, burning metal exactly as he had the last time they came. Everything in Croecia was predictable and routine. Gen envied that.

Flek burned a piece of steel with his glowing fingers. He pulled and stretched the metal like Aurelian taffy until it took the shape of a wing, then a second wing. When he was done, the metal moth fluttered its newly made wings and joined a host of other metal moths gathered along a long wire.

Flek used his MetalBending to create art, unlike others who used their magic to create things like disappearing coins and unbreakable chains. It was one reason why he was the perfect MetalBender to join them on their trip. He wasn't seduced by power or coin. He simply believed in his craft.

When his hands cooled, he lifted his dark glasses and smiled at her.

He made his way toward them with long, graceful limbs, and Pollux tightened his grip on her hand. Gen gave him another reassuring smile, not sure what else she could do to convince him she and Flek were only friends, and they were only friends because for years, he'd been the only one who hadn't hated her for being a MindWorker.

Flek picked up a long steel rod from a bin and pushed it into the dirt.

To what do I owe this pleasure? he wrote, then handed the rod to her.

Gen unlaced her fingers from Pollux's to respond in writing. Mostly for his benefit. And Bale's. Flek could read lips. They couldn't, and they couldn't hear each other with the cocoon pieces in their ears.

I don't know if I'd call it a pleasure, she wrote, then wiped away the words with her boot. *We need your help. I didn't win my father, but I have a second chance. We are setting out for Elysium and need a MetalBender to come with us.*

Flek picked up a new piece of steel. *You want me to come with you to Elysium?*

Yes, and I can pay you. It will be dangerous.

I'm not afraid of danger, Flek returned.

We could be gone a long time.

Flek rubbed out his last words. *Why do you need me?*

Gen bit down on her lip before she wrote. *The Empresses want me to get the golden apples for them. We need a MetalBender to bring them back.*

Any MetalBender?

Gen shook her head. *One we can trust. One who is skilled enough to do it. One who is willing to do it.*

One of Flek's metal moths fluttered down from the wire and landed on his shoulder. Its silver wings gently lifted and fell with Flek's breath.

He put his metal rod to the sand. *That could create a war with the Elysiums.*

It most likely will, Gen wrote.

Pollux picked up his own piece of metal. *We can't defy the Empresses. If they are after a war, they'll have it one way or another.*

Gen brushed out his words and wrote her own. *I just want my father, and this is the only way.*

Flek flicked his gaze from Pollux to her. She wouldn't blame him if he refused them. He had nothing to lose or gain on this trip. She did.

Can you do it without a MetalBender? he finally wrote.

Yes, Gen wrote quickly. *We will find a way.* It was much easier to lie in words written on sand than in speech. Without Flek, they couldn't do it. They had no other MetalBenders to ask, and whatever ship Castor brought wouldn't hold a dozen fully grown apple trees. But Gen didn't want to force Flek into coming without him knowing the stakes.

Flek pressed the end of his metal pole into the sand. She waited for the words to appear: *Best of luck on your journey. Stop by when you get back.* It would be unwise for him to agree. It was unwise for any of them to go.

Flek's words formed in the sand. *Let me pack my things and tell Gronk where I'm headed. I'll meet you by the beach.*

In the silence of the cocoon husks, Gen heard the pounding of her own heart. *Are you sure?*

Flek looked to the metal moth on his shoulder before he wrote. *No. But all I've ever wanted to do was leave this island, and you are offering me the chance.* He rubbed those words out and continued. *I also know I can't live with myself if you leave this island and never come back.*

Pollux gave her a sidelong look.

Thank you, she wrote. *We will meet you on the beach.* She left the metal rod in his workshop, guilt settling into her stomach. She had brought another innocent person into her troubles, and this other person upset Pollux.

When they reached the beach, she picked up a piece of driftwood.

There was no one else, she wrote in the sand.

Pollux picked up his own piece of wood and wrote *It's fine* in hard, sharp letters. Gen looked to Bale, who mouthed, *"I told you so."* She glared back at him.

It wasn't her fault they knew no other MetalBenders who would come with them, or that Flek liked her. She hadn't encouraged it. She also had no choice. If she didn't bring back the apples and the

Cerberus like the Empresses wanted, she would never be free. It would only be a few weeks hopefully, and then they would either be charred by the Cerberus or done with these tasks for good. Either way, it would all be over.

CHAPTER 10

POLLUX

Pollux had thought he could handle Flek joining them on their trip. He trusted Gen. He knew she loved him. Maybe not as much as he loved her—that would be impossible. But she loved him enough. More than he could have ever hoped.

Somehow, though, he had forgotten how damned attractive Flek was and how he looked at Gen with those wide cerulean eyes like he was imagining what was underneath her jacket. If Pollux could have thought of another MetalBender who could and would do the job, he would have dumped Flek in the sea and asked someone else.

On the black rocks below, Flek waved his hands animatedly, trying to teach Gen some of his language. From watching, Pollux gathered that the hand across the air meant *day*, and the hand swinging down meant *night*. When Gen didn't make her hand-down motion fast enough, Flek took her wrist and pushed her hand down. She burst into laughter.

Pollux ground his teeth and searched the sea for signs of his sister and the ship she was supposed to bring. They had been on Stymphal for hours now, waiting for her. Pollux wondered if he had been a fool, yet again, to trust a word out of Castor's mouth.

You can trust that she wants her freedom. You can trust that she wants those golden apples.

Bale climbed up from the beach and stood beside him. "You should punch him."

"What?" Pollux turned to his friend, not sure he had heard him correctly. Whenever he removed cocoon husks from his ears, his hearing always seemed to be a little off, a persistent hum settling in the background.

"Punch the MetalBender," Bale said. "It will make you feel better."

"That's not going to happen." Pollux didn't punch people. He held all his anger and jealousy inside and let it eat at him silently. A much better solution. "He knows Gen and I are together."

"Does Gen know that?"

"What are you talking about?"

"Oh nothing, I'm just breaking all my rules about meddling in your relationship. She talked to me about you back on Athenia, and I swore I would stay out of it, but I must be some special kind of masochist."

Pollux broke into a sweat. Gen had talked to Bale? About them? What had she told him? Everything she'd seen in his thoughts?

"How do you kiss someone who can read your thoughts?" Pollux asked.

"Very carefully," Bale said. "Or not at all."

Pollux didn't want that. He tried to imagine never lying beside Gen, never tasting the sugar on her lips . . . and it felt worse than having his embarrassing memories exposed. "Did Gen tell you it bothered her? Seeing everything?"

"Why don't you two talk to each other, and leave me out of it?"

Bale stuffed his hands in his pockets and wandered down the rocks. Pollux supposed it was too much to ask of Bale to run interference in his relationship. It bothered Pollux, though, that Gen had gone to Bale for advice in the first place. Why not talk to him?

He glanced at the horizon and noticed a ship in the distance, moving in straight and fast. It looked familiar. *Cas didn't go home to get one of the family's ships, did she?*

He walked down the rocks to the beach, where he stepped between Flek and Gen and grasped her fingers to pull her away. It wasn't subtle. Pollux hadn't intended it to be.

"Castor's here." He gestured to the water.

Gen cocked her head. "I suppose it's too late to leave her out now."

"It's never too late. But I think you and I both know it's better to have her on our side than against us."

"I just hope she stays on our side."

"I think she would say the same of you." He squeezed her fingers.

Gen raised an eyebrow.

"Castor doesn't fear much, but she's wary of you," he said. "Keep that in mind."

His sister showed respect for few people. It was a curse and a blessing that Gen had been chosen as one of those few.

They gathered their things and made their way to the lone dock on Stymphal, a half-rotted mass of wooden pilings. This wasn't one of the more popular islands. It didn't have any valuable exports or tourist attractions. The only thing it did have was location. Stymphal was the isle closest to the Elysium border.

"That looks like the *Hind*," Gen said as the ship sailed closer.

Pollux squinted. He knew the ship had looked familiar. He'd seen it when Castor sailed it to Athenia to "win" the game. How did his sister get her hands on it again? Maybe she'd made a deal with the owner to borrow it. Or she'd burned him to ash to steal it. Neither answer would have surprised him.

As the ship neared, Pollux spotted his sister on deck along with another girl, a Bornean with purple hair and a gaze that held as much challenge as Castor's. Dark music played in his thoughts, the song of his own eventual downfall. One Cas was bad enough. Two would be treacherous.

"I told you I would get a ship, and I have a ship," Castor called from the deck. "Is this your MetalBender?" She pointed to Flek.

"Yes," Pollux said. "This is Flek. He doesn't speak. Not vocally at least."

"That's inconvenient," Castor said.

Flek pointed to her. *"I do read lips,"* he mouthed.

"What is he mumbling?" Castor shouted.

Thirty seconds in front of someone new, and Cas was already making enemies. His sister really did know how to get on someone's bad side.

Flek took a piece of parchment from his pocket and wrote down in large lettering: "I read lips." He held it up to her.

Castor leaned over the ship and squinted her eyes, then frowned. "Well, I don't."

Pollux couldn't read lips well, either, in part because he didn't want to stare at Flek long enough to practice. But he would have to work on it. They couldn't write in sand on the ship, and they didn't have an endless supply of parchment.

"How did you get the ship?" he asked Castor.

"I made a bargain. This is Adikia, captain of the *Hind.*"

"Pleasure to meet you." Adikia bowed and waved her hand in a lazy flourish.

"This isn't your ship," Gen said.

Adikia shrugged. "I'm the one sailing it, so I would say that makes it mine. Are you going to get on it, or would you rather swim to Elysium?"

Pollux considered this.

"We'll be there in a minute," Gen said. "I need to take care of something first." She knelt at the side of the pier and traced her bronze-and-silver fingers over the surface of the water. Bale climbed up the gangplank, Chomp following him closely behind. Bale was the only person besides Gen in the entire Empire the dog could tolerate. Pollux assumed it was because they shared a grumpy disposition.

Flek lingered for a few moments on the pier. The look Pollux gave him could have been translated into any language: *"Go away."* Flek shoved his hands into his pockets and climbed up to the ship.

In the water, Andromeda rose from the depths. Despite the fish bones and seaweed that always stuck to him after riding inside her stomach, Pollux had enjoyed traveling with her. He had never felt as safe or cared for on one of his father's ships or even in his own chariot. The little whale acted as if ferrying them from island to island was an honor. He would be sorry to see her go, though he understood why she couldn't come along.

Gen pressed her hand to Andromeda's forehead. "We have to go," she whispered, then paused. "No, I mean, *we* have to go. You can't come along." Her lips pursed and her brows drew together. "It isn't safe for you. You should be free to find your own way."

Andromeda spat water from her blowhole, showering them both. Then the little whale dove under the water and swam away.

Pollux brushed seawater from his violin case. "I'm going to assume she didn't want to be left behind."

"I never thought she would get so attached in such a short time." Gen pushed her hair behind her ear. "No matter what I do, I can't make everyone happy."

"It's not your job to make everyone happy."

"I suppose you have a point." She climbed the gangplank to the ship.

When they reached the top, Pollux set his violin down on the deck. He examined their ride, from the sleek, freshly painted deck boards to the wide linen sails flapping in the breeze. This ship resembled his father's ships, except it would go much faster. With those large sails and a strong wind, they would fly across the ocean.

"She's beautiful, isn't she?" Adikia stood beside him, her hands balled on her hips.

"Why did you agree to take us into Elysium?" he asked.

"Your sister promised me an annuity. A share of Arcadia's profits."

Pollux cleared his throat. "She did?"

That didn't sound like Cas. She never agreed to multiple payments; it wasn't in her best interest. The Borneans also didn't do much business with Arcadia. An occasional rainstorm here or there when they suffered an extended drought. Nothing more. Castor didn't usually associate with people who didn't have anything to offer in the way of alliances or coin. This was . . . strange.

"MindWorker!" Adikia shouted across the deck. "Be sure to keep your blood to yourself while you're on my ship. I don't want you messing with my head."

Gen flinched.

Pollux knew he should jump to her defense, but he couldn't help flinching, too, thinking about how Gen's magic actually did mess with his head.

To his surprise, Bale snapped at Adikia in his place. "Why don't you keep your mouth to yourself?"

"Who are you?" the girl challenged.

"I'm going to be the thorn in your side this entire trip if you don't watch it."

Pollux held his breath. It would be a wonderful start to their journey if the ship captain and Bale killed each other in the first ten minutes. Pollux waited for Adikia to pull a knife.

She laughed instead. "I like this one."

Pollux exhaled and picked up his violin.

"You, Thorn"—Adikia pointed to Bale—"pull up the anchor so we can get out of here."

"I'd rather not."

"I can do it," Gen offered.

"That's true," Bale said. "She's much better at lifting things than I am."

"I asked *you* to do it," Adikia said. "And as long as I'm captain and you're crew, you'll do as I say."

"Can we stage a mutiny?" Bale asked.

"No." Adikia pointed to the anchor. "Get moving."

Bale trudged to the anchor mechanism, grasped the crank, and wheeled the anchor up from the sea.

Pollux made his way to Cas. "Great ship you found. I'm not so sure about the captain."

"Did you want a good ship?" she asked.

"Yes."

"A good captain?"

"Yes."

"Then those two needs are met. No one asked for a 'nice' captain."

Castor probably liked Adikia more for not being *nice*. His sister didn't have much respect for *nice*.

"By the way, what did you do with my chariot and horses?" he asked.

"Sold them at Ceryneia." Of course she had. "Do you want your share of the coin?" She patted the coin purse on her belt.

"Actually, I do." Even if he didn't need the coin, she owed him something. He had liked that chariot, those horses.

"Fine." She reached into her purse and handed him a fistful of silver. Some of the coins scattered to the deck. He bent down to pick them up, but they were already gone.

Adikia flipped one of the coins in her fingers before she dropped it into her pocket. "Finders keepers," she said, and smiled.

He opened his mouth to argue when Castor nudged him in the side.

"We need wind, Lux. I don't want to waste my vials." She gestured to the flat sails.

"Maybe I don't want to waste my vials, either." He stood up to his full height and glared down at her. She pressed her lips together and sharpened her eyes into slivers. This reminded him of much of his childhood, he and Castor arguing in the halls of the manor. As a child, it hadn't taken much to send him into a fit of tears. Now he was no longer afraid of his sister. She had already done her worst, and he had survived it.

Her gaze flicked to the scars on his neck and softened. "Fine, you go first. I'll take over later. We'll split the work."

"I will hold you to that." He removed his violin from its case, tightened the pegs, and held his bow across the strings. He played a soft waltz to draw out the wind. The sails filled with air, and the ship pushed away from the dock.

"He does it so much nicer than you do," Adikia said to Castor. "I like the music."

"It's inefficient," Castor said, and stormed across the deck.

Pollux smiled. At least their salty captain gave his sister a headache too.

Adikia took the wheel, and Bale sat down on some crates beside Pollux, rubbing his shoulder. Gen picked up Chomp and looked west as Adikia brought the ship to port. They were officially headed into the Elysium Empire, and it wouldn't take long to reach the border. While it seemed like Elysium was leagues away, on a clear day, you could see it with the naked eye.

Nothing large marked the border between empires. The Empresses didn't keep a line of ships here to guard it. The Elysium Emperor, Nessos, didn't keep spies on their side, either. Both empires relied on the peace treaty to keep the waters safe. But there *was* something to show where the empires met.

As he played, Pollux spotted it ahead. Three large stones jutted up from the water, barely a black speck in the distance, but still, he slowed his song to keep from reaching them too quickly. The boundary had been set by the gods ages ago. The Oracles had put the rocks there.

They were all siblings, the Olympian Oracles and the Elysium Oracles, and of course they had disagreed on how things should be done. They'd split the islands and placed the rocks to mark the boundary. However, that didn't keep the peace between the two empires.

Over three hundred years ago, the Empresses' great-great-great-grandfather, Damian, tried to conquer the Elysium Empire and lost, mostly due to the Cerberus. The Elysium Oracle of Malice, Arai, had created the beast to guard the catacombs of the dead. But it could be called upon to defend Elysium in times of need. With it, the Elysium Emperor, Laos, was able to take Stymphal. Emperor Damian had to buy the island back with a ship loaded with gold and a vow never to cross the boundary again. Those had been the terms of the treaty.

As the *Hind* passed the three black rocks, Pollux paused in his playing, wondering if they would be shot dead this very moment for crossing the border. He remained still even as Adikia shouted, "What happened to the music?"

Why did the Empresses want this war so badly?

If he knew that, then he might be able to find another way to get them what they wanted, to get Cas what she wanted, and to save Gen and her father.

He shook his head. That was what he was always trying to do, wasn't it? Keep everyone happy while also keeping them out of danger. And maybe that wasn't possible. Maybe he had to choose.

He raised his chin and looked at Gen standing at the prow of the ship with her hair blowing behind her. If he had to choose, he knew what he would pick—Gen. Always Gen. He kept watching her as he played his waltz and pushed the ship into the Elysium waters.

CHAPTER 11

CASTOR

Castor filled the sails with wind, ballooning them outward into the sunset. They had been sailing for two days, directly northwest, into the heart of Elysium. There were isles closer to the boundary, ones farther south, but those islands didn't matter. Okeanos was where they would find the Emperor and their lead to the apples.

Adikia climbed down the steps to the main deck. She had handed Bale the helm so she could rest, something she never did for long. There was only one thing Adikia truly cared about, and that was this ship.

Adikia stood beside Castor and admired the wind in the sails. "Your brother travels with some interesting companions. The blue one—"

"Bale," Castor sighed.

"Yeah, that one. He just told me the funniest joke about a woman with three eyes on her forehead. A man kept staring at them until she said, 'Excuse me, but my breasts are down here!'" Adikia broke into peals of laughter.

Cas rolled her eyes. "Pollux's choice of friends is always decided on who will annoy the family the most. And he is very good at picking them." Bale was one of his finest examples.

Adikia tempered her laughter. "What about you? How do you choose your friends?"

Castor looked to the box on her belt where Delia slept inside.

She was the closest thing Cas had to a companion, but Delia was not a friend. She was barely tolerable as a servant.

"We should see land sometime tomorrow," Cas said instead. According to the old maps of Elysium, the far side of Okeanos was only five leagues directly northwest. At this speed, they would reach it by late afternoon or evening.

Soon she would have her golden apples and her freedom from Tegea.

"Why are you frowning?" Adikia asked.

"Because I don't have my golden apples. Yet."

"What happens if you never get them? Are you going to be miserable forever?"

Castor turned on her. "That doesn't happen. I always get what I want. Sometimes not immediately. But eventually. Did you ever worry you wouldn't get this ship back?"

Adikia laughed. A rich, hearty laugh, exactly like a thieving pirate should have. "No, of course not. I guess we have that in common." The thief batted her mysterious purple cat eyes, and Castor's insides tightened. She wanted to kiss her. Again and again and again. But Adikia had already proven to be more trouble than she was worth.

On all sides, water spread as far as the eye could see. The Elysium Empire had fewer isles than Olympia, only fifty to Olympia's one hundred, but Elysium was more expansive in size, with larger islands more widely spread apart.

The Elysiums called their lands the Isles of the Blessed, because rather than blessing the people with gifts, their Oracles had blessed the land and creatures instead. That was what had caused the "Parting of the Oracles," as it was called. The Elysium Oracles thought it was too dangerous to put so much power in the hands of the people as the Olympian Oracles had. Instead, the Elysium Oracles made wonders like the Cerberus and the apples. Their magic was tied to things, things that could be traded, destroyed, and hopefully, stolen.

The Elysium Oracles hadn't been entirely wrong about giving magic to people, not in the case of the Oracle Keres and her MindWorkers. Genevieve's father was a testament to that. Even the others, the ones who didn't make people kill each other, had this air of wicked confidence, as if they knew with a few drops of their blood, they could bring someone to their knees.

Speak of the monster.

Genevieve walked onto the main deck with her dog, Pollux, and Flek trailing behind her. Castor pulled her wind from the sails. There were some things they needed to settle before they reached land.

"We need to talk. All of us." She motioned for everyone to follow her to the bridge, where Bale held the wheel. She put her hands on her hips and stared at her lackluster crew. "We're nearing Okeanos, and I need to make sure you all know your parts."

"I thought we were acting as an envoy for the Empresses," Pollux said. "That was what you told me when you thought Gen and I were coming alone."

She had said that, but she needed something better now that her own fate depended on it. "Well, you're not alone anymore, and after much thought, I think it would make more sense if you were *my* envoy, serving the Duchess of Arcadia."

Bale coughed. "*Future* Duchess of Arcadia."

Cas closed her hand on a weather vial. It would be a miracle if she made it another day into this trip without launching him over the rails.

"Why would *you* need to see the Emperor?" Gen asked.

"To sell weather. I'll tell him we want to expand our sales into Elysium. I'll let him think I am undercutting the Empresses on lightning vials in order to gain new business. He should like that." Not only would he think he'd have access to Arcadian lightning, but he'd also get the satisfaction of stealing from the Empresses in the process.

"That sounds like something you'd do," Bale said.

"Of course it does, because it would be incredibly profitable if the Empresses wouldn't take my head for doing it."

"So you're going to tell Emperor Nessos that you are doing this without the Empresses' approval," Lux said.

"Yes."

"Then he'll know he can kill us without the Empresses retaliating."

"Not necessarily. Regardless of our reason for being here, he'd have to consider that killing one of the leaders of an Olympian isle could come back to bite him." The winners of a previous war didn't want to start a new one. The losers did.

"She has a point. Elysiums don't kill innocents," Bale said. "It's in their code, carved on the Oracles' tablets at the top of Mount Ida, one of their most sacred places. It's the Oracle Gaia's law: 'Thou shall not kill those who have not borne you ill will.' *Ill will* is a loose term, but Nessos probably won't kill us on sight."

Pollux crossed his arms. "How do you know this?"

Bale shrugged. "How do you not? Might have been a good idea to study some Elysium lore before you wandered into their waters."

Castor had studied the important things. She'd picked through the decayed old maps in the library, researched their weaponry and economy, looked for clues to the whereabouts of the apples—with no success. She'd had no need to study their moral code. Or so she'd thought.

"This all sounds like a terrible idea," Adikia said. "I've never walked right in the front doors to steal something."

"It's our only option," Castor said, "because as of now, we have no clue where the apples are. We can either sail around the Elysium seas for months trying to find them, and be caught eventually, or we can try to establish a relationship here, find a faster way to the apples, and hopefully, not get killed. I am open to other useful ideas if anyone has one."

Silence followed. Exactly as Cas thought.

Until Adikia opened her mouth. "We can steal an Elysium ship and sail right through them."

"No." Bale shook his head. "Elysium ships use rowers, not sails, and Gen is the only one who could keep up."

"That is true," Castor agreed, eyeing Bale with more suspicion. As Adikia had said, Pollux chose strange friends, ones who could apparently tell dirty jokes *and* describe Elysium ships.

The MetalBender wrote something down on a piece of parchment and held it to her.

Castor read it aloud. "*Take the Cerberus first. Gen can command it, and we can use it as leverage.*" She bit down on the inside of her cheek. That was a viable idea except she did not want to die before she reached her apples. "Where will we put a Cerberus on this ship? We're already short of bunks." Castor was crammed into one of the cabins with Gen and her smelly dog. She couldn't take another beast on this ship. "If no one else has any clever ideas, then it's settled. This is a sales call."

"There's one huge problem," Bale said. "No one likes you. I'm not sure you're the one who should be negotiating with the Emperor."

Castor's cheeks flamed. "I don't need to be liked. I only need to convince him that all I want is his business."

Pollux snorted. "You sound just like our father."

"I do not," she spat. "Father would never think of something so clever. If you haven't noticed, brother, I have been the one handling the StormMaker business for years, and I will continue to do so long after he is dead."

As her temple pulsed, she heard her father's voice in the pounding of her ears: *"Arrogant, spoiled child."* She would show him. She didn't need him. Or Tegea. Or anyone.

"If you can keep the Emperor occupied," Gen said, "I can search for something to lead us to the apples."

Castor raised her chin to the least likely of her supporters. "I can keep him busy."

Gen nodded.

"We should get some sleep," Adikia said. "You there, help me with the sails." She pointed to the MetalBender this time. Flek met her at the mast, and together they pulled on the ropes to lower the sails.

Castor made her way into her cabin, frowning when she noticed the contents of Gen's bag spilling from her bunk to the floor. Dried seaweed crusted the folds, and it smelled like the sea at low tide. Cas dropped onto her own bed and covered her face with her hands.

They would never get the apples and the Cerberus back to Olympia. Not with all of them in one piece. Castor would happily sacrifice the MetalBender and Bale. Her brother? She couldn't. She supposed she couldn't lose Gen, either. Castor needed Gen's strength to finish this. Except Cas didn't need to worry about her. Gen could handle herself either through skill or unfathomable good luck.

Adikia . . . Cas didn't know. She had the feeling if things turned too rough, Adikia would be the first to run, like a rat jumping from a sinking ship.

Outside the open door, Castor heard footsteps.

"Sorry about my sister," Lux whispered.

Castor ran her finger over a lightning jar. *Sorry for what? For having a brilliant plan to save our lives?*

"I hope we're making the right decision," Gen said.

"Castor wouldn't knowingly put herself in danger."

"That's true."

"Are you sure you're all right sleeping in here with her?"

"I've survived two nights already, and I have Chomp."

Pollux laughed. "Even he might not be enough to scare my sister."

Cas heard what she assumed was some affectionate good-night gesture followed by the pattering of four small feet. Apparently the dog didn't want to watch Pollux and Gen kiss, either. He sat on the floor in front of her and blinked at her with cloudy purple eyes.

"What do you want?" she snapped at him.

He curled his lip and snarled.

The dog not only smelled, but it also left puddles of drool on the floor and purple hair everywhere. If he dared snap at her, that would be the last straw.

"You bite me, mutt, and I will turn you to ash." She rolled away from the dog and buried her nose in the blankets. Those apples had better be worth all of this.

CHAPTER 12

POLLUX

Pollux reluctantly left Gen in the cabin with his sister and even more reluctantly went into his own. They'd decided to split the two cabins into boys and girls. On the one hand, that kept Flek from bunking with Gen. But it also kept *him* from bunking with Gen, put his sister with her instead, and put him with Bale, who snored, and Flek, who constantly reminded Pollux that he had competition for Gen's affections, affections he felt slipping through his fingers.

Even tonight, he'd left her with little more than a good-night kiss to avoid her mind magic.

Pollux sat on the edge of his cot and rubbed his thumbs against his temples. For the moment, only Bale occupied one of the beds while Flek helped Adikia on deck.

"We have very little chance of success, don't we?" he said to Bale.

"That's what keeps things interesting," Bale said.

"I wish I could be more like you and not care what happens."

Bale sat upright. "I care a great deal what happens." His tone wasn't mocking.

"I'm sorry. I didn't mean that." Pollux raised his head. "I guess I've never understood why. Why you care. Why you've stayed with me all this time." Even his own family wouldn't sacrifice for him the way Bale did.

"You're a good person, Lux. One who is stuck with terrible people."

"That's a vague answer. There are plenty of good people in bad situations, people who would pay better and not drag you into danger."

"You're more than welcome to give me a raise," Bale said.

"I'd rather have an answer. Why me?" Pollux wasn't sure why he needed the answer. Maybe it was because as soon as Bale had learned they were going to Elysium, he'd seemed less like himself. Or because they could be maimed or killed on this trip, and Pollux needed to know why Bale would be willing to go that far.

"Your charming personality," Bale said.

"I see," Pollux said. "So you can meddle in my problems with Gen, but you can't give me one simple answer. Give me one good reason why I shouldn't send you home."

"You need me."

"I do. But what do you need?"

"You don't want to know."

"Yes, I do," Pollux insisted.

"Penance," Bale snapped in his frustration, the first truth from his mouth.

"What did you do that requires penance?"

Bale laughed derisively. "What do you care? You can't see anything else beyond Gen."

"That's not true." It also wasn't entirely untrue. Pollux had been so focused on their kissing problem, and their Elysium problem, that he had been preoccupied lately. "I had hoped after all this time, you and I had become something like friends. If I can help, I want to."

"You can help by staying alive and proving . . ."

"Proving what?"

"Nothing."

"Please, Bale?" Pollux couldn't drag his friend into all of this without knowing the reason, and it needed to be a good reason, because he didn't want to be like Castor and his father, using people to get his own needs.

"I made a mistake," Bale muttered.

"What kind of mistake?"

Bale leaned forward, his elbows on his knees. "What if I told you I murdered someone? I took someone trusting and vulnerable and drove her to her death? Would you still want me here? Would you have hired me to be your assistant?"

Bale watched him intently for a reaction. All Pollux gave him was a slight lift of his eyes. He'd been raised around corruption and violence. It didn't shock him anymore.

Bale had appeared on Arcadia almost two years ago with no story and nothing more than the clothes on his back. For the past year and a half, he had traveled with Pollux for his performances, casting the lights on his smoke figures with the skill of an artist. Not once had Pollux thought Bale would kill him in the night. He didn't think it now, either.

Footsteps approached, and Flek poked his overly handsome face into the room. Bale pressed his lips together and lay back on his bed. The conversation was over. Flek could read lips and gestures more acutely than anyone Pollux knew. Pollux and the others still struggled, which was why Flek continued to write everything down.

Flek wrote on his parchment now. *Is everything all right?*

He must have sensed the tension in the room. Pollux quickly

conjured excuses. "No. You've met my sister. Surely you can see how everything is not all right."

Is this the sister who killed Gen's whale?

Pollux nodded. "Just remember, metal is highly conductive to lightning. Be careful not to make her angry."

As he pulled off his boots and lay down on his cot, he didn't miss the fear in Flek's face, or the flash of a grin on Bale's. As much as his assistant complained about Cas, Bale respected that Castor didn't let anyone get the better of her.

Flek put out the lantern, and Pollux pulled his blanket to his chest, settling into the rocking ship.

"What if I told you I had murdered someone?" If that was Bale's secret, the fact that he seemed ashamed of it spoke volumes. Of all the stern faces painted into the Othonos family tree, most of them had killed someone and never felt any remorse for it. Pollux's own father had sold the lightning that killed most of the Mazon race.

"Bale," Pollux whispered.

"Hmm?"

"I still would have hired you."

"Good night, Lux," Bale mumbled.

~

Pollux awoke the next morning with a slight headache. His lips tasted like salt. He was alone in the cabin and wondered how late it was. He got dressed and combed his fingers through his hair, picked up his violin, and made his way to the main deck. He was the last to arrive.

"Good morning," Gen said, crossing the ship to greet him. As she laced her fingers with his, his mood lifted.

Despite their problems, he loved her. Every time he saw her

face, music played in his soul, a song he couldn't ignore. The rest would work itself out. Somehow.

Across the ship, his sister spoke with Adikia, pulling on a loose thread on her jacket as she did. It was Castor's one and only nervous habit, done only when she liked someone. The last person to put her in this state was their childhood friend Ariete. But Ariete had been an idle crush. Castor had never offered *her* an annuity.

"Hey," Adikia called over Castor's shoulder. "If you lazy loafs are going to stay on this ship, you need to work. This isn't a pleasure cruise."

"No, it certainly isn't," Gen sighed. Pollux tucked a piece of silver hair behind her ear.

By now, he'd sensed that Adikia's favorite part of the day was when she handed out assignments. Usually Pollux spent his time controlling the wind in the sails, while Gen was given some task that required brute strength.

"You"—Adikia pointed to Flek—"check the rudder. It seems shaky. Some of the bolts might have come loose. You"—she pointed to Pollux—"wipe down this deck."

"What?" Pollux asked.

"Swab the deck," she repeated. "It's filthy. Castor can take the sails today."

Pollux headed to the bridge while Adikia directed Bale to make them all lunch in the galley and Gen to untangle the anchor ropes. When he picked up the ragged mop from the bucket, he thought about what Soter had said to him about leading a privileged life. He had never mopped a floor. To be honest, he had never touched a mop.

He filled the empty bucket with rainwater from one of his storm vials and dropped the mop into it. He had seen the maids mop the floors at the manor, and he tried to copy them, swirling water back and forth across the deck.

Adikia gave him a look that suggested he hadn't been paying as close attention as he'd thought. "That's too much water. Haven't you used a mop before?"

"I, um——"

"Of course you haven't," she muttered. "Spoiled royals. You have to squeeze the mop out before you use it or you'll soak my deck and make it worse than before."

"Right." His skin warmed. How had he gone this long not knowing how to clean up after himself? Despite popular opinion, he did want to be useful. This trip could be his chance to strip off the title of Lord Pollux, the Great and Talented Lux, and simply be Pollux.

This time, he squeezed the excess water from the mop before he dropped it to the boards. Adikia grunted an approval.

He mopped his way across the bridge, closer to the Bornean captain. He took her in, from the salt-crusted, weathered hat on her head to the line of lavender scales running down the back of her neck, trying to see what Castor saw in her. She wasn't his sister's usual type. Not that he really knew his sister's type. They didn't talk about those kinds of things. In fact, they rarely talked. They either ignored one another or shouted at each other.

"What are you staring at?" Adikia snapped.

"Ah . . . nothing." He continued mopping. "I just find it curious that you convinced my sister to pay you an annuity. It's not like her."

"I'm clever," she said. "And Castor was desperate. If you make enemies everywhere you go, your friends are few and far between."

"You sound like you know something about that."

"I do. Thieves like me mostly know other thieves, who are more likely to stab you in the back than give you a helping hand. But it's not like that for you, is it? Everyone loves the talented Lux."

"Not everyone." He thought about all the times his father had dragged him into his office to smash one of his violins or tell him how useless he was. Or how his own sister had burned him. Or even Gen, who had lumped him in with his family as a ruthless StormMaker who would char anything to ash for the right amount of coin. He knew as well as anyone that appearances didn't always reflect the truth.

"I was on Delos when you played one of your shows. I almost got trampled by fans," Adikia said.

"They like my music. They don't even know me."

"It's more of a welcome than I've ever gotten. You're all the same, you Makers. So superior and so spoiled. You don't know how to do anything for yourself. If you lost your magic, you wouldn't be able to feed yourself. And while people are throwing coins at you to make them magic jewelry, songs, or rain clouds, the rest of us are down here finding other ways to fend for ourselves."

She didn't say a word that wasn't true. Pollux knew plenty of people who hadn't been blessed by the Oracles. His mother for one, but even she had been blessed with fortune and beauty.

"There are easier ways to get coin than by going into the Elysium Empire," he said. If that was all Adikia was after.

"Bigger risk. Bigger pay off. This is the job that's going to make it so I don't have to work again."

"That's why you negotiated the annuity."

"Exactly. Unlike you, I was born into a family with too many kids and not enough coin. Most of my life has been spent worrying about where my next meal is coming from. You have no idea what it's like to be truly desperate, and you never will. The annuity she promised me will barely affect her, but it will change my entire life."

He was beginning to see why Cas liked her. "You sound fairly respectable, for a thief."

She laughed. "And you don't sound like a complete ass. For a StormMaker."

"I try not to be."

She sized him up with half-squinted eyes. "I like you, Pollux, Lord of Storms. So I'm going to give you a word of advice—watch that girlfriend of yours."

"Gen?" She worked on the other side of the ship, pulling massive ropes apart with her bare hands, not a bead of sweat on her skin.

Adikia nodded. "I wasn't always a thief. We used to raise chickens. Then a MindWorker helped himself to our flock. There's something wrong with that lot. Worse than the rest of you. It's like their magic has poisoned their own minds."

"That's not true. Not about Gen." If anything, his family had poisoned her when they'd helped kill the Mazons.

"It's—" Adikia stopped and pointed to the sky. "What is that?"

Pollux set aside his mop and followed her gaze. Something soared across the sun. A bird, maybe? Though it looked more like a snake, long and thin.

"Look up!" he shouted as the thing fell faster. Gen stopped working on the knots in the rope, and Castor pulled the wind out of the sails.

The thing slammed into the deck, cutting through the wood like a knife through butter—a spear. If Castor hadn't pulled the wind, it likely would have cut through the sail and come dangerously close to where he was standing.

"More are coming!" Castor shouted as she pulled a vial from her belt.

Pollux made for his violin and realized Flek hadn't heard the warning or felt the spear hit the ship. The MetalBender leaned over the stern, still working on the rudder.

Pollux lifted his violin to his chin as another spear fell from the sky, heading straight toward Flek's heart. He pulled his bow across the strings, and a gust of wind emerged from the instrument, aimed at the falling spear to throw it off course. The spear drove through Flek's shoulder. The crunch of bones echoed in Pollux's ears. Blood splattered onto his arm.

He dropped to the deck and knelt beside Flek.

"Are you all right?" He cursed himself as he spoke. Of course Flek wasn't all right. Dark blood pooled on his shirt and ran down his side, smearing across the deck. The spear had pinned Flek to the rails. He couldn't move.

Pollux knew enough to not remove the spear without medicine. "Gen has something for this," he said, thinking of her smelly lizard gunk. "I'll get it."

He got to his feet, and his breath lodged in his throat. Dozens of spears fell from the sky. Enough to cover the sun. He lifted his violin and played. Wind burst from the strings and parted the spears, which struck the deck on either side of him.

Sweat coated his palms. His bow slipped. The spears never stopped falling. One of his strings snapped, and he shifted his fingers. One of the strings sliced through his index finger, and he continued to play.

"Oracles save us," he whispered, as spears hit the ship on all sides.

CHAPTER 13

CASTOR

Castor ripped a hurricane vial from her belt and tore it open. She pushed the wind into the sky and swept up the spears. She sprayed them across the sea, then drew the wind back for the next onslaught. How had the Elysiums found them so quickly? They were still hours out from Okeanos. Unless their maps were more inaccurate than she'd thought.

Castor curled the hurricane in her fingers. She let it twine around her arms, heavy rain and wind tearing at her clothes and whipping the sails. As new spears launched through the air, she released her storm. Wind and rain exploded from all sides of her. Spears shot away like broken bits of straw and dropped harmlessly to the water. Everyone else on deck fell flat, pushed down by wind.

Castor could barely discern the outlines of the approaching ships through her storm. She couldn't tell how many there were. No matter. She sent what remained of her storm toward them. She let it hover there, dropping whatever rain and wind remained on their attackers. It wouldn't harm them, but it would slow them down.

"That should hold them until we can raise the white flag," she said.

"We're going to surrender?" Adikia called.

"I can't negotiate with the Emperor if he finds out we slaughtered his soldiers. We need to raise the flag." And if Bale's blathering about

Gaia's law was true, the Elysiums couldn't keep firing at them after they'd surrendered.

She stomped her way to the bridge, where Adikia reaffixed her hat and Pollux picked up his violin. Blood stained his sleeve. Cas grabbed him by the wrist. The one thing Gen had to do was look after Pollux, and the Mazon couldn't even manage that. "How badly are you hurt?"

"I'm not. It's Flek." Pollux nodded to the rails, where a spear pinned Flek to the ship.

Gen was already tending to the MetalBender. She gripped the spear with both hands and pulled it from his arm. He opened his mouth in a guttural moan. More blood spilled down his arm.

"I'm sorry. So sorry," Gen said, and smeared some green gunk on the wound. Her dog whimpered sympathetically behind her.

Castor blanched and turned away.

"Blood scares you?" Adikia asked.

"No, mortality does." If the MetalBender died, she would have no way to bring the apples home. Her plans were quickly unraveling. "Where is the flag?"

"The deck box, below."

Castor stomped back down the companionway, Adikia following. Bale was already at the box. He flipped it open and rifled through hooks, ropes, pulleys—no surrender flag.

"Where is it?" Castor turned to Adikia.

"I don't know. It's not my ship. Should I have asked the previous owner to confirm it was fully stocked when I stole it?"

"Yes!" Castor pointed to Bale. "Go rip the sheets off one of the beds. We need a flag. Now." Then she grabbed and opened Delia's box.

"Yes, Lady Castor?" Delia said sleepily.

"Wake up!" Castor snapped. "Elysium ships are on approach. I need to know how many ships, the number of soldiers, and details of their weaponry, understand?"

"Yes, right away," the ghost said with more energy before she flitted off over the sea.

"How is the MetalBender?" Castor shouted as she climbed back up to the main deck.

"Not well," Gen said.

"Is he breathing?"

"Yes."

Castor sighed. That was something. For now. A whistling sound cut across the sky. The first of the next round of spears.

Castor opened a vial of wind and swept up the spear. It dropped into the ocean. Four more spears launched toward her. She brought her wind back and pushed those spears to the other side of the ship. For the briefest moment, she considered sending the projectiles right back to the ships that had sent them.

They were fools to think their silly little spears could hurt her. But she had bigger plans that involved not walking into the Emperor's palace as his enemy. She also couldn't waste all of her storm vials on this assault. "Where is that sheet?"

More spears fell. Pollux's violin played. His wind picked them up and sent them spinning into the water.

Castor grabbed another vial. On the next round, she caught six of the spears and thrust them to the side, but she missed one. It zoomed over her shoulder. She turned in time to see the MetalBender raise his hand. The metal tip of the spear glowed. It veered off course and harmlessly struck the deck.

At least he was well enough to use his magic. It meant he wasn't in danger of dying. Yet.

Gen plucked the discarded spear from the deck and used it to swat away two others as Bale ran up from belowdecks with a white sheet trailing behind him.

"Get that on the mast!" Castor shouted.

"Yes, Your Highness," he said mockingly.

She pushed another round of spears out of the sky and saw Delia flying right behind them.

The spirit soared toward her, blinking feverishly. "There are five ships on approach, each with ten soldiers and armed with spear launchers."

Castor blew away another three spears before her wind sputtered dry. She scrambled for another vial. Sharp-pointed spears dropped quickly toward her head. Her brother played a quick trill, and he pushed them away. She flipped open her next storm vial.

"Did you get a count on the number of spears they had left?" she asked.

"No. It was a lot."

Castor bit back a curse at Delia's incompetence. "That's enough, then. You can get in the box."

Delia blinked twice before obeying. Castor slammed the box shut as four spears embedded in the deck near her. The spears fell faster now. The ships had to be getting closer.

"Damn the Oracles!" Bale shouted.

"What's wrong?" Castor turned.

Some of the spears she'd missed had struck the mast. One had torn through a sail, and another had cut through the rope used to raise the flag. Bale would either have to repair the rope or make it all the way to the top of the mast with the white sheet on his own.

"Hold on," Castor said. "Pollux, cover me." She shifted her wind toward Bale and wrapped it around his feet and ankles.

"I have a feeling I'm not going to like this," he said.

"You'll like being cut through with a spear much less."

She pushed out and up with her wind, lifting Bale into the air. The sound of Pollux's violin meshed with the rush of the wind and the whistling spears. More of them hit the deck. One landed within inches of her feet. Bale floated up the mast with the white sheet trailing behind him. He was almost there. Another spear whistled by her ear.

"Sorry!" Pollux shouted.

Castor focused on her own wind. Bale reached the top of the mast. She steadied him there while he fumbled with the sheet, trying to attach it to the clips. *I'll be dead before he does it.*

Another spear whistled nearby. Castor glanced upward. It flew toward her head. If Pollux missed it, it would cut right through her skull. But she couldn't hear her brother's song.

She flicked her eyes to him. He'd lowered his bow and was re-placing empty vials. The spear kept falling. Castor would have to drop Bale. She drew back on her wind. He clung to the mast.

"What are you doing?" he shouted.

"Trying not to die!"

She swung her wind around too late and saw the spear aimed between her eyes.

An arrow flew over her head. It hit the end of the spear, sending it off course. Castor dodged to the side, and the spear clattered to the deck.

Adikia smiled at her with a crooked, smug grin. "You owe me one," she said, swinging her crossbow around her shoulder.

"I dare you to collect," Castor said.

Bale dropped to the deck. "No one worry about me. I found my own way down."

Overhead, the makeshift surrender flag flapped in the wind. Castor held her breath.

A small part of her hoped the Elysiums would ignore the surrender and keep firing their spears. If they did that, she would have no cause to hold back. She could burn their ships and sink them into the sea. Maybe they could reach the Emperor before he heard about it. Or maybe they wouldn't, and then he would know she was not someone to be trifled with.

But no more spears dropped from the sky. Instead, the ships moved in closer, surrounding them on all sides. Ten ships in total with five rowers each. Delia had said the opposite. The long, low ships couldn't hold more sailors than five each, not with the spear launcher and pile of spears in the center.

Had it been a simple mistake? Or had Delia been trying to sabotage her?

The first of the Elysium ships attached to the *Hind*. Hooks slammed into the hull, wrapping around the railing. Castor kept one hand on her lightning.

Beside her, Adikia cracked her knuckles one by one. She clearly didn't like letting herself get caught. Castor didn't, either. Surrender implied she had been bested. She knew, though, there was a greater plan.

Beyond Adikia, Gen held tight to her little dog and ran her

fingers through its matted fur. Her eyes were wild. She looked like a caged beast ready to claw. Or run.

"I hope you know what you're doing," Pollux whispered, coming up beside Castor.

"I always know what I'm doing," she replied.

The metal hooks bit into the wood. Cranks raised the Elysiums to the deck. The first of the soldiers landed on the ship. Dressed in thick armor and a plumed helmet, the soldier stood tall with a long braid hung over her shoulder. She hit the deck with heavy hooves.

Castor had only seen the Elysiums in paint before. She hadn't expected them to be this large. She stood about eye level with the top of the soldier's legs. *Centaurs*, they called themselves. The Elysium word for their people.

"Laski cadera armi," the woman said, as more of the soldiers pulled themselves onto the deck.

Castor had been eight when she'd told her father she no longer needed a tutor. Primarily because the tutor he'd hired to teach her had stopped providing her with any useful information. She opted to teach herself instead by studying independently in the library. She didn't need to know which fork to use when someone served her prawns. She needed to know how to grow the business of Arcadia. She studied arithmetic, climate, and island languages.

Fortunately, the Arcadian library also held an extensive section on Elysium and the old wars. The only larger collection of books was on Athenia, in the Empresses' library. Castor had read enough to have a basic understanding of the language.

"She said to lower your weapons," she whispered to everyone. "Gen, drop the spear. Lux, put away your violin, and Adikia, lose the crossbow."

Castor kept one hand on her belt. She would remove it only if commanded to do so. To someone not familiar with the StormMakers, her belt of vials wouldn't look threatening, even if one jar could strike them all dead.

"Acceito tuva resa," the woman said. Good news. They accepted the surrender.

Another centaur pointed at a spear with a melted tip. "Kana hai fatto?"

Castor bit into her cheek. He wanted to know how they had bent the spear. She didn't want the Elysiums to know their secrets, what powers they had. Not that Flek could affect any metal at the moment. He could barely stand. He leaned against the ship rails, losing more color with every breath.

"Erano. Proprio spirito sapeva labbero," one centaur said to another.

They were right where the ghost said they would be. Cas looked down at the wooden box on her belt. Delia. She had sold them out. That was how they had been discovered so soon. Delia must have defied Castor, snuck out of her box in the night, and told the Elysiums they were coming.

Little fool. If Delia wanted Castor dead to gain her freedom, it wouldn't serve her to kill Pollux too. Without him, she'd have no owner. She would be forever bound to the box until it was destroyed or collected by someone else. Delia clearly hadn't thought through their last conversation. Next time, Castor would be more direct.

"Cosa vuoi?" the lead soldier asked.

"Parleremo soliso imperatore," Castor said. *We will speak only to the Emperor.*

The woman removed her helmet. She bore a scar down her right cheek and a scowl that put Castor's own sneer to shame.

"Your command of our words is not as good as you wish it," she said in Olympian. "Lucky for you, I speak the traitor's speech."

She didn't speak Olympian as well as she thought she did, either. But at least they were at the negotiating stage of their capture.

"I had no intention of commanding your language," Castor said. "I only wish to speak with Emperor Nessos."

The woman leaned down to look her in the eye. "I am Quintas, head of the Elysium guard. You may give your message to me, and I will deliver it. Turn your ship back now, and we may let you live."

The smile hardened on Castor's face. "Our message is for the eyes and ears of Emperor Nessos only."

Quintas shuffled her hooves. "You are in breach of the treaty."

"I know," Castor said, "and you seem like a capable soldier, Quintas. Why do you think we would risk breaking the treaty? For something unimportant? For war? If we wished to attack you, don't you think we would have come with more ships, more weapons? We are only messengers, here to offer the great Emperor Nessos an opportunity."

"What kind of opportunity?"

"The kind of opportunity that it would incense your Emperor to know an overzealous guard had kept him from hearing."

Quintas's nostrils flared, and Castor knew she had made her point.

Quintas turned to her soldiers and spoke to them in Elysium. "Put them all in irons. We will take them to Okeanos to see the Emperor. He can decide what to do with them."

Castor tried not to look smug. These hired soldiers were all the same, here or in Olympia. They all did what they were told, and they were terrified of upsetting their master.

Her smile fell when one of the guards wrenched her arms behind her back and attached heavy irons to her wrists. The chains dragged at her shoulders. They must have weighed twenty pounds. She looked down at her belt and the vials she would never be able to open. But at least they were there.

When they shackled Flek, he slumped to the deck under the weight. But metal chains should have felt like nothing to him. His injuries made Castor anxious. It was the one piece of her plan she couldn't control. Only Gen seemed unimpeded by the weight of the chains. She wore them like simple bracelets.

Quintas shouted out orders. Elysium soldiers searched the ship and the crew and pulled out hidden weapons, dropping them in a pile in the center of the deck. When they searched Adikia, they found two knives buried in her socks.

"Was this all part of your genius plan?" Adikia asked as her knives were added to the pile.

"We're alive, aren't we?" Cas retorted.

"For now," Bale said.

CHAPTER 14

POLLUX

Pollux had to hand it to his sister. She knew how to make enemies everywhere. She'd saved their heads for now, convincing the Elysium guard to take them prisoner instead of dumping them into the sea, but he worried she'd only set them up for a worse fate.

His wrists ached where the chains cut into his flesh. He couldn't feel his fingers. Would this affect his violin playing? He shifted his arms to try to bring sensation back into his limbs.

The Elysiums had dragged Pollux, Bale, and Flek down to their cabin to sleep, while Cas had convinced the guards to keep her, Gen, and Adikia locked in the captain's rooms. Across from Pollux, Bale slept soundly. Flek was out, too, but not exactly sleeping. He had fallen unconscious. His normally pinkish skin had turned a sickly yellow. Whenever Pollux woke up from the pain in his arms, he immediately checked to make sure Flek was still breathing. Gen had removed the spear and healed the wound, but Flek had lost a lot of blood, and being locked in chains probably wasn't helping with his healing.

Pollux wasn't sure why he cared what happened to Flek. He hadn't missed the sidelong looks Flek gave Gen, even knowing she was already with Pollux.

Is she really with you, though? You can barely kiss her without having a panic attack.

Still, guilt gnawed at Pollux's insides. He had not wanted Flek to come with them, and now it was possible the MetalBender's journey would end here.

Don't think like that.

He shifted onto his back and closed his eyes. He wondered what Gen was doing, if she could break free of her chains. He liked to think she could. If he'd had a chance to kiss her before they were dragged away, he would have known for certain. There were some advantages to the connection of her mind magic. He would remember to kiss her next time they were about to be imprisoned, if there was a next time.

Hoofbeats sounded overhead and made their way down the steps. Pollux closed his eyes and feigned sleep.

Hooves slammed against the doorframe so hard his cot shook. Bale jolted awake, and Pollux sat upright. Flek barely opened his eyes.

"Get up, lazy Olympians," Quintas said. "You have a meeting with the Emperor. I want you on deck in five minutes." Her smile suggested she was marching them to their own executions, which was highly probable. Even Cas couldn't talk or burn her way out of everything.

Bale sat up and rubbed his face with his shoulder. "If they do decide to kill us today, I hope they feed us something substantial first."

"I don't think I could eat if I tried."

Without full use of their arms, he and Bale did their best getting Flek to his feet. They pressed in on either side of him so he could lean on them as they walked up the companionway. On deck, Pollux squinted in the hazy light of early dawn. They had sailed through the night, slowed by the centaurs towing their ship.

Centaurs marched across the deck with heavy hoofbeats and

shouted at one another in Elysium. Beyond the railing, the sun peeked over a series of stone houses climbing up a rocky cliff.

A song twined through Pollux's thoughts. A quick staccato melody with short puffs of cloud wisp. He looked to where his violin sat next to a stack of crates, along with Adikia's knives and Bale's sword.

Gen, Castor, and Adikia stood together, with Chomp snarling at Gen's feet. He had been tied with heavy rope and lashed to Gen's waist. Pollux wondered if the Elysiums had lost any fingers in restraining the chaeri. He hoped so.

Apart from being shackled, his sister and Gen looked well. Well enough, he supposed. No one looked their best. The weight of sleeplessness and anxiety hung on all of them as heavy as these chains. His only solace was the expression Cas wore. She looked smug, as if she knew she would have her vengeance for this moment and all the indignities they'd faced.

He hoped she was right. While Cas often did get her vengeance, she more often put herself in worse trouble with her arrogance and temper.

"Get moving." One of the guards prodded him in the back of the knee with the sharp tip of a spear.

Pollux's legs buckled, and Flek tipped to the side. Pollux hit the deck, and the centaurs laughed while Bale tried to help Flek stand upright.

"Don't touch him," Castor snapped at the centaurs.

Pollux got to his knees. "I don't need you to fight my battles for me. I think you've done enough."

The Elysiums marched them off their ship and tied the *Hind* to the dock. If Pollux and the others managed to survive this, they would need to free the *Hind* because there was no way they could take the Elysium ships. They sank low in the center with high sides and could be operated either by foot pedals or heavy oars. Gen was the only one who might be able to turn the massive oars, and Pollux and Castor needed sails to push a ship. The only ship here with sails was the one they'd brought.

The guards prodded them onto the shore, which was packed with Elysiums dragging fish nets from the water and carrying their catches to market via baskets on their backs. The houses that rose up the mountain were simple stone cottages with thatched roofs. The word *rustic* came to Pollux's thoughts and included the structure at the top of the hill, a massive castle built from moss-covered stone held aloft by four thick columns.

Elysiums stopped and stared, open-mouthed, at the strange two-legged Olympians in chains as they walked past. Pollux didn't know what the gawkers were saying, but by the stares, he assumed they were unhappy to see them. He wondered if they had ever seen Olympians before. If they had, it was likely how he'd seen the Elysiums—as sharp-toothed monsters with bloodthirsty eyes like the centaurs depicted by Olympian artists in books and paintings.

One of the guards snatched Flek from Pollux's side. "Hey, wait!" he shouted.

"Where are you taking him?" Bale called.

The centaurs ignored them and deposited Flek in the back of a wagon, laying him across a sack of grain.

It was the Empresses' father, Emperor Polycrates, who had said, *"The true test of character is in how a person treats their enemy."* He'd said it in reference to the feud between the Mazons and the Gargareans and had meant to diminish both of their characters since neither had treated their enemies well. But now it gave Pollux hope. If the

Elysiums recognized Flek's injuries, it meant they hadn't written them off for execution. Yet.

A spear prodded Pollux in the back, and a guard shouted, "Tuvia!" Pollux took it to mean, *"Move, worthless Olympian, or get stabbed."*

He moved, following the line of soldiers up a stone path through the village. The road they followed wound long and thin between the houses, barely wide enough for two centaurs to walk side by side. He glanced over his shoulder and spotted Gen's silver skin far back in the procession. She and Castor were snapping at one another, until an Elysium guard separated them with the point of a spear.

"Your sister is wonderful with negotiations," Bale muttered.

"She learned from our father," Pollux said. "The only problem is the Elysiums don't care about our coin or influence." She couldn't bully them here.

"It sounds like we're about to be murdered," Bale said.

"I think we will be unless we find a way out."

"How do you suggest we do that?"

Pollux eyed a sword hanging from the flank of the closest Elysium. "We find a way out of these chains, you grab that sword, I get my violin, and we clear a path down to the ship."

"You've been reading too many hero stories."

"You did say you had . . . killed someone before."

"Not like that," Bale said.

"Then how?" Pollux wished he had asked more after Bale's confession. It bothered him that he didn't know the circumstances. How had Bale done it? Like the Duke of Storms, giving the tools to someone else so he could keep his hands clean? Or had Bale been some cutthroat killer in his previous life? They could use a violent swordsman at the moment.

"I was hoping the MetalBender could free us." Bale nodded to Flek in the back of the wagon. "But that's not going to be an option."

"Then we need to think of something else. Any suggestions?"

The road took a sharp turn out of the village, and Pollux stumbled. He received another jab between the shoulders. He righted himself and turned on the Elysium guard with a glare. He could take a great deal of punishment, but he was tired of being prodded like a pincushion.

"Keep moving," the guard said in choppy Olympian.

Pollux took another step forward and stumbled again, this time by no fault of his own. The ground shook under his feet.

Quintas shouted something at her soldiers. They all pressed in close to the mountain and raised their shields over their heads to protect themselves from the rocks dropping from above. Pollux followed their lead and pushed his chest into the rock wall. Small rocks plinked off armor and shields and struck Pollux's unarmored limbs and skull.

Is this an earthquake?

He closed his eyes and listened. A low growl rumbled through the mountain.

The last few rocks bounced off the soldiers, and Quintas waved her spear and pointed to the road. She said several words Pollux didn't understand, and one he did.

Cerberus.

His mouth went dry. The tales described the Cerberus as a vicious beast larger than a manor with three heads that burned hotter than any flame. Each jaw held rows of teeth the size of grown men and as sharp as freshly honed blades. He'd assumed at least some of it was an exaggeration.

Now he wasn't so sure.

As soon as the ground settled, they continued up the small path, stepping over fallen rocks.

"Was that the beast?" Bale asked. "The one Gen is supposed to catch?"

"I think so," Pollux whispered.

Bale muttered several curses.

Pollux had seen Gen defeat the supposedly immortal Hydra. It had been a thing of legend, too, but this . . . this would be something else.

After stumbling for hours, they made their last winding circle around the mountain. Sweat rained from Pollux's cheeks and pasted his filthy shirt to his ribs. The Elysium castle rose from the rocks into the late morning light. Massive columns held the structure aloft, made from rocks that were each twice Pollux's height and ten times his girth. The castle likely had to be made of strong material to withstand the rumbling of the Cerberus.

The guards pushed open the heavy doors and prodded Pollux and the others into an open-air courtyard. Splashes of color burst from every corner in bright orange blooms and lavender vines. Like everything else here, even the plants seemed larger. Pollux formed the beginnings of a song in his thoughts, "The Gardens of Elysium." He only hoped they would live long enough for him to play it.

We're not dead yet.

He had gotten out of worse situations. His eyes went to his violin, tied to the flank of one of the Elysiums ahead. If he could reach it and even one of the vials inside, he could do something. The problem was the chains.

Across the courtyard stood a raised throne carved from marble.

It was made for a centaur body, wide and low enough that the centaur on it had settled on his haunches. Pollux guessed this was Emperor Nessos. He had a broad chest plated in gold armor and wore a crown of twisted vines. His long, silver hair blended with his beard and fell to his shoulders. He watched them warily, as he should. He knew there had to be either a very bad or a very good reason a small group of Olympians would break the treaty.

Emperor Nessos picked up the spear beside his throne and pointed it at them, speaking in a gruff voice. A hand slammed down on Pollux's shoulder, pushing him to his knees. Other hands pushed Bale, Cas, Gen, and Adikia down. The wagon with Flek was gone. He had been taken somewhere else.

Nessos stood from his throne and marched slowly across the expansive courtyard. Each click of his hooves sent tremors through Pollux's bones. Nessos eventually stopped before them and peered down.

In fluent Olympian, he said, "What message do you bring me from Olympia?"

Castor raised her head. Even on her knees, she looked defiant. "Emperor Nessos, I come to you with a proposition."

He laughed. "I'm in no need of a proposition from the Empresses. I should send you back to them in pieces for being so arrogant."

Pollux swallowed. Her ego was going to get them all slaughtered.

"This is my own proposition," Castor said. "Not from them. They don't even know we're here. If they did, Your Highness, they would likely cut us into even smaller pieces."

"I see." He ran his fingers through his beard. "Then who are you and what do you bring me?"

"Power," Castor said.

"I have that."

"Then vengeance. I am Castor, Duchess of Arcadia, Ruler of Storms."

Nessos's brow lifted. "Storms? You are a child of Tartarus?" That seemed to interest him.

"Yes, Your Highness," Castor said, "and I want to give that power to you. We bottle and sell our storms. It's how our island survives. Except the Empresses have recently decided to impede our business. I need new customers outside of Olympia, which has brought me to you."

"You want to sell me your power, against the Empresses' wishes?"

"Yes."

Nessos continued to rub his beard, considering. Pollux held his breath. Maybe Castor *could* talk her way out of this.

"I'm interested in hearing more of your proposal," Nessos said. "With the understanding that if I find out you are lying to me, or you annoy me in any way whatsoever, I will feed you to my Cerberus."

"Understood," Castor said coolly.

"Then release them," Nessos said to his guard. "They have nowhere to run."

His low laugh sent a chill through Pollux's veins.

CHAPTER 15

GEN

The chains dropped from Gen's wrists, and she rubbed the raw skin they'd left behind. Nothing a little stink-lizard pus wouldn't fix. If she had any left. She had used most of it to close up Flek's wound. It had kept him from bleeding to death, but he would need better care to survive.

The Elysiums had taken him somewhere. To heal him? It seemed unlikely, but then why had they taken only him?

Beside her, Chomp snarled low in his throat. He was tied to her waist by a thick rope, and he hated being restrained. She waited until their guard looked away, then casually spat on Chomp's back. As soon as her saliva soaked into his skin, and he felt her in his thoughts, he turned his snarl on her.

I'm sorry, she said through their connection, *but I needed to talk to you.*

It had been a while since she'd used her influence on Chomp. When he answered—*No talk! Bite!*—she immediately remembered why connecting with him never worked out as well as she hoped.

No bite. Patience.

Even though their chains had been removed, four guards surrounded them, spears pointed at their chests. They stood so close, Gen could make out her own reflection in the metal tip of the spear poised at her collarbone.

She had looked better. Trapped overnight in a room with Castor and Adikia had done as much damage to her hair as it had her temper.

The Emperor escorted Castor to his throne to speak more about her proposition. Nessos settled onto the marble dais, and Castor knelt beside him. Behind his throne, four marble statues stood, their four Oracles. Unlike the Olympian Oracles, which included two men and two women (brothers Ponos and Tartarus, and sisters Keres and Hecate), the Elysium Oracles were all women. Gen didn't know which was which. One of the statues bore long, curling antlers. She stood closest to Nessos's throne, with her carved hand resting on the back. Another wore a mask, and yet another had pointed horns and a cruel smile on her stone lips.

Gen guessed that was Arai, Oracle of Malice.

Castor and Nessos were speaking, but Gen couldn't hear them across the wide courtyard. She didn't know if the negotiations were going well or not. Either way, Castor had Nessos distracted. Gen needed to sneak away and find information on the apples before their plan fell apart.

She closed her fist, and her skin gleamed silver in the sunlight. Could she punch her way through Quintas and the three other guards? Possibly. But she couldn't slam her way through Emperor Nessos's entire arsenal. She needed to think of something else.

"Where is our friend?" she asked Quintas.

The centaur stared at the ceiling and acted as if she couldn't hear her.

"Our friend," Gen repeated. "The one who was injured." If they were healing him, then they cared something about his well-being. "Please. I need to see him. I am, um, a famous Olympian healer. I need

CLASH OF FATE AND FURY

to tend to his injuries." She had played many parts in her life: circus star, orphan, creature caretaker . . . never a healer. And it showed.

"We are tending to them," Quintas said.

"You don't know how to treat Olympians. I do."

"Your Oracle Gaia forbids you from killing an innocent," Bale said from Gen's left. "Your spear hit our friend, even though he had done nothing against you. If he dies . . . well, I wouldn't want to incur the wrath of an Oracle."

Quintas crossed her arms over her chest. "You could consider sailing into our waters an assault." It was a shaky excuse. Fear showed in her face, which meant Bale had touched on something true. Gen didn't know when or where he had learned his Elysium lore, but she was grateful he had.

"You could," Bale said, "but Gaia wouldn't."

"We don't know that you are innocent yet," Quintas countered. "Our Oracle of Malice encourages vengeance for those who betray us."

"You can keep a guard with us," Pollux suggested, coming to Gen's other side. "What's the difference between watching us here or watching us there? We're clearly not in the position to stand against you." He gestured to himself, and Quintas almost smiled.

There was something to be said for looking small and innocent. Lucky for them, the Elysiums didn't seem to have their own expert on Olympian lore or they would have known not to underestimate him.

"Two of you may go," Quintas finally said. "You and you." She pointed the tip of her spear to Gen's nose, then Pollux's. "The blue one and the untrustworthy one will stay here." She tapped her spear on Bale's shoulder, then Adikia's. Adikia stuck her tongue out.

"And if you do cross us," Quintas said, "I will be sure to enact Arai's vengeance on your friends, starting with the girl."

Adikia pulled her tongue back into her mouth and crossed her arms.

"Of course." Gen swallowed.

Quintas gestured to two of the guards. They broke from the group and jabbed Gen and Pollux in the shoulders, nudging them out of the courtyard and into one of the long hallways that extended from it. Gen paid attention to their path so she could find her way back.

The Elysium palace seemed to be set up like a wheel. Different stone structures branched from the center courtyard, rising on all sides into multilevel buildings. They took the hall to the left, then went up, hiking up a steep ramp that had been worn down from years of heavy centaurs marching up it.

Chomp trailed behind Gen, tied to the rope on her waist, panting as he tried to keep up.

Tired! Hungry! Bite! he growled in her thoughts.

No bite, and I'll see if we can find you some food.

Their golden-haired guards stood tall, shadows looming as they prodded them along. In a way, they reminded Gen of the Gargareans because of their size. But the Elysiums had an integrity that the Gargareans didn't have. That the *Empresses* didn't have.

On the fourth floor, the guards led them down another hallway. A warm breeze blew in from an open window at the end of the hall. Gen heard the call of strange birds on the wind. The guards stopped at a heavy wooden door with chipped paint that had been carved in ornate swirls and patterns.

Gen shared a look with Pollux, glad he had come along. She

didn't have a plan beyond getting away from the throne room. She would need his help.

The guards pushed open the door to a light and airy room with silk curtains, rows of white beds, and an incredibly large stone vase near the entrance.

Gen looked at the vase, then at the guards, and acted on impulse. She snatched the vase with both hands, lifted it over her head, and caught a look of shock on the guards' faces before she dropped the vase on top of their heads.

The crack of stone echoed in the hall. The heavy guards made even more noise as their spears and armored bodies hit hard tile.

"What did you do?" Pollux said.

"Took care of the guards." She grabbed one of them by the legs and yanked him away from the door. She pulled the door closed and flipped the bolt in place to lock it.

"Someone would have heard that," Pollux said. "And now you've violated Gaia's law. We're no longer innocent."

Gen looked down at the two unconscious centaurs. A gash on one of the guards' heads leaked blood onto the stone. She had hit him too hard. He would need a healer, and she wasn't one as she had promised to be. Pollux was right. "We were never innocent anyway. If we move quickly, we can be gone before they find us."

She looked to see if anyone else was in the room. She found only Flek, resting on one of the beds. The clamor of her knocking out two guards hadn't woken him. She went to his bedside and touched his cheek. Pinker than it had been before, at least. The centaur healers had cut away the shreds of his bloody shirt and wrapped the healing wound in gauze. An empty cup sat beside his bedside. She lifted it and held it to her nose.

It smelled like spice. "They must have given him a sleeping draught," she said.

Pollux paced the floor and ran his fingers through his white hair. "Gen, they are going to find the two men eventually, and they are not going to think the guards knocked themselves unconscious. I wish you had told me you were going to slam two guards to the floor."

"It was a spur-of-the-moment decision." In her circus, they'd frequently had to improvise. She had done her best with what she had.

"That's why you should have waited." Pollux rubbed the space between his eyebrows.

She grabbed his hand and laced her fingers with his. "I'm sorry."

Maybe this hadn't been a good time for improvisation. She had spent the last four years acting on instinct. She'd had nothing to lose and, more importantly, no one to hurt by her actions. Now she did.

"Gen." Pollux ran his thumb over her knuckles. "This isn't Olympia. Apart from Bale, none of us know our surroundings. You need to be more careful."

"I will. I promise." She would be as careful as she could. "Stay with Flek and try to wake him up in case we need to leave quickly."

"What are you going to do?"

"Try to find a clue to the apples," she said. "Carefully."

He released her fingers and ran his hand up her arm, clasping her by the elbow. "I love you, Gen. Promise me you'll be safe."

"I will. I love you too."

She stood on her toes to kiss him, then stopped when he subtly pulled away. He didn't want her kiss. He didn't want her to know what he was really thinking about her.

"I should go." With a knot in her stomach, she pulled her arm from his and picked up Chomp. She untied the rope from around him but kept it latched to her waist, in case she needed it.

Food! Chomp demanded.

Soon.

At the windows, she parted the curtains and looked down below. Two guards marched along the walkway. When they passed, Gen swung herself through the window with Chomp under her arm. She grabbed a piece of jutting stone and lowered them down through an open window on the floor below.

Her boots hit an ornate rug. In the center of the room sat a massive bed of oiled wood and velvet canopy. She set Chomp on the rug. He sniffed the edge of the sheets and snarled. A painting hung on the wall of a warrior centaur rising up on his hind legs with a spear in hand. Gen ducked underneath it to the table beside the bed, where a small stack of books sat.

She leafed through them. The symbols on the page looked nothing like Olympian letters. Thankfully, this page had pictures. Of centaurs. Nothing about the golden apples. Gen set it aside. How was she going to find what they needed when she couldn't read Elysium?

Food! Chomp growled in her head.

Not now.

Food here!

He growled at something in the corner. A gilded cage hung from a hook, and inside, a bird with long red feathers fluttered its wings.

It's not food.

For one thing, the bird was larger than she was. Outside of the cage, its wings would probably spread as widely as a winged horse's. Gen would even be able to fly on its back, if the bird would let her.

Bright red feathers ran down its entire body, ending in long white tail feathers. On the top of its head, a golden plume burst out above its blue eyes. The bird tilted its head and blinked at her.

Gen stepped closer and spat through the bars onto the bird's feathers. It made a loud squawking noise and flapped its wings.

"Shhh," Gen whispered.

How dare you soil me with your spittle! This bird didn't speak Elysium. Creatures had their own languages, ones Gen could understand with her mind magic, and this bird sounded very self-important.

It's the only way we can talk. I apologize.

The bird settled onto its perch and preened its feathers. *Why would I want to talk to you?*

I don't know.

Foul two-legged beast, the bird muttered.

What kind of bird are you?

A Phoenix. The bird lifted its wing and small flames burned across the feathers. Gen stepped back from the heat. A creature like this, brought home to Olympia and circling around the top of her circus tent, would guarantee endless sold-out performances.

It would also likely peck her to death before she could bring it home.

Unless you intend to release me from this prison, leave me be. The Phoenix turned its back to her.

Gen eyed the thick lock on the bird's cage. This wasn't a pet. It was a prisoner. *Why are you kept here?*

I lit one of their ships on fire.

This bird sounded like an enemy of Nessos, which could make it a friend of hers. *Do you know anything about the golden apples?*

The apples of Hesperides?

Yes. Do you know where they are?

Only the Emperor knows where they are.

Then do you know of a library?

Yes, and I can tell you where it is . . . if you get me out of this cage.

Gen eyed the bars. She could probably pull them apart to make a wide enough space for the Phoenix to squeeze through. But she was trying not to draw attention to herself, and setting a giant red bird loose on the island could do that. Pollux was right. She needed to be careful.

I can't.

You're trying not to be found, aren't you? If you don't let me out, I will make so much noise, they will catch you. The Phoenix stretched its neck and opened its beak to release a shrill cry.

Chomp howled in response. *Too loud!*

Gen covered her ears and looked to the door, listening for hoof-beats. *Fine, I'll set you free. Be quiet!*

The Phoenix closed its beak and settled on its perch. *Your library is one floor down, in a room with two large wooden doors.*

Gen reached for the bars. *No lighting ships on fire once you leave. Try to be discreet.*

I will be very discreet, the Phoenix said indignantly.

Gen's time ran short. Either someone would find her here or they'd find Pollux upstairs with the unconscious guards. She grasped the bars and flexed her arms. Mazon strength flooded through her. The bars whined and groaned as she pulled them apart. Sweat beaded on her skin. Flek would have made this a much easier job.

When the bars stopped moving, she stepped back. The Phoenix stuck its head through first, then twisted sideways to get one wing out, followed by its body, second wing, and tail.

Then it stretched its wings across the entire room. They touched the walls at each tip.

Thank you, two-legged beast. For this, I will not light you on fire.

The Phoenix tucked its wings into its sides and leapt through the window. Shouts soon followed. Gen winced, sensing she had made another mistake. She leaned out the window. Below, guards streamed from the main courtyard into the surrounding grove. They chased the bird, shaking spears at it as the Phoenix ignited its wings and set fire to the tops of several trees.

Before it flew too far, and the threads of their connection snapped, Gen heard the Phoenix cackling in her thoughts. This wasn't good.

"We need to be very fast," Gen whispered to Chomp. The bird had put everyone on alert, which might mean more guards sent to check on her and Pollux. She had minutes to find what she needed and get back to the hospital room.

She picked Chomp up and swung out through the window to one below. She landed on the stone sill and pushed on the glass. The window was locked. Behind her, the air filled with smoke, screams, and, in the distance, the high shriek of the freed Phoenix.

She looked at Chomp.

Food! He demanded.

Gen rolled her eyes. She supposed things couldn't get worse.

She pulled her fist back and slammed it through the window. Some of the glass cut her knuckles. She shook it off and dropped into a dark room that smelled of parchment and oil. She pulled the curtain wide, and in the sunlight and residual flames from the Phoenix, she saw books. Shelves and shelves of books.

At least the Phoenix hadn't lied about the library.

Gen picked up the nearest book. It was the size of her entire arm, bound in some sort of animal hide with foreign characters stamped into the cover. She dropped it on the nearest table and flipped it open.

Food! Chomp said.

"Here, make yourself useful." She set a second book in front of him. "Look for food in the pictures, fruit to be specific."

Not good food, he growled, but did it anyway.

She flipped through her own book and listened to Chomp's thoughts as he pushed aside pages with his paw. *Not food. Not food. Not food.*

She wasn't finding any apple trees, either. Only images of centaur warriors sketched in ink, including one of a centaur holding up the severed head of a man, dripping with blood.

She grabbed another book.

Hoofbeats stomped across the stone overhead, along with angry voices. They'd found the broken cage above. Would that keep them away from the healing room? Or would they go straight there for answers?

Gen dropped another book on the floor for Chomp. She heard a sound. The library doors creaked open. Gen picked up Chomp and ducked into the shadows behind one of the massive shelves. She covered his mouth with her hand.

Quiet.

A bright white light shone across the floor. Gen tried to move away from it, but the light touched everything. She pressed her back to the wall, breathing in and out. How many guards would she have to fight?

"You won't find what you're looking for in those books," a voice said.

She turned. A golden figure stood before her, one Gen thought she would never see.

Her mouth fell open. "You're a . . . a . . ."

"Yes. I am."

CHAPTER 16

POLLUX

As fists banged on the door, Pollux knelt beside Flek's cot and shook him by the shoulder. "Wake up!"

Flek's head flopped back onto the pillow; his pale blue hair splayed across his forehead.

Guards in the hallway shouted in Elysium and jerked on the door handle. Pollux's heart thrummed in his chest. He didn't have his violin, a storm vial, or anything to defend himself.

Abruptly, the shouting moved away, and he heard screams outside. He ran to the window and saw a giant red bird light the tops of the nearby trees on fire. Half of the Elysium guard chased it. Somehow, Pollux knew Gen had something to do with that.

He returned to Flek and grabbed him by the shoulders. He shook him hard. The Croecian's head fell to the side, and his mouth dropped open. *Damn the Oracles.*

"This is going to hurt you more than it will hurt me." Pollux drew his hand back and swung it toward Flek's cheek. His palm cracked against Flek's skin with enough force to leave a red mark. Still, Flek didn't stir.

Behind him, the door rattled again. Pollux spun around. *What would Gen do?*

She would run at the intruder with everything she had. Well, even if he had less, he could still try. He picked up a large, sharp piece of the broken vase and held it in front of him. Music played in his thoughts, minor notes, the song of "Pollux's Last Stand."

The door opened, and a bright light stung his eyes. He turned away, shielding himself with the piece of broken vase. The entire room lit up so bright it blurred the edges of the stones on the wall and the cots in the room. Everything disappeared into light.

Pollux had looked into the hearts of lightning storms and the midday sun. Neither had been as blindingly white as what came at him now.

The light spread across the room in tendrils and wrapped around his arm. He could feel it, in the same way he felt a wisp of cloud or the strings on his violin. It hummed through him. He lowered the broken vase shard and stared at the light, trying to make sense of it. The edges of it blurred, and it took a shape.

The tall figure stretched as high as the room, like a statue made of pure gold. Her face held wide eyes and pert lips, and long, curling antlers sprouted from the top of her head. The light surrounding her became the folds of her gown, hanging on to her like beams of sunlight. Every part of her shone the purest hue of gold. It all blurred together, her arms and legs melting into her gown as if it were all the same.

"Who are you?" Pollux asked, even though he already knew the answer. Not in words. Inside his soul.

What he felt was old magic, original magic. It made his StormMaker powers seem so worthless in comparison. The amount of magic he could hold or manipulate was a drop in a vast ocean of power.

This was the source, or at least one of the sources. A living, breathing Oracle.

"I am Phoebe," she said in a voice that rivaled his greatest songs. It spoke to him through his heart. "The Oracle of Prophecy."

Pollux dropped to his knees out of deference or shock, he didn't know which.

The Olympian Oracles had been reduced to legend. For so long, it had seemed impossible they had ever been real. But here was an Oracle standing in front of him, as real as the stone on the wall.

"I have seen you in my dreams," she said. "You and your travelers. You seek my sister's apples, and the great Cerberus."

"Yes," he said, wondering if she would smite him right now for attempting it.

"It's not for me to judge," she said. "It is my role to see the story as it unfolds, told by the choices people make. I have made my choice to tell you the story I see." She stepped closer. "Listen closely, Pollux of Arcadia, Son of Tartarus, for I have seen the success of your venture, the return to your homelands with both prizes in tow."

"We manage it? We capture the Cerberus?" Then everything they wanted would come true. The Empresses would have their prizes, their war. Castor would have her apple orchard. Gen would have her father, her freedom. And he . . . he would have her.

"*They* manage it," the Oracle said. "The ship you brought does not carry all its passengers on its trip home. If you continue on this journey, Son of Tartarus, you will not return to your homeland. At least, not as you are."

Pollux stared at the calluses on his fingertips. "I don't make it home as I am? What do you mean?"

A pit landed in his stomach. Cold sweat burst on his palms. *The ship does not carry all its passengers on its trip home.* He doubted she meant he would swim back to Olympia.

"Your friends will mourn you terribly," the Oracle said.

Pollux swallowed the knot in his throat. If there had been any question as to why he wouldn't return home, the Oracle had just answered it. He would not return alive. *Not as you are.*

He thought about Arcadia, and the way the manor looked in the autumn, with vines climbing the walls in yellow and gold. He thought about his mother and the sound of her singing in the music room, the way it echoed through the halls. He thought about the isles of Delos and their expansive, golden beaches, and the market on Ceryneia, where you could find any treasure or trinket your heart desired. He thought about never seeing any of those things again, and it pained him.

"Is there anything I can do? If you're telling me this now, there must be a way to change it. What if I don't go any farther? What if I go home now?"

The Oracle closed her ethereal eyes. "Then the venture fails, and you will be the only one to return. The journey succeeds only if you are part of it, and you succeed only if everyone else fails. This is the story I have come to tell you, Son of Tartarus. It makes no difference to me which path you choose, but I believe we both know that you have already chosen."

She was right. He couldn't let Gen fail. But he also didn't want to run headfirst toward his own demise. How were these his only choices? "If you knew what I would choose, why are you telling me this? Why do I need to know I'll die?"

"Because part of this venture's success comes from you knowing how it will end."

He pressed his palms into his cheeks. "I don't want to do this. I don't want to die." He had barely begun to live. He and Gen hadn't even had a chance to start a life together.

"Pollux, take some heart in this." She reached inside her light-made gown and removed a violin. *His* violin. He reached out to take it from her. His violin hummed with her magic. He ran his fingers down the strings, listening to the sound. He fell into a familiar song, "The Girl in the Circus." He did know which path he would choose. It was always the same—Gen. She would get the apples, capture the Cerberus, and go home to her father, and he would die knowing he had given her everything she wanted.

"Stay strong, Pollux, and maybe we will meet again." She gave him a wan smile and began to fade, turning dimmer, like a shadow of herself before she disappeared.

CHAPTER 17

CASTOR

Castor ran her fingers over one of her storm vials, wondering how long she would have to sit here and placate the Emperor.

"It's been ages since an Olympian has dared to cross our borders. Probably because they know better than to stand against us." Nessos laughed and drank red wine from a silver chalice draped in a decoration of vines. Some of the wine dribbled from his mouth into the threads of his silver beard.

The word *unkempt* came to Castor's mind. She bit it back with a false smile. Over the last half hour, she'd not only convinced him to release them all from chains, but she had also shown him rainbows and handheld clouds and struck a bargain for purchasing storms at well below her usual price. It was one that she had no intention of upholding anyway.

"When should we expect our first shipment of storms?" Nessos asked.

"It could be months," Castor said.

"What?" Nessos set his chalice aside and twisted one of the rings on his large, knobby fingers. Unlike the Empresses, Nessos commanded his kingdom with strength and respect. Castor could tell his soldiers admired him and weren't simply here because they were paid well or afraid of being poisoned. They trusted him to lead. What he lacked, however, was refinement. "I had no idea it would take so long."

"I do apologize, Your Highness, but as I mentioned, the Empresses are forcing our hand in Olympia, demanding we serve them first. There is only so much weather in the sky over our Empire, and as I will be doing this without their knowledge, I'll have to be careful. We can't make the storms. Only bottle them."

He nodded. "Another one of your weaknesses."

Cas gave him a tight smile. If she ever had the chance, she would happily show him her *weaknesses*. "As you say, Your Highness. Where is your spouse? Maybe they would like to join us?" If she couldn't twist Nessos, maybe she could work his better half. Surely the other half had to be better. They couldn't be any worse.

"No, never married. Why give up half the fortune? Better to keep a powerful woman under control than give her a shared seat." He glanced at the statue behind him, the one of an Oracle molded to look as if she doted upon him like he was a god.

"Of course." Castor fought the urge to kick him in the knees. "Well, I suppose we should return to Olympia so I can begin collecting your weather. Shall I return in . . . six months?"

Nessos ran his fingers through his thick beard. "We have plenty of storms here," he began.

Cas straightened, trying not to look pleased with herself. Finally, she'd gotten through to him. This was exactly what she needed: free reign of his Empire to search the isles under the guise of collecting storms. Lux and Gen had walked away with two of the guards since she'd been with Nessos. Surely they must have found something about the apples by now.

Nessos leaned toward her. "What if you—"

"The Phoenix has escaped!" The shout came from the other end of the courtyard.

"What?" Nessos stood and knocked over his chalice of wine. It bled across the stones in deep red. Castor turned toward the shout. Quintas and her remaining guard ran to the entrance, spears aimed where something red streaked across the sky, leaving a trail of flames behind it.

Adikia, unguarded, broke into a run for the nearest exit. Bale hesitated for a breath before following suit. Castor had known Adikia would bolt the moment she had the chance. She also knew this fiery bird had to be Gen's doing.

She closed her fist. She'd had Nessos exactly where she'd wanted him. He had been about to give her free passage through Elysium, and Gen had ruined it.

Nessos turned on her. "*Traitors*," he said through his teeth.

Cas clung to her plan, hoping she could talk her way out of this. "I have no idea what this bird is or how it got free."

"Where are the others?" Nessos shouted at Quintas. "You were to hold them here."

The centaur ducked into her massive shoulders and bowed her head. "My apologies, Your Highness. I let them tend to their injured to uphold Gaia's law. I will go find them."

"No, you've done enough."

"It must be a mistake," Castor said. "The bird must have freed itself." Her last, desperate attempt at an excuse.

"My only mistake was trusting you foul Olympians." Nessos turned back to Quintas. "Hold her. Her companions will return for her, or she will pay for their crimes."

Quintas smiled. She had been waiting for such an order. Castor also smiled, because she still had her storm belt and no intention of being held or paying for anything. She grabbed a vial of wind, flipped it open with her thumb, and released the gale inside.

She aimed it first for Quintas's second guard. She coiled the wind so tightly, it struck him in the chest with the force of a rock. He blew across the courtyard and slammed into one of the stone posts. He dropped to a heap at the bottom, and Castor yanked her wind back like a whip.

She caught Nessos by the ankle.

"How dare you?" He drew his sword and waved it over his head. Castor tugged on her wind, yanked him off his feet, and pushed him into the opposing wall. He struck it with such force, the stones cracked.

"As you can see, *Your Highness*, I am not weak," she spat at him.

"You have insulted us every way possible, Olympian," Quintas said.

Castor released the wind and drew open a vial of lightning. The white-hot current traveled from the vial, up her hand, and around her elbow before collecting in a ball on her palm. Her diplomacy had failed. And she wasn't terribly upset about it. She preferred to do things this way.

CHAPTER 18

POLLUX

Footsteps skidded up the hallway.

Pollux raised his violin and pressed his bow to the strings, poised to play something strong and fast. He relaxed when Gen and Chomp ran into the room.

"You're all right," he said.

"Yes. And I have the answer. I can tell you as we run." She made her way around the fallen centaurs. One raised his head and slowly blinked.

"I can't wake Flek," Pollux said.

"What do you mean? He's awake."

Pollux turned around. The breath caught in his chest when he saw Flek sitting upright and wide-eyed. How long had he been like that? Had he been awake when the Oracle told Pollux he would die? Had he read her lips?

"Come on." Gen reached Flek and helped him out of the cot. He leaned his bandaged chest against her side.

Outside the window, screams echoed on the air and the strong smell of smoke pervaded the room. They had to get back to Cas and the others. Quintas had threatened to kill them if Pollux and Gen deceived the Elysiums. Pollux would call setting the island on fire a pure sign of deception.

They ran for the door. Behind them, the fallen guard climbed onto his elbows and shouted, "Stop!" They ignored him. Gen supported

Flek down the hallway. Pollux kept his violin poised and ready to play. However, the halls were empty. *Everyone must be chasing the flaming bird.*

"You want to tell me about the bird?" Pollux asked Gen.

"It promised to be discreet. I didn't know it was going to light the island on fire."

"At least it has drawn away the guards," he said. "But we need to hurry."

They circled back down the long ramps. One, two, three, four. When they reached the last one, they jogged to the courtyard. Pollux's arm hairs rose. He sensed something familiar in the air. He snatched Gen by the arm and jerked her and Flek backward.

"Wait," he said through his teeth.

Castor stood in the middle of the courtyard facing Quintas, a ball of lightning dancing on her palm. Another guard already lay on the ground with coils of smoke rising from his tail, and Nessos lay at Castor's side in a motionless heap.

Pollux should have known Cas could take care of herself. But he couldn't see Bale or Adikia. Were they too late?

Quintas drew her weapon. "I will cut you open like a fish."

"No, you won't," Castor said. "You'll already be on fire."

She flung her lightning as Quintas released her spear.

Castor's lightning engulfed the spear, setting it aflame and sending it off its trajectory. It dropped and skidded across the floor to land at her feet.

Then lightning coiled off the end and struck Quintas in the chest. The centaur cried out as crackling lightning raced around her body. She fell to the stones, quivering and smoking.

Pollux released Gen's arm. "It looks clear now."

He made his way to Cas, who gathered up what remained of her lightning and fed it into an Illumium vial. He held his fingers to his nose. It smelled like charred flesh, an odor he knew well.

Cas leaned over the fallen Elysium soldier with a slight smile. "You probably should have killed me when you had the chance."

"You don't have to be cruel, Cas."

His sister spun around, her eyes wide, like a feral cat.

"I did what I had to do. What I was *forced* to do." She pointed to the flaming trees outside. "Do you intend to tell me you had nothing to do with that?" She jerked her finger to Gen.

"I did," Gen admitted. "I set the bird free."

"You fool," Castor spat. "I had the deal set. Nessos was about to give us free reign of his waters. Now we'll have to escape like fugitives. I hope, for your sake, you at least found the apples."

"I know where to go," Gen said. She adjusted Flek against her hip. The MetalBender's head dropped to her shoulder and looked far too comfortable there.

"What did you find?" Pollux asked.

"I know it sounds impossible, but I saw an Oracle. She told me where to find the apples. She told me how to escape."

Pollux sighed. "It doesn't sound impossible. I saw her too." *Except she gave me much worse news than yours.*

"We can talk about it later," Cas said. "Where do we go?"

"This way." Gen waved them from the courtyard to a surrounding garden.

"Where are Bale and Adikia?" Pollux asked his sister.

"They made an escape, and if they're not at the ship when we get there, or they've sailed off without us, they will have more to fear than the centaurs."

In the garden, smoke filled the air, blanketing the lush flowers in a sooty haze. Pollux covered his face with his sleeve and narrowed his eyes. Shouts echoed in his ears along with the crackling of fire. Centaurs threw water on the fire and launched spears at the flaming bird above.

Gen stopped at a shrub with bright orange flowers and bent down to a seemingly decorative stone beside it. But when she pushed on it, it moved, and a dark hole opened up before them.

The last time he followed Gen into a dark tunnel, he'd leapt into Queen Hippolyta's underground lair and almost been killed.

"Is it safe?" he asked her.

"The Oracle told me this is our only way out," Gen said.

"We had other options until you released the bird," Cas snapped, before diving into the hole first. Gen climbed down carefully with Flek in one arm, Chomp in the other. Pollux took one last look at the burning sky before he followed.

They will all make it home, he told himself. *But only if I stay.* He closed his eyes and leapt into the darkness.

CHAPTER 19

CASTOR

C astor regretted leaping into the hole instantly.

A rank odor seeped into her nose. It smelled like the inside of a tomb, rotting corpses and ancient bones. The air hung still and thick. It pressed to her chest and clung to her skin like rancid dewdrops.

Gen dropped beside her with the MetalBender, still breathing, thankfully, and her dog. Pollux came down last, slipping on the rocks to fall to his knees. He picked himself up and inspected his violin.

"What is this place?" he asked, wrinkling his nose.

"These tunnels run deep in and out of the mountain," Gen said. "One way will take us out. The other way will lead us to the Cerberus."

"You're leading us out, I assume," Castor said. She didn't want to go after the Cerberus until she had her apples.

"Yes, I don't think any of us are in a state to face the beast." Gen nodded to the MetalBender in her arms.

She took the lead and started walking through the darkness. Pollux played a soft song on his violin, and a sunlight serpent slithered from the strings to the bottom of the tunnel, lighting their way. A little showy, but it did the trick.

"Keep to the right," Gen said as she shuffled along with Flek.

"Is that what the Oracle told you?" Castor asked, suspicious. The Olympian Oracles had been reduced to legend, all dead because the Oracle Keres had used her mind control ability to slaughter the rest of her brethren, then killed herself in despair. Castor hadn't thought about the Elysium Oracles until recently.

"She told me I'd find a rock in the garden and the entrance to the Cerberus's tunnel underneath. Going right would lead us out, going left would lead us to the Cerberus." Gen took another turn to the right, Pollux's glowing serpent slithering along the dirt beside her.

"What did she say about the apples?"

"She told us to sail northwest."

"Anything else?"

"No."

"What did this Oracle look like?" Castor asked.

"Beautiful," Pollux said, "and terrifying. She was made of pure light and magic."

"Exactly," Gen said.

"What did she tell *you*?" Castor asked her brother, more inclined to believe him than Gen.

"She told me"——he took a breath——"you would get the apples. I think it's getting lighter." He stopped playing his violin, and his glowing snake disappeared. Hoofbeats clamored overhead, and the tunnel became less black, more a dingy gray. The rotting odor also subsided somewhat.

They took their last turn to the right. At the end of the tunnel, cracks of light shone through a pile of rocks.

"Hold him," Gen said, and passed Castor the MetalBender. He smelled like spice and dried blood and was much heavier than he looked.

Castor looked from him to her brother. The supposed Oracle had told Pollux she would get her apples. As much as Cas wanted to believe it, she wouldn't leave anything up to prophecy. When she did get the apples, it wouldn't be because of some Oracle; it would be entirely her own doing. Her brother, however, held a firm belief in stories, so why did he look so miserable about the Oracle's prediction?

Gen pulled away one of the larger rocks from the bottom of the pile. When she did, the rest tumbled downward, and they had their escape.

Gen dusted herself off and reached for Flek. "I can take him."

"He's all yours." Castor rubbed a smear of blood from her sleeve that the MetalBender had left behind.

They crawled from the tunnel into thick, overgrown brush and tangled vines. Thorns scraped against Castor's arms. She pushed her way through the overgrowth.

They had emerged from the mountain on the outskirts of town, a much quicker journey through the mountain than winding around it. Below, Castor made out the docks. Above them, smoke rose from burning trees. Centaurs rushed around in a panic to protect their homes, catch the bird, or put out fires. Gen might have ruined her negotiations by letting that flaming bird free, but she had at least given them an easier escape. No one spotted them here, hiding in the weeds.

"Keep to the thicket until we reach the road down there"—Castor pointed—"then get to the ship as fast as you can." They wouldn't be able to hide themselves in the open. Not in a city of centaurs, even with a bird lighting everything on fire.

From here, at least, it seemed as if the *Hind* was still in one piece. Cas couldn't tell if Adikia was on it and, more importantly, didn't care. At the first chance, Adikia had left her. Castor could have been trampled by centaurs, and Adikia hadn't lifted a finger to help.

Worthless thief.

They worked their way through the thicket until they reached the edge of the road. Their next steps would lead them into the open. They ducked down as three centaurs ran by them. The dog snarled. Castor gave the beast a warning glare.

"Keep your violin close," Castor said to her brother. "And you"— she looked at Gen—"punch anything that gets in our way."

"I'm not your—"

"Go now." Castor stepped into the road and broke into a run. Gen quickly surpassed her, even with Flek in one arm and the dog in the other. Pollux stayed a step behind Castor. On purpose, she believed. With his longer legs, he likely could have outpaced her.

Stares followed them, as to be expected. Castor ignored them and kept running, heart pounding.

They hit the docks. Gen's feet slammed against the wood. Three royal guards dressed in metal armor shouted, "Maren!"

Stop. Castor had no intention of stopping. Not until she reached the ship.

Gen charged up the gangplank first. Castor followed. She heard the Elysium guards galloping behind her. Her lungs ached. Sweat beaded on her forehead. She had never been forced to run like this, and she had to make a choice. Keep running or stop and fight.

Gen had already untied the *Hind* from the dock and raised the anchor. Bale appeared on deck and pulled the sails. Castor was reaching for a vial of wind to beat back the Elysiums when someone tossed a rope to her from the side of the ship.

"Climb up!" Adikia shouted.

Castor hesitated a beat before she grabbed the rope. At least Adikia hadn't set sail without her. Castor climbed, while Adikia pulled. When Cas reached the top of the rails, she rolled over the side and caught her breath.

"You left me," she panted.

"I knew you'd make it here," Adikia said.

Something plunged into the side of the ship. Castor sat upright. The guards had already gathered more troops, and they were climbing into their own ships and launching spears.

"Pollux, play us out of here!" Castor shouted.

Her brother lifted his violin to his chin and played a song that billowed wind into the sails and pulled them from the dock. Castor reached for another vial on her belt, one she had been saving. Inside the confines of its metal case, this storm begged to be released.

It was an older storm collected over a year ago from the middle of the Aegean Sea. Before one of the StormMakers had gathered it and delivered it to Arcadia, it had sunk three ships. Castor might have used it in the Empresses' labors if it hadn't been safely stored at home. She'd brought it with her this time, and now it would have its chance to sink more ships.

"Cas, don't," Pollux warned. He could sense what was inside the jar too.

"If they follow us, we won't make it two leagues away from here before they sink us into the sea. I'm only beating them to it."

She tore open the jar, and the sudden burst of wind ballooned their sails. The ship jolted forward. This storm had been contained for too long. In such a small, constrictive space, it had wanted to be freed. It had *needed* to be freed. Castor knew exactly how it felt. She was this storm. Always being shoved into one role or another, when the truth was, she only thrived with no boundaries. Her father thought she was selfish. Her brother thought she was cruel. Adikia thought she was replaceable. Nessos thought she was weak.

Maybe she was all of those things. And none of those things. Maybe she just *was*.

Wind ripped at her clothes. Her hair beat against her cheeks. Rain poured down on the docks with such fury, the vendors gathered up their wares and ran for cover.

Castor held her storm and pushed it toward the line of Elysium ships paddling out toward them. They were so tiny, so helpless. The wind picked the ships out of the water and tossed them yards away. Elysiums dropped into the sea and struggled to swim with their heavy armor.

Who is weak now, Nessos?

"Castor, stop." Pollux played his violin, mixing high-pitched notes with the rain beating on the ship.

He was trying to take the storm from her. And he was *succeeding*. Castor felt the tendrils of wind leaving her fingers. But he couldn't steal this from her. He was the weak one. Then she remembered their battle in the jungle before she faced the Hydra.

"Did you ever stop to think I was going easy on you?"

"Fine!" She pushed what remained of the hurricane away from them, out to sea. To the south, away from where they would be sailing. With her secondary wind, the *Hind* already cut through water on a direct path north. And with her hurricane, the entire seaport of Okeanos was so damaged, it would take days to get a handful of ships after them. Nothing Castor couldn't handle later.

Pollux pushed his wet hair back from his face. "You always go too far, Cas."

She spun on him. "What do you think we're doing out here?

What do you think will happen once we leave with Elysium's prizes? We are not friends with these people. We are enemies. If they'd had that power, they would have drowned us too."

"You can be someone's enemy and not be cruel," Pollux said with the same ferocity as the storm's.

"I had to save us from what *she* did." Castor jabbed a finger at Gen.

"What I did?" Gen said.

"You released that damned bird and set the island on fire. I had Nessos exactly where I wanted him until that happened."

"It was an accident," Gen said.

"Your accident almost ruined us. You should be thanking me for stepping in to fix your mistakes." Castor stalked off to her cabin to avoid facing any more judgment. Pollux could die with his pity. Gen could burn with her mistakes.

And Castor would live happily with her cruelty.

CHAPTER 20

POLLUX

Pollux tossed and turned in his bed, trying to find a comfortable position. He couldn't. In part because the mattress was hard and small, and in part because the discomfort lingered mostly in his thoughts.

The journey succeeds only if you are part of it, and you succeed only if everyone else fails.

He kept going over the Oracle's prediction, hoping to find a loophole. Her words twisted through his mind and chewed at his insides. His friends would mourn him. The ship would return without him, or it would return without any of the others. There was no way around it. He would die if he continued on this trip, and if he didn't, Gen would fail.

The only path he hadn't explored was what would happen if they all abandoned the quest. If Gen knew he would die trying to help her, she would turn back. But then what? The Empresses would enact some cruel revenge for not getting their way. They would make Gen's life more miserable than it was or possibly kill them all as an example.

Pollux also knew his sister would never abandon the quest, not before she had her apples, even if she knew it would kill him. Castor didn't take much stock in prophecies or fate. She would think she could outwit or burn her way out of destiny.

He snorted. He wished he felt the same way. The Oracle had given Gen the right path out of the Emperor's palace. Her words were already coming true. If she led them to the apples, too, then there would be no doubt his fate was coming up next.

His throat closed. He buried his face in his pillow and let silent tears fall.

It wasn't fair. What had he done to anger the Oracles? Why did he deserve this? He had been punished his entire life. By his father. His sister. And now fate would punish him too.

Gen . . . his fierce, strong, and beautiful Gen. With his eyes closed, he felt the touch of her skin on his and caught the wild spark in her eyes right before she raced off to do something dangerous. He heard her excited gasp when she encountered a new creature, saw the subtle way she chewed on her plush bottom lip when she was working out a problem.

He raised his head and drove his fist into his pillow. He'd barely had her for a fraction of a second, and soon it would all be gone.

Pollux sensed he was being watched. He scrubbed the tears from his cheeks and turned. A silent Flek stared at him through the darkness from the other side of the room.

They watched each other for an uncomfortable moment before Flek wrote something on his parchment and held it up in the stream of moonlight coming through the porthole.

Can't sleep?

Pollux decided this was his chance to ask Flek how much he knew. "Were you awake when the Oracle spoke to me?"

Flek took a breath and nodded.

"Do you know what she said?"

Flek nodded again, and Pollux exhaled. In a small way, he was glad he didn't have to bear this burden alone.

"You didn't happen to catch any loopholes, did you? I go and die, or I don't go and everyone else dies? Right?"

Flek lowered his eyes before he nodded. The knot in Pollux's throat tightened. There was his second opinion. He had no way out.

"You can't tell Gen," Pollux said once Flek looked up again. "If she knows, she'll turn the ship around and put herself in worse trouble with the Empresses. Are we agreed?"

Flek nodded, and Pollux knew he could trust him on this matter, at least. Flek cared about Gen. He wouldn't want to see her hurt.

"Good." Pollux lay back down on his cot to try and catch some sleep. He could rest knowing Gen would succeed. She would get her Cerberus. She would have her father. She could find happiness.

There was just one more thing.

Pollux swallowed before he turned back to Flek. He would rather become the next Storm Duke than say what he was about to say, but he supposed in a few days or weeks, however long he had left, it wouldn't matter.

"You need to look after her when I'm gone," he whispered. "Gen can get herself into trouble, and she will need a friend. Can you do that?"

Flek hesitated before he nodded. At least he gave Pollux that slight hesitation before agreeing.

"Good night," he said, and buried his head under his thin blanket. He curled his knees into his chest and pinched his eyes closed. No music came to his thoughts. He had too many worries in his head to make room for songs.

Pollux slept on and off, then woke to a nightmare of being burned alive by the Cerberus, his skin flaking off into charred bits while Bale,

Gen, Castor, and everyone else stood by and watched. He sat up and combed his fingers through his sweaty hair. He needed some fresh air.

He pulled on his clothes and made his way above deck. The chill wind bit at his cheeks. He closed his eyes and breathed it in. He enjoyed the cold. It didn't settle into StormMakers' bones in the way it did for other people. Not that they were impervious to chill. Just not as affected by it. Maybe that was why his sister was up here too. Cas stood at the prow of the ship with her pale hair blowing over her shoulders.

He was still angry with her for what she had done on Okeanos. He knew her. She hadn't done it solely to protect them. She'd wanted to make a point. It had been cruel and unnecessary, and he had the feeling it would come back to bite them.

But she was his sister. And he didn't have much time to make amends with her.

Pollux cleared his throat as he approached. It was a terrible idea to sneak up on Cas, unless you wanted to be struck with lightning.

She turned and rolled her eyes in one of her classic warm greetings. "What are you doing here?"

"Can't sleep. You?"

"Me neither."

"Something bothering you?" he asked. Maybe she felt some remorse for what she'd done. He leaned on the rails beside her.

"You are," she said. "You and Gen. You *need* me on this trip because you know I'll do what you won't. Then when I do it, you hate me for it. I was only cleaning up after Gen's mess."

This was interesting. No guilt for what she'd done, but she felt some remorse for him not approving it. He'd had no idea his opinion mattered that much. Or at all.

"You didn't have to burn it all down to clean it up."

"Technically, I drowned it all. Gen was the one responsible for the burning."

He sighed. "Gen's mistake was an accident. Yours was intentional."

"You always take her side."

"You always force me to choose sides."

"Not true. If I did that, I would always force you to choose mine."

"Thank you, Cas. I appreciate you not burning me *every* time we have a disagreement. Only sometimes." His fingers trailed to the scars on his neck.

Cas winced. "That was an accident."

"Then you admit people can make mistakes and be forgiven?"

She narrowed her eyes. "You know, brother, I liked you much better when you hid in your room and played silly songs all day."

"I liked you better when you only wreaked havoc on Arcadia."

Cas snorted out an unexpected laugh. "You won't be saying that when we reach the Cerberus."

"*If* we reach the Cerberus," he corrected as the cold sea air rolled across his skin.

"You're having doubts?" Her eyebrow raised, and he lost his tongue. He had no doubts they would reach the Cerberus. He only doubted if *he* would make it that far. The Oracle hadn't specified how long he would be a part of this journey.

"No, no doubts." He turned to the water.

"I know you, Lux. Something is bothering you, and if it pertains to this trip, I need to know what it is. What else did the Oracle tell you?"

He flexed his jaw. He couldn't lie to Cas. As different as they were, she was still his twin sister. They had a connection beyond blood. He also couldn't tell her the truth. Not because he worried she would tell Gen or want to turn around and go home—because she wouldn't. He didn't need an affirmation about how little she really cared about him. "The Oracle said we would win the prizes, but it wouldn't be easy. Some of us would get hurt."

There. He had lied and told the truth at the same time.

"That's a paltry prediction. Of course some will get hurt. But it won't be you or me. It likely won't be Genevieve, either."

"Why do you say that?"

"Because I make my own fate. I've worked my entire life to make it, setting up Father's deals, pushing my way into his meetings and sales calls, becoming one of the best StormMakers our island has ever seen. And I am not about to let some foul three-mouthed dog, meddling Empresses, or oversized centaurs take it from me."

She said it with such force, he believed her. "What about me? What about Gen?"

Castor sighed. "Your obnoxious girlfriend has unfathomable good luck, and you have an obnoxious girlfriend with unfathomable good luck. Along with the ability to crush rock with her bare hands. You'll be fine."

High praise coming from Cas. "I worry Gen's luck is going to run out if she's not careful."

"As long as it doesn't run out on this trip," Cas said.

Pollux tilted his head back and watched the stars shine overhead in the cloudless sky. That was the problem, wasn't it? The Oracle had told him he needed to know his fate in order for the venture to succeed, and he had a feeling he'd see that moment when there was no luck left.

"I'm going to try and get some sleep," he said. "You should too."

"I'm going to keep watch for a while. I'll sleep later."

Pollux made his way belowdecks and winced when he peered into his cabin. He dreaded going back in there. Then he realized he didn't have to. With Cas on deck, Gen would be alone in the other room, and he had such precious little time left with her.

He leaned against her doorframe and watched her sleep. It reminded him of months ago, before he'd told Gen about his feelings. Really, Bale had told Gen about his feelings, and when she'd confronted him about them, Pollux hadn't outright denied them. This still felt more right to him, to be standing outside the door instead of in the room with her.

He sighed, and Chomp rose from the bed and broke into a growl.

"Who is it?" Gen asked sleepily.

"It's me," Pollux said. "I didn't mean to wake you." He glared at Chomp. He supposed he wouldn't have enough time to make amends with the dog. It could take years for the beast to tolerate him.

"Is everything all right?" She rolled over to face him, her black-and-silver hair cascading over her tanned shoulder. Even though he had slept beside her many nights with her curled in his arms, she still seemed like something he couldn't touch. *Shouldn't* touch.

"It's fine. I just couldn't sleep."

"Where's Castor?" Gen gestured to the empty bed on the other side of the cabin.

"She's on deck. Keeping watch."

"Oh . . . do you want to sleep in here?" She pulled back the blanket on her own bed, and yes, a thousand times yes, he did want to sleep in here.

"Is Chomp going to eat me?" He nodded to the snarling dog.

"Oh, don't mind him." She scratched the sharp-toothed beast

behind the ears. "He's in a mood because I spat on him and made him read books."

"He can read?" Pollux lay on his back, and Gen curled into his shoulder, fitting perfectly against his lean frame.

"No, not really. But I can see what he sees, and honestly, I couldn't read any of the Elysium books, either. We were lucky the Oracle appeared."

"Yes, so lucky." Warmth rolled off Gen's skin. It always did. She burned hotter than anyone else he knew, always ready to break into a run or strike through a rock wall.

Gen's fingers grazed across the buttons on his shirt. "For the first time, I feel like we can actually do this. Even after killing the Hydra . . . the Empresses giving the win to Castor made me feel like I always have—like I'm not good enough."

"You were always good enough," he said.

She huffed. "For you." She twisted to put her chin on his chest, her mouth only inches from his. "I wish I could see myself the way you see me."

"I wish you could too."

She squinted. "Something is wrong. I can tell."

He was terrible at hiding his emotions. "We're in an enemy empire where you set a flaming bird loose and my sister drowned half the guards. We're about to steal some magic apples and capture a fire-breathing beast. I think I've earned the right to be worried."

"You're upset with me."

"No, not really," he lied.

"You are. I promised I would be careful, and then there was the bird—"

"I know, Gen. There's always something."

"It's not always my fault," she said. "The bird sounded trustworthy."

"My father sounds trustworthy, too, until he's selling you half-used storms for a mountain of coins. You need to think longer before you act, Gen, that's all I'm saying."

"I don't always have time to think."

"Someday you or someone else close to you is going to get hurt. Badly."

Gen went quiet. "I'm sorry," she whispered. "Do you think this trip is a mistake? Should we turn back?"

"No," he said quickly. That was exactly what he didn't want for her.

"The Oracle really told you we would get the apples? The Cerberus too?"

He took a breath. "Yes."

"Then you don't need to worry." She traced her finger along the collar of his shirt.

"There could still be a cost for that, Gen. I need you to be more careful. More careful than before." He didn't know if he could change his fate, but maybe, just maybe, if Gen didn't release any more flaming creatures, or run headfirst into the nearest danger, there was a chance.

"I will. I promise. I will no longer trust strange birds." She curled back into his neck, and her warm breath came across his collarbone. "You know I won't ever let anything hurt you. Again." She ran her fingers along his scars.

"Yes, I know." He grabbed her fingers. He knew she would always fight for him. He also knew she wasn't infallible. "I do recall you stabbing a Hydra in the chest with a giant crab claw to save me."

"You shouldn't have been there anyway. Not without your violin."

"Everything I loved was in the swamp. Where else would I be?" As soon as he said it, he realized how true it was. Everything he loved was on this ship too. Even knowing it would kill him to be here, he would never leave by choice.

"I love you, foul StormMaker." Gen pressed her palm to his cheek.

"I will always love you, Genevieve the Whale Rider."

She kissed him then, and he kissed her back, gently. He focused on keeping his mind completely blank. He could do this. He *had* to do this. Because if he thought of Oracles or prophecies—no. He thought of something else. He thought about Cas. No, not Cas. That was a bad idea. He thought of his usual song, "The Long Cold Winter."

His tongue brushed Gen's, and his body shuddered. He held tight to his song, the only thing that could claim his focus. He loved her, and he had little time left with her.

Gen pulled him in and wrapped her leg around his thigh. Pollux pinched his eyes tight and played his song louder in his thoughts. *Bah-duh-dum-bah-dum.* He tilted his head and kissed her deeper. She slid her hand from his neck to his chest. Her fingers were warm against his skin. He curled into her. How many nights had he thought about this exact moment?

She moaned and slid her hand lower, to his stomach. His muscles tightened, and he followed every note to his song in his mind, every movement of his fingers along the strings. He knew she could see it. He wasn't doing a good job of blocking his thoughts. Only working to divert them.

When her hand slid lower, he wondered if she was trying to break him.

He jerked away. "What are you doing?"

"Trying to be with you." She wiped the corner of her mouth, and he could see the hurt in her eyes.

He sat up. "I can't."

"Why not?"

"You know why." He rubbed his temples. This had been a mistake.

"You think we're a mistake?"

"You read my thoughts? Right now?" He refocused on his song.

"I didn't mean to. You're so loud. I can't *not* see them."

She reached for his hand, and he snatched it away. Gen looked at him as if he had slapped her.

"I'm sorry," she whispered. "I'm trying. I don't know how to do this, either."

"No, I'm sorry," he said, and stood up. "I'm not in a good place for this."

"Why? What's wrong?"

"It's everything." He turned for the door.

"Why can't you trust me with your secrets?" she asked.

"Why can't you let me keep my secrets?" he countered.

"Because I want to be trusted."

"So do I."

Her beautiful lower lip quivered. He left before she could break into tears because that would destroy all of his resolve. He was still connected to her thoughts though, and for once, she wasn't doing a great job of hiding them.

If he can't love the part of me that's a MindWorker, he can't love me.

CHAPTER 21

CASTOR

Something smelled foul. Three days they had been sailing northwest, following the Oracle's direction, and they had seen only sea and the occasional distant island. Castor tapped her fingers on Delia's box. She'd left the troublesome little ghost in there after her stunt with the Elysium ships. But Castor could use her now to see if they were headed in the right direction.

She flipped the box open. Delia emerged in a slow blink.

"Before we go any farther," Castor said. "I need to know two things. How did you get out of your box without me knowing? And why did you tell the Elysium soldiers where to find us?"

"The box came unlatched in your sleep," Delia said, "and I think we both know why I sent the ships after you."

Defiant, treacherous little spirit. Castor closed her fingers tightly around the box. "I could crush this."

"Then do it," Delia said. "Because I would rather be a lost soul than your eternal servant."

"How dare you speak to me like that?" The wood creaked under Castor's fingers. She should do it. She should crush this box to splinters and let Delia never find peace.

Except that would leave her without a ghostly servant.

"Get in the box," Castor commanded.

Delia didn't move, so Castor scooped her into the box and slammed it shut. "Worthless ghost," she muttered.

"Something bothering you?" Adikia stepped up beside her, chewing on an apple.

"I'm having trouble with a disobedient spirit." Castor leaned against the ship rails and let the sea air tangle through her hair.

"That must be unfortunate for you. How do you threaten something that's already dead?"

"I threatened her with eternal solitude, but that doesn't seem to work anymore. She's called my bluff. I need to find a new threat. One that works."

"You could always try negotiating."

Castor shot her a glare. "I don't negotiate with servants."

"It doesn't sound like she's much of a servant anymore, if she's not doing what you want." Adikia handed Castor her half-eaten apple. "Do you want a bite?"

Cas took the apple and bit into the uneaten side.

"Is something else bothering you? Are you still mad about the girl back home?" Adikia tugged her salt-crusted hat down to shade her eyes.

Castor laughed. "It's amusing that you think you and your love life hold any importance to me whatsoever." Although they did. As soon as Adikia had mentioned the red-haired woman, Castor smelled her foul perfume in the air.

"Good," Adikia said after a pause. "Because she wasn't important."

"Wonderful."

"I would have rather been with you, but as I recall, you left me because you had important Duchess things to do."

"I always have important Duchess things to do."

"Exactly. So in your life, I'm second tier."

"Most things are."

"Then it shouldn't upset you to be secondary in my life."

Cas pitched the apple over the side of the ship. "I am secondary in no one's life. I am the future Duchess of Storms. What are you? A second-rate thief? There are hundreds of you in the Empire and only one of me. You should feel privileged I even speak to you."

Adikia laughed. "You don't hide your jealousy well, Lady Castor."

"I'm not jealous," she snapped. But she was. Adikia was supposed to be hers in the way Pollux belonged wholeheartedly to Gen. If anyone was to be caught with someone else in her bed, it should have been Castor.

"You are," Adikia said. "And I'm sorry. I had no idea you wanted to be serious."

"I don't want to be serious."

"Then why are you so angry?"

"Shouldn't you be steering the ship?" Castor crossed her arms over her chest.

"Bale gave me a break so I could come talk to you." Adikia nodded toward Bale, who held the wheel lazily in one hand. She dropped her apple-sticky fingers to the inside of Castor's wrist and gently traced the lines of her veins. "Why don't you move out of your cabin and into the captain's rooms, with me?"

Cas stared hard into Adikia's catlike eyes, always playful and challenging. This was what Castor wanted, wasn't it? To be Adikia's choice? Then why didn't it feel like enough?

"You think it's that easy? You think you can just invite me into your bed and I'll leap into it?"

"No." Adikia blinked her slitted eyes. "You're not easy at all,

Castor, in any way. Since you'll never ask me, I'm asking you. Please come stay with me."

Castor's heart raced. "That sounds more like begging."

"If that's what you need to hear, then fine. I'm begging. My ego isn't so large that I need to push it out of the way to get what I want."

Castor frowned. Somehow the purple-haired thief had managed to turn begging into an insult. "I don't have an ego."

Adikia burst into laughter, clutching her stomach. "Then what in the Oracle's name do you call that attitude you have?"

"Pride. Worth. When you are the best, why should you settle for anything less?"

Adikia crushed her laughter. "I see your point. I know I'm the best thief, which is why I want you—the unobtainable prize."

Castor's cheeks burned, and she knew her pale skin wouldn't hide it. "That's the only reason you want me?"

"Does there need to be another?" Adikia leaned against the rails in a gentle swagger. Damn the Oracles. Cas wanted to kiss her hard and drag her to the nearest bed so she could tear off her clothes piece by piece.

But she couldn't do it. Her affection for the thief kept her from pitching Adikia off this ship, and her pride kept her from giving in. Cas wanted something more. Like always, she wanted it all. Adikia's heart, soul . . . everything.

Castor looked to the bow, where her brother and Gen coiled rope. Gen did most of it. Lux tried. He struggled with the heavy sail rope until Gen snatched it from him, easily coiling it around her wrist.

Castor could tell they were in a mood. The atmosphere around them felt like a storm cloud ready to burst. She didn't care enough to ask the cause. Whatever it was, they could barely look at each other, and when they did accidentally make eye contact, they both paused, as if on the verge of breaking into tears. Gen's work was certainly suffering for it. She was tying the rope into knots at her feet.

That is love, Castor thought. *The mind-altering, disgusting, painful side of it.*

She turned to Adikia. "I suppose—"

"What's that?" Adikia looked to the sea, where something rose from the water and sank back to the depths.

"Probably some sea creature. You should ask Gen. She's an expert in slimy things."

"I'd be more concerned about *that*," Bale called, pointing from the bridge to a wall of rock rising into the sky in front of them.

It was far off yet, but it nearly blocked out the sun, casting long shadows across the water.

"We need to turn the ship to get around it." Adikia made for the wheel.

"No, wait." Castor grabbed her arm. "The rock isn't solid. There's a break."

A small strait passed through the center of the cliffs. Barely a sliver from here, but Cas was sure when they reached it, it would be wide enough for them to pass. That had to be its purpose, a passageway for sailors.

Adikia pulled the spyglass from her belt and held it to her eye. "We have no idea what is through that pass."

"We have no idea what is around it, either. I didn't know you were such a coward."

"Not a coward, a thief. I like to avoid getting caught."

"And I would like to avoid getting caught by Nessos and his army,"

Castor said. "It will take more time for us to go around, letting him close the distance."

Adikia frowned. "I still don't like it."

"Neither do I," Pollux said. He and Gen joined them at the railing.

Cas groaned. "Then we take a vote. I say we go through the pass."

"I do too," Gen said. "If the Emperor catches us, he will kill us on sight."

Castor raised an eyebrow. She didn't think Gen would be the first to agree with her.

"I say we go around," Adikia said.

"Me too," Pollux added.

Flek raised a hand and pointed to Gen, then to the pass. He wanted to go through, which left only Bale.

Castor shot him a glare and tapped her belt of storm vials. If he sided with Pollux and Adikia to make it a tie, she would char him to ash and change the numbers.

"I'd rather not get impaled by a spear," he said. "Let's go through."

Castor released her vial of lightning.

"I guess we go through," Adikia sighed. She took the wheel and kept the ship on a direct course toward the rock wall.

Castor opened a vial of wind and let it gently billow into the sails. She pushed them along carefully. As they got closer to the rocks, she realized they would barely fit through the pass. One bump or gust of wind in the wrong direction and they would hit the rocks. Whoever had carved the pass into the mountain had been a poor craftsman. They hadn't left any extra space.

The *Hind* sailed into the rock wall's shadow, and the water turned dark. Cas pulled back on her wind and slowed the ship. Everything turned silent apart from the sea slapping against the hull and the wind billowing in the sails. A shiver ran down her spine. Something didn't feel right.

Did we make the wrong choice?

Even if they had, Cas couldn't say anything. She would look weak. Whatever sat within this mountain, she would face it with dignity and her remaining storm vials.

Adikia held the wheel steady as the front of the ship passed the first few rocks. White cliffs rose up on either side of them. The only sunlight broke through from the sliver at the top. Ledges and shelves had been carved into the rocks, places for guards or archers to keep watch for passing ships. Now they were all empty. Overgrown trees and long vines spewed from the top of the rocks, unkempt from years of neglect. If this strait had been watched once, it wasn't anymore. Cas exhaled.

"We're almost through," Lux said.

A column of white appeared in front of them, the other side of the pass. Cas knew she'd made the right choice. She could only imagine how much time they would have wasted going—

The wood hull splintered, and the ship slammed into something. Castor flew forward. She hit the deck, landing on her arm. Pain lanced from her wrist to her shoulder.

Adikia cried out a thousand different curses as she tried to keep the ship from breaking to pieces. "Someone go below!" she shouted. "See if we're taking on water."

The entire ship groaned. Castor tried to pick herself up. But she couldn't put any weight on her right arm without pain shooting through her like lightning.

Bale thundered up the companionway from belowdecks. "We've got a leak."

"Damn it!" Adikia shouted.

Pollux and Gen peered over the edge of the ship.

"Did we hit a rock?" Adikia called to them.

"No," Pollux said.

"What did we hit?"

"I don't know," Gen said. "It looks like . . . a net."

As soon as Cas heard that, she stood and fumbled for a storm vial.

"I wouldn't do that if I were you," a voice growled.

Castor raised her gaze to the white clifftops, where a series of archers appeared on the rocky ledges. The same overgrown vines and leaves that grew from the rocks were draped over their backs and hooves. And they held rough-hewn crossbows aimed directly at Castor's face.

CHAPTER 22

GEN

For the second time since they had crossed the border into Elysium, their ship was being taken over by centaur soldiers. Except these soldiers were different from Nessos's army. They wore armor carved from wood bark, and their hair hung long and tangled around their suntanned faces. Their weapons had all been hand-carved, made with tools that left deep grooves behind.

The soldiers spoke in Elysium, shouting orders. One of the centaurs aimed a crossbow between Gen's eyes. Chomp broke out from between her legs and snarled at the man. He re-aimed his bow at the chaeri.

"Don't hurt him!" Gen grabbed the crossbow and snapped it in two before elbowing the centaur aside.

The other soldiers paused for a breath, then every single bow aimed in her direction. The centaurs shouted at her. She raised her arms and stood protectively in front of Chomp and Pollux. One of the centaurs loomed over her, piercing her with sharp green eyes. His finger wriggled on the trigger to his crossbow. Gen held her breath.

Castor spoke in Elysium, and the centaur flinched.

"You come with us to Kyknos," he said in rough Olympian. "She will decide your fate."

Gen exhaled as the guard prodded her in the shoulder with the end of his crossbow.

"You need to be more careful," a voice whispered behind her.

She turned to see Pollux. This was the most he had said to her in the past few days. She wanted to let it go. Whatever secret he had, he could keep.

Except he couldn't keep it and be with her. She'd made a mistake in trying to get it out of him. She knew that. She also knew the secret he held was making him miserable. *Why doesn't he trust me enough to share it?* She could see it in his face: *"I wish she wasn't a MindWorker. I wish she were someone else."*

The guard tapped the side of her cheek with the tip of an arrow. He led her and the others off the ship and onto a thin walkway up the cliffside.

"We should have gone around," Adikia whispered behind Gen.

"Quiet," Castor hissed.

Castor couldn't take all the blame for this. Gen, Bale, and Flek had voted with her to go through the pass. And for all they knew, there would have been worse dangers for them if they'd gone around the island. What worried Gen now was how they would escape this. She envisioned another hurricane sweeping centaurs into the water where they would drown. Another island shrouded in flames.

She truly didn't want to leave a wake of destruction everywhere she went.

At the top of cliffs, the centaurs marched them into a thicket of trees and vines. It crawled with various creatures. Gen heard them clicking and clawing and scraping. Chomp heard them, too, and snarled at the undergrowth. She tapped him with the end of her boot.

"Be still," she whispered as a flying creature with leathery wings and a long-feathered tail swooped overhead.

If she lived long enough to meet one of those, she would love to spit on its wings and learn more about it. Her father had always been enchanted by unusual creatures. His excitement for them had captivated their audiences, made the circus even more magical. She wondered if she would ever see that man again, the one with infectious delight.

He will heal. As soon as you get back to him.

But returning to him seemed less likely as the centaurs prodded her up a cliff with arrow tips, even though the Oracle had told Pollux they would succeed.

The soft ground beneath their feet gave way to buried stones. The archers' hooves clomped across them. Then the trees parted into a clearing where a tall, open-air building rose from a series of twisted columns.

This building wasn't as grand as the Emperor's. Twined with flowering vines, and with a floor covered in moss, it seemed like it had grown from the ground, like a flower or tree.

The archers stopped and tapped Gen on the shoulder as a signal to kneel. She did so, dropping her knee into the moss. Her companions all did the same behind her.

A woman in the center of the clearing stood up, rising tall on her four hooves. Her hindquarters were steely gray, the same hue as her silver hair, which twisted into braids that fell down her back. She wore wooden armor over her chest, oiled into a glossy sheen.

The guards spoke to her in Elysium. She nodded and turned to Gen.

"I am Kyknos, keeper of the pass," she said in Olympian. "Who are you?"

"We are travelers seeking passage, my lady," Castor said.

Kyknos waved her away. "I wish to speak to your leader. Your warrior."

"I *am* the leader," Castor said.

"Be quiet," Pollux whispered.

Kyknos approached Gen. "Who are you?" she asked again.

"I am Genevieve Drivas, from Olympia." Gen spoke to the ground.

"Raise your chin when you talk to me. Now tell me again, who are you?"

Gen lifted her head to look the woman in the eye. "I am Genevieve Drivas, from Olympia."

"Why do you want to pass through this island? What do you hope to find on the other side?"

Pollux had told Gen the Oracle said she would get her apples and the Cerberus. But there was something else he wasn't telling her. He'd warned her to be careful. It made her worry their fate wasn't carved in stone, that one wrong choice could change it all.

She swallowed, wondering what the right answer would be. She wanted the apples, which sounded greedy. But she didn't want the apples for herself. She wanted something else.

"My father," she said.

"Your father is through this pass?"

"No, but the means to save him is. If we don't get through, he's lost to me."

"I see." Kyknos walked in a circle around her, her tail swishing against her hind legs.

Gen watched her from the corner of her eye.

"It's a noble cause, protecting one's family. I admire it." Kyknos stopped pacing. "This is my family, and we have guarded the Strait of Euripus for eight thousand years. Only those worthy can pass."

"Am I worthy?" Gen asked, hopeful.

Kyknos smiled. "We shall see. Passage through here is simple. You must defeat me in battle. You win, and you sail through the mountain. You lose, and I keep your ship and your crew as payment. Do you accept?"

It was never simple. There was always some multiheaded monster or giant centaur warrior trying to beat Gen to pieces.

She looked to Pollux. He subtly shook his head.

"Can I refuse?" she asked Kyknos. "Can we sail back the way we came?"

"No," Kyknos said. "You are halfway through my pass. Either way, you are asking for my permission to travel it. Permission you already stole from me to have made it this far. Our Oracle Arai demands penance for your trespass." She pulled a sword from the sheath on her hindquarters and swung it in a silver blur. "You fight, or you all die. You pay with your loss, or you redeem yourself through victory."

Gen rose to her feet, hating that these were always her only two options. "Then I guess I'll fight."

"Wonderful." Kyknos waved her arms, and her fellow centaurs stepped back to clear a circle. The ones holding Pollux and the others dragged them to the edges.

"Gen," Pollux called. "Be careful."

"I will," she answered, and shooed Chomp off with the others.

But as she stood under the shadow of the centaur warrior, her confidence wilted.

This wouldn't be like her battle with the Hydra. Gen didn't want to hurt Kyknos. She also had never been trained in hand-to-hand combat. Not like her mother. Zusma had been raised as a warrior. She probably could have knocked Kyknos off her hooves with one punch. Gen would have been much better poised to win a song-and-dance competition, assuming Kyknos didn't have any unknown musical talent.

"You have no weapon." Kyknos sounded concerned.

"I need no weapon." Gen would most likely injure herself with a sword. Her goal would be to disarm Kyknos as soon as she could without getting stabbed.

"Then I will take no weapon, either." Kyknos dropped her sword to the moss-covered stones and kicked it away, making disarming her unnecessary and hurting her much harder.

Kyknos had honor.

"I appreciate your sacrifice," Gen said.

Kyknos laughed. "It is not a sacrifice. I don't need a weapon to defeat someone as small as you."

Her confidence stirred Gen. *Remember, you are the Hydra-Slayer.* But looking back on that fight, Gen found more luck, daring, and strength than skill. Also, as much as she hated to admit it, Castor had helped a little with the beast. Gen wished Kyknos had chosen Castor for this fight. It would be over with one blast of lightning.

She swallowed as Kyknos walked in a slow circle. At the edges of their fighting pit, the other centaurs cheered and stomped their hooves. Gen flexed her arms, darting a quick glance to Pollux.

If she lost this battle, Kyknos would crush her and keep the others as slaves. Gen immediately thought of Mr. Percy's son, held by the Empresses. Gen couldn't let that happen to her friends. She had to win.

She and Kyknos walked a full circle on the mossy ground, never breaking eye contact. Gen didn't want to be the first to lunge. Her entire plan rested on not getting trampled to death and using her brute strength to get one solid hit on Kyknos, enough to knock her flat.

Another circle, and neither of them attacked. The centaurs continued to yell and stomp their hooves. A bead of sweat ran down Gen's neck.

Then Kyknos charged.

Gen panicked, leapt out of the way, and skidded across the moss. Kyknos doubled back, and one of her massive hooves came down toward Gen's chest. Gen didn't have time to escape. She grabbed the hoof with both hands and pushed it away. Kyknos stumbled back three steps.

"My soldiers told me you were strong." The centaur pushed hair away from her face. "I did not believe them. Impressive."

So, it had been Gen breaking the crossbow that had marked her as the challenger. If Kyknos hadn't seen something in Gen's strength, they might have all been dead already. Not all her rash decisions were mistakes.

Kyknos lunged again. Gen shoved the centaur's fist aside, but Kyknos kicked out with one of her hooves.

It struck Gen in the shin, and she buckled. The pain burned like fire through her entire body. Tears sprang from her eyes. Kyknos came at her with another fist, and this time it hit her on the shoulder. Gen spun like a children's toy until she collapsed to the stone.

She took a moment to catch her breath. Kyknos reared up on hind legs and came down toward her skull. Gen rolled aside purely on instinct. She could barely see through the tears. She couldn't think. All she felt was pain.

"The show must go on," she heard Alcmen's say in her head. *"Show them the dream, not the reality."*

"I thought you would be more of a challenge than this," Kyknos said.

Gen wiped the tears away with her fist and crawled to her knees. The show must go on, and that was what this was. A show, a dance. Except it was a dance where Gen couldn't hear the music. She didn't know the steps. She hadn't been trained as a warrior like her mother.

She had been trained as a performer like her father.

This time when Kyknos lunged, Gen spun a little more gracefully to the side. When Kyknos stepped over her, Gen grabbed her by the ankle. She tugged hard, and Kyknos fell over in a clatter of hooves.

"Watch your step," Gen said, and got to her feet. She leaned heavily on her right leg, her left shoulder stiff from the punch she'd taken. Her entire body pulsed with Mazon strength, fueled by throbbing pain.

Even so, she made a gentle bow.

Kyknos pushed herself back to her feet. Her nostrils flared, and her eyes sparked with life. "I see you decided to fight after all."

She came at Gen with a kick. Gen tugged off her jacket, wincing as her left arm twisted. She threw the jacket at Kyknos's face, wrapped it around Kyknos's head, and grabbed it by the sleeves. The jacket tore as she pulled on it and slammed Kyknos to the ground, headfirst. "I'm not sure if that jacket is your size."

Adikia let out a snorting laugh. Bale clapped his hands.

Kyknos tore the jacket from her face and stumbled to her feet. Her soldiers, no longer cheering, moved in from the sides to help her.

"This is not your fight. It's mine," Kyknos growled at them. She flashed her gaze to her discarded sword, likely wishing she had kept it now. Then she looked at Gen. "Are you mocking me?"

"Not at all," Gen said. "This is the only way I know how to fight."

They resumed their circling. Kyknos wiped the end of her nose and cracked her knuckles. Gen tried to ignore the throbbing in her shin and keep moving. She didn't know what to do next. This was the only show she'd ever done with no rehearsal.

"Why don't you attack?" Kyknos asked.

"I don't want to fight."

"Unbelievable. You must be a warrior in your home, with strength like yours."

"No, I'm a performer."

"A performer?" Kyknos laughed. "What a waste of skill."

"I suppose that depends on what you consider 'waste.'"

"Fair point, little Olympian. I'll admit, your technique is unusual. But you have promise. You could be great if you live through this day."

"I would prefer to see tomorrow," Gen said, and stumbled on her injured leg.

Kyknos lunged, snatched Gen by the wrist, and twisted. Gen's arm went in a direction it was never intended to go. Her muscles pulled and stretched, then something popped. Gen screamed in agony as Kyknos tried to tear out her arm. On the other side of the circle, Castor fought to hold Pollux back. Bale fought to hold Chomp.

Kyknos brought Gen to her knees. "Yield. I could use a warrior like you. With training, you could be great. Let me teach you. I vow you and your kin will have a place here with us."

Gen could hardly think through the blinding pain. This was a good offer. Better than any her other challengers had made. She could live, and the Empresses couldn't touch her here.

But they could hurt her father.

There was no other life for her besides the one she'd chosen. Maybe because she couldn't imagine one. Maybe because she didn't want to. Maybe because she had held on to hers for so long, it had fused into her bones. She couldn't separate her dreams from herself anymore.

The only life for her remained in Olympia. With Pollux, with her father, with her circus.

Gen closed her eyes, took a breath, and braced herself. She spun her entire body, which only twisted her arm more. But with her left fist, she landed a strike on Kyknos's jaw that sounded like shattering glass. Kyknos released Gen's arm as she flipped backward.

Gen's right arm hung loose at her side, screaming in pain. Gen bit it back and took her chance while Kyknos lay on the ground. She pushed her foot into the centaur's neck, tears streaming down her cheeks.

"Give up," she begged.

"No," Kyknos choked, and struggled to rise. Her legs kicked out with such force, they cracked stone.

Gen pushed her foot down harder into Kyknos's windpipe. This was the last chance she had. If Kyknos struck Gen again, she wouldn't get back up. She knew that in her bones.

"Please," Gen whispered. "I don't want to be a warrior. I don't want to die. Please, let us pass through the mountain."

Kyknos's face was turning purple. She stared hard at Gen with bloodshot eyes and then nodded, ever so gently.

Gen removed her boot from Kyknos's neck, and the centaur soldier gasped for air.

"The Olympian has won her passage," Kyknos coughed. The

crowd remained silent for two more of Kyknos's choking breaths, then it broke into raucous applause.

Gen clutched her injured arm to her chest. Mazon strength pumped through her muscles behind the pain. But it didn't matter that she had the strength to be a warrior. She didn't *want* to be a warrior. She was like her mother in that way. Zusma had run away to join the circus because she, too, hadn't wanted to fight.

CHAPTER 23

POLLUX

Sweat rolled down Pollux's forehead, one stream for every hit Gen took. Another for every scream that echoed from her lips. This was the hardest part about loving her: watching her always in battle. Always in danger. He wondered if it would ever end for her.

It will. When it ends for me, and she goes home with her prizes.

When the guards released him, Pollux dodged between hooves and bodies to reach Gen. But she and Kyknos were lifted onto the backs of other centaurs and carried into the trees in a flurry of loud horns and scattered rose petals. Chomp chased after her, snarling and barking.

"She's not bad, that Mazon of yours," Castor said as she approached him. She spoke with the most admiration for another person she had ever shown. Cas tended to look at other skilled people as competition, which was why she tolerated him. She didn't think he was capable enough to be her competitor.

"She almost got her arms ripped from her body," he said.

Castor cradled her own injured arm from her fall on the ship. Still, she had managed to hold him back when he'd tried to rush in to save Gen from getting crushed. He had been ready to snatch one of the wind vials from Castor's belt and knock Kyknos off the cliffs.

If Gen had been killed, he never would have forgiven Cas. And if he had knocked the warrior centaur into the sea, he probably wouldn't have forgiven himself.

"Gen always seems to pull out her best work when she's under pressure," Cas said. "Too bad she can't bottle that talent and use it sooner. Can you believe Kyknos thought *she* was the leader?"

"Yes, I can. This is her venture. The Empresses asked *her* to come to Elysium. Not you. If I recall, you had to beg to come along."

"I did not beg," Castor snapped. "I never beg."

Some of the other centaurs approached them. Pollux's muscles tensed. So far, his experience with the Elysiums had been as expected—not good.

The first soldier stopped and bowed. Flower petals dropped from her long, golden hair.

"Lady Kyknos has asked us to help you bathe and prepare for dinner," she said in rough Olympian. She spoke the right words but with the wrong inflection. Her knowledge of the language came from books instead of practice. "If the women will come with me." The woman waved her hand to Adikia and Cas.

"The men can follow me," a male soldier said. He towered over Pollux with tanned skin and black braids that reached down his back.

Pollux heard a song in his head, loud and choppy, with a cloud centaur as large as this man riding into battle. It would be an epic performance . . . if he ever played again. He could be dead before he played another song. The Oracle hadn't specified how long he had to live or how far he would make it into Gen's journey.

She also hadn't mentioned anything about this mountainous island or the battle with Lady Kyknos. Why would she tell him so little? And so much? Why was it so important that he know he would die?

He stumbled over a tree root, and Bale caught his arm. "Watch your feet, Lux. You don't want to go stumbling off the rocks."

Pollux, Flek, and Bale followed the centaur through an over-grown forest. Colorful blooms and strange creatures popped out on the branches. Pollux heard a babbling brook, and the forest opened to a series of hot springs cut into a hill. The largest one fed into the ones below. The steam rose into the trees.

"You can bathe here. I will have someone fetch you clean clothing," the man said.

"Thank you," Pollux said. "Can I ask you where Gen is?"

"Who?" The centaur raised an eyebrow.

"Our friend who fought with Kyknos."

"Oh." The man nodded. "Your warrior has been bestowed a great honor, favor by Lady Kyknos. She is being tended to by our healers, along with your other injured. You will see them once you've bathed and been made presentable." He gestured to the hot spring again.

Pollux had to admit days at sea had left a gray film on his skin he wasn't sure even this spring could remove.

"What about our ship?" Bale asked. "Your trap damaged the hull."

"Your ship is being repaired. We apologize for the inconvenience. Please enjoy the hot spring."

Flek took off his shirt to reveal the muscle underneath and the round scar in his shoulder from the spear. Pollux waited until Flek had sunk below the water before he removed his own shirt, showing his gaunt ribs and pale skin. He wondered what would happen after he was gone. He'd given Flek his blessing to look after Gen, which had seemed like the right thing to do at the time. Now it felt all wrong.

He sank into the water with a scowl as Flek surfaced.

"What's bothering you?" Bale asked. "You look like you ate some Borean beet root."

"I hate watching Gen almost get killed," Pollux said.

Flek mouthed, *"Me too,"* copying the words in the Croecian language at the same time. One hand swept upward and two fingers touched his lips. After spending more time with Flek, Pollux was beginning to understand the gestures.

Bale ran his wet fingers through his blue hair. "You know Gen. She'll go looking for trouble even when it's not looking for her."

"I wish she'd break that habit," Pollux said.

"It's not her fault. Certain people attract danger. They can't avoid it. Like you."

"I avoid danger," Pollux argued.

"Really? I guess racing into Hippolyta's cave and pitching rocks at the Hydra was *you* avoiding danger? Was sailing into the heart of an enemy empire also *you* avoiding danger?"

Pollux looked to Flek, who shrugged in agreement. "All right, so I haven't always made the safest decisions."

He regretted lecturing Gen so often about being careful. He regretted a lot of things.

The centaur who had led them here dropped off some clean clothes.

"Here," he said, setting them on the flat rocks beside the warm spring. "These are from other Olympian travelers."

Bale picked up one of the shirts and held it out. It had soft, ballooned sleeves and a lace tie at the collar. "I don't think anyone has worn something like this in over three centuries." He eyed the sleeve. "Is this a blood stain?"

"You probably don't want to know," Pollux said.

Other Olympians must have come through here, either during the last war or before. Or perhaps others had gone in secret to search for the apples. That would explain why Kyknos and her people spoke

Olympian. They must have a collection of Olympian goods somewhere, taken from failed travelers: books, clothes, other artifacts.

Flek reached for some of the clothes. Pollux looked away as the MetalBender changed. When he turned back, Flek wore the billowing shirt and loose pants like they had been made for him.

"*I'm going to go down and check the boat,*" Flek mouthed and signed at the same time. Pollux was doing better with reading lips. He'd also managed to capture some of the hand language. *Boat look Flek go.*

"We'll meet you shortly," Pollux said.

Flek nodded and made his way back down the tree-lined path. Pollux closed his eyes and sank into the warm water. He held his breath as long as he could, then let out the bubbles and rose to the surface. When he cleared the water from his eyes, Bale was watching him.

"What's really bothering you, Lux?" Bale asked.

"I told you." Pollux slicked back his wet hair.

"That's not all of it. I've known you awhile now, enough to know that look in your eyes. Faraway, wistful. Something's not right."

Pollux sat upright. "How about we go back to your thing about murdering someone?"

"I'd rather not."

"And I'd rather not talk about my worries."

"How about we trade? I tell you mine, you tell me yours."

Pollux wasn't that desperate to know about Bale's past. But he also hated that he shared this secret with Flek and no one else. "The Oracle gave me some bad news about this quest."

"How bad?"

"Very bad," Pollux said. "Bad enough that I don't want Gen to know, which is making it difficult to be with her."

"Because of the kissing," Bale said. "I warned you. The only way—"

"I know." Pollux pinched the bridge of his nose. "I don't need another lecture." He gave himself enough of those.

"What exactly did the Oracle say?" Bale asked.

"How exactly did you murder someone?" Pollux countered. He was shocked at how adept he had become at avoiding the truth.

Bale sighed and picked up a wide leaf that had fallen on the water. He twisted it in his fingers, his way of avoiding the truth. Good. They could stay at a standstill. Bale could keep his secret. Pollux could keep his.

Then Bale opened his mouth.

"I forced a girl to swim out to sea, knowing it was unsafe, and she drowned." He released the leaf onto the warm water.

"Why did you do it?"

"Her boat had come loose from the docks. I convinced her she could swim out and get it."

"That doesn't sound like murder," Pollux said. Coercion, maybe, which was something his sister did on a daily basis. "You've been punishing yourself for an accident."

"It wasn't an accident." Bale's expression turned dark.

"Did you hold her at knifepoint?"

Bale shook his head. "There are many ways to kill someone. You can hold the knife to their throat, or you can give them the knife and tell them where to cut. I did the second, and it feels the same as if I'd cut her myself."

"I'm sorry," Pollux said.

"Do you feel better knowing that?" Bale asked.

Pollux chewed on his thoughts for a while. Did he feel better? Knowing Bale had suffered? Still suffered?

"I do," he said. "Not because of what happened, but because you trusted me enough to tell me."

"Your turn. Tell me what the Oracle said to you. Exactly."

Pollux rose out of the water and grabbed one of the blousy shirts. He pulled it over his head and tugged on the loose pants. "I can't."

Bale grabbed him by the wrist. "You can tell me, Lux. I told you my darkest truth."

"And I will keep it to my grave, friend." Which might not be that far away.

"You don't trust me to do the same?"

"No, I trust that you would do the right thing if you knew the truth. Which is why you can't." Pollux pried his wrist free. "I'll tell you when it's part of my past and not part of my future. Like your secret."

He left Bale in the hot spring, feeling guilty. But Bale would figure out the truth soon enough. If he knew now, he would tell Gen to protect Pollux from his fate, and Pollux couldn't let him do that. Especially now. He didn't want Bale to feel responsible for another life.

On the way back toward the clearing, Pollux heard music: loud horns, stomping hooves, banging drums. Where Gen and Kyknos had tried to kill one another an hour ago, tables had been set up—though the centaurs had missed some of the blood. Drops of it stained the mossy stones as a reminder of the fight.

Bowls of bright-colored fruit and flowers sat in the center of each table, and some kind of charred meat turned on a spit over a blazing fire. Gen stood with Kyknos on the steps of the stone building. A moss-covered arch hung over them, draped in chains of flowers.

Gen wore a simple blue dress tied over her left shoulder, another ancient Olympian artifact. Her arm no longer drooped. The healers here had done miraculous work. She looked better than she had when they'd arrived. At her feet, Chomp scratched at a crown of blue flowers.

When Gen spotted him, she smiled, wider than she had in days. He'd missed that smile. He'd also missed the way she'd rush toward him when she saw him, as if walking at a normal pace would take her far too long to reach him.

She rushed across the stones now. Pollux opened his arms, and she fell into him. She squeezed him hard, pushing the wind out of his lungs. It was as if the last few days hadn't happened. That was one nice thing about her "almost dying" again. They could forgive each other without words.

He buried his nose in her black-and-silver hair and breathed deeply. "Are you all right?" he asked.

"I'm fine—are you? I didn't know where you were."

"Bathing." He pulled away from her and ran his thumb down her cheek. "They must have some great healers. You look . . . perfect."

"They have a drink here called ambrosia. It's like stink-lizard pus, except better. Kyknos gave me a vial to take with us." She bent down and reached into her boot. She removed a small jar with gold liquid inside. "It's rare. It was a gift from their Oracle Gaia, the same one who made the apples. This vial will heal only one person, so we need to use it sparingly."

"Who is this?" Lady Kyknos came up behind them. She wore a fresh set of leather armor across her chest and a red cape with golden clasps draped over her shoulders.

"This is Pollux of Arcadia," Gen said.

"It is a pleasure to meet you, my lady." Pollux bowed his head. It would have been a greater pleasure if the lady hadn't tried to pull Gen's arm from its socket earlier.

Kyknos smiled at him. "What a handsome and polite mate you've chosen, Genevieve. May your children be strong and bountiful."

Pollux cleared his throat. He would love to be at the "mated" part of their relationship, but he doubted it was a place he would ever see.

"We're not quite there yet, but thank you," Gen said.

"You must be a sage in your land," Kyknos said to him. "You have the look of someone wise and well-traveled. It's in the eyes. And here." She pointed to the center of his forehead. "The two lines here. They are the mark of someone who spends much of his time in thought."

Castor called that his "lost expression," when he stared at the walls composing songs in his head. Where was she, anyway? He looked around the crowd and spotted her with Adikia by a table of food.

"I do," he admitted, turning back to Kyknos. "About music."

"He's a performer," Gen said, "like me. A musician."

Kyknos slammed a front hoof into the stones, hard enough to shake the ground. "You must be joking! What is it with you Olympians? You take your wise men and strong women and make them performers instead of sages and warriors! I have a great love for music, but it's only secondary to one's true pursuits. Ah, one day, if my duties ever release me, I should like to see your land. It must be a fascinating place. I would like to see your best warriors if you, Gen, are one who can be spared for performance."

Gen gave Pollux a look, one he understood without a word. If Kyknos did ever see Olympia, it would be in battle once the Empresses launched their war.

Just then, Flek entered the clearing carrying Pollux's salvation—his violin. Pollux gratefully took the instrument from him and ran his fingers over the strings.

"Thank you," he mouthed. Flek tipped his chin.

"You must play," Kyknos said. "I demand it. I wish to see the skills of someone who focuses his wisdom on song."

"As you wish." He had planned to play regardless.

He took his violin and joined the other musicians. He did his best to play along with them. But it wasn't only their off-kilter rhythm that kept him from following in time. He couldn't concentrate. Every time he thought he had a grasp on the song, it slipped away from him.

You are going to die.

The words played with every beat.

He shook them off and tried to make some semblance of a song. It took every ounce of his will to make it happen. He had to focus on every note, every pull of the strings. He hadn't worked this hard on his music since he'd first learned to play.

His fingers picked up the pace, and finally the song began to take shape, literally, in a wisp of cloud that took the form of Kyknos. Then he played another wisp of cloud for Gen, and the two entangled in battle.

He lifted his chin and turned to Kyknos to see if she enjoyed the song—or if she'd noticed his many mistakes. Then he saw Gen with Flek, both speaking animatedly with their hands.

Pollux watched as Flek fanned his fingers on either side of his head, then dropped his hand in front of his face. *Understand me . . . know me . . .* What was that last word? Then it struck him. *I know the secret.*

That snake was about to tell Gen about the prophecy.

CHAPTER 24

GEN

Usually, Gen loved to watch Pollux play. She would watch him for hours, even if he wasn't actually playing. Sometimes he only put his fingers in the positions and hummed the tune he wanted to make. He had to have everything right before he brought his bow to the strings. Music came as naturally to him as breathing.

But not tonight. Tonight, he struggled. She could see it in his face, the way he held his bow . . . everything.

Flek came up beside her. *"What's wrong?"* he mouthed as he drew a finger across his forehead and down the side of his jaw.

"It's Pollux." She stretched one hand overhead and waved her fingers. *Storm violinist.* "Something is bothering him, breaking him, and he won't tell me what it is. And I think—" She couldn't say the rest. *I think it might be me.*

Flek shook his head and mouthed, *"I know what's troubling him. I know what his secret is."* He fanned his fingers on either side of his face.

"What is it?" Gen's heart beat faster. She would finally have answers.

Flek raised his arm in the air—and another hand grabbed him by the wrist.

Pollux stood between them, cheeks red and nostrils flaring. Gen hadn't even realized the music had stopped. She had been so intent on Flek.

"You promised" was all Pollux said before he shoved Flek's hand aside.

"What is going on?" Gen reached for him.

"It's not your concern!" Pollux shouted at her before storming into the trees.

Tears brimmed in her eyes. She turned to Flek, who shook his head. He wouldn't tell her now, either.

Gen left Chomp grazing scraps under the food table and chased after Pollux. Enough of this. She couldn't take being held at arm's length by some invisible wall anymore.

Away from the lanterns and music, the woods turned dark. The only light came from glowing insects crawling in the dirt.

Gen spat on their backs. "Where did he go?" she asked them.

The insects formed a line and moved down the path. She followed, careful not to step on them. They walked in a straight line for several feet before taking a sharp turn to the left.

"Thank you." Gen pushed her way through the brush. The trees broke open to a wide night sky. Below, she heard waves crashing against the cliffs. Pollux sat on a rock, staring into the darkness, his pale hair shining in the moonlight.

She remembered when she'd first seen him up close at the Lion's Den, right after she'd watched him play his violin. She'd hated him, mostly for being a StormMaker, but also for being so irritatingly talented. He'd gone out of his way to turn her feelings around. He had forced his way into her heart. Now it felt like he was trying to claw his way out.

"You shouldn't have yelled at me like that," she said as she approached him. "Of course it's my concern. *You* are my concern."

She had beaten the Hydra to save him once. Whatever this was, she could beat it too.

"I'm sorry," he said.

She sat beside him, and the little illuminated bugs swarmed around her feet. "I can't do this. I can't keep wondering why you're lying to me."

"I know. It isn't fair to you."

She took his hand. "Then tell me, please. Whatever it is, we can fix it."

"We can't fix it."

"At least let me——"

He took his hand from hers. "Gen, if I tell you the truth, it will only hurt you more. Trust me."

Her throat tightened, and she swallowed the knot. "Then this does have to do with me. It's because of my mind magic, isn't it?" What a struggle it must have been for him to be with her while she was constantly prying into his thoughts.

"It's not your fault," he said.

Tears ran down Gen's cheeks. She scrubbed them away with the back of her hand. "I can try harder. I promise."

"I don't want you to." When he turned to face her, he had tears on his cheeks too. "I just . . . I can't do it." He shook his head.

"Then don't." She reached for his hand again. "We can pretend like we never had this conversation. We can find a way to make it work."

"I can't." He pulled his hand back and buried his face in it. "I love you, Gen. So much, but I can't do this."

Her breath hitched. "You made me believe in you. You made me believe you didn't care about my magic or what I could do with it."

"I'm so sorry."

Gen stood and wrapped her arms around her ribs. The pain cut through her chest worse than when Kyknos had nearly torn off her arm. Pollux cut her much deeper inside. To her heart. Her soul. She had to get away from him.

She made her way back to the path. One way would lead her to the music, lights, and dancing. She couldn't go that way. She couldn't bear other people's joy. She turned and stumbled into the darkness instead. Her eyes burned with tears as she tripped over tree roots and rocks. *Foul StormMaker.* She never should have trusted him. Yet all she wanted to do was run back to him and fall into his arms.

She wandered deeper into the trees, hoping to get lost, and found a rough wooden building at the end of the path with an oil lantern dangling from a hook out front. She wiped the tears from her cheeks and stepped closer. A moldy, broken chair sat out front. It had a missing leg, and it was made for Olympians, not centaurs. Beside it sat an old, rusted sword, also Olympian-made.

Gen picked it up. The four-diamond imprint of Olympia was inscribed in the hilt. But the design was old. At least a few hundred years out of fashion.

She heard laughter and dropped the sword. Castor and Adikia emerged from the shack. They stopped when they saw her.

"Oh, Gen," Castor said. "What are you doing here?"

"I was out . . . walking. What is this place?"

"Apparently where Kyknos keeps what she takes from ships that don't make it through her pass," Castor said. "We're lucky you beat her in that fight, or our things might have been shoved in here too."

"We found something useful, though." Adikia waved a rolled piece of parchment.

"What is it?"

"A map. To the apples," Castor said.

Gen's wounded heart lifted slightly. This put one of their prizes within reach. "You can't take that. Kyknos has been kind to us." *And she could tear off our arms if she wanted.*

"She wasn't so kind when she was knocking you into the dirt," Adikia said.

"It's also not her map," Castor said. "It's Olympian-made. We're only taking it back."

Adikia lifted her tunic and tucked the map into her pants. "There. No one will know we have it."

"Fine." Gen didn't have the energy to argue. Her spirit had been drained.

Maybe if you'd tried harder to control your mind magic. Or maybe if you hadn't pushed so hard. Pollux had warned her to be careful, to take caution, and she had pushed through their relationship with as little care as everything else.

They made their way back to the celebration. Gen sat down at a table and picked at pieces of fruit. She plucked some remnants from a plate of roasted fowl and dropped the bird bones on the ground for Chomp to gnaw on. While he ate, she leaned her cheek into her palm and stared into the blackness of the trees. She had been alone for so long before. She didn't want to do it again.

Someone sat down across from her.

"Pollux?" She jerked her head upright and frowned when she saw Bale.

"Sorry to disappoint." He grabbed a sweet roll from a wooden platter and took a bite. "Where is Lux, anyway?"

"I don't know. Last time I saw him, he was sitting by the cliffs."

Pollux chose that moment to return to the party. He kept his eyes down and his shoulders hunched. This hurt him too. So why did he do it?

Because it hurt him more to be with you.

The knot re-formed in her throat.

"Is something wrong?" Bale asked.

"You were right," she said. "We can't be with people. Not the way they want us to be. Pollux couldn't do it anymore."

"I'm sorry, Gen. I didn't think—"

"What is that?" someone in the crowd shouted.

Gen turned around. In the center of the clearing, Adikia stood under Kyknos's glare, the stolen map on the ground between them.

"A parting gift?" Adikia snatched it up and shoved it back into her pants.

"How dare you steal from me!"

Gen scooped up Chomp. "I think we should run."

"I agree." Bale snatched up two more sweet rolls before he leapt from the table and made for the path down the cliff.

"Archers!" Kyknos waved her arm, and her soldiers fumbled for their bows. Thankfully the centaurs had been drinking wine for the past few hours. They aimed with slow reflexes. Gen grabbed Pollux by the elbow and pulled him toward the cliffs. Her breath hitched. It hurt her to be this close to him. But it would hurt her more to see him impaled by an arrow.

The first round of arrows fired. Flek held up his hand, and the metal tips glowed red. The arrows stopped in midair and dropped to his feet.

Gen and the others reached the path and wound their way down to the ship. It felt miles away. More arrows plummeted from above.

The crew kept tight to the stone walls, and the arrows soared over their heads.

Gen held tight to Pollux's arm.

"You don't have to help me down the mountain," he said.

"I do," she argued. She could lose him, but she couldn't *lose* him. There were some heartaches even she couldn't bear.

They reached the ship and leapt onto the deck.

"Pull the sails!" Adikia shouted.

Gen set Chomp down and helped Bale tug the sail ropes. The yellowed sails dropped. Pollux lifted his violin to his chin to play them out of there. The sails filled with wind, but the ship barely moved.

"Have we been freed from the nets?" Adikia shouted.

"I think so." Gen leaned over the bow. No ropes held them in place.

"We still have water belowdecks!" Castor shouted. "They didn't fix the leak."

Pollux played harder and louder, and long notes filled the sails with wind. The *Hind* slogged through the canal while arrows dropped onto the deck.

Flek waved his hands in the air. *"I can fix the leak."*

He and Castor went belowdecks. An arrow sliced Pollux's hand. He dropped his violin, and the sails went flat. He slumped to the deck, blood running down his wrist.

"I thought that was it," he said numbly. "I thought that was the end."

"What are you talking about?" Gen asked, but he didn't respond. He must have been as emotionally spent as she was.

"We need wind!" Adikia shouted.

Castor emerged from belowdecks. "What are you doing?" she shouted at Pollux.

Gen put her hand on his shoulder. "It's all right. I can fix your hand. It's just a cut. It won't affect your playing."

"Enough of this!" Castor shouted, and released a strong gust of wind. The ship surged forward. Adikia lost control, and the *Hind* scraped against the rocks. Bits of stone fell onto the deck, along with a few more arrows.

Adikia straightened the ship, and it burst through the end of the pass into open water. The last of the arrows dropped into the sea behind them. Gen stood upright and exhaled.

"I hope that map was worth it," she snapped at the thief.

Adikia smiled. "It was."

CHAPTER 25

CASTOR

Castor leaned over the map they'd taken from Kyknos's crumbling shack of stolen treasures. She and Adikia had run off into the woods looking for a place to be alone, when they'd found the moss-covered hovel, and Adikia had been too distracted by the trove to do anything else. But it hadn't ended in a complete loss. They had found precise directions to the apples.

Weathered, torn, and burned, the map was barely readable. But she could clearly make out the smudge labeled *Isle of Hesperides* and the swath of water around it that read *Death Awaits*. No explanation was given. Was it a rocky reef that would sink them? Or a giant sea monster that would devour them?

Either way, Cas would cross that water. She had to if she wanted her apples. She only worried that someone else would have concerns about the warning and make them turn around. Like Pollux. A tiny arrow had grazed the back of his hand, and he'd fallen to pieces. Cas had always been able to count on him being calm. Sensible. Stoic.

Not anymore.

Castor rolled up the map and tucked it into the inner pocket of her jacket. She counted the vials of storms on her belt. One, two, three, four ... all the way to twenty-four. She'd captured a bit of wind here and there, no storms of significance. She had only six vials of lightning and two tornados. She hoped those would be enough to avoid whatever death awaited.

She slogged her way across the damp floor belowdecks, the warped floorboards creaking. They'd managed to stop the leak and remove most of the water. But they'd had to toss out two bags of wet bread and grains, and nothing down here would ever smell the same.

Still, she preferred the mold to the tension above.

On the surface, everything looked fine. Gen and Bale coiled rope on the foredeck. Adikia held the wheel. Flek bent strips of metal into new bolts to replace the ones that had degraded from rust. Pollux pushed a mop back and forth on the bridge. All normal.

Until she looked closer.

"It's not right," Gen muttered as she uncoiled the ropes and recoiled them . . . in exactly the same way. "I can't seem to get them straight. I can't do anything right."

Above her, Pollux mopped the same circle of wood again and again. He'd mopped it so many times, he'd cleaned it of varnish.

Castor didn't think there could be anything worse than Gen and her brother fawning all over each other. She had wished for them to break up a thousand times. Pollux was far too good for the Mazon. She was a MindWorker, and she came from poor stock. Circus folk. She was handy in a fight, true, but she wasn't worthy of becoming family.

Now Cas had her wish, and she wanted to take it back. She needed Gen and Lux at their best to face whatever danger awaited them on the isle. According to the map, they would reach the danger by tomorrow afternoon. Pollux had to cover her on storms, and Gen needed to smash, break, crush, or control everything else. Cas couldn't do this on her own.

She made her way to Adikia and carefully unrolled the map.

Pieces of the brittle corners broke off in the wind and floated out to sea.

Castor traced her finger gently across the paper. "According to this, as soon as we pass that small isle"—she pointed out to sea—"we need to head south."

Adikia squinted one eye. "I know that."

"How?"

"I memorized the map." Adikia tapped her forehead. "When you're stealing information, it's best to keep it in a place where no one can touch it."

"Then we were shot at by that horse woman's arrows for no reason? We could have left the map and you could have just . . . memorized it?"

"No." Adikia tugged her hat slightly lower. "I didn't have it memorized then. I do now. I needed to look at it a few times."

Cas shook her head and pulled out a vial of wind to push the sails. They ballooned outward, and the ship rose on the gentle waves.

They neared the small island. Cas picked up the spyglass and made out a mound of rock overgrown with grass and wildflowers and crumbling stone structures that looked long abandoned. The ship bobbed along on the breaker waves until Adikia cut the wheel and Castor shifted the direction of the wind. They circled around the island and cut back the other way.

Gen dropped her ropes. "We're going south."

Castor rolled her eyes. "You are such a gifted navigator. How did you figure that out?"

"The Oracle told me to go northwest."

"And we did," Castor said. "Now the map is telling us to go south."

"The Oracle didn't—"

"Maybe the Oracle sent us northwest to find Kyknos and the map," Adikia suggested.

"Or maybe the map is wrong," Gen said.

"Maybe your Oracle was wrong," Castor said. "When did you become so devout? What has your Oracle Keres ever done for you? Apart from making you an outcast?"

Gen flinched.

"I'll trust a map I can see with my own eyes over some half-thought-out directions from an Oracle who, may I remind you, serves our enemy." Castor wondered if she would have trusted the Oracle's word even if she had seen it for herself. Doubtful.

Gen chewed on her lower lip, stewing. "Let me see the map."

Castor's eye twitched. That was exactly what she didn't want. "It's fragile. The more I unroll it, the more damaged it becomes. Adikia has seen it. She can vouch for me."

"It says south," Adikia concurred.

Somewhere behind Castor, a mop dropped to the deck.

"Why won't you let her see it, Cas?" Pollux sounded more like himself than he had in days—at the most inopportune time, of course.

"I want to see the map," Gen said, her tone more demanding.

"Fine." Cas reached into her jacket. She held out the map to Gen, and then, with a flick of her pointer finger, lashed it in wind. The gust shredded the parchment and carried the pieces into the air, where they floated before disintegrating into the sea. She hoped Adikia wasn't lying when she said she had it memorized.

"Look what you've done!" Castor shouted. "I told you it was too fragile."

"You did that on purpose." Gen closed one of her silver fists.

Castor took a step back. "How dare you accuse me of such a thing?"

Pollux knelt and picked up a shred of map that lingered on the deck. He twisted it in his fingers for a few seconds before it crumbled to dust. "What are you trying to hide, Cas?"

"Nothing. Do you honestly think I would do anything to hurt my chances of getting those apples? They are the only way I can save Arcadia."

"You mean they're the only way you can save yourself."

"Same thing."

"That's what worries me," he said. "I know you would do anything to get those apples."

"Yes, so the one thing I wouldn't do is purposely sail us in the wrong direction."

"That is true."

"We've followed your Oracle's directions for days," Cas said. "I think it's only fair we follow mine for a while. If the map was correct, we'll find the Isle of Hesperides by tomorrow afternoon. If it was wrong, we'll lose only a day, and we can turn back."

Her brother looked to Gen for a response.

Gen threw up her arms. "Fine, do whatever you want." She returned to Bale and her ropes.

"As usual, you get your way," Lux said to Castor before he tromped across the deck to retrieve his mop. This time, he pushed it across the boards to clean a different spot. A marked improvement.

Castor held her hand over her eyes to shield her face from the sun. A natural wind pooled in the sails. She stopped using her own wind to conserve the vials. Twenty-four. She worried they wouldn't be enough. They were never enough.

She approached her brother on the bridge. "How many storm vials do you have left? I might need to borrow some."

He ignored her, staring out to sea.

"Pollux."

"Something is behind us." He pointed to where the waves broke in a straight line.

"Dolphins frequently travel in ship wake. I'm sure it's nothing to worry about. I only want to know if you see one of Nessos's ships. How many vials do you have? Because I think I should hold on to them." He was too distracted to be holding on to vials of lightning. She should have them. For safekeeping. "Never mind, I'll just go get them myself."

"No, you won't." Lux dropped his mop. "The last time you went into my room unguarded, I came back to it flooded with three inches of rainwater."

"Lux, we were ten, and besides, you had tattled to Mother that I was the one who'd ruined her blue dress. It was the least you deserved."

"I'm coming with you."

"Fine," she sighed, and went with him belowdecks, into the damp underbelly of the ship. It had already been flooded. It wasn't like she could flood it more.

Pollux's cabin smelled slightly worse than the rest of the ship. It had the distinct odor of three unwashed young men. Castor held her nose. This made Gen's dog smell like a bouquet of flowers.

Pollux sat on his bed and removed a box of storm vials from underneath his bunk. When he flipped it open, Cas quickly counted thirty vials. He had been holding out on her.

"I think I've done something horrible," he said.

"Yes, you have." She reached for the box. "You've hidden your best storms from me."

Pollux slid the box away from her. "No, with Gen."

Cas rolled her eyes. She supposed he would hold the vials until she listened to his whining. "Lux, as long as I've known you, you have never done anything terrible. I'm sure it's fine. Can I see those vials?"

"It's not fine. I've hurt Gen. Irreparably. I thought I was helping her, but I'm wondering now if I made a mistake."

Cas slumped on the bed beside him. "If it was a mistake, then apologize and get back together." That would shake off their poor moods and put them in better shape to reach the apples.

He turned to her, his ice-blue eyes rimmed red. "I lied to her, Cas. I let her believe the reason I didn't want to be with her was because I couldn't handle her power. When we kiss . . . she can see my thoughts."

"She can control you through kissing?" The depths to which the MindWorkers sank never ceased to surprise her.

"She can't control me. I can't control myself. She can see . . . everything."

"Then you were right to dump her. That is unsettling."

"I don't care. I mean, I do care when there is something I don't want her to see. If I had been better at controlling myself . . . but I didn't know how else to do it."

"Do what?"

"Not let her know."

"Know what?"

He took a long breath and stared at his folded hands. "I didn't tell you everything the Oracle said to me. She was much more specific about the danger we would face on this trip than I led you to believe. She told me . . . she told me I wouldn't survive it."

Cas looked at her brother, with his high cheekbones and pale hair. He was almost the mirror image of their mother, right down to the long, slender fingers and thin-lined nose. She had always hated him for that. For being their mother's favorite. For much of their lives, he had been the knife in her side, the one that caused her great pain. But if she yanked it out, she knew she would bleed to death.

"I'm wondering now, though," Pollux continued, "if it was a false prediction. Or maybe she didn't know everything. She told Gen to go northwest, but if your map is correct, and we find the apples to the south of us, then she either led us in the wrong direction on purpose, or she made a mistake. And if so, maybe her prediction about me is a mistake too." He shook his head. "I don't know. Maybe that's just what I want to believe."

"Then believe it, Lux."

He turned to face her. "What?"

"Believe it. Make it true. The Oracles don't control me. I make my own fate. You do too. You wanted Gen; you got Gen. You never wanted to be Duke of Storms, and now you won't be. No Oracle told you to do those things. You did them on your own."

Some of the bleakness left her brother's face. He spent far too much time inside his own thoughts. She was glad, sometimes, that she could be the rope to lead him out of them.

"Maybe you're right," he admitted.

"I'm always right."

He laughed. "I would have to argue with that."

Despite his insult, it was good to hear him laugh again. She could prod him later about what a fool he'd been to let some Oracle prediction turn him into a sappy-eyed mess.

"You can't tell Gen the truth," he said.

"I don't plan on it." Castor reached down and picked up a couple of his storm vials. Wind, rain . . . lightning. Yes, she would take this one. And this one.

"She would do what she had to do to save me," her brother continued.

"I know." The last thing Castor wanted was for Gen's complete focus to be on Pollux. The Mazon needed to save her strength for the apples, and the Cerberus.

Castor grabbed three more lightning vials and tucked them into her belt.

"I'm going to take these for safekeeping." She started for the door, then stopped. "When this is all over, you can tell Gen everything, and she'll forgive you. She's actually not the most unreasonable person I know."

"Such high praise, Cas."

"It is. From me. Considering she almost killed me once, I think I'm being more than generous."

She left with her lightning vials and returned to the bridge, in-haling deeply of the salt air to clear the boy smell from her nostrils. Then she shook her head. Pollux. Always believing in prophecies and songs instead of the things that were real, like wealth and power.

"Oy!" Adikia shouted to Bale. "Take care of that loose rope on the mizzen mast, before the whole thing tears loose. Lazy crew," she muttered under her breath.

Cas smiled. Maybe, in the rarest possibility, Adikia could be something real one day too.

~

Castor awoke hours later to the rumbling thunder of an impending storm. She sat upright. Gen and the mutt slept soundly, the dog snoring as loud as the thunder. Castor removed her box of empty vials from under the bed and made her way upstairs. She could stock the vials with the fresh storm.

When she reached the deck, she found Adikia near the rails with the spyglass to her nose, focused on the dark clouds ahead. A spark of lightning shot across the sky. Her heart sped up.

"Storm ahead," Adikia said, without turning around.

"Perfect."

Adikia folded up her spyglass and hung it on her belt. "I know you like storms, but most seafaring folk don't."

"It's a good thing I'm here, then," Cas said. When Adikia smiled at her with her slightly crooked front teeth, Castor's cheeks warmed. She couldn't help herself. She always liked to chase the most violent of storms.

"It would be nice to keep one of you StormMakers on board. Too bad that once you have your apples, you'll have to go back to doing Duchess stuff."

"You could——" Cas stopped before she made a fool of herself.

"I could what?" Adikia tilted her head to the side.

Not that it would be ridiculous for Adikia to come to Arcadia. There was a place for her there. "You could sail for Arcadia. We're always in need of good captains to run shipments." There. She'd said it. She didn't want Adikia to go once this was all done, and she always needed people around her she could tolerate.

Adikia laughed. "You want me to turn legitimate?"

To be fair, not all the Arcadian shipments were legal. "You'll have your annuity. It's not like you'll have to steal anymore."

"That doesn't mean I want to work for you."

"Forget I mentioned it."

"That's exactly what I plan to do."

Adikia clearly didn't want to stay with her. Castor grabbed an orange from their stores and peeled it with her thumb. She ate one of the withered segments. Their food supplies were getting thin. What they hadn't lost in the flood was either half-rotted or dried out. She hoped they could find some real apples on Hesperides, along with her golden ones.

She dropped the peels over the side of the ship, where they bobbed on the smooth sea. Odd. A storm this close should have some wind. Enough to affect the water.

She made her way to the prow and breathed in the air. She tasted the tang of electricity, but there was something else, something sour. Something unnatural.

"There is something different about that storm," she said. "Where does it fall on the map?"

"Once we get through it, we should see the Isle of Hesperides."

Castor remembered the *Death Awaits* warning on the map. Was this it? This unnatural storm? She smiled. If so, they had absolutely nothing to worry about. Magic storm or not, it was still a storm, and she had yet to meet a tempest she couldn't control.

Behind the storm came the gray light of dawn, struggling to break through the clouds. The rest of their crew ambled onto the deck. Gen and her dog came first, followed by Flek and Pollux and eventually Bale. They picked through the crate of oranges, trying to find the least spoiled of them. Gen and Pollux grazed hands, reaching for the last orange.

"You take it," he said to her.

"No, you should."

"I'm not hungry." Pollux shoved the orange at Gen and walked away.

Castor wasn't sure she could suffer this polite indifference for the rest of the trip. It reminded her too much of her parents.

She watched Pollux approach the prow.

"There is something not right with that storm," he called. "It sounds wrong."

"It *is* wrong," Castor agreed. The closer they sailed to it, the more *wrong* it felt. Usually, the storms reached for her. This one wanted to push her away. "I think it's enchanted. But I can handle it."

"I hear music," he said. "Singing." He tapped his fingers on the rail in a rhythmic beat.

Castor leaned over the rail and strained her ears. She heard only the rumble of thunder and the patter of rain.

Gen set down her uneaten orange and tilted her head. "I hear it too. It's a sad song."

"Not for me," Pollux said. "It's cheerful. Don't you hear the staccato rhythm?"

Adikia took off her hat. "I feel like I know this song. But I can't quite remember it."

When Castor closed her eyes and shut out the storm, she finally heard it too—a song carried on the wind in ghostly notes. It made her feel powerful. Strong.

"Cover your ears!" Bale shouted. "No one listen!"

Cas stared at the blue man. "What are you going on about?"

He grabbed her by the wrist and shoved her hand toward her ear. "Cover your ears. *Now.* Your map has led us right to the sirens."

"The what?" Gen asked.

"The sirens," Bale said. "They're women. Sea creatures. They lure sailors into the sea and devour them. They're children of the Oracle Arai."

"How do you know this?" Adikia asked.

"I read. Now cover your ears!"

Adikia clamped her hands over her ears. "I can still hear them."

Castor could too. The longer she listened, the more she wanted to grab the wheel and use her strongest wind to push them directly into the heart of the storm despite knowing the danger.

"I know what to do." Gen reached into her bag and pulled out a small tin filled with cotton. "Whisper moth cocoon."

She tore it into small pieces and looked at the lumps in her hand. Castor counted only six.

"I don't have enough," Gen whispered.

Flek nudged her and mouthed, *"I don't need it."* He was the only one unbothered by the song. As much as Castor hated struggling to read his notes and lips, this would be a great advantage for them—one less person the sirens could control.

The siren's song turned louder, tying itself around Castor's heart and pulling her to the sea.

Come to us for what you seek,

We have the prize beneath the sea.

Castor shook her head to drive the voices out. "That still leaves us with only enough for three. Two of us will have to go without."

"Keep some for yourself," Bale said to Gen. "Tie me up and anyone else who doesn't get the cotton." He jabbed a finger at her. "You'd better do everything in your power to keep us from jumping into that water."

"I will," Gen said. "I promise."

Flek waved his hands toward Adikia and mouthed, *"We need someone to sail the ship."*

"You're right." Gen handed two pieces to Adikia, which left only enough cocoon for one other person.

You don't need them, you will see,

We have everything you need.

Castor turned to the water, and the storm. Of course the sirens were right. She didn't need Gen or her foul bug carcasses. The sirens would help her.

No. She pressed her fingers to her temples. The monsters had invaded her mind. She needed to close them out. She turned to the last two wads of cotton on Gen's palm.

Gen reached her hand to Pollux. "Take them. They're yours."

Pollux picked up the cocoon husks, his fingers grazing Gen's palm. Cas bowed her head. Of course Gen would give them to him. Gen would probably be delighted if Cas drowned herself in the sea.

"She told me this would happen. She said I needed to know my fate to make it true. This is it. This was why," Pollux said.

"What are you talking about?" Gen asked.

"Here." Pollux tapped Castor on the shoulder and handed her the cocoon. "You take them. To control the storm. You'll do better than I will."

"Are you sure?" Castor asked.

"I'm sure."

Cas closed the cocoon husks in her fist.

A mistake was made, your choice is wrong,

You need to listen to our song.

"No!" Gen grabbed Lux by the arm. "You need to take them."

Pollux ran his thumb down Gen's jawline. "I trust you, and Cas, to look after me. I know you won't let me drown."

"No, never."

Pollux leaned down and kissed Gen on the forehead.

Cas turned away and shoved the cocoon husks into her ears before she had to witness any more sad farewells. Everything went silent. The siren's song, the sound of the storm, the waves slapping against the ship . . . all gone. Only her heartbeat thudded in her ears.

While Adikia steered the ship, Bale and Pollux sat back-to-back against the mast. Gen, Flek, and Cas twisted heavy ropes around them. When Cas dropped the rope over Lux's legs, she noticed a bead of sweat running down the side of his face. He was fighting hard against the sirens' song. She wondered what they sang to him.

Maybe she should have felt guilty, taking the cocoon husks from him when she knew he'd only given them up because he thought he was fated to die. But he had made a valid point. She *would* contain that storm better than he would. And Gen would do everything in her power to keep him on this ship.

To make sure, Cas turned to Gen and mouthed, *"He gets off this ship and you die."*

They'd all gotten better at reading lips with the MetalBender on board, so when Gen jabbed her finger and said, *"That storm sinks us and you die,"* Castor understood every word.

As Gen picked up her dog to secure him belowdecks, Cas turned to face the storm. They were close enough now that it hummed across her skin in delicious electricity. Lightning shot across the sky and buzzed through her bones. She flipped open the caps on all her empty vials. Oh, the things she could do with an enchanted storm.

Adikia kept the ship on a steady path directly toward the clouds.

The sky went dark, and the wind tore through Castor's clothes and hair. Still, the sea remained smooth.

At the mast, Bale clawed at the ropes holding him down. "I have to get off the ship! I need to save her!" she saw him say.

Gen emerged from belowdecks and tugged on the knots to make sure they were secure.

"Let me go!" Bale writhed against his bonds. Gen pressed her hand to his chest to calm him. He turned and snapped at her, trying to bite her fingers.

Castor pushed the cocoon husks farther into her ears, glad she'd silenced the siren voices before they'd driven her to that kind of madness.

On the other side of the mast, Lux sat quietly pensive with his jaw clenched and his forehead beaded in sweat. *Keep fighting*, she thought. Her brother had always excelled at enduring.

Up ahead, a pile of rocks rose out of the water in the one patch of sunlight that broke through the clouds. The sirens sat upon them, singing their foul songs. From here, Cas made out only their silhouettes.

A gust of wind struck the ship and rocked it hard to port. Castor grasped the railing to keep herself steady.

Adikia held tight to the wheel with both hands and mouthed, *"Do something!"*

"I am!" Castor shouted back. She stood upright and reached her hands to the sky. She called to the storm, and it didn't come to her. Impossible. She stretched her fingers and demanded it. How dare it refuse her? Small wisps of the storm separated from the mass and curled down to her, like a sweater unraveling one thread at a time. The enchantment on this storm didn't want to let go.

She reached her arms higher, stretched her fingers wider.

You will come to me, Storm. Do you know who I am? I am the Duchess of Storms, the Wielder of Lightning, the Mistress of Rain, and you will obey me.

Larger gusts of wind peeled away from the mass. She ripped them free, like tearing a piece of cloth.

The gusts wrapped around her arms, and she dumped them into an empty storm vial. The ship settled back against the ocean. Castor continued to shred the storm to pieces. She would never let a storm get the best of her.

Behind her, something hit the deck. The rattle of it shook her boots.

Lux had lost his battle against the sirens. He writhed against his ropes so violently that he managed to wriggle an arm free. Gen tried to grab his wrist to restrain him. He raked his claws against her cheek instead.

"I have to go to save you!" he mouthed.

Now Cas saw the problem. If she had been in Pollux's position, Gen would have broken both of her arms to keep her in place. Gen was being too gentle with her dear Pollux, trying to negotiate him back into his bonds like she would an unruly child.

Flek tried to help. He melted metal in his palms to make handcuffs. But Bale kicked him in the shins, and the metal slipped from Flek's hands.

A blast of lightning struck the front of the ship. A piece of the smoking rail dropped into the water. Castor raised her hands to the sky to control the storm. They had reached the rocks and the sirens, who settled in the one break in the clouds, draped in sunlight. The beautiful creatures opened their mouths in song, and even though Cas couldn't hear them, she couldn't look away.

They were lightning, wind, rain, coin, power . . . all the things she loved made real. They beckoned to her with bodies of soft, supple flesh and arms adorned with jewels. Below their waists, long, shimmering tails licked at the water.

Temptresses, she thought, and wondered how they would like to have their own magical storm shoved in their faces. She reached up to pull more wind from the sky.

Something slammed into her shoulder. She lost her hold on the storm and tumbled to the railing. *How dare—*

She spun around to find Gen and Pollux wrestling on the deck.

Gen held both of his arms, trying to get him under control. Pollux screamed and writhed, fighting to get free. Gen wasn't holding him hard enough. Cas had seen her break apart a giant crab, and she was treating Pollux like porcelain.

"Break him!" Castor shouted, but only Pollux and Bale could hear her, and Bale was wrestling with Flek. The MetalBender had one band of metal wrapped around Bale's arm and was trying to get the other end attached to the ship while Bale clawed at him.

She would have to do this herself. She reached for a vial of lightning as Pollux shoved Gen aside, sending her skidding across the deck. Pollux snapped his head to Castor.

Before, she would have said he'd looked like their mother. Now he looked exactly like Father: cold and calculating. She flung her lightning toward his shins. She would burn him into submission.

The white light exploded—and shrank.

Pollux caught the ball of lightning in his palm. He bounced it up and down on his hand, grinning at her.

But Pollux couldn't do that. *Didn't* do that. Except he had.

Gen rushed at him from the side. He tossed his lightning at her.

Castor grabbed some wind from the storm and pushed the spark out to sea. When Pollux returned to normal, he would never forgive himself if he'd lit Gen on fire.

Gen ran for the ropes to retie him. She lashed one around his legs, and Pollux grabbed a gust of wind and swirled it in his hands. When Gen swung a rope around his arm, Pollux unleased the gale.

The tunnel of wind struck Gen in the chest. She slid across the deck and slammed into the prow, hard enough to snap the railing. She tumbled over the side and held on to the ship with one hand.

Pollux straightened his jacket and turned toward the sirens. He made for the rails and lifted himself over. The fool was going to jump. Castor yanked wind from the sky and curled it around his chest. She pulled hard.

He didn't move.

He turned over his shoulder and smiled. A cruel smile. This wasn't the brother she knew. This wasn't the brother she loved. The sirens had turned him into something else—a monster that wore his skin.

Lux reached his hand to the sky, and the enchanted storm obeyed him, swirling down around his fingers. He shoved it at her.

Castor held up her hands and pushed it back at him, straining every muscle, bone, and nerve in her body. She dug her boots into the deck. Pollux reached his arms out farther, and she slid back an inch. Her elbows buckled. The wind pushed her another inch, and Pollux's smile widened.

"Did you ever think maybe I didn't strike you as hard as I could because I didn't want to?"

He'd asked her that once, and she had considered it. She'd known Lux never used the full reach of his abilities.

He used all of it now.

This was Pollux unleashed. No conscience. No forgiveness.

And she couldn't hold him.

He pulled back on the wind, and she stumbled forward. She lost her hold on the storm, and when he shoved it back, she couldn't catch it. It struck her in the side and knocked her to the deck. When she looked up, she caught one last glimpse of him before he leapt from the ship.

"No!" she screamed, the sound echoing only in her chest.

She saw Gen open her mouth in the same cry. The Mazon ran to the rails and kicked up her leg. She was going to jump too.

Castor got to her feet and grabbed Gen by the arm. The fool would only kill herself trying to save Pollux. He wouldn't want that.

Gen tried to twist free, but Castor held strong. Then Gen drew her fist back and cracked her knuckles into Castor's cheek. Pain lanced across Castor's jaw as she fell to the deck. And Gen disappeared over the rails.

CHAPTER 26

GEN

G en hit the icy water and sank. Hands snatched her before she could drop too far. Cold, sharp fingers pulled at her clothes and hair. Nails raked her skin. Salt water stung the wounds. Gen punched and kicked in every direction. Her fist made contact with something soft. She broke free and swam for the surface.

She took a deep breath and screamed, "Pollux!"

With the cocoon husks, her scream fell silent on her own ears, but he would hear her. He *had* to hear her. A hand snatched her leg. She kicked it away. Another grabbed at her waist. She twisted herself free. One of the sirens leapt onto her back and pushed her under.

Gen managed a gasp of air before the dark water swallowed her. She opened her eyes, and one of the cruel, beautiful sirens stared back at her. She jerked in the siren's grasp and searched the waters for a sign of Pollux. His white hair or ivory skin. His piercing blue eyes.

She shouldn't have let him give away the cocoon husk. She should have made him take it.

Her lungs screamed for air. She twisted from the siren's grip and swam upward. Her head broke through, and she coughed out green water. Another siren lunged for her, opening her mouth, some of her glamour peeling away to reveal sharp teeth and black eyes.

Gen pushed the siren away. Another hand scratched her arm. She sucked in a small breath and sank into the sea. She couldn't fight them in the water. They had the advantage here. But she couldn't give up on Pollux. She elbowed another siren in the side and caught a flash of white—Pollux. She snatched at his arm and kicked her way to the ship.

She reached for one of the ropes and heaved herself upward, dragging Pollux behind her. Holding him with one hand, she scrambled her way up the ship. She threw him over the rails and followed. She coughed up seawater and looked down at the figure sprawled across the deck.

It wasn't Pollux.

It was one of the sirens.

Her white hair clung to her bronzed skin. She opened and closed her mouth, screaming or singing. Whatever sound she made caused Bale to bury his head in his arms and cry. Gen looked back to the water. She could no longer see the other sirens. They were gone. So was Pollux.

No, that couldn't be. Even when she had tried to run away from him, he'd always appeared. Even after he'd broken her heart, he'd still been there. He wouldn't leave her like this.

Gen gazed down at the shrieking siren, and fire burned in her veins. This creature knew where Pollux was, and she would bring him back.

She snatched the siren by the neck and lifted her from the deck. "Where is he?"

The siren pulled at Gen's fingers with her mouth wide open. If she spoke an answer, Gen couldn't understand it.

Enough of this. Gen held her bleeding arm to the siren's open mouth. A few drops of blood fell onto the creature's lips, and Gen's mind magic snapped into place. The siren exuded great fear and great hunger. It reminded Gen of when she had briefly connected to the Hydra. This was a creature with no empathy, no thoughts, no dreams. She wanted only one thing: to devour anything that sailed these waters.

"Where is he?" Gen shouted at her. This time, she got an answer.

We ate him. So delicious.

Gen's lip quivered. Her grip on the siren tightened. "You're lying."

So delicious, the siren repeated. She licked her lips and fed images of her sharp teeth sinking into Pollux's pristine flesh and ripping pieces of him free.

Bile rose in Gen's throat. Hot tears burned in her eyes. "What did you sing to him? What made him leap?"

She had heard only a few lines from the sirens' song before she'd clogged her ears with the cocoon husks. They had promised her they would get her the apples and the Cerberus and they would set her free. But what had Pollux wanted so desperately?

We told him if he came to us, all his friends would live.

Tears rolled down Gen's cheeks. Of course that would be his greatest desire, to sacrifice himself for everyone else. And Gen . . . she had wanted only her prizes. She had been such a fool. She'd already had her prize—Pollux. And now he was gone. She had gone into this quest thinking only of her father and her own future. She had rushed into it, and she had sacrificed Pollux to do it.

So delicious, the siren repeated, sharing thoughts of the taste of Pollux's skin. Gen tightened her grip on the monster's throat.

Someone touched her arm.

She spun around to Flek, who pointed to Bale and mouthed something to her. Gen tried to make out the words on his lips through her tears. Something about being owed a favor. She shook her head. She didn't understand.

She flicked her eyes to Bale, whose lips formed the words, "You caught the siren! She owes you a favor." He returned to clawing at his ears.

Gen turned back to the siren. She dug her thumb into the creature's neck. The siren's scaled tail flipped back and forth wildly as she clawed at Gen's fingers with her sharp nails. Blood leaked down Gen's wrist, but she didn't feel it. She couldn't feel anything except anger at this thing. At herself for letting Pollux go.

"I've caught you," she said. "You owe me something."

I owe you nothing.

Had Bale been mistaken about the favor? No. He had been right about everything else in Elysium so far.

"If you owe me nothing, then I owe you nothing." Gen squeezed the siren's neck tighter. The creature's bronzed skin turned pale, and the veins burst around her eyes.

I can give you something, the siren screeched in her head. *I can give you the apples.*

"We know where the apples are."

You know the location, but you will never reach them without my advice, and I will tell you the secret if you set me free.

Gen loosened her fingers. Without Pollux, the quest was all she had left. "How do we get them?"

Find the man named Atlas on the isle if you want any hope of survival.

"That's it? That is all you have to give me after taking away—" A knot closed in her throat. She couldn't say his name. He had been her love. Her partner. Her soul mate.

That is all you need, the siren hissed. *Now set me free.* The siren showed her a memory of Pollux shrieking in pain. Gen couldn't bear to see any more. She flung the siren out to sea.

When the creature hit the water, she swam away far and fast. The tether of the mind magic snapped, and Gen sighed with relief. But she would never forget the things the siren had shown her of Pollux's pain, his last moments of being alive.

She threw up over the ship's edge. Everything hurt: her chest, her eyes, her arms, her legs, her ears, her hands. She tore the cocoon husks from her ears and threw them into the sea.

They had passed through the storm. Ahead, the Isle of Hesperides rose out of the ocean. But she didn't care. She would get the apples. She would catch the Cerberus. She would save her father. But she would never, ever feel joy again.

She broke into a sob. All her Mazon strength poured through her, unspent. She spun around, drew her fist back, and punched the first thing she saw: the main mast. Flek yanked Bale out of the way just before her knuckles smashed into the wood. A crack split down its center, the break running from the bottom of the mast to the top.

Everyone was watching her, afraid and unsure. Even Castor. She should have been as miserable as Gen. He'd been her brother. Why did she look so calm and collected?

"Why didn't you stop him?" Gen asked.

"I tried," Castor said. "He wasn't himself. I—couldn't."

"He's *gone*," Gen said, because Castor didn't seem to understand. He wasn't coming back. "They *ate* him. The siren showed me how they tortured him. How they tore him to pieces." Gen's stomach turned again.

"I know."

"Then why aren't you crying?"

"He knew," Castor whispered. "He knew it was coming."

"What?"

"The Oracle told him he wouldn't survive. I didn't think it was real."

Gen shook her head. No. If the Oracle had told him something like that, he would have . . . done exactly what he did.

He would have kept it to himself. Suffered silently. Sacrificed himself to keep her from throwing away her hopes at saving her father. He would have lied to her about why he didn't want to be with her. Because he would have known she'd discover his secret if they kissed enough times.

Gen clutched her stomach and bent over. It had been happening all along. Right in front of her. And she had been so preoccupied with her own needs, she had completely missed it.

"I'm sorry," Castor said.

Gen turned on her. Castor *should* be sorry. So very sorry. "You should have told me. You knew, and you didn't tell me because you had to get your precious apples. You knew why Pollux was giving up the cocoon husks, and you took them anyway. What did the map say, Castor? What else were you hiding?"

"Nothing," Castor said.

"Liar!" Gen shouted. "You could have saved him, and instead you let him die so you could get your way."

Castor flinched. Gen made out the red marks on Castor's pale cheek from where she had punched her. Not hard enough.

"I want you gone," Gen said. "I never want to see you again." Looking at her reminded Gen too much of Pollux. They had the same pale eyes. The same wispy white hair.

"You need me if you want your father. He's all you have left."

Gen lunged.

Bale grabbed her by the wrist. He looked almost as wrung out as she felt. "Gen. I hate her as much as you do, but now is not the time."

Gen shook herself free. "You're right. The time was when Pollux told her he knew he was going to die and she did nothing."

She stormed belowdecks to Pollux's cabin. She sat on his bed and picked up his violin. Pain cut through her insides. *I knew he was upset about something. I should have tried harder to find out what it was. I should have told him that having my father and my freedom would be worthless without him.*

She ran her finger down one of the strings, and it made a humming sound. Fresh tears spilled from her eyes. She took the violin in both hands and twisted. The metal whined and groaned, and the strings snapped. She dropped the unrecognizable piece of metal to the ground.

No one would ever play it again. She never wanted to hear music again. She buried her face in his pillow and breathed in fresh rain and summer winds, the last scents of him.

CHAPTER 27

CASTOR

Castor held a cold cloth to her swollen cheek while Adikia examined the skin around it.

"You're probably going to have a black eye." Adikia's small fingers gently prodded the wound.

"Wonderful." This was the appreciation Castor got for trying to stop Gen from throwing herself into a sea of murderous sirens. And it hadn't worked. Gen had launched herself into the sea anyway, and she hadn't returned with Pollux.

The ache twisted in Castor's chest. She pushed it aside and buried it with the rest of her pain. His death knotted inside her so tightly, she felt like a tangled rope. But sobbing over him, or childishly smashing the mast, wouldn't bring him back.

The ship bobbed on the water in front of the Isle of Hesperides. The dark storm cloud loomed behind them. Castor had filled three vials with it, and that had barely calmed the wind.

Death Awaits.

Behind closed eyes, she saw the warning on the map. She had thought she was above death. She had thought she could blast it away with a sharp gust like everything else.

"I never thought he would die," she said to Adikia. "Or I would have done more." She thought of her advice to Pollux to control his own destiny. Well, he had. He'd controlled it when he'd given her the cocoon husks, and she'd helped him fulfill it by taking them.

Another knot formed in her insides.

"I don't believe much in prophecies, either," Adikia said. "Fortune tellers always promise wealth and love you never get."

"It wasn't some market fortune teller. It was an Oracle who gave him the prediction." Bale stepped down from the bridge. "I knew something was bothering him. I should have made him tell me. If I had known, *I* would have made Lux keep the cocoon husks." He glared pointedly in Castor's direction. As if it were her fault.

It is your fault.

"You don't know what it was like," Bale continued. "Those creatures, they get into your head and they steal away all reason. All I could think about was that song. I wanted it. I wanted to hold it. I wanted to breathe it and eat it. They promised me everything. If I'd been able to . . ." He shook his head. "I would have jumped too."

"I know," Castor said, even though she didn't know. She'd only heard a piece of the song. But she'd seen the look in Pollux's eyes and felt the power of his storms. He had lost all control.

"I'm sorry," Flek mouthed as he came back from sweeping debris from the deck, the pieces of burned and broken railing. *"I tried to hold him. I tried to hold you both."*

"If Gen couldn't, you couldn't," Bale said.

"I'm worried about her." Flek nodded toward the broken mast.

"I am too." Bale clapped a hand on his shoulder. "Give her some time. And try to watch her fists."

Castor pressed the cool cloth to her eye. She would be the primary target for Gen's rage. She had seen it in the girl's face, the utter fury and pain. Another knot twisted in her chest. Gen had really loved her brother. If Cas could go back, she would have done things differently. But she couldn't. She could only sail onward.

"We can't go any closer to the isle," Adikia said, as if reading her thoughts. "Not without grounding ourselves. We should drop anchor here."

The Isle of Hesperides rose from the water in front of them. Green hills sprouted up from the beach, and a thin plume of smoke rose somewhere in the distance. Castor abandoned her swollen eye and led the others to the prow.

They climbed into the dinghy. Adikia sat close to Castor while Bale and Flek pulled the ropes to lower them to the water. When they reached the sea, Adikia took the oars and pulled them to the shore.

They struck sand. Castor used a vial of wind to part the shallows. Crabs, no longer covered by water, scurried to find their way back to the sea. Castor dropped into the wet sand and made her way to the beach without soaking her boots. Flek and Adikia pulled the dinghy up beside her.

"We're here." Castor inhaled salt air and something more fragrant and flowery. Birds swooped overhead and made their way inland. Bale kicked at the sand and picked up something from the ground. It looked like part of a sword. Half charred and . . . bitten?

A shudder rolled down Castor's spine. The map had said *Death Awaits*. Maybe the sirens had only been the beginning.

"We probably shouldn't go too far," she said. Not without Gen, whose rage would come in handy if some sword-chewing monster came their way.

But Castor worried that wouldn't be enough. She looked to her belt, filled with storms. Her eyes lingered on the vials of lightning she had taken from Pollux, and another knot twisted in her chest. She tapped her fingers on the wooden box where Delia slept. Castor needed all her tools and tricks if she wanted to see this through.

She opened the box, and a dull light blinked inside.

"Yes, Lady Castor," Delia said in a petulant tone. "What is it I can do for you?"

Castor had been careful to make sure the box remained latched. No more unplanned escapes for Delia to stab them in the back. She had hoped some time alone in her box would remind Delia who was in charge. Clearly it hadn't.

Castor hated that she had to negotiate with her own indentured spirit for servitude, but here she was, and she had a new piece of information that could change things.

"My brother is dead," she said.

"Oh." Delia rose out of the box. "I'm so sorry. I only hope he has risen to the afterlife and won't be bound forever to a box."

"Not very subtle, are you?"

"Should I be?"

"You are aware that with my brother gone, all my worldly possessions will go to my father if I'm lost. That includes you. I would think it would be in your best interest to make sure I stay alive."

"Why? Would serving your father be any worse than serving you?"

"Yes, because he doesn't negotiate."

"Neither do you."

"I am rethinking my stance on that in light of Pollux's death." Castor tapped her fingers on the side of the box.

"You'll let me go?" Delia blinked rapidly.

Castor swallowed, unable to believe she was about to say this. "Yes . . . eventually. First, I need your help. You help me bring home the apples and the Cerberus, and I will set you free."

"You will?" Delia blinked even faster.

"As long as you do everything I ask without hesitation and don't try to get me killed by Elysium soldiers. You must be the picture-perfect example of a devoted servant or this deal is moot. One mistake, including any unplanned outings, and I will smash this box to dust. Do you understand?"

"Yes, Lady Castor. I will do everything you ask. I swear it."

"Good. Then I need you to look around the island for some food. And let us know if you see anything that could bite through a sword. We would like to avoid that."

"Yes, Lady Castor. Right away."

Delia flitted off, and Castor smiled. Much better. That was the spirit servant she needed: efficient and eager to please.

"I see you made amends with your ghost," Adikia said. She slicked back her wet purple hair. The scales on the nape of her neck glistened in the sunlight.

"I can't take any more chances or make any more assumptions. She'll be a devoted servant until the end. Then I have to set her free."

Adikia put a gentle hand on Castor's arm. So gentle it startled her.

"I am sorry. About your brother," Adikia said. "He was a good person."

"He was." A lump formed in Castor's throat, and she choked it down. She didn't have time for tears.

Adikia drew her hand away and reached for her pocket. She removed two storm vials. "I took these from him, but I think you should have them."

Castor rolled the vials in her fingers. One was a thick fog, the other a thin cloud cover. Not incredibly useful. Not that Adikia would have known that when she'd taken them. She wouldn't have been able to sense the contents.

But even if Adikia hadn't told Castor they had belonged to Pollux, she would have known by their feel. He never chose his storms by strength or endurance. He chose them because of their rhythm, the way they moved.

Tears threatened to escape. She blinked them away and placed the storm vials into her belt. "Thank you," Castor whispered.

"You know it's not a crime if you cry over your lost brother," Adikia said.

Castor turned on her. "Gen can have the tears and fits of rage, and I will keep my sensibilities, thank you."

Delia returned then, blinking feverishly.

"I've found some food," she said. "Over the second hill."

Adikia and Castor followed Delia to a small grove of orange trees. They collected and carried as many of the fruits as they could back to the beach. The sun set over the hills to their left, casting a red-and-purple glow on the surrounding land.

Bale and Flek had managed to catch some fish, and they laid them across flat stones while they pulled together the wood for a fire. Castor dropped her oranges in the sand next to Bale, who fumbled with sticks and dried grass to get a flame. She could have easily started it with a spark of lightning, but she didn't want to waste her storms. Besides, Bale almost had it.

A spark lit the dried grass, and he and Flek fed the fire with small twigs. Flek pierced the fish with a stick and set them up on a spit. Castor sat in the sand and grabbed one of the oranges.

"What's the plan for the apples?" Bale sank back on his heels and brushed sand from his pants.

"I don't know yet." She tossed him an orange. She could send Delia out in the morning to find the apples and survey the scene.

The Hesperides—the daughters of the Oracle Nyx for whom this island was named—still sat between her and her apples. They were witches, though Cas didn't know what kind of magic they had.

Something splashed in the water. Castor turned to see Gen swimming toward them with her dog under her arm. She hadn't bothered with a dinghy. When she reached the shallows, she simply marched through the water and arrived on the beach like some sea creature, dripping with water and seaweed.

Castor could admit, on Gen's better days, she could be somewhat pretty. Now she looked as if she had been dredged out of the mud. Her skin had paled, and red lines rimmed her eyes. She also wore a blue jacket and black pants. Cas had never seen Gen in an outfit that didn't match. Or have sequins on it.

Castor had never thought she would miss the sparkling, over-exuberant circus girl. She'd always thought Gen needed to be more focused. With her talent, the girl could have been something far more than an entertainer. Now Castor would have given up her best jar of lightning for Gen to put on some silly little dog show and be more like herself.

Gen sat down on a rock by the fire. She grabbed one of the oranges and peeled it methodically while she stared into the flames. The dog shook seawater from his fur onto Castor's pant leg. She brushed it off and kicked sand into his face.

"The siren told me how to get the apples," Gen said. "We need to find someone named Atlas."

"Who is Atlas?" Bale asked, and tossed his fish bones into the fire.

"I don't know, but she said he is the only way we will get to the apples."

"Maybe he can get us past Nyx's daughters," Bale said.

"You're going to trust a siren?" Cas asked. "After what they did to Pollux? How do you know she wasn't sending you into a trap with this Atlas person?"

Gen glared at her through the flames. "I was in the siren's head. She wasn't lying."

"Okay," Adikia said. "Then Atlas it is." She tossed her half-eaten fish to the dog, and the beast swallowed it, bones and all.

"I'll send Delia out to look for him in the morning." Castor sighed. She didn't want to pick a fight with Gen at the moment, especially about this.

"Good." Gen grabbed another orange.

Bale stood up. "Take a walk with me, Gen. We need to get more firewood."

"Fine." Gen reluctantly followed Bale down the beach.

Castor's rigid spine eased as Gen walked away. Cas would never admit it to anyone, but she was scared. Gen untethered was like Pollux untethered . . . too powerful for anyone's good.

She shuddered, thinking of how easily he had defeated her on the ship. She'd struggled to snatch the smallest pieces of wind from that storm, and Pollux had played it like one of his songs. Why had he hidden that power for so long? And why hadn't it been enough to save him?

That scared her more than anything.

"I don't think Gen's going to come back from this," Adikia said. She threw another log on the fire. Sparks drifted into the night sky, and the flames curled around the fresh wood.

Flek mouthed, *"Don't say that,"* and repeated the words in sharp hand gestures.

But Castor had to agree with Adikia. Gen wasn't going to come back from this. Not entirely.

Gen and Pollux had loved each other in a way Castor had never seen before, a way she would never know. She would never crumble to pieces at the loss of one person. She had better things to worry about. Like getting the apples and securing her place on Arcadia.

Except now, without Pollux, she would have to do it all alone.

CHAPTER 28

GEN

Gen plucked loose firewood from the beach and carried it under one arm. She found solace in the mundane task. Chomp grasped a few twigs in his teeth and ambled on beside her. Bale held a branch in one hand and a flask in the other. He took a swig and wiped his mouth with the back of his hand.

"I miss him," Bale said.

"I miss him too." So much that she had to make herself numb or the pain of it would destroy her. She'd spent the last hours sobbing into his pillow until she had nothing left. She was physically and emotionally squeezed dry. Only her raw, damaged insides remained.

She had felt this way once before, when her mother had died and her father had been sent to prison. But she'd also had hope, a great, big expanse of hope. With each failure and setback, that hope had become smaller and smaller. Now she barely had any left.

"I've been where you are." Bale took another swig of his drink. "When Andromeda died, I fell. Hard."

He was speaking of his ex-girlfriend, who he had convinced to swim out to sea to rescue her boat with his mind magic. She had drowned, and Bale had become . . . the way he was. They had named Gen's new whale in her memory.

"Then you understand why I feel the way I do," she said.

Bale held the flask up. "Want a drink?"

"No. Thank you." She couldn't disappear completely. She still

265

had something to do. The small hope of reclaiming her father was barely an ember, but it was all she had.

He shrugged. "More for me." He tipped the flask back, and some drops ran down his chin.

Gen picked up another piece of driftwood for the fire. Moonlight glistened off the water near the shore. Clouds covered the rest of the sea, hiding the place where she had lost Pollux.

"After she drowned," Bale said. "I lost control. I used my magic on anyone I could. I would convince barkeeps to pour me extra drinks. I even made a man give up his ship. That ship brought me to Arcadia. Do you know why I stayed?"

"Because they would pay you large amounts of coin for menial tasks?" she said, even though she knew it wasn't entirely true. Bale had loved Pollux. More than his own sister had loved him.

Bale laughed. "That was a bonus, but I picked Arcadia out of all one hundred Olympian isles because of the library. It's the second largest in the Empire. And easier to get into than the Empresses'."

"What did you want from their library?"

"A cure. For this." He pointed to his head. "I didn't want to be a MindWorker anymore. I thought that if an Oracle gave us this power, maybe an Oracle could take it away."

Gen stopped walking. "You wanted to give up your ability?" She had wished not to be a MindWorker many times. But not because she feared her power—because people feared *her* for having it.

Not that it mattered. There was no cure. Keres, the Oracle who had made the MindWorkers, was gone.

"That must have been a waste of your time," she said.

Bale shook his head. "It wasn't. I found the answer. You want to know how I know so much about Elysium? I studied it. I studied their lore, their history, their wars, and I found what I needed in Gaia, the Oracle of Growth, of rebirth. She can take power away. She did it before, during the Elysium and Olympian War. A StormMaker named Aiolos had been making strides for the Olympians, crushing armies with lightning. Gaia stepped in and took away his magic. The Elysiums won the battle."

"That's why you studied Elysium?" Gen asked. "For a way to lose your magic? Why didn't you say something before?"

"You're the only one who knows what I am, Gen."

"Then you could have told me."

"You were preoccupied with your own problems."

Another pain shot through her stomach. Yes, she had been pre-occupied with this quest and worried about Pollux not kissing her when she *should* have been more concerned about *why* he wouldn't kiss her.

"What is your plan, then?" Gen asked. "Do you want to slip away and try to find Gaia?"

"If we find the Hesperides, I'm going to ask them where I might find Gaia. And then I'll find a way to get there." Bale tucked his empty flask into his jacket pocket. "I don't want this anymore. I just want to be . . . normal."

Gen nodded. "If there's anything I can do to help you—"

"I thought you might want to ask her to take your ability too."

"Me?" She pressed her hand to her chest. "No—that's . . . we don't even know if we'll find Gaia, and I need my power for the Cerberus. For my circus." If she hadn't been a MindWorker before, Pollux could have kissed her without worrying about his secrets. But that wouldn't have saved him. It wasn't her magic that had killed him. It was her thoughtlessness. Her selfishness.

"Just thought I'd offer." Bale bent down to pick up a piece of driftwood.

Gen examined his profile in the moonlight, his unshaven blue chin and red-rimmed eyes. It had been years since Andromeda's death, and he continued to punish himself.

Alcmen did too. The death of Gen's mother had shattered him. For a long time, Gen had blamed him for not being strong enough. Now she understood—some burdens were too much to bear. Even for the strongest people.

They made their way back to the fire. Gen tossed fresh wood on the fire and grabbed another orange. She tossed the peels into the flames and watched them char in the embers. The curls of smoke that wafted up reminded her of the cloud creatures Pollux used to make with his violin.

Fresh tears pricked her eyes. She tossed the rest of the orange into the fire. "I'm going to bed."

She picked up Chomp and carried him back into the water. Chomp whined. He didn't like being wet. But Gen needed it. She needed to feel cold and wet and slimy simply to feel something, even if it was uncomfortable.

At the ship, she pulled herself onto the deck and made her way to her cabin. She lay down, sopping boots and all, and covered her eyes with her arm. It didn't matter. The horrifying things she saw were behind her eyes, the images that the siren had fed to her.

If Gen could make a wish of an Oracle, she would ask Gaia to bring Pollux back to her. But she doubted even an Oracle could fix him after what had been done to him. Maybe if she had been able to pull him from the water still alive, she could have used the vial of ambrosia from Kyknos to save him. But she had been too late. Much too late.

Someone stepped into the cabin.

Gen wiped away her tears and sat up. She frowned when she saw Castor in the doorway.

"Oh, it's you." Gen had forgotten she still shared a cabin with her.

"I'm just going to get my things and go stay with Adikia."

"Fine." Gen pulled a piece of seaweed from her jacket and dropped it to the floor.

Castor shoved her expensive jackets and fine boots into a sack. "I miss him, too, you know."

Heat flared on Gen's cheeks. This was something to feel, too, this great and passionate hatred for Castor, destroyer of all things good. "I'm sure you miss having someone to bully and blame for all your problems."

Castor threw her bag of clothes to the ground. "You know nothing of me and my family."

"I was there when you burned him. I was there when you let him leap over the side of the ship to his death."

"And where were you in all this? You could have stopped him. All you had to do was snap his legs and he never would have made it to the railing."

Gen kicked her legs over the side of the bunk. "You wanted me to break his legs?"

"If you had, he would still be alive."

Gen shook her head. "You are unbelievable. I can't hurt people the way you do."

Castor sneered. "You have to be kidding. You hurt people plenty, and the way you do it is even worse. You put on this pretty little smile and act like the downtrodden heroine, then drag everyone into your misery with you." She snatched up her bag. "At least I have the courage to own up to what I am." She flung her bag over her shoulder and stalked from the room.

Gen picked up her boot and threw it at the wall, hard enough to split the wood.

"I hate you," she whispered, and curled into a ball on her bunk. Chomp licked her hand, and she gently nudged him away. She wasn't worth his condolences because Castor . . . Castor was right.

~

The next day, Gen woke with ringing ears and a stiff neck. She rubbed her shoulders and pulled on her boots. She slid into her jacket and swam Chomp to the beach. The early morning sun cascaded over the dunes.

Flek was the only one on the beach. He looked as if he had swum here as well. His pale hair swept from his forehead in glistening blue, not as dark as Bale's. Much lighter. Like the sky on a cloudless day. His shirt sat on a nearby rock, drying in the early sun. With it off, she could see the round scar on his shoulder where he had almost died from a spear wound.

Castor's words rang in her thoughts. *"You drag everyone into your misery with you."*

Flek tossed Gen an orange. *"Sleep well?"* he mouthed.

"No." Gen sat beside him, turning the orange in her fingers. She'd had nightmares of Pollux struggling in the water, screaming for his life while the sirens took large bites of his flesh.

"It's not your fault," Flek mouthed, and made the same words with his hands.

"It's also not *not* my fault," she said.

"We have a saying on Quisces," he mouthed, then picked up a piece of driftwood to write something in the sand.

The caterpillar's song is harmful only to those who hear it.

He set down the wood and looked her in the eye. *"The blame is only yours if you take it."* He pointed three fingers at her, then swept them over his head.

"Wise words," she said. "But I want the blame. I want to feel miserable."

"Pollux wouldn't want you to feel miserable."

"You don't know what he would have wanted."

She had known Pollux best, inside and out. She had seen his inner thoughts, the ones he'd tried to hide from everyone, including himself. Yes, he had sacrificed himself for her in the same way he'd always sacrificed something for someone else. He had done it because he believed it was his purpose. Not because he'd wanted to do it. She owed him so much, the very least she could do was mourn his loss.

Bale, Adikia, and Castor rowed their way to shore in the dinghy. At the sight of Castor's pale hair and high-collared jacket, Gen turned away and wrung her wet hair into the sand. Castor hadn't been wrong. But she'd also done what she always did—refuse to take any responsibility for her own part in what had happened to Pollux.

Castor grabbed an orange and shot Gen a glare. Gen cracked her knuckles and delighted in the flash of fear on Castor's face.

"Delia, I need you to find someone named Atlas." Castor opened the box on her belt and set her sprit free.

"Right away."

The blinking light flitted off over the hills. Gen kicked at the sand and uncovered something underneath, a rock or a shell. She cleared some space around it and realized she had found a bone, a rather large one. She quickly covered it back up.

"I've found him," Delia said, returning.

"Does he seem dangerous?" Gen pressed her boot down on the buried bone.

Delia laughed, blinking with each ghostly giggle. "Not at all."

"Good." Castor swept her hair over her shoulder. "Then let's ask him how to get the apples."

They followed Delia through overgrown grass. It nearly reached Gen's waist. Chomp trailed along behind her, barking at every small creature hidden in the brush. Unkempt orange and pomegranate trees sprouted from the weeds, dripping with fruit. Gen picked oranges from the branches and stuffed them in her bag.

Insects swarmed the isle—and Castor. She waved her arms to chase them away. "Are we almost there?" She slapped a bug on her arm.

"Almost," Delia answered.

"At least she's keeping the bugs away from the rest of us," Bale said.

They crested the hill. Below them sat a small stone cottage with a thatched roof. Beyond it were two more hills, one large, one small. Grass covered the top of the larger one and wrapped around it to the bottom, where an elderly man pulled dirt from the base and dropped it onto the second hill, a much smaller mound of dirt and rocks.

The old man was the first person they'd seen in Elysium who wasn't a centaur. He looked more like them, with two legs, smooth skin, and long, wispy gray hair.

"Here we are." Delia blinked rapidly.

"This is Atlas?" Castor pointed to the elderly man. Gen hadn't known what to expect, either. A monster with claws and teeth? A ten-foot warrior dripping with swords?

"This is him," Delia confirmed.

"At least he's not a threat." Bale scratched his chin.

"Are you sure?" Adikia asked.

"No. I'm making a solid guess based on the fact that he's at least one hundred years old and shaking like a leaf."

"We should talk to him," Flek mouthed.

"We should," Gen agreed. "I'll go first." In case Atlas was more than he seemed.

She led the way down the hill, moving carefully. Old man or not, she wouldn't make any assumptions. He could have razor-sharp claws or spit poison. Nothing was impossible.

At the base, she stood near his thatched cottage and watched him work. *Thump, clump, thump, clump.* One shovelful at a time. Grassy hills sprang up all over this island, surrounding the open fields of orange trees and weeds. Why was he shoveling this one?

Gen cleared her throat. "Are you Atlas?" She spoke in Olympian, hoping he would understand.

"Yes, I am," the man said in perfect Olympian, while he continued to shovel dirt from one mound to the next. He had made a sizeable dent in the first hill. It looked as if some giant beast had taken a bite out of it, instead of an old man moving it shovelful by shovelful.

"We were told by the sirens to ask you where to find the apples," Gen continued. A gust of wind picked up some of the loose dirt to spray it across their faces.

Atlas paused, then resumed shoveling. "You spoke to the sirens?"

"Yes." Gen brushed the dust from her cheeks.

"And you didn't get eaten?"

"No." Her voice cracked on impending tears. She hadn't been eaten, but someone had.

"Impressive." He moved another shovelful of dirt. "Then yes, I can take you to the apples."

"Wonderful," Castor said, as she and the others joined them. "Let's go, then."

"I can't now," Atlas said.

"Why not?" she demanded.

"I have to finish my work first." He gestured to the hill, then dug his shovel into the dirt, moving one more load.

"How much do you have to do?" Castor asked.

"All of it," he said. "I have to move the whole hill."

Bale sputtered out a laugh. "That will take you a thousand years."

"Yep, probably. I've been at it for a hundred and twenty-three and got this far. So come back in about a thousand years, and I'll take you."

They didn't have a thousand years. Or even two years. Gen couldn't leave her father with the Empresses that long. "Can't you take a break?" she asked.

"Nope."

"Why do you need to move the hill?" Bale asked.

"I'm being punished. I'm stuck on this island until I move it over there." He pointed to the second mound. "Then I'm free."

"What are you being punished for?" Adikia asked.

"You don't want to know."

Castor turned to the others and whispered, "We can reach the apples on our own. This island can't be that big."

"You could do that," Atlas called. "But you'd never get past the Hesperides."

"We can handle a few guards," Castor said, tapping her fingers on her storm belt.

"No, you can't," Bale said. "The Hesperides's song will put you to sleep. For years."

"Is that their magic?" Castor waved him away. "They can't sing if they're dead."

Gen shook her head. She didn't want to take any chances with deadly, singing women. The siren had told her Atlas was the way.

"You'll be fast asleep before you can raise a fist to the Hesperides," Atlas said, "but they'll let you pass into the gardens if I ask."

"Why would they listen to you?" Castor asked.

"Because I'm their father, that's why." He dropped another pile of dirt.

Gen eyed the larger hill, covered in grass and flowers, and the smaller hill, a mound of dirt and rocks. Atlas had been carving out the center of the first one. With a big enough push from the other side, and some more of the base scooped out, they might be able to topple it.

"I think we need to help him move the hill," she whispered.

Castor balled her hands on her hips and laughed. "I know you think very highly of yourself, but move a mountain? It will take a hundred years, even for you."

"It's barely a mountain," Bale said.

"I also don't intend to do it alone," Gen said. "Your wind can push the hill."

Castor shook her head. "I'd rather take my chances with the Hesperides and their sleep song."

"I won't. We already lost Pollux because we were unprepared.

I won't lose anyone else." Even Castor, who had more conceit than sense most times.

"If anyone cares——" Bale started.

"They don't," Castor said.

"Even so," he continued, "I think we should try to help the old man. Look at him." He gestured to Atlas, thin and weathered, wearing a torn rag that hung off one bony shoulder. The garment had been aged with years of stains. "If we can't do it, then we can take our chances with the Hesperides."

Flek mouthed, *"I agree,"* and touched his hands to his chin before sweeping them up to his forehead.

Gen pressed her fingers to her lips and raised them upward in what she had learned was Croecian for *thanks*. Even if Atlas hadn't offered to get them to the apples, Gen would still have wanted to help him. She knew what it was like to be burdened with impossible tasks.

"Adikia?" Castor turned to their captain, still searching for support. "What do you think?"

Adikia cocked her head to the side. "That man kind of reminds me of my grandfather. I think we should help him."

Cas threw her arms in the air, finally defeated. "Fine. I guess I'll use up all my wind blowing around dirt."

Gen smiled.

CHAPTER 29

CASTOR

Castor rolled her eyes as Flek tried to wrestle the shovel away from the old man.

"No, don't take that! I need to do my work!" Atlas fought back with brittle fingers.

Didn't the old man realize they were going to help him? Or more likely they would get crushed by falling debris trying to move the dirt.

Flek eventually pried the shovel from Atlas's weathered hands. Atlas kicked dirt at his back and wandered aimlessly in a circle, muttering to himself.

They had collected four more shovels from inside Atlas's home, all twisted and bent and tinged with rust. Flek dropped the five shovels at his feet, then held his hands over them, fingers glowing red. The metal ends of the shovels melded together. He twisted and shaped them into one giant scoop. When the metal cooled, he used his magic to raise the shovel into the air.

Castor had to hand it to Gen; she had found a capable MetalBender to bring along. Hopefully he could work the same magic with her apple trees once they had them.

"Flek," Gen said, "you carve out the dirt from this side, and Castor and I will push from the other side."

"It looks like you have everything covered." Adikia batted her eyelashes. "I'll just grab the old man and keep him out of the way."

The pirate thief hooked Atlas by one elbow and yanked him toward the cottage.

"I'll help you." Bale took the other arm.

Atlas struggled with them, fighting to get back to his shovel. "I need to do my work! I need to finish!"

Castor shook her head. Even if they moved this hill, she doubted Atlas could get them past the Hesperides. He couldn't possibly be their father. All of this dust had clouded his sense.

She and Gen walked around the first hill, the foul insects on this island trailing her every step. She smacked them away and stumbled over a rock. The sun beat down on her shoulders. When they stopped at the base and looked up, she could barely make out the top of the grassy knoll. Of all the hills and mounds on this island, he had picked the largest one to move.

"We can't do it," Castor said. "It's too large." She slapped away another insect, and it left a smear of blood on her skin.

"Even if we only move some of it," Gen said, "it will help Atlas."

"That doesn't help us." Castor didn't do favors.

"Just start blowing." Gen sank her hands into the dirt and braced her boots against the ground.

Castor reached for a vial of wind, and Gen's purple dog growled at her. "Be quiet, or I'll blow you away with the dirt."

The mutt tucked his tail between his legs and crawled under a bush.

Gen leaned into the hill. The silver bands around her arms glistened with sweat and expanded with each breath. Her muscles bulged. In the distance, Castor heard the scrape of Flek's giant shovel. She ran her fingers along the tops of her storm vials, sensing the power inside each one: rainstorm, thunderstorm, lightning . . .

She stopped when she felt the rage of a tornado against her fingers. If they wanted any chance at moving this thing, Castor needed to take the lead.

She grabbed the vial and opened the top. The tornado swirled from the jar, and bits of sand and rock slapped against her cheeks. Her hair blew straight upward. She caught the tail end of the tornado and twisted it around her fingers.

She pulled back and swung it forward, cracking it like a whip. The tornado hit the side of the hill and yanked up rocks, dirt, and shrubs. They swirled around inside the tunnel of wind, and Castor smiled. Even if this was useless, she did like tearing things apart. She closed her hands and lifted upward. The tornado reversed direction and spat the dirt on the far pile.

She had barely made a dent.

Gen repositioned her legs and continued pushing at the base of the hill. Her arms sank into the dirt up to her elbows. Castor dumped another tornado load of dirt on the other pile, then went back for a third load.

This time, her wind picked up a massive boulder that had been buried inside the hill. Castor held up both hands to make sure her tornado could hold it. The giant rock spun around and around inside the wind tunnel. Castor shoved it hard. It dropped from the funnel and hit the top of the growing dirt pile.

Gen sank into the first hill up to her shoulders, still uselessly pushing.

"This isn't going to work," Castor said. Her tornado had almost burned itself out. She drew back what remained and sealed it inside the vial. She had already wasted enough wind on this ridiculous endeavor.

"I'm not giving up," Gen groaned. She put her back heel against a rock and sank deeper into the mound, her face pressed into the dirt.

"What are you trying to prove? If you think you can move this hill, then why can't you take care of some singing women before they put us to sleep?"

"Because I couldn't stop the sirens," Gen said. "I lost him."

Castor sucked in a breath. Now she understood. Losing Pollux to the sirens had been Gen's one and only failure, and she didn't want a second one. Castor suspected if Gen failed at shaking this hill down, she would stop trying altogether, and Castor couldn't have that.

She reached for a new vial, a strong windstorm. She tore it open and pushed outward with her wind.

Dirt and rocks blasted out on either side of them. They pelted against the trees and Atlas's stone cottage. Castor's mouth filled with dust. *Re-landscape an island. Gen couldn't have picked something easier?*

The ground rumbled. Castor drew back on her wind and listened. Inside the dirt and rocks, something groaned. She gave Gen a look. Gen dug her heels into the ground, and Castor pushed outward with the full force of her wind.

The entire hill quivered.

"I think we're doing it!" Gen shouted.

"I think we are."

Castor stretched both arms and focused the wind toward the base of the hill. They might actually do this. They could move this mound. No other StormMaker had ever done this before. She would be the first. The greatest.

She struggled to keep her wind under control. The ground vibrated violently, and the dust swirled around her so thick she could barely see. The rumbling deepened. Gen shouted something at her, but she couldn't make it out. She kept pushing with her wind, tearing up rocks and dirt.

A hand latched on her wrist.

"It's coming down!" Gen shouted. She grabbed Castor by the waist with both hands and jerked her backward.

Castor lost hold of her wind. "What are you—"

Then she saw it. A loose boulder rolled down the falling mound on a direct course for her head. Gen yanked her backward, and they both fell in the dirt. More dirt and rocks rained down on Castor's shoulders. Gen took Castor by the wrist, scooped up her dog, and dragged them away from the falling rock.

The ground shook under their feet. Castor stumbled twice, yanked upright by Gen and pulled farther along until they reached the cover of a fallen tree and hid underneath the log. Gen pressed her hand on Castor's head and pushed her nose into the dirt. Castor tried to jerk her head free and found it useless under Gen's hold.

Dust clouded everything. Through squinted eyes, Castor could make out the dark shadow of the former hill, no longer in the same place. It had rolled over to the other side of the old man's cottage. She hoped the MetalBender had had enough sense to get out of the way. She still needed him to resize her apple trees.

When the shaking stopped, Gen released her hold on Castor. Castor cradled her wrist, sure there would be bruises on her arm. Gen was so rough. They crawled out from under the fallen tree, both covered in dust. Castor wiped it from her eyes and spat it from her mouth.

She opened her eyes a sliver. As the dust settled on the new hill, her lips curved into a smile. Her father had said no one could move a mountain. Technically, this had only been a hill. Still . . . she had moved it.

"Chomp, are you all right?" Gen inspected her mutt, brushing dirt from his matted hair.

"I'm fine too," Castor said as she patted dirt from her jacket.

"You're welcome," Gen said.

"For what?"

"For not letting you get crushed by a rock."

"I wouldn't have been crushed by the rock," Castor argued. "But I suppose you did keep me from using another wind vial to save myself."

Gen shook her head. "I don't know why Pollux cared so much for you. But he was the best person I knew. He saw something redeemable in you, and I guess I hope one day I'll see that too." Her voice broke apart at the end, and two tears ran down her dirt-stained cheeks.

One of the knots in Castor's chest loosened. Not that she'd needed Gen's forgiveness. Or her charity. Or anything from her except her help in getting the apples, but it was nice that Gen wanted to like her, even if she didn't right now.

"You did it!" The old man Atlas ran from the dust in his torn tunic. "You moved the hill." Bale, Adikia, and Flek followed in his wake, appearing unharmed. Atlas danced among them, skipping around like a child. "The hill is moved! I'm free!"

Castor wondered why he had been tasked with moving the hill in the first place. If someone had really wanted the hill moved, they should have chosen someone more capable. It must have been a menial task to keep him out of someone's way. Castor often sent her servants on useless errands when they annoyed her, and Atlas seemed like he could be very annoying.

"Now will you take us to the apples?" Enough of the dirt pile, they had more important things to do.

"Of course. Of course. Right this way." He waved them through the dust, hopping over fallen rocks. Very spry for an elderly man.

"Is everyone all right?" Gen asked.

"Fine," Bale said. "You?"

"I tore my blouse." She shoved her fingers through a large hole on the seam of her shirt. It hadn't been that nice to begin with, a common cotton tunic found in any shop.

"I might have a top that will fit you," Castor said. "You can borrow it if you want."

"That would be . . . nice."

There, she had made a small effort with Gen as well. It was almost as if she could hear her brother saying, *"See, I knew you could be nice if you wanted to be."* Ugh. She hated when Lux was right.

Adikia approached Castor and ran her fingers through Castor's hair. Clods of dirt dropped to her boots. "You've looked better," she said, grinning.

"I just moved that entire hill. What do you expect?"

"It wasn't that big," Adikia said.

"Coming from the person who did no work whatsoever to move it," Castor said.

"This way to the apples!" Atlas shouted, and waved them from the rocks and dirt back into the tall grasses.

A swarm of mosquitos instantly circled around Castor's head. She swatted one aside and cursed. If Atlas didn't take her straight to the apples, she was going to bury him inside his own dirt pile.

Suddenly, he stopped walking. He held his hands wide and said, "Here we are."

Castor looked around at the empty field and the swarm of mosquitos. There was nothing here. Not even a shrub. "What are you playing at, old man?" she growled. "There are no trees here."

"The garden of Hesperides only comes out at dusk," he said.

"Only comes out at dusk?" Castor repeated. It sounded even more ridiculous the second time. "We moved your entire hill, and you led us to an empty field?" She grabbed him by the shreds of his shirt.

Flek stepped between her and the old man. *"Let's wait till dusk,"* he mouthed, and pointed to the sky.

Castor uncurled her fingers. "Fine. We'll wait. And if I don't see a garden here soon, I will burn you to ash."

She wandered through the grass while Gen handed out oranges. Castor left her orange peels in a pile to attract the mosquitoes and keep them away from her. She paced the field with one eye on the sun and the other on the old man. She needed these apples. More than she had before.

She was it. The last of the Othonos StormMakers. She had no second chances. If she failed Arcadia so badly, she would either have to marry Memnon or relinquish the duchy to her cousin. She thought back to the many, many times Pollux had spoken on her behalf or offered to share Arcadia with her. Then she thought of the many times she had pushed him away.

I'm sorry, Lux. If I could go back and do things differently, I would.

The sun dipped below the hills, and the sky turned purple. Atlas stood in the center of the field, humming to himself with a smile on his weathered face. He was about to hum his last song.

"It's dusk." She touched the tops of her storm vials. "Where are the apples?"

"Right there." He pointed to the empty space, and Castor clenched her jaw. She raised her hand to slap him when the air in front of her sparkled, like dew on early morning plants. Where there had been nothing, something began to take shape, blurry at first, like it was breaking through fog.

Two high walls carved from pure marble came into focus in front of her, stretching across the entirety of the field. A wrought iron gate twisted between them. Beyond the gate, a large black stone hill rose in the distance. In front of the gate, three statues appeared: stone women wearing long robes. They were poised to look like they had been caught dancing, with their arms and legs lifted.

Finally, in a slow shimmer, golden trees appeared beyond the gate before the black hill. The trees twisted into shape, their golden trunks reaching to the sky, where bright leaves burst from the ends. Ripe golden apples dropped from the branches. Soon hundreds of trees filled the orchard, each one bursting with fruit.

Castor stepped forward, her heart pounding. She peered through the bars in search of the Hesperides and found only her golden apple trees. If she had been duped into all of that work for nothing—

One of the statues opened her eyes, and Castor jerked away.

"Wow," Bale said. "That is unsettling."

"Who are you that seek the apples?" the statue said. Her body moved stiffly, like it truly was made of rock. So these were the famed daughters of the Oracle Nyx, the witches who guarded the apples.

"Aegle," Atlas said. "It's me. Your father."

All three of the Hesperides rolled their eyes with a grinding of stone. "I thought you were occupied, moving your hill," the statue called Aegle said.

"I finished," he said proudly. "These nice young people gave me a hand. I told them I would let them see the garden if they did."

The statue in the middle sighed. "You cannot promise everyone you meet passage into the garden."

"This isn't everyone."

"If we don't get through the gates," Castor said, "I will personally move the hill back where it began."

"No!" Atlas cried. "Please, Erythea," he pleaded with the statue in the center, "just this once. Can you do it for me?"

Her stone face showed no emotion as she looked down at him. "This one time," she said, and the gate swung open. "And don't you dare ask us for another favor."

"I won't! I won't!" Atlas clapped his hands.

The old man really had come through for them. Castor took a step forward, and a stone arm came down in her path.

"Take only what you can carry. Too much gone from the garden, and it will not grow. And take care not to wake Lados." Aegle gestured to the mound of black rock in the very back. "He is nearly impossible to put back to sleep when he is disturbed."

"We will do as you ask," Gen said.

Castor took a breath. She would break this stone arm if it didn't move in three seconds. One, two . . . the arm dropped. She exhaled and took her first steps into the garden. She reached into the branches of the nearest apple tree and plucked one of the ripe, golden fruits.

The power of it seeped into her fingers. A quiet power. Not like a thunderstorm or a hurricane. It felt like warm sunlight on her skin.

She tossed it to Flek, who caught it in one hand. "Mold this into a jar. I need to see if it works."

If the apples couldn't hold her storms, they were worthless to her.

Flek twisted the apple in his hands. It melted and curled in his fingers. When it split apart, she saw golden seeds inside—what she would use to grow her own orchard. Flek melted these seeds into the rest of the apple.

He worked like an artist, turning the apple through his fingers in the same way she would twist a piece of cloud. The golden apple glowed red, then white, then returned to its original color in the shape of a small vial, almost identical to the ones on her waist. Except this one was gold. And it was free.

He handed it to her. She rolled it in her palm. It was still warm to the touch. She pulled out her strongest vial of lightning for the true test. When she opened it, the lightning clung to her palm and she curled it into a ball. She held up the golden vial and coaxed the lightning inside. It danced along her fingers, almost eager to get into the new vessel. Once it was inside, Cas closed the vial and waited.

Nothing happened. The lightning didn't rattle inside its new cage or try to break free. It stayed.

"It works." She broke into a smile. She could already imagine the new doctrine, the new mural on the wall where *she* would be at the top. Then she saw an empty black circle where Pollux should be, and her smile dropped.

She buried her sadness with the rest of her worries. "All we can carry, they said." Which could be thirty trees once Flek condensed them to a more transportable size.

Back at the gate, Bale spoke to the Hesperides. One of them shook her head, and he walked away, frowning.

"What business do you have with the moving statues?" Castor asked him.

"My own business. Don't you have apples to collect?"

"I do." She looked to the gate, where the stone women watched their every move. "We should look at the trees in the back."

"Good idea," Gen agreed.

"But let's stay away from the rocks," Flek mouthed.

Also a good idea.

They walked deeper into the orchard, between rows and rows of golden trees. Castor plucked a leaf from the end of a branch and twisted it in her fingers. Adikia grabbed apples from the trees and shoved them into her pockets—as if they weren't going to steal hundreds of them in a minute and she hadn't already been promised an annuity of Arcadia's profits. She couldn't help herself, which made Castor realize Adikia didn't take things to have them. She took them because they were there.

That was why she had taken the redhead on Ceryneia. The woman had been an easy take. Castor wasn't. It flattered her a little that Adikia continued after her even though she was a challenge.

Ahead, the black rocks rose behind the trees. The Hesperides had called them Lados. Jagged spikes stood in a long row at the base, each one as sharp as glass. If Castor stared hard enough, she could see the mound rise and fall with quiet breath.

She kept her distance.

"You, start shrinking trees," she said to Flek.

Flek raised his hands to the nearest tree. As his magic swirled around it, the tree pulled into itself, lowering to the ground. A bird that had been nesting in it flew from the branches, and Gen's mutt chased after it, barking furiously.

"Shut him up," Castor said.

"Quiet," Gen said to the dog, who ignored her.

He continued to chase after the bird, snarling and barking. Castor reached for a vial of lightning. She wouldn't kill him. A blast in his hindquarters should get his attention, though. The bird flew up toward the rocks, and Castor held her breath as the dog leapt after it.

He hit one of the black spikes and slid backward.

"Chomp, get over here!" Gen snapped. The dog scurried to her with its tail between its legs.

Too late.

The mound of rocks shivered. The ground shuddered and, one by one, the rocks shifted, unfurling into a long tail. A pair of massive stone eyes creaked open, and an even larger mouth of stone teeth appeared.

Castor was going to kill that dog.

CHAPTER 30

GEN

Now you've done it." Gen turned on Chomp, who cowered behind her. If Castor didn't kill him, whatever unrolled from the black rocks might.

The tail of the thing stretched through the apple trees, ripping up three of them by the roots. One massive, clawed foot emerged, and two eyes stretched upward on a long neck. More eyes worked open on the main mass and broke apart, splitting into separate heads, each with their own spindly neck. Gen counted fifty, no, sixty black stone heads? More than she wanted to count. Why did these beasts always have so many heads? And teeth?

As a test, Gen spat on the tail. Instead of sinking into the stone, the saliva ran down a crevice and dropped to the ground. Her mind magic was useless here. This beast wasn't made of flesh and bone. It was crafted from stone and magic.

"How are we going to kill this thing?" Castor snapped.

"You don't have to kill it!" Adikia shouted. "You only have to keep it from killing us long enough for us to steal the apples." She grabbed Bale and Flek, each one by the ear. "Come on." She dragged them to the next tree, and Flek immediately began shrinking it down.

The stone dragon raised its heads and screeched into the sky. The sound cut through Gen's chest. She covered her ears and knelt. They didn't have to kill it, she reminded herself. They only had to stay alive.

She raised her head as one of the stone feet came down for her. She picked up Chomp and rolled to the side. The foot planted in the ground with enough force to shake apples from the nearby trees. Gen covered her head, and golden apples pelted off her arms.

Castor drew her first bolt of lightning. She sent it shooting for the largest of the dragon heads. The bolt struck right between its eyes and exploded in a spray of sparks.

The stone head shattered. Chunks of black rock cascaded down the side of the dragon and landed in the dirt. One large rock crushed a golden apple tree flat.

"Nice shot!" Gen called.

"I don't miss!" Castor shouted.

The dragon's remaining heads howled in pain. Gen clamped her hands over her ears again. As soon as the wailing stopped, she lunged for the nearest head, fist outstretched. Her knuckles cracked a fissure right down its center. The thing yowled until it split in two and the pieces dropped at her feet.

At least this beast didn't double its heads every time she smashed one.

One head snaked around her back and tried to clamp onto her shoulder. Gen spun around and grabbed it by the neck. She hooked her arms around it and twisted. The entire head came off and writhed in the dirt. Chomp growled and snapped at it, as if he hadn't already done enough.

Castor blasted another dragon head with lightning. That only left seventy-two or eighty-six to go—Gen had no idea. Something bashed her in the shoulder and knocked her to her knees. She twisted around and punched another stone head in the teeth, knocking them loose. Shards of black rock tumbled to the ground.

Her arm ached from the strike. She patted her shoulder and felt something warm and wet. She was bleeding, and if this blouse hadn't already been torn and covered in mud, it was now completely unwearable.

Another dragon head came her way. She struck it down with a fist and cried out from the pain in her shoulder. Castor blasted two more. Gen kicked the next one down and shattered it to pieces.

Adikia came from the trees. "Run!"

Gen didn't need to be told twice. Castor struck down one last head, and Gen scooped up Chomp with her uninjured arm. They raced for the gate. The ground rumbled as the dragon took a step to follow them.

Bale carried a pot with twelve tiny apple trees nestled inside. That would be enough for the Empresses. It would have to be.

Gen soared through the gate first. One of the stone women shrieked as she passed, "We'll never get him back to sleep, you know!"

"Sorry!" Gen called. She empathized with the work it took to control temperamental beasts. Especially one so large. With so many heads.

She rushed through the field and stopped when she no longer felt the ground quaking under her feet. She turned. Twenty yards back, the three stone Hesperides held the dragon at the gate. One of them swatted him on his foot and scolded him like a misbehaving child. Beside them, Atlas danced in a circle through the grass, waving his hands in the air.

Castor reached Gen first, followed by Adikia, Flek, and Bale. Blood ran down Castor's neck from a slice near her collarbone. One of the shards of dragon stone must have cut her. Gen released Chomp to the ground and reached into her bag for her jar of stink-lizard pus. These weren't ambrosia injuries. Not yet.

She opened the jar and smeared a glob of pus on her own shoulder. Then she handed the jar to Castor. "For your wound."

"Thank you." Castor dipped her fingers into the jar. She dabbed some on her neck, then on the fading bruise around her eye. Despite them coming to some sort of tolerance for one another, Gen had no regrets about striking Castor's perfect cheek. She had deserved it. For so many things.

"And you." Gen waggled her finger at Chomp. "Do not anger any more dragons, please." Chomp tucked his tail between his legs and licked his paw.

Castor bent over the pot filled with miniature apple trees, running her finger over one of the leaves. "They're beautiful, aren't they?"

"They are mostly for the Empresses," Gen reminded her.

"I know that."

Gen rubbed her injured shoulder. The lizard pus closed the wound, but the bruises ran deep. "We also need to bring back the Cerberus. How are we going to get back to Okeanos without getting caught?"

"We don't march in the front doors, that's for sure," Adikia said.

"We should go after dark," Bale suggested. "Future Duchess here can send in some fog cover."

Flek mouthed, *"We can use some of these apples for armor."*

"Not a bad idea," Castor said. "But I don't want to waste apples." She still spoke as if they belonged to her, and that worried Gen.

They walked back to the beach. Despite her aching shoulder, Gen felt anxious. Adrenaline mixed with Mazon strength flooded her veins after the fight with the dragon. All she wanted was to face the next monster, the next mountain. Smashing dragon heads and pushing down rocks had kept her from thinking about Pollux. While she'd been fighting the dragon, there had been a moment where she hadn't felt the emptiness inside her. Now, as her pulse slowed, she heard his name in every beat.

Pollux. Pollux. Pollux.

They reached the dinghy and rowed back to the ship. Castor took the apples and secured them in the captain's room, where she'd moved her things the other night.

"They'll be safest with me," Castor said.

Gen peeked inside the captain's quarters. Castor had dumped her clothes in a pile on the floor. Old orange peels littered the table. Seawater-soaked boots leaned against the wall. The bed was unmade, with velvet covers balled up at the ends, and the curtains were torn at the edges. It looked as if Castor had opened one of her storm vials in here.

"Maybe we should keep the apples somewhere else?" Gen suggested, worried they might get lost in a pile of clothing.

Castor pushed aside a chess set to set the apples on the table. "I'm no fool. I know if the Empresses don't get theirs, then I don't get mine." Castor dug through her pile of clothes and tossed Gen a shirt. "Here, try this. It should fit you. It's too big on me."

"Thank you." Gen ran the blouse through her fingers. Handwoven linen dyed pale blue, the same shade as Castor's and Pollux's eyes. "I can't take this."

"I can buy another one."

Gen shook her head. "It's not the gift. It's the color. It reminds me of . . . never mind." Gen needed a shirt, and it was more than likely this one wouldn't last long. She would either burn it, tear it, or bleed on it soon enough.

"Red was his favorite color," Castor said. "He didn't really care for blue."

"I know." Gen had worn a red dress once on Lerna, the first time they'd kissed, and he hadn't been able to take his eyes off her.

"You, Bale, pull the anchor! We need to get ready to sail!" Adikia called out orders from above.

Castor slumped into the chair and picked up one of the chess pieces, twisting it in her fingers. "Something has been bothering me," she said. "About the Oracle."

"Please." Gen closed her arms around herself. "I don't want to talk about it." It was far too late to do anything about the Oracle's prediction now. It only reminded Gen how she had failed to do something sooner.

"You have to. You're the only other person who saw this Oracle." Castor returned the chess piece to the board. "Why do you think she neglected to tell you my brother would die?"

Gen swallowed. "I don't know."

"Isn't that information you would have liked to know?"

"*You* could have told me," Gen reminded her.

"The Oracle could have too." Castor stood up and paced the floor, maneuvering around the pile of clothes. "If I'm purposefully keeping information from someone, it's for a reason. Lux was questioning the prophecy, too, before he . . . you know. I should have given it more thought."

Gen sank her teeth into her bottom lip. Castor made a good point. The Oracle had told Gen only how to get out of the palace and where to sail. Why not tell her that the quest would cost her Pollux?

"She wanted us to chase the apples," Gen said. A small fire ignited inside her. This had all been the Oracle's doing. She had made Pollux's death possible by telling him, and only him, it would happen.

"Exactly," Castor said. "What I don't know is why."

Gen closed her fist, and the bands of silver tightened across her knuckles. "If I meet the Oracle again, I will get an answer."

Adikia elbowed her way past Gen into the cabin. "Sorry to break up . . . whatever this is, but to get out of here, we're going to have to sail through a nasty storm and some murderous singing women, and if I recall, we're out of those handy little ear blockers."

"We are," Gen sighed. They'd used what she'd had of the whisper moth cocoon. All the pieces had been soaked through or lost in the storm. "We won't make it. Castor, if they get into your head, with the storm . . ."

She'd seen Pollux under their influence. He had been a stranger to her, a captive of the sirens, wielding the storm with unfathomable strength. Castor in that same place would be worse. *Gen* in that place could crush everyone on this ship.

"I am not letting them into my head," Castor snapped.

"Then what do you propose we do?" Adikia crossed her arms over her chest. "Flek is the only one of us who can't hear them, and he can't hold us all."

"He can hold the sirens," Bale said, coming up behind her with Flek. "You catch one, you get a favor. Our friend Flek here can go on ahead, wrap one up in chains, and make her promise to let us pass."

"I can do that," Flek mouthed.

"We'll sail as close as we can," Adikia said, "and send Flek ahead on the dinghy."

Gen placed her hand on Flek's arm. "Are you sure you can do

this?" She had underestimated the sirens once. She wouldn't do it again.

"Remember what I said?" He brushed his fingers across his temple and fanned them next to his ear. *"The caterpillar's song is harmful only to those who hear it. The sirens fight with song. I can't be hurt. Let me do this. For you."* He reached up to sweep a piece of her hair from her face, and Gen flinched away from him. She wasn't ready for that kind of touch. Not yet.

"Be careful," she said.

"I will." He swept three fingers across the bridge of his nose.

Adikia took the ship's wheel, and they set sail for the black clouds and the song of the sirens. Gen locked Chomp in her bunkroom, unsure if the siren song had affected him before or not. She didn't want to find out.

Castor did her best to control the winds. Gen could tell it took a toll on her. The girl whose flawless skin never cracked now beaded with sweat, and fine lines cut through her forehead. The first whispers of the siren song came across the winds.

Come back to us to find what you seek,
We have him here beneath the deep.

"No." Gen shook her head. The siren had already shown her the truth. She knew these were lies.

Flek put his arm around her, planting his ten fingers tight on her shoulders. *"It will be all right,"* he promised her.

Gen swallowed and closed her eyes.

What you wish will come to be,
If you meet us in the sea.
Our sister lied,
He did not die,

We have him here with us,

Your dear, sweet Pollux.

Instead of seeing Pollux being bitten and drowned, she saw him sitting on the rocks in a white shirt and black pants, playing his violin while the sirens gathered around him, listening to his song.

"No!" Gen shouted, her arms shaking. She couldn't fight them much longer. "Stop the ship. We can't go any farther."

Adikia turned the ship to port, and Bale dropped the anchor. Tears streamed down his face as he turned the crank. The sirens must have sung to him about Andromeda, his lost love. Flek climbed into the dinghy, and Gen loaded the small boat up with chains before she pulled the ropes to lower him to the sea.

"Be safe," she said to him.

"You too." He pressed his thumb to his lip and drew it down before he took the oars and made his way toward the sirens.

Adikia watched him with the spyglass. "I hope he's quick about it," she said, her voice shaking.

Castor continued to pull at the storm, losing focus as the ship rocked back and forth. She stamped her foot on the deck and shouted, "Be quiet!" before she reached to the sky for more wind.

Gen held her stomach and paced. *The song only hurts those who hear it. The song only hurts those who hear it.* All she had to do was not listen. It was only a song.

Come, child, we have what you seek,

Hidden here in the deep.

What you wish will come to be,

If you meet us in the sea.

Then she heard something she couldn't ignore—Pollux's violin. Her pulse raced, and she ran to the edge of the ship. Squinting her eyes, she made out the rocks, the sirens—and in the center of them, she found Pollux.

He sat under a patch of sunlight shining through the clouds. His pale hair glimmered like diamonds, and underneath his chin, he held his violin. He pulled the bow across the strings, and one of his cloud figures emerged. It took the shape of her, standing tall in front of the Hydra.

Pollux lowered his bow and looked directly at her. "Come to me, Gen. I'm waiting."

"I'm coming." She grabbed the rails and raised her leg to leap into the water when a deafening screech cut through her.

She clapped both hands on her ears and fell back onto the deck. The illusion of Pollux shattered to pieces, and cold darkness fell upon her. There was no sunlit Pollux singing to sirens, and there never would be.

When the screeching stopped, Gen carefully uncovered her ears. A residual hum rang through her skull. No more songs. No more false promises. All she had was the memory of what they had shown her and the ache that it couldn't be real.

Flek rowed his way back to them in the moonlight. Bale held a lantern over the side of the ship to light his way. When Flek's dinghy butted up against the ship, Gen grabbed the ropes and hauled him back onto the deck.

Despite not having heard the siren song, Flek bore a few claw marks on his arm and the shock of someone who had seen the worst side of the creatures.

"We can pass," he mouthed.

"Thank you," Gen said.

"Let's get moving before they change their minds," Adikia said. "Castor, give us some wind."

"With pleasure." Castor took the wind she had gathered from the storm and pushed it into the sails. They cut through the water away from the Isle of Hesperides and the sirens on their rocks. The women bared their teeth and hissed as they passed. Gen stared at the empty place on the rocks where the creatures had shown her Pollux.

Flek put a hand on her shoulder. *"I tried to be fast,"* he mouthed.

"You were very fast." He had saved her from leaping headfirst to her own death. A few moments later, and she might have joined Pollux.

"What did they tell you?" he asked.

"They told me I could still save Pollux." She shook her head. "They told me what I wanted to hear."

Across the ship, Bale stared out at the sea, wiping tears from his eyes. They must have promised him Andromeda. Or a cure from being a MindWorker. She wondered what they had offered Castor. Or Adikia. She doubted either one would tell her. They would consider their vulnerabilities weaknesses.

The *Hind* passed through the storm, and Gen felt weak. "I need to lie down."

"Let me help you." Flek took her elbow and walked with her below-decks. When she opened the door to her cabin, she found Chomp had chewed through Castor's mattress and left shreds of wool all over the space. Either he'd been upset by the sirens or he'd disliked being locked in a room.

"I'm sorry, old friend." She sat on her bunk and patted Chomp on the head.

Flek sat beside her. *"Pollux was a good person,"* he mouthed, and made his sign for Pollux, waving his fingers over his head.

"He was."

"He cared so much about you."

"He did."

"He made me promise to look after you when he was gone."

Gen nodded. "Pollux would do something like—" She raised her head, snapping back into focus. "When did he tell you this?"

Flek reeled back, pressing his lips together tightly. His pale blue hair fell over his dark eyes.

"You knew." She jabbed him in the chest. "You knew what the Oracle told him and—oh, that's what you were trying to tell me at Kyknos's island. Why would Pollux tell you and not me?"

"I was there when the Oracle told him," Flek mouthed. *"I saw her words. Pollux begged me not to tell you."*

"And you did as he asked? What about me? What about what I want?"

"It wasn't my secret to share. I'm sorry." Flek swept his fingers past his lips.

Gen made her own gesture. She pointed to the door. "Get out."

Flek reluctantly stood and left her alone in her cabin. Gen hugged her pillow to her face and buried her tears in the threads. Almost everyone had known about Pollux's death prediction, and no one had told her. There had been so many places to change his fate, and she had missed them all.

CHAPTER 31

CASTOR

Castor couldn't shake the siren's song.
You will rule the land,
True love will take your hand,
Your father at your side,
If our words you do abide.

It had changed from before. The sirens no longer promised her apples and treasure; they offered her love, power, and acceptance. She had seen herself with Adikia. Her father had stood behind them, an arm around each shoulder. And she had wanted it. Badly.

Castor poured herself a glass of wine from the carafe in the captain's room. She swallowed it in three gulps and poured a second glass. The problem was that love and power didn't mix. One would always sacrifice the other, and she already knew which one she would sacrifice. She had already done it once. With Pollux.

She poured herself a third glass as the door to the captain's room opened. Adikia tore off her hat and ran her fingers through her purple curls. She tossed her hat on the table and slumped into the armchair.

"The ship is secure for the night. We can get some rest and figure out our next steps. I'd suggest we avoid going through Kyknos's pass. Especially since you tore up her map."

"I had to. Besides, we knew where the apples were. We didn't need it anymore."

Adikia kicked off her boots, revealing mismatched socks with holes in them. For some reason, Castor found that oddly charming.

"Clever," Adikia said. "With no map, no one else can find the treasure. You know, if you were a thief, you'd make a pretty good one. Though I can't say everything the StormMakers do is on the up and up."

Castor sat in the chair next to her. "Once you have enough money and power, no one questions what you do. That's why *you'll* always be sneaking in the shadows."

"Not any longer." Adikia reached into her pocket and removed an apple. "I've just become an investor in Arcadia." She tossed the apple to Castor.

Castor clumsily raised her hands to catch it. Instead, the apple dropped to her feet and rolled under the chair.

"Good thing you're not a proper thief. You'd get caught." Adikia retrieved the apple and twisted it in her fingers, smiling to herself.

Castor sipped her wine. Everyone else on this ship was miserable, even Flek. Though he hadn't heard the siren's song, Gen had said something to him that put him in a mood. But Adikia smiled as if the sirens hadn't touched her. "Adikia, what did the sirens sing to you?"

Adikia's smile dropped. "It's not important."

"It is important. To me."

Adikia sighed. "You don't really want to know the answer. It's not like you care about the real me. You like the troublesome thief. Nothing more." She ran her finger across Castor's lower lip.

"What if I want to care?"

Adikia blinked twice. "This makes me wonder what the sirens sang to *you*. It must have been something good to give the Storm Lady a heart."

Castor ran her fingers over her storm vials. "They told me . . . I would have control of Arcadia, and I wouldn't be alone. I've never had to worry about being alone before. No matter what I did, there was always Pollux." Everyone else she had pushed away, and they had stayed away. Except for him.

"I have a big family," Adikia said. "Eight younger brothers and sisters, and six little cousins. Like you said, stealing sails and ships and the odd bag of coins here or there isn't always enough. That's why I agreed to come on this trip with you. I need some regular coin. The sirens suggested you would balk on our deal and the only way I would get what I need was from them."

"I don't balk on deals." *I do alter them sometimes.* "The annuity is yours, and to be completely honest, I made that deal because I wanted to force you to come visit me. To collect. I wasn't sure if you would, otherwise."

Adikia raised an eyebrow. "I would have. I didn't think you wanted me in your palace."

"It's a manor."

"Your manor—whatever. You seemed busy and everything there was so . . . expensive."

Castor laughed. "When we get back, you'll be the most expensive thing there. I never pay out annuities. Especially not percentages. I plan to be incredibly profitable, you—"

Before she could finish, Adikia crawled into her lap and kissed her. Castor wrapped her arms around Adikia's waist and pulled her close. She was tired of pushing people away. It hadn't made her any stronger. It hadn't made her any happier.

She pressed her mouth to Adikia's and inhaled her scent of seawater and wind. She tangled her fingers in Adikia's hair and ran her hand down the line of scales on Adikia's back. She pulled away for a breath.

"I would prefer it if you did not bring any more redheads here," Castor said.

"So brunettes are fine?"

"Shut up."

She kissed her again. Adikia nibbled on Castor's lower lip, and sparks shot through Castor's veins. Adikia pushed Castor back into the chair and kissed the underside of her jaw, her neck . . .

Something hit the ship.

They rocked to the side, and Adikia snapped her head up. "I swear I leave the helm for ten minutes . . ." She crawled off Castor's lap.

Castor combed her fingers through her hair. Her lips still pulsed from Adikia's kiss. Adikia straightened her jacket as she made her way above deck, Castor right behind her. Castor was sure the horrid dog was behind this. If she had lightning to spare, she would light his fur on fire.

They reached the deck. No one was there. The sails were down. The anchor had been dropped.

Something glinted in the moonlight.

Castor grabbed Adikia and yanked her back. A spear hit the deck right where she'd been standing.

"They've found us. We're under attack!" Adikia said. "We have to raise the sails! Pull the anchor!"

Another spear struck the ship. Castor squinted in the distance and found a mass of black ships on the water. They were too far for the centaurs to have decent aim, but that didn't stop them from firing.

"Wake up!" Castor shouted belowdecks before moving to help Adikia with a sail.

Gen came running up first. "What's wrong? What is it?"

Castor pointed to the spear embedded in the deck. "They've found us."

"Get the anchor!" Adikia yelled. A spear cut right through the sail as they lifted it.

"Damn the Oracles," Castor cursed.

Gen hauled the anchor out of the water. Bale took the wheel. Castor pulled a vial of wind from her belt and pushed it into the sails to get them moving. The ship lurched forward and away from the Elysium army. Castor looked down at her belt. Her wind was sparse. She had the lightning vials she'd taken from Pollux. Enough to take down a few ships, but not all.

"Now might be a good time for that armor!" Bale shouted at Flek when another spear hit the ship.

Flek nodded and went to get the apples.

"Don't use too many!" Castor shouted at him. This would all be worthless if they survived Emperor Nessos's soldiers only to come home empty-handed.

Castor's windstorm died quickly. She pulled a vial of rain and released the clouds from the jar. She pushed them toward the oncoming ships. She could sink a few ships with the rainwater. Or at least slow them down. Another spear launched toward them. Gen grabbed it from the air and flung it back—then bent over her knees and groaned. She grabbed her shoulder and pressed on it before she got back to her feet. That cursed dragon had damaged her.

Gen plucked another spear from the air, and this time, she threw it left-handed. It didn't have the same strength, but Castor heard the thud of it lodging into . . . something.

Flek returned with five golden chest plates. He handed one to

Castor, and she quickly strapped it to her shoulders. She wondered how many apples he had used to make it. When a spear hit the deck and a shard of wood glanced painlessly off the golden armor, she decided she didn't care.

She threw another rainstorm at the oncoming centaurs. Squinting into the darkness, she saw she had successfully removed some ships. Fewer shadows approached. But more spears launched. Gen picked them up and threw them back. Flek twisted them around and flung them at the centaurs by controlling the metal tips.

Then a spear hit the mast. It lodged in the crack Gen had left when she'd punched it. The wood groaned. Castor took a step back. The crack spread up and down the mast, which split down the center and bent outward at both sides. The sails flapped loose in the wind. Castor leapt out of the way as the broken mast fell.

She rolled onto her side and covered her face as the mast crashed through the railing. Splinters struck her arm. She raised her head. Half of the mast had rolled into the sea. The other half lay in pieces on the deck.

Castor turned over her shoulder to glare at Gen. The girl's mental breakdown would cost them their lives now.

Castor tried to get up, but she was stuck. A piece of the broken rail had caught on her belt. She tugged harder, and the waistband of her pants ripped. Her belt slipped free. She snatched at the end of it, but the leather strap slipped through her fingers. She managed to grasp only Delia's box. The rest dropped into the sea.

The belt held all her storms. *All* of them. She moved to dive for it, when a hand caught her wrist.

"Don't do it," Adikia pleaded.

"But—" Castor looked at the dark water and the errant spears falling into it. Yes, she could drown or be impaled. She could also save her storms.

"It doesn't matter," Adikia said. "You don't need them."

"Fine." It would be too late now. Her storms would have sunk too far.

Without Castor's wind, the ship coasted on momentum, then slowed to a crawl. Spears hit the deck at an alarming rate. *Thud! Thud! Thud!* They stuck out from the wood everywhere. Adikia got to her feet, and a spear struck her armor.

Castor screamed as the force of it knocked Adikia onto her back and sent her skidding across the deck. Castor raced for her. Adikia raised her head, battered and bruised. Castor picked her up from the deck.

"I think we should go below," Adikia gasped. The strike had winded her.

Castor nodded. "We're going to the captain's room!" she shouted, and shoved Delia's box into her pocket.

She helped Adikia get below. Then she went to find what remained of her apples. The twelve little trees were mostly intact. Flek had used only a few of the apples. Spears continued to hit the deck above. *Thud! Thud! Thud!* One broke through the window into the captain's room and hit the bed. Broken glass and feathers filled the room.

"Where can I hide this?" Castor asked Adikia.

"Here." Adikia opened a hidden panel in the floor where she had stashed quite a few things: jewelry, knives, lengths of fur, coins . . . and now, a pot of twelve golden apple trees. Bale, Flek, and Gen and her dog rushed into the room.

Adikia sealed the door closed, and they all huddled on the floor, behind the armchairs. This was a true surrender. Not like the planned one before. Castor had no plans. No power. No storms. She had nothing.

They listened as more spears slammed into the ship. Then they heard something worse: the sound of hooks attaching to the railing, followed by heavy hoofbeats tromping across the deck.

"Are we just going to wait here for them to find us?" Bale whispered.

"Yes," Castor hissed. "Unless you'd like to fend them off by yourself."

"No, I'd rather wait."

He didn't have to wait for long. Someone kicked their door in, shattering the wood. It was Quintas. She looked down at Castor and smiled. The centaur guard had recovered from being struck by lightning, but she carried long scars on her arms as a reminder.

"You were right," Quintas said. "I should have killed you the first time we met. I won't make the same mistake again." She pulled a sword from the sheath on her haunches.

"I should have cooked you fully last time we met." Castor reached for her belt. Her heart stopped when she felt nothing on her waist but Delia's box in her pocket. Nothing she could use to fend off centaurs.

Quintas shifted to the side, and Emperor Nessos stepped in beside her. The two of them filled the doorway, which hadn't been made for Elysiums. Nessos laughed when he found Castor and the others cowering in the corner.

"Like true rats," he said. "Scurrying to the shadows."

He walked around the room, purposely knocking maps and pictures off the walls. He stepped on the glass and shattered it under his front hoof.

"I offered you hospitality, and you drowned a hundred of my soldiers." He knocked over the desk, and a bottle of ink spilled to the floor.

"Your mistake," Castor said. "You hire incompetent soldiers." She flicked her eyes to Quintas, who set her jaw.

"Indeed," Nessos agreed. He eyed her carefully. When his gaze dropped to her golden armor, he frowned. "Where did you get that armor?"

Castor's eyes widened. They were fools, wearing the stolen apples right in front of him.

"It's ours. From Olympia," Gen answered. She said the lie quite well in Castor's opinion. Not a hint of remorse.

Nessos grabbed the sword from Quintas and thrust the blade at Gen. It struck her in the chest plate. The tip broke, and Gen gasped.

The sword hadn't left a mark. Not even the barest scratch.

Nessos tossed the broken sword to the ground. "You have the apples. Where are they?"

"What apples?" Adikia said.

Nessos grabbed her by the collar of her shirt and lifted her into the air. "The golden apples," he said through his teeth. "The Hesperides let you into the orchard. How did you find them? Why did they let you pass?"

"I have no idea what you're talking about," Adikia said.

He tossed her aside like a doll, and she landed in a pile of broken glass. Castor gasped, then cursed herself for it immediately. This was her fear, the balance between power and love. Now Nessos knew she cared for Adikia, and he would use it to his advantage.

Nessos grinned as he pulled a crossbow from his saddlebags

and aimed it between Adikia's eyes. "Tell me where they are, or I pull the trigger."

Castor got to her feet. Her gaze darted from Adikia's face to the golden armor on her chest. Castor needed the apples. She also needed Adikia. How could she choose? How could she not choose?

"You have three seconds," Nessos said.

"Don't do it," Adikia said. "Take your prize."

"My prize," Castor repeated. *Adikia* was her prize. Castor had made it to the Isle of Hesperides once. She had moved Atlas's hill, fought a stone dragon. She could do it again, but she would never find Adikia again, even if she searched a thousand isles. "The apples are—"

Something hit the ship. Something large.

The ship rocked. Cas fell backward. Broken glass and furniture slid across the floor, and Nessos fired his crossbow over Adikia's shoulder. Quintas stumbled and hit the wall, and Gen leapt to her feet. She grabbed Quintas by her leather armor and yanked her to the ground.

The mutt snapped at Quintas's leg and sank his teeth into her flank. Quintas howled. Castor dragged herself to her elbows and smiled. She supposed the beast could be useful. Sometimes.

She looked between Adikia and the hidden compartment with the apples. The ship rocked again, this time in the other direction. Castor heard centaurs drop into the sea. She abandoned Adikia and went for the hidden compartment. Adikia wasn't in danger of being shot anymore. She could take care of herself. The apples couldn't.

Nessos met Castor there with a knife under her chin. "I'm going to send your skins back to the Empresses in a box," he said.

"I'd like to see you try." She picked up a fallen bottle of wine and cracked him across the face with it, sending him reeling back.

Something hit the ship a second time.

Nessos rolled across the room and slammed into the wall. "What is happening out there?" he shouted.

Castor tumbled away from the apples. The ship was near sideways now. Gen, Bale, and Flek slid across the floor. Adikia kept herself wedged against the wall. The dog held on to the doorframe by his teeth.

Castor clawed her way to the secret hatch, digging her fingers into the cracks in the floorboards. She needed to get the apples before the ship turned over.

"Here!" Adikia threw Castor the end of a blanket. Castor grabbed it and pulled herself across the floor. More like a climb now. A broken mug hit her in the shoulder as it toppled. She coughed on a mouthful of feathers, and broken glass cut her arms.

Adikia pulled, and Castor reached the hatch. The ship groaned. The bed slid across the floor and struck Nessos in the chest. Adikia slid with it—right out the broken window. Castor held on to the hatch in the floor. She could hear the contents inside, and her apples, turning around.

The ship tipped to its side and hit the water with a heavy splash. Water poured in through the broken window. The remaining lanterns went out. Broken furniture and people slipped out. Water rushed into Castor's mouth.

"Castor, we have to go!" Gen shouted, and crawled on her elbows toward her.

"Not without the prize."

Seawater filled the cavern. Castor took a deep breath, then

plunged under the water's surface. She tried to lift the hatch as salt water stung her cuts and eyes. But the door wouldn't budge. The heavy seawater pinned it down. Then Gen reached her. Gen wrenched the door from the hatch, Castor grabbed the pot of apples, and Gen closed a hand around her elbow.

Gen yanked Castor into the open sea. A centaur dropped into the dark water between them, and Gen's hand slipped from Castor's. Without Gen holding her up, Castor's heavy golden armor and the pot of apples weighed her down. Cas kicked her legs wildly while centaurs continued to sink. She saw the terror in their eyes as they struggled to swim. She felt their same fear. She pulled at the metal armor with one hand to tear it off, but she refused to release the apples. She looked for Gen. For anyone. Her lungs tightened. She needed air.

Cas gave up on the armor and reached for Delia's box. She flipped the latch, and the blinking light emerged into the water.

"Help," she said in a swarm of bubbles.

The last thing Castor saw was Delia flitting off into the darkness.

CHAPTER 32

GEN

Gen had lost Castor. She had lost everyone. She frantically scanned the water for a sign of them. Even Chomp. They had all slipped through her fingers like Pollux. The sea swarmed with casualties from whatever had hit the *Hind*: centaur soldiers, pieces of the ship, broken furniture, pots . . . even Pollux's broken violin. She snatched it and stuffed it into her bag. Then she went up for a gasp of air.

She surfaced and saw more centaur soldiers and overturned ships. What else was in this water with them? What had tossed their ship? She dove back down. A blinking light flashed below. She swam toward it, ignoring the ache of her shoulder.

Out of the darkness, Castor appeared. Gen caught her by the arm and kicked toward the surface. A dark shadow loomed—likely whatever had sunk the ship.

Gen kicked harder, but the sea monster moved faster. It opened its mouth to swallow them, and a rush of water sucked them in. Gen kicked with everything she had but failed. The sea creature pulled her and Castor into its mouth. Gen waited to be gnashed to pieces against sharp teeth.

Instead, she landed on something soft and squishy and breathed *air*. She sputtered out mouthfuls of water and heard Castor cough violently beside her. They sat in a few feet of seawater. A faint, pink light glowed all around them.

"Gen, it's okay." Hands took her by the shoulders, and Gen swung around to see Bale.

She realized she knew this light. She knew this mouth.

"Andromeda?"

It had to be. She pressed her hand to the inside of Andromeda's cheek and remembered the slimy, soft feel. The fool whale had followed her all the way from Olympia. And she had rescued them from imminent death. Brave, reckless whale.

"Gen, you should see something." Bale turned her to face the back of the whale. She did a quick count of heads. Andromeda had already scooped up Chomp, Adikia, Flek, and Bale. She and Castor had been the last ones. But there was someone else inside too.

Gen's heart stopped.

"Pollux," she whispered.

She slid across the whale's tongue to reach him. It wasn't possible. The siren had said he was gone. She said they had eaten him . . . but the siren had only shown her images of Pollux screaming as the sirens took bites of him. Gen touched his ice-cold skin and traced a circle of missing flesh.

Weathered bloodstains covered his torn clothing. More bites marred his skin. Gen rolled him onto his side, and when she saw the slight rise of breath in his chest, her insides broke open. Tears streamed down her cheeks.

"You're alive." She kissed his forehead. "You're alive." She kissed his cold knuckles. Then she reached into her sopping wet bag for the ambrosia. She prayed it hadn't floated into the sea.

"What is going on back there?" Castor asked.

"It's Pollux!" Gen called as she grasped the bottle. She wrenched open the top and spilled the entire contents down his throat.

"He's alive?" Castor gasped.

"Barely."

A day, maybe a few hours later, and they would have been too late. Even now, there were no promises. Gen didn't know how much the ambrosia could do.

As the whale swam, cold water sloshed over Pollux's skin. Gen pulled a few of her hairs and pressed them to the whale's tongue. A familiar connection lashed her thoughts to Andromeda's. As usual, the whale broke into a string of rambling thoughts.

It took me so long to find you. I had trouble keeping up. Then I saw the nasty water women, and your mate. I scooped him up—

Please, Andromeda, we can talk later. I need to get Pollux to dry land. Can you find an island?

Yes. I will find an island.

And thank you. For ignoring me and coming to save us.

You're welcome.

Andromeda swam faster. More seawater and fishbones rolled to the back of her mouth. Gen covered Pollux with her own body to protect him from the cold and wet. If Andromeda had saved him from the sirens, then he had been in here, bleeding and without food or water, for more than a day. Gen had lost him once. She wouldn't lose him again.

In the glow of Andromeda's insides, Gen found Castor. Pollux's sister looked on with no expression, but Gen noticed how tightly she held Adikia's hand, to the point where her knuckles almost burst through her skin.

I will save him. I will save him for both of us.

Gen held her hand to Pollux's cheek. Did she only imagine the color slowly blooming on his skin?

"We're almost there," she whispered into his ear. "I'll get you warm."

Andromeda rose from the sea and opened her mouth to a small, rocky isle. Gen picked up Pollux and held him close to her chest. She walked him to dry land and set him in a patch of sand. The early morning light cascaded over the beach.

"We need a fire and something dry to wrap him in," Gen said without tearing her eyes from Pollux. "We need fresh water."

His eyes twitched behind his eyelids. Gen pushed his wet, tangled hair from his face. *Please, please bring him back to me.* She worried this was a dream. That she had actually drowned in the ocean and none of this was real.

Bale started a small fire near them. Flek brought Gen some large, dry leaves. She snatched them from him and laid them over Pollux's chest. Castor watched, unmoving, like she thought if she dared to help or believe he could come back, it wouldn't happen.

It had to happen.

Gen rubbed her hands furiously down Pollux's arms. If she rubbed any harder, she would take his skin off. Color flooded his cheeks. He opened his mouth and sucked in a breath. Then he fluttered his eyes.

"You're ... you're ..." Gen couldn't manage anything else before the tears came. She wrapped her arms around him and sobbed into his chest. "I'm sorry. I'm so sorry." She would never let him go again.

CHAPTER 33

POLLUX

Am I dead?

Pollux had hoped death would be more peaceful than this. Less painful. Every part of him ached. He felt dried out—like an autumn leaf that had been crushed to dust under someone's boot. He couldn't move anything. The effort it took to wriggle a finger or tilt an eyebrow seemed insurmountable. But he sensed someone was near. Waiting for him.

He lifted his eyelids the barest sliver. Through pale eyelashes, he made out a shadowy figure. Someone familiar. He would have known her anywhere. The Girl in the Circus.

"Gen," he whispered with a dry, scratchy throat.

"You need some water." She lifted his head and held a cup to his lips. Cool water washed over his parched tongue and down his desert throat. His eyes opened slightly. The figures around him began to take shape. He gazed into Gen's heart-shaped face. She had seaweed in her hair and tearstains down her cheeks.

"I thought you were gone," she whispered.

I thought I was too.

Then he heard a raw and guttural choking screech. He'd heard it once before. Only once. He and Castor had been very small, playing outside of their mother's room, and their mother had been talking to her sister, their aunt.

"I don't know what to do with her. She burned her own brother and showed

no remorse for it. I'm afraid she might do something worse. That girl was born with cruelty in her veins. I sometimes wish I'd had only the one child."

His sister had run away to their room, and Pollux had heard this sound, the sound of Castor's tears. It was the one and only time she had cried like that, at least that he had seen. It took a lot to break his sister. He never thought he would be enough to do it.

He watched his sister cover her mouth and walk away. Adikia tried to follow her, but Castor shooed her away. She didn't like to be seen crying.

"That was unexpected," Gen said.

She raised his head and fed him more water. After a few more times, he was able to hold his own head upright and drink on his own. The chill, however, set deeper into his bones. He scooted closer to the fire. Bale threw more wood on top of it, and the flames grew higher.

Gen sat as close to him as any one person could. Her heat radiated almost as warm as the fire, even though her clothes were as wet as his.

He didn't remember much about his venture with the sirens. He'd only come back to himself as they were tearing him apart. He'd fought and kicked as much as he could, the water filling with blood around him. The last thing he remembered was the sirens' pale, wicked faces before the whale appeared and swallowed him up.

The whale had saved him.

Was this the death the Oracle had seen? He'd been as close to death as anyone could be without taking their last breath. Maybe he had escaped his fate. Or maybe it still waited for him somewhere else.

On the other side of the fire, he saw a pot filled with golden trees, drenched in seawater.

"Did you get the apples?" he asked, looking from the pot to the golden chest plate hanging from Gen's shoulders.

She nodded. "I caught one of the sirens while I was looking for you. In exchange for her life, she told us how to get the apples."

That was one task done. The Oracle had said Gen would succeed only if he died. She had also said he needed to know his fate to make it true. Had he done it in refusing the cocoon husk? Or maybe she had only told him what she needed him to hear.

Bale placed a hand on his shoulder. "Welcome back, old friend. Flek and I are going to find some food. You look like you could use some."

Pollux nodded. "Thank you."

Gen placed her hand on Pollux's back and rubbed up and down to keep him warm. Chomp, who usually despised him, curled up by his feet.

"You should have told me about the prophecy," Gen said.

"I'm sorry. I made a mistake."

"I did too," she said. "I let you think that saving my father, the circus, the apples . . . that all of it was more important than you. It's not. I don't want any of it if you're not there."

"That's not true. You would hate yourself if you let the Empresses take Alcmen away."

She closed her hand around his. "I hated myself more when I thought I had pushed *you* away. I'll call Andromeda back right now. I'll tell her to take us home. Maybe the apples will be enough for the Empresses without the Cerberus. Or I can—"

"You don't have to do that." He ran his thumb across Gen's knuckles. "I'm beginning to think the Oracle made a mistake."

He ran through what the Oracle had told him. *Your friends will mourn you. The ship you brought does not carry all its passengers on its trip home.* Did she ever say specifically, "You will die?" Or had he assumed? The broken *Hind* wouldn't return with any of its passengers now. It lay in pieces at the bottom of the sea.

The Oracle hadn't lied. She hadn't been entirely truthful, either.

"Castor said something like that too," Gen said. "She wondered why the Oracle hadn't told me about your fate."

"If Cas senses plotting, she's probably right," Pollux said. He should have sensed it too. He'd been raised in a household of half-truths and colorful lies. He'd also been raised to believe he wasn't good enough, strong enough, or worthy enough. It hadn't been hard for the Oracle to convince him he was expendable. "I'm sorry, Gen. I should have been honest from the start."

"I should have made it clear to you that there is no happy future for me without you in it." She leaned in to kiss him, then stopped, pressing her lips together.

He had done that to her. He had made her believe he couldn't handle her mind magic.

He bent forward and closed the kiss, pressing his lips hard to hers. She tasted like salt air and sweet oranges. He had missed that taste. He had missed the way she exhaled ever so slightly when they kissed. Sort of a small sigh.

He slid his hand to her cheek, parted his lips, and let down all his walls. He let her see the embarrassing childhood memories. The Oracle's prediction. How he used to hide at the back of her circus performances, watching her with delight. He knew it was a risk. Once Gen knew everything, she could leave him. But if she knew everything and stayed . . .

A throat cleared.

Gen pulled away from him and smiled. "You really did love my circus."

"Always."

Bale tossed him a green apple. "Here, you should eat something. Unless your mouth is otherwise occupied." He flicked his eyes to Gen.

"I can come back to that later." Pollux flicked his eyes to Gen, too, and she laughed inside his thoughts. That would still take some getting used to.

Pollux ate three apples before he started to feel like himself. In that time, Cas still hadn't returned. It wasn't like her to sulk this long. Thinking of her, he rubbed his hand down his neck and felt smooth skin. No scars. Did the ambrosia heal all of his injuries?

"I should find my sister." He moved to stand and almost toppled backward on shaky legs.

Gen helped him upright. "Do you want me to come with you?"

"No, I'll be fine, and if Castor is in a mood, it's best if I go on my own."

He navigated the beach carefully, stepping over rocks and crushed shells. He found Castor throwing rocks into the water with Adikia.

"Cas," he called. "Can we talk?"

She dropped her next rock and lifted her head. His sister was not an easy person to rattle, but here she was, shaken. If he had pictured how she would be after his death, he wouldn't have pictured this. He'd have thought she would be unchanged. He was glad to be wrong.

"I'll meet you back at the fire," Adikia said, and winked at him as she passed. "Glad to see you're not dead."

"Glad to not be dead."

Adikia crawled over the rocks, and Castor fidgeted, clearly unsure what to do with herself. Her usual confidence had been stripped away.

He didn't know where to start with Castor like this. "I was talking with Gen about the prophecy, and I think the Oracle made a mistake."

"Of course she made a mistake, you fool!" Castor shouted, before exploding into another choking sob. She clamped her hands over her mouth as if she could shove it back down. When that failed, she bowed her head and tears dropped from her cheeks to her boots.

Pollux stepped tentatively toward her. He couldn't remember actually hugging Castor. Maybe he had when they'd been very little. Or maybe his mother had been right, and Castor had been born unfeeling. But if she had been born that way, things had changed. She felt something now.

He wrapped his arms around her, and she didn't push him away or burn him with lightning. She held him tight and cried into his shoulder. Tears spilled from his eyes too. He felt like he had been without a sister for a long time. But she'd always been there, just out of reach.

She abruptly stepped back and wiped the tears from her eyes. "I hate crying," she said. "Don't make me do it again."

He laughed. "I'll try not to. I heard you got your apples." He pointed to her golden armor.

"I also fought a one-hundred-headed stone dragon with your girlfriend."

"I'm sorry I missed it." He wasn't. He liked being on the other side of things, the battle already fought and won.

"We still have to get the Cerberus," she said. "You showed up right on time."

"I'm more worried about the Oracle. Why would she tell me what she told me?" That was the piece that nagged at him. Had she wanted him to throw himself to the sirens? Or had she simply wanted him to sacrifice the cocoon to Castor? Trying to figure it out made his head ache, but he felt like he was almost there—he needed only a few more notes to finish the song.

"The best way to find out will be to go back to Okeanos and demand an explanation," Castor said.

"I'll let you do the demanding. I'd rather not see another Oracle for a long time," Pollux said. "Now let's go back and join the others. Figure out our next steps."

"I'll be there in a minute." Castor turned away to scrub any remnants of tears from her face. He knew if he ever brought up this moment to her again, she would outright deny it. But she would also remember it.

Back at the campfire, he moved in close to the flames. Gen, Flek, and Adikia were at the water's edge, digging up clams. Gen seemed to be keeping her distance from Flek, which Pollux was glad to see. If something had happened between them, he would have no one to blame but himself. He was the one who had told Flek to look after Gen.

Bale sat on a rock next to him. "You look terrible, you know."

"Thank you." Glad to see his "death" hadn't drawn Bale to tears.

"I should have known that when you said the Oracle predicted something bad, it was something bad for you."

Pollux picked up a stick and poked at the fire. "If I had told you the truth, you would have told Gen."

"No. I would have told *you* to tell Gen. She's not that girl you used to have a crush on. Not some idol. She's a real person, and it broke her when you left."

"I made a mistake. It won't happen again."

"It better not." Bale poked an apple with a branch and held it in the coals. "We all saw a bit of who we would become without you.

Gen without hope is a scary thing. Castor without you . . . well, she actually wasn't that unpleasant. She finally understood what it was like to lose something she cared about, and frankly, I hope it sticks. I think Adikia does too." He nodded toward the water, and Pollux cracked a smile. It would be nice if Cas found someone to torment on a regular basis, someone like Adikia, who could weather it.

"What about you? What did you become?" he asked.

Bale removed his steaming apple from the flames. "It's not so much me." He touched the apple and hissed when he burned his fingers. "It was Gen. I saw her, and I knew what she could become if she kept blaming herself for your death." He touched the apple again and this time pulled it from the stick. "She'd look a lot like me."

"There are worse things to become."

"There are better ones too." Bale bit into the apple.

Gen, Adikia, and Flek returned with armfuls of clams.

"What are you two talking about?" Gen asked. She knelt by the fire and buried her clams in the coals.

"Just telling Pollux how glad we are he's back," Bale said, and chewed on his apple.

Gen sat in the sand and laced her fingers with Pollux's. "I am never letting him out of my sight again." She squeezed his hand tighter, and Pollux saw in her eyes a bit of that fear that Bale had mentioned.

Pollux had returned from the grave, but none of them would ever forget what it had been like for him to be dead. Neither would he.

CHAPTER 34

GEN

A s much as she hated having wet boots, Gen had missed traveling by whale, her beautiful, wonderful whale. It had been a mistake to travel by ship. Under the sea, inside the protection of Andromeda's belly, they didn't have to worry about Nessos's ships or singing sirens. They were safe.

Andromeda swam on a direct course to Okeanos. Even if Nessos recovered his ships and his soldiers, it would take him time to reach the isle. They would beat him. They could reach the Cerberus and be gone before he arrived.

"How are we going to get the Cerberus inside this whale?" Castor raised her hand and picked a piece of seaweed from between her fingers. She made a face before she flung it aside.

Size was a problem. Andromeda already carried six people and one ornery chaeri. They crammed together on the center of her tongue, and she had to surface for air every thirty minutes or they'd start gasping for breath.

"We'll have to steal a ship," Adikia said.

"One of the ships we can't row because they're made for centaurs?" Castor said.

"We can make it a sail," Bale suggested.

"Out of what?"

"Andromeda can pull it," Gen said. "Until we can find something to use for a sail. Or I can find some other obliging sea creature to help." She pressed her hand to the inside of the whale's cheek.

Andromeda's blubbery inside reminded Gen of the siren's wet skin. Gen saw that image again of Pollux screaming as the beasts ripped hunks of his flesh free. She snapped her gaze to him sitting calmly across from her. Unharmed. Healed. Alive. She stared at him for a long moment, waiting for him to disappear or collapse in front of her. It had been so easy to lose him the first time.

"You wouldn't happen to know what happened to my violin, would you?" Pollux asked, shaking her out of her daze.

"Here." She reached into her bag and handed him the twisted piece of metal that she'd saved from the sea, along with a few other meager possessions. "I'm sorry. When I thought you were gone . . ." She had never wanted to see the thing again. She didn't want to see it now. It reminded her of the hopelessness that had almost consumed her.

Pollux tipped it upside down, and seawater poured out. "Well, it had never been my favorite violin."

"I can fix it," Flek mouthed, and reached for the instrument.

"You can try." Pollux handed it to him.

Gen glared at them. Those two, thick as thieves, keeping the Oracle's prediction from her as if she were a child. It would take her a while to trust either of them fully. Gen expected Castor to lie to her. But not Flek. Not Pollux.

Flek held his glowing fingers to the twisted metal and pulled and stretched it like taffy. It made horrible creaking sounds as the neck stretched long and the strings snapped into their preformed grooves. Pollux winced more than once. When the violin looked almost like a violin, Flek took one of the empty Illumium vials from inside and stretched it long to make a bow.

"*I hope this works.*" He handed the bow and violin back to Pollux.

"We'll see." Pollux held the violin to his chin and pulled the bow across the strings. The soft and familiar sound of his music floated through the whale's mouth, along with a small wisp of cloud. "That should do." He rested the violin in his lap.

"You had storm vials in there?" Castor asked.

"A few. Nothing you would care about. You already took my lightning vials."

"And they dropped into the sea. Hand me your empty vials. If we pass a storm, I can refill them."

Pollux untwisted a few empty jars from the inside of his violin and handed them to her. "What about the apples? Can you make vials out of those?"

"Yes," Castor said. "But we can't waste any more. We already used some for armor." She tapped her fingers on her chest plate. "The rest of the trees have to make it to Olympia."

The miniature apple trees already drooped from being dashed around a sinking ship and falling into the sea. They needed to get the trees planted and back into the sunlight soon.

On Andromeda's next air break, she emerged near a small island. They all stepped onto dry land to pluck the seaweed from their clothes and relieve themselves. To Castor's delight, a thunderstorm cracked across the sky in a swath of black clouds. She reached her hands into the air and yanked lightning bolts from the sky, while Pollux coaxed the rain and wind into his vials, playing them like he would a song.

Gen remembered him on the ship when the sirens came. He hadn't played the storm like a song then. He had wielded it like a sword, slashing at everything that stood in his way. He had almost knocked Gen into the water. Then he'd fought Castor and defeated her. He could strike as hard as, if not harder than, his sister. But he chose not to. That was what made him different from his family. That was why Gen loved him.

"That's much better," Castor said, when she had her vials filled.

They decided to camp on the island for the night. They would need their rest before they faced the Cerberus. Gen curled up next to Pollux and buried her nose in his arm. Each time she woke up from her nightmares, she had to grab his hand to make sure he was still there. She wondered if her father had done the same thing after her mother died, if it had broken his heart each time he reached to her side of their bed and felt nothing.

When Gen had thought the sirens had killed Pollux, she had wanted to kill them too. She had fed her blood to the siren to make it answer her. What if Alcmen had done the same thing to the Gargareans? And what if it had all gone wrong?

For the first time since her father had gone to prison for killing the Gargareans, she couldn't convince herself that it had been a mistake.

~

They awoke early the next morning and ate green apples taken from the last isle.

"Did you sleep well?" Pollux asked as he ran his fingers through her hair.

"Fine," she lied. He had been through enough. She didn't need to burden him with her bad dreams. He had lived them too.

After they ate, they stepped inside the whale's mouth. Andromeda chatted while she swam.

I like this water better. It's much clearer. I saw some interesting fish. They each had four eyes and two tails. They tasted like the fish off that island you called Lerna. I liked those fish. Do you think we'll be going back?

I hope so, Gen answered.

She had missed Andromeda's chatter. The whale kept Gen's head so filled with her thoughts, Gen couldn't focus on her own.

The little whale navigated to Okeanos and found a small cove on the far side of the isle, away from the ships.

Are you sure it's clear? Gen asked.

There are no ships here, the whale assured her, and carefully opened her mouth. Gen stepped to the edge and looked around before exiting to the beach. She was prepared for anything this time. Birds that could light islands on fire. Warring centaurs. Meddling Oracles. Flesh-eating sea creatures. But the small beach was empty.

"Come on." She waved to the others. "It looks safe."

Before Gen walked away from the water, she pressed her hand to Andromeda's forehead. "Thank you," she whispered. "I owe you my life. We all owe you our lives."

You are my home, Andromeda said.

Gen hadn't known this whale very long. She'd found her when she'd been lost and stranded on Flek's home island. She hadn't realized that the whale had needed her too. Two lost and stranded souls who had happened to find one another in this great big sea.

"I'll call for you when we're ready to leave. I promise," she said. She would never leave Andromeda behind again.

The little whale whistled before she sank back into the sea, carrying the golden apple trees inside her belly. That was the safest place for them until Gen could get the apples home to the Empresses.

Gen plucked a piece of seaweed from her shoulder. The blouse

Castor had given her was, no surprise, ruined. Water-stained, grimy, and torn, as was her last pair of pants. The rest of her clothing had sunk to the bottom of the sea. She couldn't see a future past the Cerberus, but if it existed, she hoped it had a full wardrobe.

Bale wrung out his wet shirt onto the sand. "I certainly don't miss traveling by whale."

"It's better than swimming," Adikia said.

"True."

Castor opened the box on her hip and released the spirit inside. The white light blinked fervently in front of her.

"Stay ahead of us and watch for centaurs," Castor said.

"Yes, Lady Castor. Right away." The spirit flitted up the rocks and into the trees.

"You made up with Delia?" Pollux asked.

"Yes, we've made an arrangement."

"No doubt one that suits you," Pollux muttered.

Gen hadn't even known Castor and her spirit had been at odds, though she had seen much less of Delia this trip. Gen had never trusted the Spirit Watchers or their creations. The Watchers spoke to ghosts in the way that she spoke to creatures, except in most cases, no one else could see them—unless they made one an anchor, like Delia's wooden box.

Gen picked up Chomp in one arm and reached her other hand to Pollux. He took it, and she pulled him upward along the sandy dunes into the copse of trees, following Castor and her ghost. A walking path had been carved through the brush. Not wide enough for a centaur. Probably some animal used it to get to and from the water.

"How are we going to get the Cerberus to the beach once we have it?" Adikia asked. She stretched her arms, measuring the width of their path. If the Cerberus was as large as its legends said, it would never fit through here.

Gen hadn't reached that far in her planning. Her only wish—no, her only requirement—was that they all walk out of here alive. Even if they had to leave the Cerberus behind.

"We'll have to take the main road to reach the ships," Bale said.

"You can control the thing, can't you?" Castor asked.

"Hopefully enough for Flek to get chains around it," Gen said. "We should also hope this armor is fireproof." She tapped the metal plate on her chest.

As they walked through the trees, Gen kept one eye on Pollux and another on the path. Her ears tuned to every sound in the forest. Every broken branch, every rustle of leaves, every chirrup and squeak. Her muscles sat tensed and ready to leap at anything that might attack them. She would not be caught off guard again.

They stopped at midday, collapsing on moss-covered rocks and half-rotted logs. They ate the few apples they had left in their bags, along with some of the steamed clams from the other isle. Gen threw bits of clams into the air, and Chomp snatched them in his jaws. The little ghost came buzzing back from the trees.

"I've found it." The spirit bobbed up and down.

"You've found the Cerberus?" Castor's pale skin turned a shade lighter.

"The entrance to the underside of the mountain. This way."

"I guess this is it." Bale stood up first, followed by Flek. Gen slung her bag over her shoulder and turned to Pollux. Her heart beat faster.

"You don't have to go in there, you know," she said. "I can call the whale, and she can take you away from here."

"Why would I want to be away from here?"

"I can't lose you again."

"I don't want to get lost." He traced his thumb down her jawline. "So we either turn back together or go on together."

Gen looked along the path, first toward the Cerberus and then toward the beach. Could she give up when she was this close?

No, not yet.

"We go on. For now," she said.

He nodded and followed her down the path. At the front of the line, Gen could just make out the bobbing figure of the ghost. It stopped at a mound of rock where bars covered an opening large enough for a massive three-headed beast to pass through. Vines twined around the rusty bars, untouched for years.

"This looks promising," Bale said. "If I had a massive, fire-breathing dog, I'd put it in here."

"You." Castor pointed to Flek. "Can you do something about this?"

"*I can*," Flek mouthed, and raised his hands. The rusted bars twisted and bent, spiraling in two different directions until they made a space wide enough for them to pass through.

The air inside the cave smelled damp and stale. Musty. Like something had died in here, not recently, but ages ago. This had to be part of the network of caves and tunnels they'd used to escape the Emperor's palace before. Except this part belonged to the Cerberus.

Pollux played his violin, and a small wisp of cloud emerged from the strings. It took the shape of a bird, illuminated by sunlight. The cloud bird lit the inside of the dark cavern.

"Don't tell Flek," Pollux said, careful not to face their MetalBender, "but I think my violin is better than before."

"I won't," Gen said.

They followed the bird down the tunnel. If not for Pollux's bird song and their shuffling footsteps, the tunnel would have been eerily quiet. The air felt as clammy as Pollux's cold skin when she'd found him in the whale's mouth. She rubbed her hands down her arms, trying to shake off the feeling that this was all wrong.

"What was that?" Adikia whispered.

"What?" Castor said. "I didn't see anything."

"It was up ahead. There."

Gen squinted into the darkness and found nothing, apart from the glow of Pollux's musical bird. "No, wait. There it is." A shadow moved across the wall in front of them, about the size of a centaur. Except it made no noise. No hoofbeats. Chills raced up Gen's spine. "What was that?"

"The Elysium legends say the Cerberus guards the path to the dead," Bale said.

"Are you suggesting this tunnel is haunted?" Castor asked.

"Doesn't it feel like a crypt down here?"

It did. The air around them turned cold, almost frigid. Gen felt it in her lungs. A gust of wind blew, and Pollux's cloud bird disappeared. Darkness swallowed them. She scrambled for his hand and latched her fingers around his wrist.

She couldn't do anything about ghosts. They wouldn't succumb to her strength or her mind magic.

"Don't move," she whispered to Pollux, blinking rapidly to adjust her eyes to the dark.

"Lady Castor," Delia said, "I think something's wrong."

"Of course something's wrong," Castor said.

"No, with me."

A faded glow appeared in the corner, a smudge of light that spread across the wall, stretching up and down from the center.

Arms pulled from the sides. Wispy legs from the bottom. A round shape appeared on top, a face. The features slowly took shape. She had a wide nose and high cheekbones, a stoic chin. She was lovely.

"Delia?" Castor's jaw fell open as the ghostly shape raised her hands, leaving trails of smoke behind.

"I look like myself again," Delia whispered. Even her voice sounded more complete. Less of an echo.

"Yep," Bale said. "I would say this is a clear sign we're headed toward the Underworld."

CHAPTER 35

CASTOR

Castor gaped at the new Delia. Or the old Delia, she supposed. This must have been what Delia had looked like when she'd been alive. Probably not so pale and wispy. But petite, thin, with a round nose and soft cheeks and wide eyes. She had been cute. Innocent. She looked like someone who had been easily bullied when she'd been alive.

Castor tapped her fingers on Delia's wooden box. She wondered if Delia would still fit inside, if she would still be bound to it. Castor decided not to ask. If being in this cavern had somehow set Delia free, she didn't want to draw attention to it.

"I've missed having fingers." Delia spread her ghostly fingers apart and laughed as they became separate units.

"Let's keep going," Castor said. "I want out of this place."

"I wonder if this is what it will be like when I'm free." Delia picked up her wispy skirt and twirled in a circle. The skirt blended into her pale legs, becoming one translucent blob.

"You can find out after we return home with the Cerberus. *If* we return home with the Cerberus. That was the deal, remember? No Cerberus. No freedom."

Delia's smile disappeared into mist. "Yes, Lady Castor. Of course, Lady Castor."

At least Delia still knew her place.

"You're going to set her free?" Pollux said. "That's the deal you made?"

That *was* the deal she had made. However, deals could always be changed. Delia under control had proved useful. Castor could use that help a little while longer. At least until she had her golden apple orchard planted and Arcadia secured. But with Pollux returned, she couldn't threaten Delia with transferring her to her father after Castor's death. She would have to think of something else.

Delia's new glow lit up the cavern enough for them to see. Pollux put away his violin to conserve whatever weather he had left. More ghostly shadows appeared against the walls. Darker shadows. Less-defined shadows. Delia was not the only spirit here, just the most corporeal.

Testing her new form, Delia bent down to pick up a small rock. She pinched it in her thin fingers and lifted it into the air. "Look at this." She held it out for Castor, a child with her prize.

"Wonderful," Castor muttered. "Maybe next you can hold a piece of twine. Or a blade of grass."

Delia dropped the pebble and sullenly continued onward. Castor was more impressed than she'd led Delia to believe. One of the issues with her ghostly servant was her inability to collect or take anything with her. What if she kept this shape, this ability, when they left here?

Castor imagined a servant who never complained. Who could walk through walls and travel long distances in hours instead of days. A servant who never grew tired or old. Who never had to sleep. Castor would have the means to claim Arcadia when she returned, but would she have the means to keep it? Even after she appeased her father, there would always be someone to challenge or question her. She needed to find a way to convince Delia to stay.

The tunnel continued downward. With each step, the air turned thicker and warmer. It weighed on Castor's chest. She shuffled along the corridor, barely picking up her feet.

Adikia collapsed against the wall. "I need a break," she gasped.

She sat down on the nearest rock and tried to catch her breath. Castor took shallow breaths too. It was like trying to inhale soup.

She slumped on the ground beside Adikia. Bale dropped his bag and sat on top of that. Flek leaned against the wall and mouthed, *"How much longer do you think it is?"*

"I don't know," Pollux answered. He leaned against Gen, who seemed only minutely affected by the pressure, which was a good thing. Castor didn't feel like she could fight off a fire-breathing beast at the moment. At least Gen stood a chance.

Castor opened a vial of wind she'd collected and let it fill the cavern. Everyone took grateful breaths. It wasn't like she could use the breeze in battle. Better to sacrifice it to keep them breathing.

She inhaled the cool air and delighted in the faint scent of rain it carried with it. She took one last deep breath before she sealed the jar to save what remained.

"We should keep moving. It's only going to get worse from here." She turned to Delia. "How much farther?"

Her ghost spoke to the other shadows in the tunnel. "They say to keep to the left if we want to find the beast."

"Why are they the way they are," Pollux asked, "and not more like you?"

"They are lost souls," Delia said. "They can't get past the beast to go to the Underworld, and they can't leave this cave. They will be stuck here forever. Like this." She paused. "The same would happen to me if my box broke before I was freed."

Castor ran her fingers on the wooden box and smiled. The fool spirit had given Castor her new bargaining chip.

The tunnels split, and they followed them to the left, always to the left. The air turned hotter. Castor wiped away the beads of sweat that ran down her face. She imagined this was what it would feel like to be buried alive. She pulled her hair up and away from her neck and kept walking.

Adikia slowed considerably. Sweat dropped off her lavender curls and fell onto the toes of her dusty boots. Castor fell back to walk with her. It pained her to watch the normally spry and vivacious thief melt into a puddle. She opened her vial of wind and blew a gust of it in Adikia's direction.

"Thank you," the thief gasped.

"You can go back if you want," Castor said.

"No," Adikia panted. "I want to earn my bounty." She pointed to Delia up ahead, waltzing her ghostly way through the cavern. "She's quite a useful thing, isn't she?"

"That depends," Castor said, "on whether or not she's trying to kill me."

"She tried to kill you?" Adikia smiled, as if that were a hilarious joke at Castor's expense.

"She tried to kill us all," Castor said. "When she gave us up to the Elysium ships."

Adikia stopped smiling. The joke wasn't so funny now. "She seems to be behaving now."

"Because I told her I would set her free if she helped us get the apples and the Cerberus."

"That was kind of you."

"Too kind."

When Pollux had been gone, she'd realized the true burden of running the StormMaker legacy on her own, and it had been ... overwhelming. During their battle over the enchanted storm, Pollux had defeated her—meaning Castor wasn't the strongest StormMaker. To thrive as Duchess and prove to the people she was up to the task, Castor needed more. More resources. More allies, like Delia.

"When we get to Arcadia, I plan to renegotiate the terms with Delia," Castor said. "She's too valuable to be given away."

Something rumbled through the tunnel. Castor braced herself against the wall and covered her head. Rocks and dust tumbled from the ceiling. Gen swatted away the largest rocks and shattered them to pieces, reminding Castor of the hill they'd moved for Atlas—until a deafening roar in triplicate echoed down the tunnel.

Atlas's mound hadn't done that. It also hadn't spouted flames.

The cavern lit up orange. All the shadow ghosts disappeared. Even Delia's ghostly form faded to a watery mist. When the beast roared a second time, Castor clapped her hands over her ears and bent to her knees. The growl echoed through the metal of her chestplate and rattled down her ribs. She felt it in every bone, every nerve, and every fiber of her being.

The snarling subsided, and Castor uncovered her ears. She brushed dust from her shoulders and stood up.

Gen had cut herself swatting away rocks. She stanched the blood with torn pieces of her blouse.

"Great," Adikia muttered. "She's bleeding her mind poison everywhere." She made a face with every drop of blood that ran from Gen's arm. Castor didn't want to get close to it, either, but she had learned that even Gen's disgusting magic had its uses.

"Save those bloody rags," Castor told Gen.

"What?"

"Save the rags. You can feed them to the beast unless you'd rather let it drink your blood from the source."

"Good idea." Gen put the first bloody rag in her pocket and held a new one to her arm.

They dusted themselves off and made their way down the next tunnel. The air hit Castor's cheeks with a hot sting. Bale tore off his golden armor, cursing about the burns. Adikia did the same after a few more steps. Pollux had no armor to remove. Castor felt the heat, but she could stand it. It seemed Gen and Flek could too. The MetalBender must have been immune to burning metal. Hopefully he would be immune to direct fire too.

Flek gathered up the discarded pieces of armor and molded them into two golden cuffs that he locked around his wrists. Good. They couldn't afford to leave any precious gold behind, even if it was melting through their flesh.

"We have to be close now," Pollux breathed.

The beast roared again. Louder this time. Castor covered her ears, but the sound rattled through her skull like thunder. Falling rocks bounced off her armor to the ground. One struck her arm, tearing through her skin and bashing against bone. She pulled her arm close to her chest.

Smoke billowed into the cavern, along with a blast of orange light.

"The beast is near," Delia whispered.

Castor cleared her throat. "Gen, you take the lead. We'll be right behind you."

Far behind her. This wasn't Castor's beast to slay.

CHAPTER 36

GEN

Gen's beating heart slammed against the inside of her armor. The light from the Cerberus's flames lit up the cavern. The heat from it blasted against her skin. The Cerberus waited around the next bend, and this was it. Her last battle. This would be the fight to either kill her or buy her ultimate freedom. She would walk out of here a hero or not at all.

If Gen survived this, if she won it, she would make sure it truly was her last favor for the Empresses.

"What's your plan?" Pollux asked. Sweat beaded on his forehead while he panted through every word.

Gen dabbed more blood from her arm with a torn shred of shirt and tucked it into her pocket. "I'm going to feed the thing these bloody rags and hopefully get enough control over it to wrestle it into submission. Then Flek can make some golden chains to hold it captive . . . assuming it doesn't light me on fire first."

Flek nodded. *"I'll do my best."*

He slid the two golden bracelets he'd made from Adikia's and Bale's armor off his wrists. With a twist of his fingers, he stretched them long and flat into a golden shield. He handed it to Gen.

"You might need this too." Then he mouthed his next words to her so only she could see them. *"I hope you can forgive me."*

She took the shield and nodded. "I can. I do." She didn't want to hold any grudges heading into this last cave. "And I'm sorry too. We wouldn't have made it this far without you." She threw an arm around his neck and pulled him close.

He draped his hand around her waist. Gen moved away when Pollux cleared his throat.

"What can I do?" he asked.

"Play," Gen said. "Play something with lots of rain to douse the flames, something that might distract the beast."

"I will."

She stood on her toes to kiss him. Quickly. She was about to have a fire-breathing beast in her thoughts. It would be too crowded with Pollux in there too.

She clutched the shield in one hand, her bloody rags in the other. "Stay behind," she said to Chomp. "I don't need any heroics in there."

Her poor chaeri, sweltering in the heat with his thick fur, happily cowered in the shadows.

Gen took a breath and stepped forward. It felt oddly reminiscent of when she'd gone to the Hydra's swamp. That time, she had rushed in to save Pollux from his sister. This time, she had no reason to hurry. She could take her time and plan her steps.

Her muscles pulsed with strength. For a few brief moments in moving Atlas's hill and fighting the stone dragon, she had found some joy in using her strength, and not simply as a means to an end. Focusing on each punch, each kick, each push and pull, she'd been able to clear her head of anything else.

All she had to do was focus on the fight.

The Cerberus's footsteps rumbled through the ground. The light ahead turned orange. Gen stepped forward and stumbled. When she looked down, she found a few blackened bones at her feet. Her mouth went dry. She brushed off her fear and continued forward.

Around the next bend, the cavern opened. It smelled like charred meat and burned dog hair. The beast was there, reaching almost to the top of the cavern. It paced idly around massive piles of bones, watching the dark shadow ghosts against the wall. It paused in front of a second tunnel. When one of the shadows moved too close to it, the Cerberus shifted, and a growl rumbled in its throat.

Sweat ran down Gen's cheeks. Her pulse pounded in her ears. She felt the beast pacing the floor. She hid behind a pile of bones and focused on breathing. The creature reminded her of the Lion's pet orthus, the much smaller two-headed dog that had tried to eat Livia Kine. Gen had been able to subdue it with a small amount of her blood. But the Cerberus towered over her and had a third head. It also breathed fire. She wouldn't be able to break this beast that easily.

Another shadow ghost tried to slip past the Cerberus's defenses. The right head turned on it and snarled, baring yellow teeth. If Gen removed the beast, all these trapped spirits could make it to the Underworld.

She clutched the bloody rags in her fingers. *This is your last fight. Finish this, and you can go home.*

She stepped into the open and held up her shield. "Hey, Cerberus!" she shouted.

The beast lifted all six ears and waggled three pink tongues. Drool ran from the three mouths and hit the ground with a splash. It thought she was a meal.

The center head opened its mouth. From deep inside its throat, a red glow burst forward. Flames shot from between its teeth in a stream directly toward her. She raised her shield and cowered behind it. The metal burned hot around her arms. Pieces of her hair singed to ash as fire shot around the edges. But the golden metal didn't warp or melt. Thank the Oracles they had these shields and armor.

When the flames subsided, Gen stood up from behind her shield. The center head cocked to the side, confused. She should have been charred to a crisp. All three noses sniffed at the air. Then all three mouths opened into a howl.

Gen bent down and covered her ears. The sound ripped through her skull. As soon as it stopped, she knew she had to move. Fast. She straightened as the left mouth opened for a new round of flames. Curiously, the two other mouths remained closed, though it would have been much easier to cook her if all three mouths lit up this cave in fire.

Could they not all spit fire at the same time? That would be helpful.

She skirted to the right, stepping over mounds of bones. She needed to get close enough so she could shove a bloody rag in one of the mouths.

One of the beast's paws swatted at her. She leapt out of the way, and it toppled a pile of bones instead. She skidded on the fragments, landed in the dirt, and hit her chin on a rock. The left head spewed its flames, and Gen rolled, covering herself with the shield until the fire passed. Before she could get up, a paw pressed on the shield.

She pushed back. The paw pressed harder.

She couldn't breathe. Her arms shook. A head peered at her from around the edge of the shield. Yellow drool leaked from its mouth and dropped onto her shoulder.

Pollux's music filled the cave, and a soft rain pattered from the ceiling. The Cerberus turned its heads and lifted its paw slightly. Gen yanked one of her bloody rags free and tossed it into the Cerberus's center mouth. It stepped back and gnawed on the rag, and Gen's thoughts lashed to the beast's.

They always send meals too small. We are so hungry.

Gen responded. *Clearly Emperor Nessos doesn't treat you well. Come with me, and I can free you from this place.*

She had its attention. The center head cocked to the side, while the right head prepared to blast her with more flame. This wouldn't work unless she had all three of them.

She dove to the side, and Pollux continued to play. More rain pattered from the top of the cave, dousing the flames. Smoke billowed in the cavern, obscuring everything in a gray haze.

Gen stayed low, sneaking under the fog. The Cerberus snarled. She made her way to the right head and stood. She tossed a bloody rag into its mouth, and another line of strings connected her thoughts to it.

Why does he think he should be the first to eat? I'm always the last to eat.

The center head responded. *I do not. You ate first last time.*

There is plenty of food if you come with me, Gen said, not mentioning that they all shared the same stomach.

Why is the food talking? the right head asked.

She's offering more food, the center head replied.

Where? I don't see more food. Why is it raining in here?

Oh, I see it. That must be the more food, making it rain. The center head focused on the mouth of the cavern, where Pollux stood with his violin.

Well, make it stop.

I'll eat it. Then it will stop.

Gen gasped. "No, you will not eat him!" She used whatever

influence she had on the beast to make Pollux sound unappealing. "He tastes like rope and old shoes."

That doesn't sound very good.

More and better food is out there, outside of this cave and these tunnels, if you'll just come with me, Gen said.

We're hungry now! the two heads shouted simultaneously.

Gen sighed. Her influence on the beast wasn't strong enough to convince them, and the leftmost head remained free. Smoke unfurled from its nostrils. It bore a long scar across its face that cut through one eye, and when it opened its mouth to spit flames at her, she saw a femur bone stuck between its yellowed teeth.

Focus on the fight.

Gen lunged at the beast. She dropped her shield and threw herself at its neck. She tangled her fingers in fur, and the beast howled. Her ears burned. The Cerberus shook back and forth, trying to knock her off, but she held tight. When it stopped shaking, she grabbed one of her bloody rags and threw it toward the left head. The beast snarled and jerked away. The rag fluttered uselessly to the ground.

Rain pattered overhead, making the Cerberus's fur slick. The left head twisted violently back and forth. Gen tangled her fingers in wet fur and fought to hold on. If it shook her off, she'd have a long way to fall.

She lost her grip with one hand and pulled out a tuft of fur. The Cerberus howled, and Gen took her chance. She shoved her cut arm in its mouth and scraped it along its teeth. Her blood flowed across its tongue, and she felt the last head connect to hers. She snatched her arm back and listened. This head wasn't like the others. She felt its strength as a slap to her thoughts.

I am not as foolish as my brothers. We will not trade this prison for another. I would rather eat now.

It snapped at her. Gen released her hold and slid down the Cerberus's leg. She hit the ground and rolled. A glint of gold caught her eye. Her shield. She snatched it as a heavy paw struck her back.

She crashed through a pile of bones, scraping her arms on their sharp edges, then slammed against the wall. The air shot from her lungs. She sat up, and everything spun. Something wet ran down her head. She touched her hair. Her hand came away with blood on her fingers.

Inside her head, the Cerberus laughed.

Foolish mortal. You can't defeat me.

I don't want to defeat you. I plan to tame you.

The Cerberus laughed again. *You will make a nice snack ... before I eat your friends.*

Gen held up her shield. *We will see about that. I am the Hydra-Slayer. The Tamer of the Thracian Mares.*

You sound delicious. The Cerberus lunged.

CHAPTER 37

POLLUX

Here they were again: Gen about to get eaten by some giant beast while Pollux could do nothing to help her. No, not nothing. Just not enough. The Cerberus lunged, and Pollux played louder from his spot inside the tunnel. Rain poured on the fallen bones between the beast and Gen. Its foot slipped, giving Gen enough time to run to the other corner of the cave.

"Castor!" Pollux shouted. "I'm running low on rain. I need your help!"

"Gen looks like she has it handled," his sister replied.

"Does that look handled?" The left side of the Cerberus snapped at Gen again. Gen pressed against the wall and lashed out at it with her shield. She barely kept it back. "Throw me a vial of lightning! We can hit it from both sides and drive it back from her."

"Fine." Castor tossed him a vial and kept one for herself.

Pollux quickly twisted it into place and held his violin to his chin. He pressed his bow to the strings. "On three. One, two—"

Cas released her vial of lightning, always having to be one step ahead of him. It struck a pile of bones to the left of the Cerberus. Pollux pulled his bow across the strings, and his lightning shot next.

Sparks and smoke filled the cavern. A large head with sharp teeth lunged through the cloud. It had worked. They had the Cerberus's attention. Flames shot from its nostrils as it snapped at them.

"Run!" Bale shouted.

Pollux picked up Chomp and held him under one arm. "Head into the cave!" he shouted. If they stayed in this tunnel, the flames would shoot farther down it than they could run.

He dove onto a pile of bones, burying himself in them and holding Chomp tight. Flames closed over him. Pieces of his jacket burned away. His exposed knuckles blistered. When the flames subsided, he tore off the smoking pieces of his jacket and tossed them aside.

He coughed and looked for the others. He couldn't see anyone else. The room was clouded with smoke, dust, and steam.

Chomp licked the side of his face.

"So now you like me." Pollux tucked the dog aside and reached for his violin. He played a breeze to clear out the cavern and spotted Gen. She slammed her shield into the Cerberus's left head.

"This is the one we have to worry about!" she shouted. "Flek, I think we're going to have to chain him down. He won't listen."

Pollux saw Flek on the other side of the cave with Adikia and Castor. Adikia repeated Gen's words so Flek could read them. He nodded and lifted the chains he'd made. Gen continued to strike the beast with her shield. It bared its teeth and snarled at her. She cowered under the shield and tried to cover her ears.

The other two heads seemed unsure what to do, if they should help their brother fight or stop it from killing Gen. Whatever hold she had on them was tentative at best. Pollux searched the cave for Bale and saw him at the very back behind a pile of bones.

The beast raised a paw and knocked the shield from Gen's hands. Pollux played another blast of lightning to give her the space to roll after it. The beast reared back, and Flek sent his golden chains after it to tie it down. The Cerberus ducked underneath them and snapped back with a blast of fire.

Flek molded his armor into a shield and held it up to keep from being cooked like a roast pig. He pulled his chains back and sent them again. Again, the Cerberus dodged them, eyes flicking to Gen.

Of course. Gen had lashed herself to the thing. It could sense her thoughts as she sensed its. It knew what she planned to do. *Intelligent beast.* Pollux could see why this was the monster that had won wars.

Flek tried again with the chains. This time, the Cerberus swatted at him with a paw. Gen leapt forward to slow it down, but she didn't stop it. The Cerberus knocked Flek flat to the ground. His shield skidded from his fingers.

She and Flek stood underneath the beast's glare. Pollux raised his violin to play another blast of lightning. Possibly his last. The vial Castor had given him was running short. He couldn't kill the thing. But maybe he could wound it.

He played a series of notes, and lightning burst from the center of his violin. It struck the Cerberus directly in the chest—

—and glanced off its skin, as if he'd pitched a handful of pebbles at it. He'd only singed its fur and made it angrier.

"Castor!" Pollux shouted. "I need more vials!"

She didn't answer him.

"Castor!" he shouted again, and looked for her across the cave.

He couldn't find her. She had been right beside that pile of bones, and now she wasn't.

CHAPTER 38

CASTOR

The beast blew out another blast of fire. She and Adikia scrambled behind a pile of bones to hide. The flames careened over their heads and left scorch marks on the walls.

"I think I want more coin for this," Adikia said.

"It will be difficult to collect anything if we're both dead." Castor snatched another vial of lightning from her belt.

She peered between the charred bones. Her brother blasted the thing in the center of its chest with lightning. It did nothing. The beast howled and snapped at Gen and Flek on the other side of the bones.

"Castor!" her brother shouted.

She had given him a weak vial. Maybe the monster needed something stronger.

"Lady Castor."

Castor snapped her head up to Delia, who stood before her, glowing brighter than ever. Maybe the beast didn't need stronger lightning. Maybe it needed a more direct strike.

"Good." She handed Delia a vial of lightning. "Now that you can carry things, and can't die a second time, pitch this into the beast's mouth. See if that makes it more accommodating."

She doubted the lightning would kill it. The thing breathed fire. But hopefully that would bring it down so Gen and Flek could catch it.

Delia closed her wispy hand around the vial. "I think not."

"What?"

"I'm tired of listening to you." Delia twisted the cap to the lightning and released it into Castor's face.

Castor held up her hand to push the lightning back. She barely reached it in time. A few sparks landed on her skin and left blisters behind. "How dare you!"

She moved to stand, but Delia pushed her back down. "How dare *you*? I heard you two talking. You promised to set me free as soon as we got home. Now you want to keep me longer?"

Damn. Cas shouldn't have spoken so openly. "It was only talk. A negotiation. Clearly you're not interested, so we will continue with our original bargain."

"It's too late for that."

"It's never too late." Castor put her hand on Delia's box and squeezed. "You want to spend your life in this cave? Like one of those shadows?"

The pile of bones quivered as the beast thrashed on the other side.

"Never." Delia lunged for her. Ghostly nails raked across Castor's arm. Adikia jabbed a knife at Delia's face, which only split her features apart temporarily. When she re-formed, the deviant ghost snatched at the box. "Give it to me. It's mine."

"I'll crush it first and leave you lost here forever."

The box cracked. Something flared in Delia's misty eyes. She drew her hand back and slapped it against Castor's cheek. It stung more than Cas thought it would. Delia snatched at Castor's belt.

"Stay away from her!" Adikia screamed. She pushed Delia aside, but the ghost had won her prize. She held the box in her hands.

"It's mine. I'm finally free." She turned to Castor. "And like you said, I can't be killed a second time. But *you* can be killed a first, and I want you to know what it is like to be someone's dead servant."

Delia held the box in one hand and picked up a large femur bone with her other.

Adikia pulled out her crossbow and aimed it at Delia's face. "Don't move," she warned, looking more beautiful than ever, holding a deadly weapon at one of Castor's enemies.

"Don't you know? That can't hurt me," Delia taunted.

"I know," Adikia said. "But it can do this."

She lowered her aim and pulled the trigger. The arrow hit the box, spiking a hole in it and knocking it from Delia's hand. Delia's form flickered as the damaged box skittered across bones to the top of the pile. Her features blurred. She looked less like a doll-faced woman and more like one of the shadows on the wall.

"No!" Delia scrambled for the box. Castor lunged for it too.

They reached the box at the same time, Castor grabbing one side, Delia the other. They struggled over it, cracking it further. Delia paled to cool gray, like she was made of chalk and being washed away by rain.

"Let go now," Castor said, "before it breaks any further!"

Adikia tried to pull Delia away from the other side, but she couldn't hold her. Delia's solidity wavered in and out. The only thing real was the wooden box.

Delia grabbed Castor by the hair and pulled. "I hate you," she spat. "A thousand times I hate you."

"I'm not the one who pinned you to the box. Blame the SpiritWatcher."

"You're the one who kept me. You could have set me free at any time. You're a selfish, spoiled brat."

"And you're a worthless spirit!"

Delia slammed her elbow down on Castor's hand, and the box slipped from Castor's fingers. It rolled down the pile of bones toward the center of the cavern, and the Cerberus. Cas dove after it and slid down the pile. She grabbed the box and landed on the dirt floor. Above her, a head of the Cerberus bared its teeth. A glance to her left, and she found Gen and Flek halfway across the cave, battered and dazed. Pollux hid behind another pile of bones.

"Looks like I won't have to kill you after all," Delia said. "The Cerberus can do it."

The Cerberus lunged. Castor felt its hot breath on her skin. She looked to the box, then smiled at Delia.

"If I go down, you do too." She threw the wooden box in the Cerberus's open mouth, and it shattered to pieces on yellowed teeth.

CHAPTER 39
GEN

Castor had the beast distracted. Gen reached for the nearest rock. She picked it up, lifted it over her head, and threw it with all her strength.

Something in her injured shoulder popped, and she cried out in agony and dropped to her knees. But the rock struck its mark. It shattered against the left head.

Why do you damage our brother? the center head asked her.

Because he's trying to damage my friends. I'll keep fighting until you convince him to come with me.

The pain racing through her arm called her out as a liar. She couldn't fight indefinitely. That might have been her last stand.

We can't convince him of anything, the right head said.

The beast prepared to blast her with fire again. Sweat rained down her cheeks, pain pulsed in her shoulder, and bruises marked both of her shins. She couldn't control the beast. She couldn't defeat it. She had to think of something else.

Bale.

He was the better MindWorker. The stronger one. He could make the left head leave them alone.

"Bale!" Gen shouted, already breaking into a run. Flames chased at her heels. She passed by Pollux, who picked up his violin to play more rain, to wash away the fire at her back.

I'll burn you, then eat you, the Cerberus warned.

Bale was her last hope. Her mind magic had failed, and her muscles were weak. Whatever power she'd held had been spent. She needed help.

She reached Bale, snatched him by the arm, and pulled him behind a pile of bones. Flames shot over them and the ground shook as the Cerberus shifted direction. Bits of charred bones dropped on their shoulders.

You can't hide from me, the beast said in her head.

She crouched with Bale in the shadows. "Why did you bring it over here?" he asked.

"I need you."

"To do what? Be the bait?" Fear shone in his cerulean eyes.

"I need you to take control of it. I'm not strong enough. That left head is stubborn. But you can do it. You can make it listen."

He shook his head. "I don't do that anymore."

I smell you, the Cerberus said. *You smell delicious.*

"You did it for Argos, when he went wild." She'd been connected to the little monkey and then she'd gotten upset. Argos had tried to destroy a hotel lobby, but Bale had stopped him before he could.

"That was a mistake. I want to be free of this. I don't want to use it. It was a mistake to tell you."

The beast stepped closer. Heat from its three mouths spread across her injured shoulder.

"I know you don't want to do it. But this is our last chance. I can't persuade the other two while the left head is fighting me. It's either you help, or we run for our lives and hope we make it out of the tunnel before we're charred to ash."

"Then we should start running."

Here I am.

The left head of the Cerberus looked down at them over the pile of bones. Gen stared up into its red eyes. This was it. Her only hope would be to keep her shoulder together long enough to buy the others time.

"Run!" she said to Bale.

She raised her fists, trying not to wince. It didn't matter. The Cerberus knew.

You're injured. You're weak.

So are you, she responded. *The Emperor's pet.*

The Cerberus curled its lip. She had hit a mark somewhere deep inside. It lunged at her, and she grabbed it by the tooth, pushing back. Bones crumbled underneath her. The Cerberus tried to fling her off. She held tight. She would snap the tooth right out of its mouth.

Footsteps ran behind her. Bale was making his escape. Except the footsteps came toward her, not away, and she knew.

She flinched as Pollux climbed the bones beside her, as he raised his violin. She fed the Cerberus all her fear and worry about losing this one person. Pollux played a gust of wind that glanced off the Cerberus's nose.

The beast laughed. *I'll kill him first and make you watch.*

She used both hands to shove the head aside, and her shoulder screamed. She faltered, and sharp teeth grazed her arm. The beast's throat glowed with fire. She and Pollux couldn't avoid the flames this time.

Bale leapt in front of them and thrust his hand into the creature's mouth. The jaws closed, and Bale released a horrifying scream. He pulled his arm back short one hand. A bleeding stump.

The Cerberus stumbled back.

No, I won't listen.

Those were the last cries Gen heard before the head's connection to her snapped free and lashed to Bale instead.

Bale stood up, cradling his arm to his chest. "You'll do what I say!" he shouted.

The Cerberus shook its left head, like it could drive Bale out of its thoughts. It howled so loudly, rocks shook from the ceiling. Gen covered her ears.

The other heads cried out in her thoughts.

What is happening?

What have you done to our brother?

She could negotiate with the beasts. She could communicate with them. She could nudge them. But Bale . . . he could force the beast to its knees. He could turn this vicious dog into a mewling pup.

The dog stretched out its paws, and all three of the heads lay in the dirt, defeated.

Gen ran over and clamped her hands around the third set of jaws. Looking into the left head's eyes, she saw its internal struggle, where it fought against Bale and his superior mind control. She pitied it, like she did all creatures. But this beast would eventually leave this cave and fight a great war. And she was sure the Empresses would feed it well.

"Flek!" she shouted. "Chain him now."

She held tight while Flek stumbled forward with his length of golden chain. He wrapped it around the Cerberus's left muzzle once, twice, three times. He sealed the ends, and Gen slowly released her grip. She waited to make sure the head couldn't snap them open.

Though a low rumble echoed in his throat, the left head seemed cowed.

Does this mean we're leaving? the center head asked.

Yes, Gen said. *Soon.*

She turned back to Bale. He lay in Pollux's arms. Blood pooled across his chest where he cradled his severed arm.

He was the hero today. Not her. The Tamer of the Cerberus. She was glad to give up the mantle and only hoped Bale would live long enough to claim it.

CHAPTER 40

POLLUX

Pollux held Bale tight, not sure what had happened. Not sure if he needed to know. His friend was hurt. The closest friend he'd ever had. Bale was the first person to ever see him. To know him. Bale had never treated him like the Lord of Storms, or even Lux, the violinist. To Bale, he was just Pollux, the annoying rich boy who paid him to travel around.

"Stop crying," Bale moaned. "You're dropping tears on my face."

"Why did you feed it your hand?!" Pollux smeared the tears away with the back of his hand.

Gen slid in beside him. "Don't touch his blood," she warned.

"Why?" Pollux asked.

"Because I'm a MindWorker," Bale said. "And I promise you, with my dying breaths, I will make you stand on your head and shout dirty poems if it's the last thing I do. It *will* be the last thing I do."

Pollux pulled back slightly. A lot made sense now. Why Bale blamed himself for someone's death. He had more influence than other people, more influence than even Gen by the look of it. He alone could control the Cerberus.

"You're not going to die," Gen said. "Come on. We're getting out of here." She leaned down to pick Bale up.

He waved her away. "You have the Cerberus under control?" he asked her.

"For now."

"Good, then I can die."

"No!" Pollux shouted.

"I did what I needed to do. I've made amends. I used my magic to save someone. I call it even." Bale's eyes rolled back into his head. His blue skin turned ashen.

"Stop!" Gen cried. She shook him awake. "You're not going anywhere."

Castor and Adikia appeared from the shadows, covered in char marks and bone dust. "What happened here?" Cas gestured to the blood seeping from Bale's arm.

"I fed my hand to the Cerberus," Bale said. "Now I'm bleeding to death." Even in his last breaths, Pollux's friend kept his dry wit.

"Did the Cerberus choke on it?" Castor asked.

Bale's laugh turned into a cough.

"Stop it, Castor," Pollux warned.

"He's a MindWorker," Gen explained.

"Ah, I knew something was wrong with him." Castor tapped her finger on her chin. "Can't your smelly lizard spit or whatever fix him?"

"No." Gen shook her head. "It only works on superficial wounds."

And Pollux had drunk the ambrosia, the one thing that could have saved Bale.

"Then I suggest everyone stand aside." Castor pulled a vial of lightning from her belt.

"You can't char him with lightning," Pollux argued.

"I can seal the wound closed."

"What if it doesn't work?"

"Then I kill him. He's dead anyway." Castor shrugged. "You

should be grateful I'm willing to waste one of my last lightning vials on him."

Sometimes Pollux appreciated her way of setting aside emotion for logic, but this wasn't one of those times.

"She makes a good point," Bale moaned. "Let her try the lightning."

"No, I'll do it. Give me the lightning." Pollux didn't trust Castor's control, or lack of it. He lay Bale on the ground, and Castor handed him the lightning vial. Everyone took a few steps back.

"Why did you do it?" Pollux whispered to Bale. "Why did you give it your arm?"

"I already told you. I saw how Gen was when you died once. I wasn't going to let it happen again. Now burn me before I change my mind."

Pollux nodded and slowly opened the vial. He coaxed the lightning from inside and let it sit on his palm, a small ball of fire. He felt its power in his bones. If he used too much, he could turn the rest of Bale's arm to ash.

"This is going to hurt." He held the lightning to Bale's arm. Bale cried out and arched his back in agony as the smell of charred flesh hit the air. Gen rushed in to hold Bale down by his shoulders.

Pollux flinched. He'd never wanted to cause anyone this type of pain.

"Finish it," Gen said to him. "You can do it."

Pollux nodded and let the lightning swirl around Bale's arm. He played music in his head. Loud, fast notes. Bale screamed louder. Blisters formed on his arm where sparks hit other parts of his skin. When the wound seemed as closed as it could be, Pollux pulled away.

"Enough." He revealed the smoking stump of Bale's arm. No more blood leaked from the wound.

Bale let out a soft breath. "Next time, let me die."

"There won't be a next time," Pollux assured him. This was their last adventure. Nothing would gnaw off their hands once they went back to performing . . . unless Chomp lost his temper.

The purple dog gazed up at him with wide eyes and crooked, sharp teeth. Pollux could see why Gen liked him so much. He did grow more endearing with time.

At Gen's or Bale's command, the Cerberus dropped to its knees and let Gen place Bale on its back. She climbed up behind Bale and held him in place.

"Come on," she called.

"You want us to ride on the beast that just tried to cook and eat us?" Pollux asked.

"They say they won't now, at least two of the heads do, and the other one is in chains. We should be fine." Gen held out a hand.

"*Should* be fine?"

Gen smiled. "It's the best I can do. There are never any guarantees with wild creatures."

Pollux took her hand, carrying Chomp and his violin with the other arm.

"He seems to have warmed up to you." Gen nodded to Chomp.

"For the moment." The dog settled in his lap, and he ran a careful hand through his fur.

Flek climbed up next. Then Adikia. Cas hesitated. She looked behind them, to the other tunnel leading from the cave. Shadowed figures made their way toward it, disappearing inside. Without the

Cerberus blocking the path, the spirits had free passage to their afterlife.

One of the shadows, the one trailing behind, looked slightly grayer than the others. A little rounder and more cherubic.

"I guess Delia gets her wish," Castor said. "She gets to cross over."

"You sound disappointed," Pollux said as she climbed onto the Cerberus.

"I am. She tried to burn me with my own lightning. She deserved another decade or two of servitude for that."

Pollux sighed. "If you think burning someone with lightning is cause for servitude, you owe a few decades yourself."

"I serve no one," she said, and wrinkled her nose.

Once they were all settled, the beast tore out of the tunnel. Gen held tight to Pollux with one arm and Bale with the other. She held on to the beast with her knees. Blood crusted half of her face. Dirt crusted the other. Still, she had never looked more beautiful to Pollux. Underneath all the grime, he could make out the immense relief on her face.

They bounded over the rocks, away from the heat and the oppressiveness of the cave. As they rose from underground, the air turned thinner, cooler. Pollux took a deep breath. He filled his lungs with air he'd thought he'd never breathe again.

The Cerberus took a different path than they had followed before, and different from the one they had taken out of the palace the first time. When they burst into the light, the town and the docks appeared below.

Gen whispered something in the center head's ear, and it raced downward. It leapt over rocks and trees and landed on the main road.

The Elysiums, when they saw the giant beast, screamed and dove for cover. The ones that didn't, the Cerberus snatched up in its jaws.

"Stop that!" Gen shouted.

The Cerberus swallowed what remained of an arm and continued to the docks.

"Are you sure you want to give this thing to the Empresses?" Adikia asked.

"I don't think we have a choice," Gen said. "But in my experience, some creatures aren't meant to be kept, and I think the Empresses will regret trying to keep this one."

A small number of the Emperor's soldiers tried to block them from reaching the docks. The center head opened its mouth and blasted them with a round of fire. The soldiers dove into the water to put out the flames. Gen scolded the creature again, but it was obvious her hold on it was precarious.

Gen brought them to the nearest ship. The centaurs that remained on the docks quickly ran for safety. Gen slid off the Cerberus's back with Bale. Pollux followed. Adikia and Flek moved to untie the nearest ship. Gen carried Bale and coaxed the beast toward the water. It balked and pushed back on the wood. It clearly didn't like the sea.

A flash of light shone across the docks. Pollux spun and froze. He knew this light, the soft ethereal glow of old magic. The Oracle of Prophecy, Phoebe, had returned. Her circle of light cast wider, engulfing the ship with Gen and the others and the Cerberus. Everything outside of the circle stopped moving, as if it had been frozen in time.

Ice filled his veins. He had learned his lesson. Whatever she came to tell him, he didn't want to hear.

"Leaving so soon?" the Oracle asked. She held out a hand with long fingers. Pollux took a step back.

"What are you doing here?" Gen stepped forward. Covered in blood smears, cut from elbow to shoulder, and with patches of her hair burned, she looked terrifying.

"I came to say farewell. I see you've collected your prizes." The Oracle gestured to the Cerberus.

"No thanks to you."

Phoebe bowed her head. Sparks of light drifted from her golden antlers. "I only told you what I saw."

Castor, Flek, and Adikia came closer. His sister crossed her arms and raised an eyebrow, skeptical. Adikia took her in from head to toe, likely to see if the Oracle had anything to steal, and Flek, who had also seen her once before, focused on her lips, so he could catch her every word. They had both learned that she told only pieces of the truth.

"You told us what you wanted us to hear," Pollux said.

"Perhaps." Phoebe twisted a long piece of her hair in her fingers.

"You didn't tell me enough," Gen said.

Phoebe looked down upon her. "I didn't tell you anything."

The Oracle's circle of light parted, and in it stepped a dark figure with pointed horns and cheekbones as sharp as glass. Spiders crawled across the figure's fingers, and smoke curled around her legs.

"Sister," Phoebe said. "How good to see you, Arai."

"And you, Sister." The Oracle of Malice bowed. When she did, her darkness peeled away to white, and she appeared as a mirror image of the white-shrouded Oracle of Prophecy. "*I* spoke to you, Genevieve the MindWorker." In a blink, Arai returned to her shadow form.

"Why?" Gen asked. "Why would you pretend to be your sister?"

"My dear Phoebe cannot lie. I can. I sent you to Kyknos to get her riled up for the coming war. She and her troops will be integral in fighting it, and now she has a personal vengeance against the Olympians who robbed her."

"But you did lie, Phoebe," Pollux said to the Oracle of Prophecy. "You told me I wouldn't be going home as I was." And yet here he was, very much alive. His sister wouldn't be bringing back his corpse as he'd suspected the Oracle meant.

"Have you not changed on this venture, Pollux? Where are the scars you bore when you first arrived?"

Pollux touched the smooth skin on his neck, healed from the ambrosia. He flexed his jaw. She had fooled him with the details.

"I may not have spoken all truths," Phoebe continued. "But I did not speak any lies."

"Why speak at all?" he asked. "Why did you want me to know I'd die?"

"Love," Phoebe said.

"Love?" Castor scoffed.

Phoebe held up her wrists. Two golden cuffs cut into her skin, linked with a golden chain. Pollux hadn't noticed them before. They had blended with the gold of her dress and skin.

"I loved him once, and I thought he loved me. But he had only fooled me into believing he did so he could have these chains made, from the very golden apples you sought."

"Who?" Gen asked.

"Nessos," Phoebe hissed. "He only wanted to keep me here for my power of prophecy. I wanted to destroy him for it, and so I began searching the future for an answer. But I couldn't find it. I had to reach farther, into Olympia, and there I found the Empresses, and a possible future where they would destroy this empire and Nessos would fall to their hands. But how to bring that future about?"

"I had some ideas." Arai curled her finger around her smoke. "Chaos is my specialty. I told her to look further."

"Magic flows in a line," Phoebe said. "I followed that line of the Empresses' victory back to its origins. I saw the Cerberus, and soldiers outfitted in golden armor, and vials of lightning, but it all had to come from somewhere, didn't it?"

"You." Arai pointed to Gen. "The Empresses needed you."

"I visited them in dreams," Phoebe said. "I showed them their glory. I told them they would have everything they wanted; they only needed a champion. But you weren't ready. You had no faith in yourself, which is why you needed a challenge"—she gestured to Castor—"and love." She pointed to Pollux. "But when I saw your love, I grew envious."

Pollux flicked his gaze to Gen. Her mouth had fallen open as she realized how long these two Oracles had been using her. The first ten labors had been a test, Castor had been a push, and he had been thrown in as her support. He shook his head. No. He had gone to Gen of his own volition, hadn't he?

"I told her how we could destroy your love," Arai laughed. "By telling you part of the truth, we would force you to lie to one another. To mistrust each other. We would break you like Nessos broke Phoebe." Arai closed a shadowy fist.

"It pleases me that we failed," Phoebe said softly. "It makes me believe true love does exist."

"Ah, but vengeance is much more tangible, and you will have that, Sister, when the Olympians come back to destroy Nessos with his own toys." Arai waved her hands together. "I simply love a good war. It's been far too long."

"That's why you did this?" Gen asked. "You used me all this time so you could have vengeance?"

"That depends on what you want to believe." Phoebe pointed to Castor. "Your Duchess believes her fate is hers alone. She will never believe that I told the Empresses to take the Illumium so she would be forced to come on this venture, which is why she will walk away from this conversation feeling no different than she did before."

Pollux shook his head. The Oracles had played all of them in the same way he played his violin. They had known exactly which strings to pluck. Even Castor's. Without the Oracle feeding the Empresses her suggestions, they wouldn't have picked Gen for their lottery. They wouldn't have picked Cas, and Pollux wouldn't have had his excuse to know Gen. They wouldn't be together now. He would still be a lonely musician with a crush on a girl who didn't know he existed.

"If that's the case," Castor said, "then why are you revealing this to us?"

A good question.

Arai smiled. "I am sure you will figure it out, Lady Castor. All in good time."

"You know," Adikia said. "I'm kind of glad all *our* Oracles are dead. They seem like more trouble than they're worth."

"That was our siblings' failing," Arai said. "They always worked against each other instead of with each other. My sisters and I will not make the same mistake."

"You owe us something," Gen said, "for all you've put us through."

"And what is it you want?" Phoebe asked without any real question on her lips. She already knew what Gen wanted.

"Your sister, Gaia," Gen said. "She can take away Bale's magic. He wants it gone."

"No," Bale moaned. "I think I'll keep it." He clutched his charred arm to his chest.

"Why now?" Gen asked. "What changed?"

"I took someone's life with it and saved someone's life with it. I'm curious to see what happens next. I think I'll give my mind magic one more chance."

"There," Arai said. "He has refused. Now go home with your prizes. We will see you soon enough, on the battlefield. Come, Sister. Let us prepare for war." Arai held her hand out to Phoebe, and the two Oracles walked through the circle of light, arm in arm. When they passed through it, they disappeared, and so did the bubble surrounding them. It was like waking from a dream. Pollux even had the sensation that none of it had been real. But the Cerberus in their ship was very real.

Notes and chords formed in Pollux's thoughts, a song dark and angry, mysterious and raw. He would call it "Clash of Fate and Fury." It might be his greatest yet. The tale of a heartbroken Oracle and her vengeful sister who planted the seeds to start a war and destroy an empire.

CHAPTER 41

CASTOR

astor stood on the prow of the Elysium ship. Gen's whale had towed them a safe distance from Okeanos. Then they'd tied together some canvas they'd found in the ship to make a usable sail. Castor pushed her wind into the ragged sail to push them east, toward home. Even in the larger ship, the Cerberus barely fit. She felt the beast's hot breath on her neck. Disgusting. Beside her sat the pot of golden apples. In the moonlight, they looked bronze and wilting. If she didn't get them planted soon, they could die. She used a little more wind to push the ship faster across the waves.

You will figure it out, Lady Castor. In good time.

The Oracle's words nagged at her. If *she* had been conjuring a year-long plot of vengeance, she would never reveal it, especially at the point of fruition. So, why?

"You look lost in thought," Adikia said.

Castor raised her chin to the purple-haired thief. At night like this, her eyes sparkled, like she was made to be viewed only after daylight. It made sense. Adikia was more of a night creature. It was easier to steal things in the cover of shadow.

"I want to know why the Oracles told us their plan. What do they get out of it?"

"Who says they get anything out of it?" Adikia brazenly brushed the Cerberus with her fingers. Even asleep, it snarled. Castor wouldn't dare touch the thing. She didn't trust Gen's or Bale's hold on it for a second.

"There is no point in plotting if it doesn't better serve yourself," Castor said. "They must gain something from it."

"Maybe they just want to annoy you," Adikia suggested.

"There are easier ways to annoy me."

"Fair . . . so what are you going to do with the information now that you have it? Tell the Empresses that they have been fooled by two evil Oracles?" Adikia stuffed her hands in her pockets and placed a boot on one of the rails.

"Possibly, if I find a way that it benefits me. As it is, I want the Empresses to have their war. They will buy massive amounts of lightning from us. So will everyone else. Even with the discounted price for the Empresses, I'll be selling more lightning than before. I'll make up the loss in quantity, and eventually I'll profit with my apple trees." She touched a finger to one of the small trees. "Arcadia will make a fortune. If I tell the Empresses they were only the Oracle's pawns, they could call off the fight."

"Don't do that," Adikia agreed. "Since I'm entitled to a percentage of those sales, I want them to be as large as possible."

"Then I guess you will be returning to your family," Castor said, remembering the many siblings and cousins under Adikia's care.

"For a while."

"Then what?"

Adikia slid her hand down Castor's arm and twined her fingers through hers. Castor let her wind fall from the sail and curled her hand around Adikia's.

"I might keep an eye on my investments," Adikia whispered. "Make sure this new Duchess isn't wasting her coin."

Castor trailed a finger through Adikia's curls. "I never waste coin." She kissed Adikia and wrapped her arm around her back, running her hand down the thin line of scales between Adikia's shoulder blades.

Her father was going to hate Adikia. She couldn't wait to introduce them.

~

After three days of sailing, they reached the shores of Arcadia. Castor had never been happier to see her childhood home because it was now hers. Completely hers. She had gained the means to secure Arcadia's future. There would be no discussion of marriages. She would never be forced, urged, or nudged to give up her inheritance or share it with some imbecile.

As they pulled into the port, dockworkers stared at the foreign ship and the giant beast riding on top of it. The troublesome head on the beast snorted smoke and pulled at its chains. One dockworker dropped his crate of fish and broke into a run. The others followed.

"It is a useful creature," Castor said. "If you can handle the smell." She reached for the pot of golden apple trees and scooped up only one. She hated to leave the others behind, but she could plant more with the seeds inside the apples on this tree. The Empresses would need their prizes to launch their war.

"Flek," she called. "I need you to help me plant it. I don't trust the Arcadian MetalBenders. They like my father too much."

Flek turned to Gen. *"Do you need me?"* he mouthed.

"No. You can help Castor. We're going to take the Cerberus and the golden apples to the Empresses and collect my father. Castor can give you a lift to Quisces when you're done."

"I'm not sure I want to go home to Quisces," Flek mouthed.

Castor leapt at her chance. "You can stay here. I am going to need an experienced MetalBender to handle the golden apples." Flek was both skilled and incredibly quiet. Two excellent qualities in reliable staff.

"*I'll think about it,*" he mouthed, and stepped off the ship with Adikia.

"Are you coming, brother?" Castor asked Lux. "I'm sure our mother would love to see you." *To dote on you and tell you how perfect you are.*

"Tell her I'll visit soon. I have to see this through with Gen."

Castor nodded, having suspected that would be his answer. He would follow Gen to his death. He already had. "Just remember, you're always welcome, Lux. I mean that." And she did. She wanted to see him again. Soon.

"And I'll always set aside a pair of tickets for you," he said. "Every performance."

She smiled. "Maybe I'll take you up on that offer." She wouldn't. But she did like knowing that if she ever did show up unannounced at one of Lux's grand performances, there would always be two tickets waiting for her.

Her brother, Gen, and Bale sailed away with the Cerberus and the golden apples, and Castor carried her single precious apple tree to the manor, cupping it with both hands. "Soon you'll be in the finest garden in Olympia. With all the rain and sunshine you could want."

"Are you talking to the tree?" Adikia asked.

"I'll sing it lullabies if it will save this island."

They reached the gate of the manor, and the two guards standing on either side gawked at them.

"Lady Castor," one said, and pushed open the gate. "You're home."

"Why wouldn't I be?" She had no idea what excuse her father had used for her absence, and she didn't care. She carried her precious apple tree to the gardens and knelt in the grass to dig a small hole. Adikia helped her, their fingers intertwining as they pulled away dirt. Then, gently, Castor placed her apple tree into the hole and covered the roots with soil.

"Make it bigger, Flek. Show everyone what we've done."

She and Adikia stood back while Flek raised his hands to the tree and let his fingers glow. The tree twisted and bent, stretching branches high and wide. Great golden apples dripped from the ends.

Castor plucked one free and twisted it in her fingers. Then she tossed it to Flek.

"Plant them everywhere. Anywhere. I want these trees all through the gardens."

Flek nodded. *"I'll do my best."*

Castor took another apple for herself. "Time to speak with my father."

~

Castor pushed her way into her father's office with the golden apple in hand. Her father, per usual, sat at his enormous desk with a stack of parchment in front of him.

"How dare you—" He raised his head. "Castor, you're home?" He sounded pleased to see her for the barest moment, until his frown returned. "Who is this?"

"Adikia, sir." The thief ducked her head.

The Duke ignored her. "Where have you been, Castor? You leave me with little more than a note. What kind of future Duchess runs off and abandons her people?"

"The one who solves our metal problem." Castor held out the

golden apple. "It's from the garden of Hesperides. I'm having an orchard of them planted right now. A free, renewable source of metal that can hold our storms." She removed the one golden vial from her belt and opened it to release a small spark of lightning. She let the spark crawl from her fingers to her father's before flicking a finger to call it back to the vial. "I told you I would find another way."

She smiled, waiting for her father's words of approval. *You've done it, Castor. You've done the impossible. You will make a fine Duchess.*

"I see you're the reason the Empresses took our Illumium." The Duke leaned across his desk. "Oh, I know exactly what the Empresses are planning, and what you've done. You're not the only one with spies, dear daughter. I did some of my own searching after you left. If you have this one apple, it means you've given the Empresses the rest. Did you and your brother get them the Cerberus too?"

Castor tightened her arms across her chest and said nothing.

Her father slammed his hands on the desk. "You haven't saved us, Castor! You're the reason the Empresses stole our metal! Don't you see? If you had failed to get their prizes, they would not have cause to start their war. These apples you have will take months to grow. We'll be bankrupt before that happens, and you thought that would make me happy? I would have been happy if you'd simply married Memnon and done your duty."

"You think the Empresses would abandon their war even without their prizes?" Adikia asked with a laugh. Castor flicked her gaze to her, regretting bringing her in here.

"Why is she speaking?" her father snapped.

"War is good for us, Father," Castor said. "We'll sell more lightning than ever."

"At a discount. To the Empresses. Oh, I know their price. It's ridiculous. You've made us servants to them."

"We will keep Arcadia alive by selling in bulk. Then, once the apples are grown, we will need no one. It will be pure profit, Father," she said through gritted teeth. "It's what we've always wanted. A means to sell our weather without depending on Tegea."

Her father shook his head, and his pale hair fell over his stern shoulders.

"You have taken our independence and sold it for a few golden apples. When will you learn, Castor? What is best for you is not always what's best for our people."

Castor's body shook with anger. With shame. She should have returned here under rainbows. Under fanfare.

Then she understood. She was never going to get that. Not from her father. And that was exactly why she'd wanted control of the duchy in the first place, to do things differently, to change the Arcadian Doctrine and take their island to the next generation. Castor didn't need his approval, or the blessing from her deceased male ancestors painted on the wall. When the Elysium Oracles were abused by Nessos, they spent a year plotting his downfall. Maybe that was why they'd told Castor their tale, so she could do the same. Just like Nessos, her father would rue the day he had crossed her. She smiled as an idea took hold.

"Then I'll be on my way to talk to the MetalBenders about some changes in production."

"What?" Her father raised his head. "You'll do no such thing. I still run this island, if you recall. You will talk to no one."

She planted her hands on his desk and looked him hard in the eye. "I will do as I please, and if you interfere, I will remind our people that the Empresses named me your successor. You wouldn't want to look like a traitor to the Empire by defying their rule, would you? A bad look, especially during wartime."

The Duke's fingers tightened on a stack of papers, crumpling them to nothing. "Get out of my office," he said in a low voice.

"Gladly." Castor took Adikia's hand and pushed through her father's office doors.

She didn't exhale until the doors closed behind her. Her body quivered with adrenaline. Lightning raced across her skin. Her father might technically own the title of Duke for now, but the island had outgrown him. And soon enough, he would see there was no place for him on it. Castor saw her mistake now. She had been begging for control when she should have just taken it.

"We need to go." Castor started down the hall with Adikia by her side. She had much to do before the Empresses called for their lightning.

"That was impressive," Adikia said. "But he made a fair point. You won't have all these riches until those trees grow."

"I know." Castor walked under the portraits of her ancestors and stopped under Tyrus's glaring face. "That's where you come in. How would you like to return to piracy?"

"What are you suggesting?"

Castor smiled. "There should be cargo ships leaving Tegea soon for Athenia, loaded with very heavy and very sinkable Illumium. Wouldn't it be a shame if something happened to those ships and they lost all of the Empresses' Illumium?"

She raised her head to Tyrus at the top of the family tree. She couldn't think of anything that would anger him more than purposely losing some of his precious metal.

Adikia's eyes widened "You'd sink the metal?"

"Technically *you* would be sinking the metal. I can't be seen anywhere near it. The Empresses can't know I'm involved." She would be sure to craft a foolproof alibi, and Adikia could steal a new, undistinguishable ship and crew it with sailors who could stay quiet.

"Even if I sink the Illumium, the Empresses would just hire some MetalBenders to pull it out of the sea," Adikia said.

"True." Castor tapped her fingers on her chin. "But it would take weeks to bring it all back up. Then more time for the Empresses' MetalBenders to mold the Illumium into vials, and even more time for the vials to be shipped here, filled, and sent back. Nessos could already be gathering his army to reclaim his Cerberus. The Empresses can't wait that long."

"I'm sure you have a plan for that, though," Adikia said.

"I do. The Empresses can have their next shipment of Illumium sent directly here. *We'll* mold the vials and send them back filled before the first batch of Illumium can be dredged from the sea. Of course, I'd have to raise my prices. To cover for the extra work."

Arcadia employed more than fifty MetalBenders to receive the Illumium from Tegea and mold it into vials. She could have them work on what Illumium they had in storage and reuse any empty vials until her golden apple trees bore more fruit. If she could convince Flek to stay, he might be able to work with their MetalBenders on some new vial configurations that used less metal to buy them more time. All of that plus charging the Empresses a molding and shipping fee would make up for any temporary losses.

Adikia grinned. "I told you, you'd make a great thief." She slid her hand into Castor's. "But if I'm going to do this, I'll need cannons. Lots of cannons."

"I am happy to provide."

Castor raised her gaze to the Othonos family tree and winked at Tyrus sitting so pious at the top.

You lose, Old Man.

CHAPTER 42

GEN

Gen used Bale's pocketknife to cut into her arm. When the blood pooled, she pressed a cloth to it. Red soaked through the rag. She tore the bloody rag in half and fed one piece to the right head of the Cerberus and the other to the center head.

Pollux tied a clean cloth to her arm to bind the wound. "I'll be glad when you don't have to feed that thing your blood."

"So will I." Gen handed the knife back to Bale. He took it with his golden hand—or tried to. As he reached for the knife, the gilded hand wandered off to the side and pointed to the sea. On the journey back from Elysium, Flek had made Bale the metal hand from one of the plates of golden armor. He'd infused it with MetalBender magic, so it could respond to Bale's command. Somewhat. The golden arm tended to be a bit fickle.

Bale grabbed the knife with his other hand, the flesh one. "I don't know what's more annoying," he grunted. "This hand or this beast."

We are hungry, the center head said in Gen's thoughts. *How long until we can eat again?*

Soon, Gen promised.

For the entirety of the trip, Andromeda had been scooping fish from the sea and spitting them onto the ship to keep the Cerberus fed. But no matter how much fish they shoved into the Cerberus's belly, it always wanted more.

Gen looked to the left head, the one under Bale's control. Smoke continuously poured from its nostrils. She couldn't hear its thoughts, but she knew creatures, and this one would never be fully controlled. It was simply biding its time, waiting for its moment to break free and wreak havoc on everything in its path.

Gen hoped to be long gone by then.

Pollux's fingers curled around her shoulder. "You look worried," he said.

"I am. I don't trust this beast and I don't trust the Empresses. They fooled me once. What if they try again?" The last time she'd assumed she had defeated the Empresses at their game, they had simply changed the rules.

"You hold the beast," Pollux said.

"I hold two-thirds of it." She nodded to Bale, who wore his exhaustion in his heavy-lidded eyes and unshaven chin. He could only rest when the beast rested, and only a half sleep at that.

"We're going to be sure the Empresses think you hold all of it," Bale said.

"That is the plan."

If the Empresses knew what Bale could do, how powerful he was, they would toy with him as they had toyed with her.

Their sail fell flat. Pollux picked up his violin and played a song to push them forward. They were close to Athenia. Gen shifted her weight from foot to foot, anxious to rid herself of this beast, and even more anxious to see Alcmen and make sure he wasn't in worse shape than when she'd left him.

"Do you think we should tell the Empresses they've been duped by the Oracles?" Pollux asked.

"I don't know." Besides the beast and the golden apples, it was the one thing they held that the Empresses did not—the truth. But

Gen wasn't sure it would change anything. The Empresses wanted their war. Knowing their prophetic dreams hadn't been their own wasn't likely to deter them. It would only convince them that their war was sanctioned by a higher power.

"I see the tower," Bale said, and tried to point with his golden hand. Instead, it flailed in the air until he cursed and clamped it to his side.

Gen turned to the isle of Athenia, where the Empresses' golden spire rose into the clouds. Apprehension twined with relief inside her chest. As glad as she was to be home, she always regretted setting foot on this particular island.

Pollux drew the wind from the sail and slowed their approach into port. Gen took one of the oars and gripped it with both hands to steer them to one of the docks. The Athenian dockworkers made to help them secure the ship, took one look at the beast, and backed the other way.

Gen leapt from the boat and tied it to the dock. For the first time in days, she stood on solid ground. Pollux picked up the pot of miniature golden apple trees, and Bale handed Gen the Cerberus's chain.

Is this it? Can we eat now? the right head asked.

Soon, Gen promised.

She thought back to the stables of Elis, where she had washed away mounds of cow manure by tearing open a dam that held back a river. For completing that task, the Empresses had gained half of the herd. Plenty to feed a hungry Cerberus. It made Gen realize how long these plans had been in the making. How long she had been the Empresses' fool.

The left head of the Cerberus snorted out a puff of smoke.

"Can I trust it?" Gen asked Bale.

"No," he said without pause. "But I'll do my best to keep it under control."

"And I'll be ready to play some rain if we need it," Pollux added. He held the pot of miniature apple trees in one hand and his violin in the other.

Gen nodded. It was the most she could ask for. Creatures were always unpredictable, even under a MindWorker's control.

Bale climbed out of the ship with Chomp, and Gen gently tugged on the Cerberus's chain. It hesitated. She held her breath and tugged again, and the beast took a step forward. She exhaled and began walking.

As they walked through the garden, people stared.

Can we eat him? the center head asked.

No, Gen said.

What about him? the right head asked.

Not him, either. We're taking you to the people who will feed you, and if they don't, you can eat them.

All three Cerberus heads smiled. Gen had the feeling the Empresses would regret asking for this beast before the next month.

They reached the palace bridge, where Gargarean guards stood on either side, trying not to look terrified. Gen pulled the Cerberus between them.

Would you mind growling at them? Gen asked the center head, the most amicable of the three.

Not at all.

The center head bared its teeth, and a snarl ripped from its throat. One Gargarean guard dropped his spear and leapt from the bridge. Gen smiled.

Bale raised an eyebrow. "Remind me to never fall out of your graces."

"Who said you were in them anyway?"

"I think Castor has been a bad influence on you," Pollux said.

"Maybe doing things Castor's way isn't always the worst way," Gen said. Castor was cruel and malicious, selfish and spoiled. She also lived without regrets and fought fiercely for the things she wanted. Gen could admire that, even if she didn't always agree with Castor's methods.

"I'm surprised to hear you say that," Pollux said.

"Don't expect me to say it again."

They reached the palace entrance. Gen kicked open the front doors.

Gregor, the Empresses' assistant, scurried across the polished floors. "You don't—"

He froze when the Cerberus ducked under the doorframe and planted its massive paws on either side of her. Its sharp nails cut into the tiles.

"We don't need an appointment today." Gen tugged the Cerberus into the great hall. Maids and dignitaries screamed and ran. Gregor scurried off across the tiles, slipping twice on his way, likely to warn the Empresses they were here. *Good.*

They shoved their way into the solarium. The Cerberus knocked down poisonous plants and crushed them under its massive paws. The right head bent down to sniff them.

Careful, Gen said. *They're poisonous.*

Bale set Chomp on the ground, then pinned down his golden arm when it tried to pull a leaf from an oleander. "What's the plan?"

he asked, as Chomp hurried to hide under a table with his tail between his legs.

"The Empresses don't get their prizes until I get mine," Gen said.

Gregor pushed through the dais doors, wearing a sheen of sweat. "Uh, the Empresses will be here in good time."

"Be sure to bring my father," Gen said. "It's time for him to go." She tugged on the Cerberus's chain, and a puff of smoke emerged from the left head's nostrils.

Gregor clutched the red curtains next to the Empresses' thrones. "Yes, of course. I will collect Master Alcmen right away. He has been treated very well, you know. The best of care, food, everything."

"I should hope so," Gen said. "For your sake."

The Cerberus growled again, and Gregor escaped through the door.

Gen's heart beat furiously. *Play the part*, Alcmen had always said to her. She just had to continue acting confident, as if the beast were under her complete control.

The doors behind them opened. They turned as Alcmen marched through, clean-shaven, dressed in a black suit, and looking well— almost like his former self.

"Gen," he whispered. "You're back." He came toward her. No fear for the beast she held.

Gen smiled, and tears sprang to her eyes. This was the father she remembered. There was no creature Alcmen met that gave him pause. He treated the Cerberus as if it were a harmless stink lizard or milking goat.

"I'm sorry," she said. "You told me not to go."

He touched his hand to her cheek. "And like your mother, you defied everything I said and went anyway. And like your father, you succeeded where everyone else thought you'd fail." He balled his fists on his hips. "I see you've brought back the Cerberus. Impressive." He touched the beast's flank. He trusted so completely that it was under her control.

"Have the Empresses treated you well?" Gen asked.

"Better than prison. Don't you worry about me." He folded his hands in front of him. "I've had some time to think—"

Before he could say more, the dais doors opened, and the Empresses appeared, dressed in their finery, a gown of red and white covered from chest to skirt in crystals. From a casual glance, they appeared to have spent hours preparing for this meeting. But Gen noticed the earring missing from one of the Crystal Empress's ears, the smudged rouge, and the loose hairs.

Crystal dragged Mr. Percy's son on a length of silver chain, and Gen flinched, unable to distinguish between this young man and the three-headed beast she held on her own chain.

"Well done, Mistress Genevieve," the Red Empress said. "We knew we had made a good choice in selecting you."

Gen nodded, knowing they had done nothing to choose her. The Oracles Phoebe and Arai had nominated her.

"I've brought your apples and your Cerberus," she said. Pollux set the apples on the edge of the dais. "I'd like to leave with my father now."

Red cocked her head, eyeing the apples. "They are so small."

"We had to resize them to transport them. One of your MetalBenders should be able to grow and plant them." A bead of sweat ran down Gen's cheek. She sensed the Empresses were on the verge of asking for more favors, more promises.

We're hungry. When can we eat? the right head asked.

Quiet, Gen snapped.

Behind her, the left head snarled and pulled at its chain. She tugged on the metal with sweaty palms.

"Oh my." The Crystal Empress fanned herself. "The beast is quite impressive. May I ask how you contain it?"

"With some blood"—Gen gestured to her bandaged arm—"and the promise of food." She reached toward them with the chain. "The creature is delivered as asked. With your permission, I'd like to leave."

"So soon?" Crystal asked. "We wish to honor you with a luncheon."

"I've already eaten," Gen lied. The walls of the solarium closed in on her. The plants reached out with long, green tendrils. She was going to be trapped here. Again. She needed to leave now.

She dropped the chain. "Thank you for caring for my father while I was gone. We will take our leave."

She'd taken one step toward the door when the Red Empress said, "Wait."

Her heart stopped. She looked to Pollux, who pulled his lips taut. He held his violin to his chin. He would play a storm like no other to give her time to escape if she asked for it. But then he would end up in chains like Mr. Percy's son. Or worse. He had sacrificed himself once for her. She wouldn't allow it again.

"You seem to have such a way with the creature," the Red Empress said. "Perhaps you could stay on, in our employment?"

"I have plans of my own, Your Highness. I regretfully must refuse." Not to mention, she held only two-thirds of the beast, and she'd promised Bale she wouldn't reveal him. "I am sure any number of MindWorkers could manage the beast," she lied.

"That wasn't a request," Crystal said. "We demand you stay and help us manage the creature. You will be well compensated for it."

"It is a great honor to be counted among our staff," the Red Empress added. "You would do best to remember that."

Pollux drew back with his bow. Played one note. Gen shook her head. She had known this was coming. She'd been a fool to convince herself otherwise. The Empresses had their fingers so tangled in her flesh, she could never escape.

"I—"

"Your Highnesses," Bale said. "There is something you should know."

"No," Gen said through her teeth. "There is nothing."

Bale had done enough. He'd already given his hand for her. Pollux had given his life. She couldn't take any more from them.

"There *is* something you should know." Alcmen shoved her aside and dropped to one knee in front of the Empresses. "I cannot allow my daughter to steal such an opportunity from me, Your Highnesses. A great honor indeed. And if I may, as skilled as she is, she has much to learn. This Cerberus is barely under control."

He sliced his palm open on one of the clasps of his jacket, and of all three heads, he reached for the left one, the one in chains.

"No!" Gen said. "Don't."

He turned and winked at her. "Gen, no need to be ashamed. I've been practicing far longer than you."

He shoved his hand at the creature's mouth. It snarled as he smeared his bleeding hand on its teeth.

Gen closed her eyes. After all this, her father was going to be eaten. She waited for the snarl, snap, and swallow, but she didn't hear it.

She cautiously opened her eyes. Her father stood in front of the stubborn head, his eyes narrowed. The left head pulled back its lip and warred inside itself. Gen looked to Bale, who shrugged and mouthed, *"I don't know."*

Alcmen had stolen the head from Bale, the most skilled MindWorker she knew . . . or thought she knew.

After several long minutes and a whimper of defeat, the left head stood cowed in front of Alcmen. Gen's father proceeded to feed his blood to the right and center heads. As soon as his hand touched their lips, Gen felt the strings connecting them to her snap free.

"There we go." Alcmen raised his arms. "Now, why don't we sing for the lovely Empresses?"

He waved his hands through the air and, one at a time, each head lifted and broke into a howl.

Gen covered her ears. The glass windows on the solarium rattled, and the plants shook from their containers, shattering to the ground. When the howling stopped, Gen uncovered her ears. The Empresses sat on their dais, expressions frozen until the Red Empress broke into a cruel grin and clapped her hand on the side of the throne.

"Wonderful, Alcmen. Simply wonderful! I had forgotten how skilled you were, buried under that grime and ennui. How wonderful!"

Gen's father bowed, transporting Gen back to when she'd been a child, watching her father perform in the center ring. Except that was not what this was. He was signing himself up for another prison sentence.

"Your Majesties," Gen tried to speak.

Her father waved her away. "I think you can see, with a beast such as this, you can't leave its control up to a novice. Your success— Olympia's success—depends on having complete command of it."

"Of course, Alcmen." Crystal waved her fan. "We would be delighted to have your expertise."

He paced in front of them, rubbing his chin. "Of course, I will need an assistant. Someone strong and capable. This young man"—he pointed to Mr. Percy's son—"looks quite strong. Perhaps you will deign to put him in my employ."

"Well . . ." Crystal bit her lip. "I am quite fond of him."

"As I am sure he is fond of you," Alcmen said. "But it's not fair to all the other young men who must be vying for your attention, now is it?" He winked at her, and the Crystal Empress giggled.

"I suppose," she said, fanning herself.

"Now, let me take these young folks to their ship, and then we can discuss the beast's training plan." Alcmen tipped into a bow, grabbed the beast by the chain, and shooed Gen from the solarium. "Go now," he whispered. "Before they change their minds."

Gen grabbed Chomp under one arm and took Pollux's hand with the other. Her heart pounded in her ears. She had just watched one of her father's best performances, and like always, he had left her stunned.

She didn't dare breathe until they'd crossed the bridge and reached the gardens. She kept waiting for the Empresses to send their Gargarean guards after her, or for the Cerberus to break free of Alcmen's hold and spray them all down with fire.

"Why did you do that?" Gen asked. "I had set you free."

"You had," Alcmen said, "and this is what I want to do with my freedom—prevent you from selling yours." He waved to Pollux and Bale. "Go on ahead, gentlemen. Prepare your ship. I need a moment alone with my daughter."

"Thank you, sir," Pollux said. "If there's anything—"

"You can," Alcmen said. "You can look after my daughter. Not that I have to ask. You could barely take your eyes off her in that room. Make sure you never do."

"I won't."

"You," Alcmen said to Bale, "are a bit out of practice with your abilities. You made it far too easy to snatch the beast from you."

"Probably because I didn't want it," Bale said.

Alcmen laughed. "And the creature knew it too. Go on. Get the ship ready. Gen will be along in just a moment."

Pollux let his fingers slip from hers one at a time. "I'll see you soon."

She nodded. "Soon."

Pollux and Bale made their way toward the docks, and her father sat down on a nearby bench. Gen sat beside him. The Cerberus calmly settled in the grass and watched a nearby butterfly float on the wind. The thing looked as docile as a kitten. Any doubts about her father's ability disappeared.

"You shouldn't have done that," Gen said to him.

"Of course I should have. What I shouldn't have done was leave you behind for four years, then let you chase after the beast in the first place. If I'd been in a better place then, I wouldn't have. But I've had a lot of time to think, Gen." He picked up her hand. "Mostly about the mistakes I've made. The wrongs I've done."

"It's in the past."

"It's not in the past." Alcmen took a deep breath. "Gen, I've been lying to you for a long time."

"About what?"

"About us." He nodded to Chomp. "Do you remember that time

you got so angry with your mother, and Chomp nearly bit her fingers off?"

"I do. You took control of Chomp and calmed him down. I couldn't control him."

"That's the problem, Gen. You *could*. You had such great control over him, he would have eaten his way through a wall if you'd asked. I took him from you because I was scared."

"Of what?" Gen narrowed her eyes.

"That you'd learn how much strength you really have." Alcmen sighed. "Our family is powerful. Very powerful. I learned that when I was a young goat herder. I had been playing around with the goats and sent three of them leaping to their deaths over the edge of a cliff. After that, I knew I had to gain control of myself or I could be very destructive.

"When you were born, I decided that, rather than letting you run wild with your abilities, I would put limits on them. I would *tell* you how far you could go. I let you believe you were weaker than you are, but Gen—if you wanted, if you believed, you could have this beast licking your palms too."

Gen looked up at the massive Cerberus. "No." She shook her head. "I tried."

"Did you?" he asked. "Or did you push yourself only to the limits I let you believe you had?"

Gen pinched her eyes closed, trying to remember all the times she had set her mind magic free with no boundaries, no limits. Twice it had happened: when Chomp had gone wild like her father remembered, and when the monkey Argos had torn apart a hotel. Both times had been chaos.

"I'm not like you," she said. "I don't have that ability."

"You do, Gen." He squeezed her hand. "As I said to the Empresses, you just need more practice, practice I've denied you. In doing so, I've denied you something else too. Knowing when and how to use great power is the greatest power of them all. I misused that skill"—he sighed, releasing her hand—"when I used my mind magic against the Gargareans."

Gen sucked in a breath.

"You did it," she whispered, shattering the last fragments of the illusion she'd held of her father. She'd had her suspicions, cracks in his perfect picture. Now those cracks splintered it into pieces.

Great MindWorker, loving husband, doting father . . . Alcmen was still those things, but other things now too: a murderer and a liar. She had fallen victim to his performance like everyone else. *Show them the dream, not the reality, Gen.* Her entire childhood had been a dream. Now she saw the reality.

Tears rolled down her cheeks. "I think I should go."

"You should," Alcmen agreed.

She stood up and hesitated. "You'll be all right here, with the Empresses, with him?" She nodded to the Cerberus.

"Oh, we'll be fine." He patted the Cerberus on the leg. "Don't you worry about us, and don't count us out yet. I'll be back in the circus before you know it." He winked at her and wiped one of her tears away with his thumb. "Go live your life, my darling Gen. Go discover love, and heartache, adventure, fame, defeat, joy, sadness, regret, and happiness. Do it all. Because it's all worth it."

She pressed his hand to her cheek and nodded. "I love you."

"I love you too. Always."

Gen pulled away from him, collected Chomp, and walked to the docks, rubbing tears away with the back of her hand. The Amazing

Alcmen was just a man. He had always been just a man. One with flaws and imperfections like everyone else.

Thank the Oracles. Gen was so tired of trying to be as great as her parents had been. She felt like she could finally rest.

When she reached the ship, Pollux waited for her, one boot on the prow's railing.

"Is everything all right?" He reached for her hand and helped her onto the deck.

She set down Chomp and fell into his arms. "No, but I think it will be."

He pulled her close and leaned his chin on the top of her head. "I think so too."

"Are we ready to leave?" Bale had one hand on an oar. "I'd like to get very far from here in case the Empresses try to catch up to us."

"Yes, please." Gen released Pollux and made for the oars. She would be able to row them much faster. She flexed her muscles and pulled on the nearest oar to get them moving. Pollux drew up his violin and played a soft wind to fill the sail.

"Where are we headed?" Bale asked.

Gen looked down at her torn, blood-stained, mud-splattered blouse. "The nearest tailor. I need something suitable to wear before we begin planning our first performance."

"Then to Ceryneia it is," Pollux said, and smiled as he shifted the wind to push them north.

Show them the dream, not the reality, Gen.

Instead, Gen would make her dreams into her reality.

She imagined sold-out shows, cheering crowds, and a shimmering new dress for each performance. Pollux would play his stories of song and cloud, and her menagerie of creatures would accompany every note. Together, they would stay as far as they could from the Empresses and their war.

Gen was done playing the warrior, the Hydra-Slayer, the Amazing Alcmen's daughter, the Mazon, and the MindWorker. From now on, she would simply be . . . Gen.

ACKNOWLEDGMENTS

After years of waiting for my debut to be published, I feel like *Clash of Fate and Fury* happened in a whirlwind. I started spawning ideas for this sequel almost as soon as I wrote "The End" on *Game of Strength and Storm*. As always, I leave loose guidelines when I plot in case my characters decide to run away with the story, and they did. (Can you imagine Castor being told what to do by anyone?) I like where they landed, though, and I hope you do too. It's sad to think of their adventures being over, but I always imagine them living their lives somewhere off the page, and who knows? Maybe Gen, Castor, and Pollux still have some stories to tell.

I am grateful that I had the honor to tell them, and even more grateful to all the people who helped bring them to you. I have to first and foremost thank my life partner, Barry, for his continued support of my creative endeavors. He has never once doubted me. And my son, Jaxson, for screaming, "My mom's famous!" at the playground. He said it so loudly, I almost believed him. To my agent, Valerie Noble, who shouts out her praise almost as loudly as my son, and my editor, Meg Gaertner, who took the mess of the first draft and shaped it into another nonstop adventure.

To Mari Kesselring, who, even though she is no longer with Flux, has been cheering for me from the sidelines. To my publicity team, Heather and Taylor, who I swear answer every email within the hour. To my cover designer, Sanjay Charlton, who outdid himself with this second book cover, and to the rest of the Flux team who worked tirelessly behind the scenes to make this happen. To my sister Jenny Lee, who has been my unofficial publicist and one-woman cheering section, and to my sister Melissa and our parents for their continued support. Also thanks to Stacey Donaghy, who has been working to make sure this duology gets even further reach.

I also want to shout out to all the amazing authors I've met on my publishing journey who have shown their love and support: Riss M. Neilson (I would not have survived debut year without you), Claire Winn, Rosaria Munda, Laura Reuckert, Amanda Pavlov, Leslie Vedder, Lindsay S. Zrull, George Jreije, and everyone else in the Class of 2K22 debuts. Marissa Meyer, who made me feel like I was finally in the author club. Joelle Charbonneau, who did the same, and my agency sibling, Erin Beaty, for making me feel like I had always been in the club.

To all of my friends who have shown up at my events, bought my books, and cheered me on along the way, I love you all so much, and to all the readers, bloggers, Bookstagrammers, and BookTokers who read, reviewed, and shared my books, I want you to know how much your kind words have meant to me. For a long time, I never thought people would read my stories, let alone have favorite characters and ships, and so I wrote this for you. I really hope I did your story justice.

ABOUT THE AUTHOR

Rachel Menard is an author of strange and fantastical stories for teens that feature unapologetic young women. Her work has been featured in *Writer's Digest* and on *Cast of Wonders*, and her short story, "Blame it on the Bees," was chosen as a "Best of 2019" by *Diabolical Plots*. Her novels include *Game of Strength and Storm*, a Junior Library Guild Selection, and *Clash of Fate and Fury*. Visit her online at www.RachelMenard.com.

Twitter: @missusm
Instagram: @menardrachel
TikTok: @rachel_writes_books